Born In Space

Unlocking Destiny

Jeremy Clift

ElleWon
PRESS

BORN IN SPACE

IN

SPACE

UNLOCKING DESTINY

Praise for "Born in Space"

Comments from readers around the world

"Clift masterfully intertwines themes of sacrifice, romance, and redemption, all set against a backdrop of celestial conflict and human resilience. The narrative explores the ethical quandaries of space colonization, the exploitation of interstellar resources, and the profound connections between a mother and her children, even under the most extraordinary circumstances. As alliances shift and betrayals unfold, the fate of entire worlds hangs precariously in balance."
— **Melissa Caudle**, United States

"This book is an easy read with a great peppering of human interaction, machine learning, and scientific problems that will need to be solved as human life expands beyond Earth's surface. A great read!" -- **John Brenneman**, United States.

"Funny, Factual, Futuristic, & Fascinating: A science fiction novel on the next likely frontier, not so far in the distant future but just 44 years from now in a story that starts in 2068. Most acclaimed Sci-fi bestsellers have imagined technologies unimaginable at the time of writing, and they have been mind-stimulating. The difference with 'Born in Space: Unlocking Destiny' is that looking at where present-day science stands, the author's forecasts look feasible in our foreseeable future, which makes you either joyful or fearful depending on which side of the glass half full versus half empty divide you are on." -- **Uday Khandeparkar**, India.

"Watch out, science fiction writers, a huge new talent has arrived. Compelling and ingenious, this fast-paced and epic tale has fresh ideas and twists galore." -- **John Fullerton**, United Kingdom.

"As a fan of modern science fiction, I found myself engrossed by how the novel seamlessly weaves together advanced robotics and thrilling space escapades while staying true to the emotional and philosophical essence that defines this genre. A must-read for those who value storytelling intertwined with high-stakes cosmic thrillers." – **Dana SF**, France.

"The plot races along. I was kept entertained and engaged the whole way through, helped by the writing which is light-hearted and humorous. I thoroughly enjoyed the pace and the twists and turns... right up to the final shocker! I definitely recommend this book, whether you're a sci-fi reader or not. — **Jenny C.**, Spain.

"Clift's exceptional skill can pull readers into becoming sci-fi enthusiasts who may have been overlooking this genre in the past." **Pacific Book Review**, United States.

"Vivid and fast-paced story-telling about seven infants, artificially conceived aboard a rotating space habitat as an experiment to populate the solar system. What would life be like for the first children born away from Earth? Clift successfully weaves familiar earthly challenges of supply chains, resources, and moral dilemmas with chillingly realistic scenarios of how our successors might all be living." — **Andrew Lord,** UK.

"Jeremy Clift has crafted an epic science fiction novel which takes cues from today's concerns - on the impact of AI, synthetic biology, and the quest to become a multi planetary species - and reimagines a troubled future for mankind where current divides are turbocharged. Besides being a superb writer, Clift is a fantastic world-builder who redefines what it means to be human." — **Vasuki Shastry**, United States.

ElleWon Press,

Virginia, USA

This is a work of fiction. Names, characters, businesses, places, events, locales, and incidents are either the products of the author's imagination or used in a fictitious manner. Any resemblance to actual persons, living or dead, or actual events is purely coincidental.

ISBN (hardback) 979-8-9900107-2-7

ISBN (paperback 6 x9) 979-8-9900107-3-4

ISBN (paperback 5.25 x 8) 979-8-9900107-0-3

ISBN (eBook) 979-8-9900107-1-0

Cover design by Liam Relph.

Visit: jeremycliftbooks.com

ElleWon
PRESS

BORN IN SPACE

IN

SPACE

UNLOCKING DESTINY

JEREMY
CLIFT

"Our passionate preoccupation with the sky, the stars, and a God somewhere in outer space is a homing impulse. We are drawn back to where we came from."

Eric Hoffer, American philosopher, 1902-1983

Prologue

The Summons

Tucson, Arizona, October 19, 2063

PERHAPS THE SPAGHETTI WAS a mistake.

Claw's pasta was always delicious but maybe this time it wasn't the best idea. Teagan Ward, her stomach rumbling with anticipation, couldn't resist ceremoniously twirling a delicious big bite onto her fork and shoveling it into her mouth as she and her brother, Hunter, watched the hilarious antics of their favorite animated characters.

The marinara sauce smeared her mouth and dribbled down her chin as she laughed uncontrollably while slurping the long strands through her lips. Every few minutes, they would burst into fits of giggles or gasps of excitement as the cartoon animals tricked their latest dupe. Their affectionate dog, Chester, lay beside them, hoping a tasty morsel prepared by their multi-limbed robotic chef, Claw, might fall her way.

Teagan was busy wrapping a long strand of spaghetti around her tongue when she snorted with laughter, ejecting the pasta in her mouth across the sofa and hitting her brother in the eye. In mock outrage, Hunter darted across the sofa and acted as if he was strangling her.

"I didn't mean to. I'm sorry!" spluttered the six-year-old Teagan, as she continued to shake with laughter.

"Apologize, you sniveling grasshopper," her brother, three years older than her, demanded.

"It won't happen again, Your Majesty."

Drawn by the playful mayhem, Teagan's vigilant AI companion, Betty--who had helped bring her up since she was an infant--dropped by to advise them that it was bedtime.

"Time to head for the land of Nod," she said in her distinctive computerized vocal timbre.

Hunter had told Teagan that she could adjust the speech pattern, but Teagan rather liked it. Betty was a sleek humanoid with fluid movements and a soft, almost friendly face. Her eyes glowed with a faint blue light, and her skin was a smooth metallic silver, with small panels and wires visible under her transparent joints.

Betty instructed the room to dim the lights and turn down Teagan's bed. Teagan groaned, not wanting to go to sleep yet, and faked resistance, but knew it was past time. Hunter always got to stay up a little later. She couldn't wait until she could too.

"But first," Betty said as she cleared up the dinner plates, "we need a short visit to Gummy in your health pod for a quick clean of your teeth, to keep your smile bright."

The health pod, a regular feature in most homes, gave her an instant checkup and reported back her vital signs. Teagan liked Gummy, her personalized dental robotic assistant. Not only was Gummy very gentle—using a water jet flossing system and whitener to meticulously clean her teeth—she always did it while telling jokes. Once Gummy had finished her task, Teagan reluctantly made her way to bed, dragging her feet as she went.

Betty gave Teagan a hug. "Mummy says she loves you and Chester gives you a wet nose. Go to sleep now."

When Betty hugged Teagan, the skin on her outer frame felt a little cool to the touch. It was a strange sensation, but Teagan had grown used to it and found it comforting. She hugged Betty back.

"Don't let the bed bugs bite," Betty said, giving her one more kiss.

Teagan's laundered sheets smelled fresh like the sea breeze. She snuggled under the covers and wiggled around, trying to get comfortable.

The bright full moon shone through her window, unhindered by the curtains embroidered with graceful butterflies that her mother had put up last year, making the small nightlight unnecessary. Since the night of the great blackout when her mother's car had gone berserk and driven itself off the road, Teagan insisted on keeping a light on.

She could hear the howling of coyotes in the Arizona desert nearby, accompanied by their occasional yips and barks as they marked out their territory.

She pulled her soft pink sheets tightly over her ears, wrapping them around her head to keep out the sounds and the light, and closed her eyes.

But her sleep was disturbed and irregular. She began to toss and turn as she started to dream.

She soon found herself in a strange place, in the presence of a huge octopus with eyes like black orbs the size of basketballs. Its slimy, wet, sucker-covered arms stretched around her, enveloping her, making it hard to breathe. Its suction cups wavered and flexed against her skin.

Teagan tried to fight back but, despite her kicking, she was too small and dainty to break free of the octopus's grasp. She screamed her voice raw, but the octopus only tightened its tentacles around her.

Awaking with a start, she found the sheets wrapped around her neck, mimicking the cephalopod's grasp. She screamed and cried for help, but no one came. Betty was shut down and Hunter was oblivious.

The dream was so real, she felt she was suffocating. Tears streamed down her face. She ran down the dark corridor to her parents' room. Chester, her russet-brown Labradoodle, looked startled at the sudden intrusion.

Her mother, Clara, hugged her and comforted her. "What happened? Your PJs are all damp with sweat."

"Don't worry, darling. It's just a dream," her father, Noel, said as he rubbed the sleep out of his eyes.

"It was so horrible," cried Teagan. "I'm scared."

"Just sleep here for now." Her mother patted the sheets beside her. "You're safe here. You can tell us in the morning."

Teagan snuggled in beside her parents. Her mother smelled good and comforting.

"Get some sleep now." Clara put her arm lovingly around her daughter, and soon Teagan was drifting back off.

But it didn't take long for the dream to return.

Teagan was standing in a dark and cavernous space. The air was thick and humid. As her eyes adjusted to the dim light, she saw that she was surrounded by a chanting crowd of strange beings.

A voice boomed out from the darkness.

"Welcome, Chosen One," it said. "You have been summoned to serve the all-knowing spirit of the Octopus."

Teagan tried to scream, but no sound came out. The giant arms of the octopus wrapped around her again, and she was lifted into the air as though on a huge crane. The next thing Teagan knew she was standing on a stone platform, the beings all looking up at her. Her feet were bare, and the stone was rough and irregular.

She wasn't a child any longer, but a full-grown woman, wearing a flowing white robe and a headdress made of seashells and pearls. In her hand was a golden scepter with an octopus-shaped head.

The figures chanted, and the look in their eyes was of awe and worship.

She was their priestess now, and she raised her scepter to lead them in a hypnotic dance, singing words in a curious language she didn't know.

The scepter gave off an intense light of pure energy that coursed through her body and filled her with a feeling of immense power as if the worshippers were at her command. Their chanting was intoxicating, and she began to become unsteady on her feet. Her body swayed and trembled.

On the floor of the cavern, light from the scepter created shapes that danced across the naked rock. It traced a familiar pattern, but Teagan couldn't think what it was. What did it remind her of? She wished her father was with her. He would know for sure.

Gradually, the shapes helped her recall how one clear night her father––a professor of planetary sciences––had pointed out to her the patterns in the stars, and how one bright cluster, the constellation Orion, looked like a rectangle and belt. Her father said he'd once used Orion to navigate a boat out at sea, and it had saved his life. She had grown to love the bright constellation.

The lights seemed to enrapture the worshippers, who still moved in their hypnotic dance. She was being sucked into an alternate world, somewhere far into the universe.

As the throbbing, mesmerizing dance continued, Teagan sensed a deep connection with these strange beings. The dance sapped all her energy, and she drifted into a deep sleep.

In the morning, her mother asked her if she was okay. "You were such a pest last night, jiggling around, almost like you were dancing."

"I'm fine, Mom," she replied.

Teagan knew better than to tell her what had truly transpired, but the mysterious spirit of the Octopus seemed to linger, tugging at something deep inside her. Its bewitching power had a strange allure that would remain within her and beckon her on a journey of a lifetime.

"Lifting my head,

I watch the bright moon;

lowering my head,

I dream that I am home."

Li T'ai-Po, Chinese poet,, 701-762 AD

1

The Construction

T HE MOON WAS BECOMING a big construction site. The piercing din of rivets being drilled into prefab structures was the music of the morning, and Clara Ward was disturbed by the harsh sounds of fabrication above her.

She missed the birdsong that used to wake her up with the early light in Arizona. She missed Claw's breakfast pancakes and the children's laughter. She missed her family and Betty's nasal tones. She even missed the sound of Noel's snoring in bed beside her.

Saying goodbye to them had been the hardest thing she'd ever had to do, but Clara was a botanist with ambitious plans. Creating a seed bank on the Moon and ensuring a lunar food supply was an opportunity she couldn't pass up. Her ultimate goal was to ensure the future of plant life across the universe. Clara had been collecting and storing seeds for years, but she still needed funding, and more seeds from different parts of the world.

The kids had mixed feelings about her assignment: They were equal parts excited about the idea of their mother working on the Moon, while also afraid of Clara being gone when Earth was in such turmoil. Her contract was only for six months though, and she commuted back and forth from their Arizona home.

Lately, though, she had been spending more and more time away from her family. Phone calls and video chats became brief and sporadic, filled with rushed conversations and interrupted moments. Clara's mind was often preoccupied with calculations, strategies, and problem-solving, making it difficult for her to be fully present.

"Why don't you come home? All you care about is your research and seeds," Hunter said one time.

"That's not true, Hunt. You know that! Besides, I'll be back in a couple of weeks for some R&R."

"Yeah, we know," said Hunter. "But then you'll be gone again."

"Maybe I need to quit," she told Noel on one call. "They miss me too much."

"Stick with it," he advised. "This is too important."

She knew that Noel would be able to handle things, with the help of their family friends Ray and Desiree, along with Betty and the two household robots, AJ and Claw. But she couldn't help the guilt she felt at being away.

Clara sighed. She thought she could have it all—a professional life and a family life—but now she wasn't sure if she could do it like this.

Shaking her head, she forced the thoughts to the back of her mind.

At the Malapert Lunar Base Camp, much of the grunt work was done by specialized robots. Private sector companies had taken the lead in establishing mostly robotic mining facilities and factories; robots had none of the patter of human workmen, none of the coffee breaks, and they worked at a constant speed. They were part of a growing population, with bots outnumbering humans six-to-one on the Moon.

From her dugout, Clara could hear two of them outside, repairing a refueling pipeline. Regular shuttles moved men, equipment, and product to and from the south pole region, which had become a refueling center for intergalactic traffic. Those who didn't want a lunar stop could also refuel at the ElleWon facility, stationed in orbit at an equilibrium point between the Earth and the Moon known as Lagrange point, L1.

Through the window, Clara watched the pair of bots tightening the valves again after clearing the blockage. The spillage from the pipe had turned to ice, and one of the bots slipped as it tried to tighten the valve fully. In a slow-motion dive, it rolled onto its back and, because of the ice, was left flailing like an upside-down cockroach. The other bot came to its rescue, proffering an outstretched claw-like metallic "hand" and pulling its companion up slowly.

"Thank you," it said.

"You're welcome."

Hearing that conversation made Clara uneasy, but she understood that they had learning subroutines that made them able to copy human interaction.

Her daily schedule involved scientific research, as well as maintenance and upkeep of the moon base. The base had laboratories equipped with state-of-the-art instruments, where scientists from different fields collaborated on groundbreaking research. Clara was looking into lunar geology and biology, including how low gravity affected plant growth.

Living on the Moon required constant maintenance and upkeep of the base. Everyone had to do their share, and Clara participated in routine checks and repairs to ensure that all systems, including life-support, were functioning properly. This included tasks such as monitoring air quality, checking water supplies, inspecting equipment, and conducting repairs as needed.

But today, Clara had a big day in front of her.

The intercom summoned her to see Alain Gagnon, the French head of the international team of researchers at Malapert.

"Be there shortly," she responded.

Malapert, near the Moon's south pole, comprised a base camp of prefabbed capsules and 3D-printed cylinders covered in a thick layer of lunar soil to shield them from micrometeorites, extreme temperatures, and radiation. The Malapert base was in some ways more constraining than the ElleWon space station: On the Moon, they were constantly bothered by the sharp regolith dust that clogged machinery and coated space gear unless they were extremely careful and cleaned everything regularly. This grainy, abrasive, and sometimes powdery material that covered the Moon's surface had a low thermal conductivity and a high resistance to solar radiation, meaning it had strong thermal insulator qualities—the deeper the colony, the greater the thermal protection.

She took an elevator down three floors below the surface to see her new boss, and wondered once again why he was here. He didn't have the research background needed for this type of role. More military, it seemed. Nevertheless, he was tall and good-looking—always welcome, even on the Moon—with dark hair, a well-defined jawline, and protruding eyebrows. He greeted her with an outstretched hand and warmly embraced her.

"I wanted to have this opening meeting to clear the air. I know I don't have the research background of my predecessor, so I don't plan to interfere in your work."

Clara was relieved, although she feigned indifference.

"I know you're passionate about your job, and I fully support your plans to grow food here and create our own seed bank."

Clara nodded.

She'd already made significant progress in her research. By studying the effects of microgravity on plant growth, she'd developed new methods for growing plants in space. With each breakthrough, she came one step closer to her dream of one day walking in a garden on the Moon. Who knew? Maybe someday people would flock to the Moon to see her work firsthand.

"But we need you to add an important responsibility," continued Gagnon. "This is highly confidential, of course. But we, and in particular our funders, want us to keep an eye on what the Chinese are doing. You can liaise with them about crops, what food grows best, and how to improve yields. These are all legitimate things to cooperate on. At the same time, I need you to report to me whatever you find out about what they are planning, especially anything that might threaten us. Do you understand?"

She nodded, a part of her she didn't know existed suddenly excited at the assignment. "I'm to be a sort of spy?"

"Exactly. You should try to come across to them as a bit zany and not very well informed."

"Ha, I think I can do that!"

She smiled, and Gagnon seemed to relax.

"Okay, I'm counting on you. They are very advanced and we don't want to be caught by surprise."

Clara excused herself and headed to the nearby kitchen unit to get some breakfast. The cuisine—packets of premade meals—reflected the international nature of the base: Food from all over the globe, all reduced to storable sachets. She watched the news from around the world as she got ready: An election in South America, the collapse of a bridge in India, and renewed efforts to agree on sharing fresh water in West Africa. The base hadn't got big enough yet for its own radio station, but she could already imagine the hyper-jaunty "Good Morning Lunatics" cry of the DJ in a few years, once more scientists and engineers had arrived.

Malapert did, however, already have a light system designed to support the normal circadian rhythm. During the "day," the system increased the cold, bluish light that promoted activity and concentration. Toward "evening," the cold light was replaced by a warm, yellowish light, causing the body's level of melatonin to rise.

Right now, the ridges around Malapert were bathed in natural sunshine. It had a good landing spot nearby and excellent comms with Earth. Clara often joked with Noel that he had prepared her well for a job up a mountain. They had met on a hiking trip when they got stranded in the Rockies, and Noel had built a fire to keep them warm while they waited for a rescue team to arrive.

"I can honestly say he saved my life," Clara would tell her new colleagues. "He set my heart afire."

"Sounds like a song," said Choo-hee, one of the researchers from Korea.

Although it was stimulating to work with so many talented people in close proximity, she had to admit that being constantly "international" was a strain, and a bit lonely. Clara loved tango dancing and spent more time than she would confess at Malapert dancing with her imaginary partner in the evenings when she wanted to escape from the international repartee of the base. She missed America, and the normal cultural banter that helped her unwind and let her guard down: "How are those Mets? They suck, as usual."

But soon, Clara would get a chance to begin her new assignment. She was scheduled to take a trip to meet the legendary Li Jie, one of the founders of the Chinese lunar complex, at the nearby Huashan Chinese base, where she was hoping to track how they were doing with their vegetable cultivation.

It was a journey she would later wish had never begun.

2
The Discovery

Guiyang, China, April 2068

GENERAL LIN WENYI KICKED a rock on the ground. Her walks no longer brought her the tranquility they once had, and she was constantly angry, blaming others for her failure.

She went over and over in her mind the reasons for the country's dramatic defeat in the Great Cyber War: Her team had been incompetent; they had let her down; they had failed to exploit obvious advantages; they had given the enemy room to retaliate. Even four years later, that day still played on in her mind.

The cyber war had been designed as a dramatic chance to cripple the West in a blow so fast that there was no chance for retaliation. General Lin had formulated the perfect plan—a plan designed to give China not conquest but mastery, to put right centuries of humiliation.

China's hackers would activate the ultimate attack, supported by a network of secret underground communications bunkers, and protected by an arsenal of satellites and new missile systems. This is what they had been training for—all the mock attacks, monitoring and response, testing for vulnerabilities, noting the weak spots, and checking the reactions.

A strike without warning would immobilize the enemy and leave China ready to dictate the terms for a new world order. And with China's working-age population declining rapidly, Beijing had had to strike before demographics started dictating policy.

With much of its population online, China was home to a highly trained army of hackers, phishers, and cyberspies, and over the years China had probably stolen more secrets from businesses and governments, and inserted more crippling malware into rivals' systems, than any other country. All were to be transformed into a potent weapon of coordinated attacks designed to cripple U.S. power, aviation, banking, and industry in one move.

General Lin gave the go-ahead at 9.03 am Beijing time – the time suggested as auspicious by her *Suan Ming* or fortune teller – early evening on the U.S. East Coast when attention spans might be waning.

The visible signs had been almost immediate. U.S. military bases in Japan, South Korea, the Philippines, Guam, and the Indo-Pacific region were immobilized by a strange electronic cloud that shut down computers and made communications impossible. Guidance systems malfunctioned, and missile sites were locked tight or refused to function. Swarms of minute drones, unleashed from suitcases by prepositioned agents, confused controllers at hundreds of sites.

Across North America, the power grid began to fail. Patients in ICUs across the country were left without oxygen, traffic systems became gridlocked, and the world's major stock markets entered panic mode as millions of trades refused to register.

Air traffic control went into lockdown as flights across the Atlantic and the Pacific were grounded, and major companies blacked out. Ports could not operate, and GPS went haywire. Millions of self-driving cars came to a halt or crashed as satellite uplinks and downloads were interrupted, damaging navigation and early warning systems.

Nevertheless, despite China's advantage of surprise and coordination in the initial chaos, the countries in the Five Eyes Alliance, along with Japan, Korea, India, and Indonesia, were soon ready.

They switched to dedicated communications which used random quantum cryptography to safeguard control data and commands, as well as avoid hacked networks. China's control of the vital electromagnetic spectrum over its territory was degraded, satellite guidance was disabled, command and control satellites were fed false orders, missiles were immobilized on launch, and secret bunkers were rendered inoperable.

Simultaneously, the U.S. and its allies struck back with every covert weapon they could muster, from crippling cyber attacks to artificially induced typhoons, tsunamis, landslides, and floods, all of which deluged huge swathes of Chinese farmland and burst through the aging concrete of dozens of hydroelectric dams, creating an inland tidal wave that swept aside towns and cities. China's huge industries were rendered inoperable, highways were crippled, and trains were tossed aside like toys.

With China severely weakened in the botched cyber strike, Chinese triad gangs took over many of the cyber networks that General Lin Wenyi had developed for the covert attack, feeding off a new era of poverty and hardship while inflicting financial misery on millions. Many around the world lost their jobs in what became known as the Great Unraveling, initiated by the fallout from the devastating cyber war.

People became desperate. Everything was suspect and hack-prone.

General Lin was forced into a period of compulsory hibernation following the short-lived attack, which China had blamed on "renegade elements."

Several officers had endured show trials for "rebellion" and sedition. But, able to rely on the friends she had prudently bought in high places, General Lin had deflected blame for the disaster and was only strongly reprimanded.

"Just stay out of the public eye," she was told.

She had taken up residence in the southwestern city of Guiyang, where the summers were not too hot and the winters not too cold. She would chat with the monkeys in Qianling Park, and occasionally make an offering at the Hongfu Buddhist Temple, before reciting a wish at the Nine-Dragon Wall.

Her wish was always the same: To be reinstated.

And eventually, her wish was granted. She was to be given a new chance—this time to participate in the history-changing scramble for space.

The apparatchik who brought the news was a short, thin, mean-looking man, but Lin knew that he was a high-ranking officer and not to be trifled with. His eyes were like bullets, and he assessed her with an unflinching gaze. After a while, he seemed to nod, and she assumed she had passed his inspection.

"General Lin, in light of recent events you have been assigned to oversee the space industries based here in Guiyang," he said in a deep voice that did not match his size.

She nodded slowly, noticing that she had not been offered a seat.

"I will gratefully accept, but can I ask why I am being given this honor?"

His eyes narrowed, and Lin was frightened that he would withdraw the offer.

"For now, it would be too risky to bring you back into the public eye. Personally, I don't think that you deserve the opportunity, judging by your incompetence so far, but others have decided that you have a flair for leadership. Officially, you will be supervising and overseeing these industries, but unofficially, there is an important additional role."

"How may I serve?" she asked, eager to prove herself after so long in the shadows.

He was quiet, as if trying to decide if she was worthy of the task he was about to give her.

"You will cultivate a relationship with an American billionaire called Howie Rich. He's a big mine owner but, more importantly, he heads a consortium exploiting asteroids to be harvested for building material in LEO. Low earth orbit."

She nodded slowly. "I know of him. I'll do my best."

"You will not do your best. You will do what you have been assigned to do. Do you understand?" he asked her, and she nodded again. "Keep an eye on his activities, maybe throw him some business. Keep in with him."

"Yes, but where do I find him?"

"Your AI will know. He's either in Arizona or a new space habitat he's building called Halona. Maybe he could be fed a bit of data from the Tianyan FAST dish when we spot a viable asteroid," he suggested.

"And Lin," — she noticed that he did not add her rank — "there will be no additional chances."

She saluted sharply. "I won't let you down."

The Guiyang job gave General Lin good access to lucrative new projects on the moon and beyond. She did not care that it was low visibility. In fact, that suited her. It got her back in the game.

And on her appointment, although she was unaware of him at the time, General Lin became the boss of an energetic, constantly curious young graduate named Zhu Yan, who would go on to locate several commercially lucrative asteroids, including one called Valdenia 53.

Few would suspect that Yan's discovery would ignite a battle of greed and deception that would shake the entire space industry, not just in low earth orbit but far beyond into the galaxy.

3
The Siblings

Tucson, Arizona, June 2068

A s Teagan grew older, her interests began to diverge from her older brother's. They were only three years apart, but at eleven and fourteen, three years spanned a lifetime. While Hunter became increasingly interested in space, Teagan was firmly rooted in the now of Earth. She shared her mother's passion for nature and collecting seeds, and had adopted a baby octopus she found one day. She had called him Tentikal.

"Who's Tentikal, when he's at home?" enquired Noel's buddy, Ray, when he heard chatter about the friendly cephalopod.

"Come over and see. Teagan adopted him after he was found washed ashore. Heaven knows how he got there. For some reason, Teagan's become obsessed with octopuses."

They moved over to a small aquarium on the corner next to Teagan's piano, which she loved to play Bach and Mozart sonatas on.

"Tentikal, meet Ray," said Noel. "He's Teagan's favorite member of the family, apart from Chester, of course!"

"Tentikal is a mimic octopus and can impersonate many other animals and fish, including jellyfish, a sea snake, the lionfish, a shrimp, and a flatfish."

"Versatile!" said Ray. "He's fascinating," he said as he peered through the glass. I feel you could have a conversation with him, or play chess. Look how he's stretching out his arm in greeting."

Ray excused himself to go to the bathroom. As he relieved himself, the toilet came alive. "Uric acid high," said the appliance.

"Oh, shut up, you porcelain pisspot," shouted Ray, unimpressed by the diagnosis.

While Hunter lazed in bed, playing games that took him to far-off planets, Teagan would get up early to avoid the sweltering heat. Her favorite spot was the splash pad at the sprawling Brandi Fenton Park, where she would relax with her best friends, Alec and Tate, under bio-synthetic botanic structures and arboreal systems that not only mimicked nature, but also harnessed solar energy and purified the air, creating a sheltered haven for their gatherings.

Tens of millions of people around the world were thrown out of work by the Great Cyber War and subsequent economic unraveling, compounding the upheavals of climate-induced migration as rising seas and failed harvests forced people to flee their homes and home countries. Even qualified professionals, including trained doctors and pilots, found it difficult to get work, with robots displacing many humans. This in turn had prompted the rise of lawless gangs that roamed the countryside, scavenging what they could and kidnapping for ransom. The rich were voting with their feet, moving off-Earth to secure luxury rotating habitats the size of small cities, built by big corporations with the promise of all needs taken care of.

But as Clara pioneered a career in lunar research, Noel still preferred for his family to grow up on Earth, and for Clara to visit when she could. And so Teagan spent her days meeting up with her friends in the local park while her mother made a life on the Moon.

Sometimes Sofia and Maya would join Teagan, Alec, and Tate in Brandi Fenton Park. Even their docile labradoodle Chester liked to slump in the shade after a playful stint in the dog park.

As they settled onto the park benches, Sofia, whom Teagan had been friends with since kindergarten, asked if she wanted to try her new virtual reality headset.

"It's really cool. You can go anywhere," Sofia said.

The sleek headset boasted advanced brain-computer interface technology, known as BCI, that enabled a seamless connection between the user's brain and the virtual world. It directly transmits sensory information, allowing users to experience virtual reality with unprecedented realism.

After putting the headset on, Teagan gingerly activated it. To her astonishment, she suddenly found herself standing in the rugged terrain of a volcanic landscape, surrounded by an array of strange crested yellow and black creatures. Their forms were unlike anything she'd seen—some had shimmering scales, others sported luminescent wings, and a few exuded an ethereal glow. Their eyes sparkled with curiosity, and she felt their long fingers against her neck.

The sensation made her squirm, and she started to run to the entrance of a dark and foreboding tunnel. The air hung heavy with heat, and eerie red hues bathed the rocky surroundings. Teagan's heart raced with the sense of imminent danger lurking behind her as she sprinted into the depths of the lava tube, the walls seeming to close in around her. Her breath grew ragged, her muscles throbbed, but she refused to give up. She knew stopping meant those long, menacing fingers would get her.

Finally, a glimmer of hope appeared—a faint light beckoning her forward.

But she abruptly came face-to-face with a giant, ant-like creature, almost the size of a human, with large mandibles and antennae sticking out from the sides of its head. Teagan tried to scream, but no sound came out.

Despite the fearsome sight, the creature had a calming air. "Do not be afraid. I mean no harm," it said. "We will meet one day."

Teagan's fingers shook as she yanked the VR headset off her head, her turquoise Hopi bracelets jangling on her wrist. She stumbled back, knocking over a water bottle on the ground, her stomach churning in fear and confusion. She looked as though she was about to vomit.

Sofia's concerned voice broke through Teagan's dazed thoughts.

"What happened in there?"

But Teagan refused to say. Instead, she just sat quietly, trying to process the encounter. It was eerily similar to her dream.

Why do they want me? she asked herself.

Sofia put a comforting arm around Teagan's shoulders. "Let's go home," she suggested gently.

Teagan stood up. She was still shaking and uneasy. She tried to convince herself that it was all just a twisted game of no importance, but deep down, she knew there was something more ominous at play. Why did it keep coming back to her, and what did it portend?

4

The Hunt

Eye of Heaven, China, June 2068

A FEW TIME ZONES away, in southern China, the young student called Zhu
Yan was dreaming not of aliens, but of valuable rocks.

Yan, an energetic and industrious graduate in his mid-twenties, worked at a
giant radio telescope that was hunting for signs of life and trying to pinpoint
prized asteroids. Nestled in a valley among the limestone peaks of southern China's Guizhou Province lay the Five-hundred-meter Aperture Spherical radio Telescope—FAST—also known by the more poetic nickname of Tianyan, or the "Eye
of Heaven."

Every day, on his walk to work from the cramped, one-room flat where he stayed
with a local family, he watered a small Osmanthus tree he had planted on the
path nearby. It rewarded him with its beautifully fragrant flowers, smelling of ripe
peaches or apricots, lifting his spirits.

An only child, Yan had grown up with his grandparents after his mother died
from a malignant tumor when he was five. His grandparents doted on him but did
not have much, and he was often lonely. He had adopted a small Asian mongoose
as a pet, whom he named Kuai and played with all day, feeding him scraps from
the dinner table. Kuai was his best friend, until he was killed by a farmer with a
shovel; he had been scurrying along a drainage ditch after escaping. Yan had been
heartbroken and refused to eat for a week.

Yan grew up watching the stars, not far from the vast silvery-grey aluminum dish
that would eventually become his life. He had dreamed of one day living on the
moon, but Kuai had taught him not to take anything for granted.

The curve of the giant dish glinted in the early morning sun. The air was crisp
as Yan grabbed his breakfast of steamed baozi––dumplings and bean juice––at the
canteen before starting the early shift at the lab. The giant reflector, supported by a
mesh of steel cables hanging from the rim, towered above him as a slight rain started
bouncing off the telescope's intersecting perforated aluminum panels.

"Keep your hard hat on," a guard shouted. Yan, his protective headgear dangling
from his belt, bounded up the iron stairs to his lab—a series of cabins behind the

giant dish where he and a team of researchers monitored the constant stream of cosmic data and bursts of radio waves.

Building the FAST receiver had been part of a huge push by China to explore space. The giant dish was designed to scan the universe, listen for signals of alien life, promote further understanding of dark matter, and help map the Milky Way. When construction was completed, a lifetime ago in 2016, China's FAST receiver was the largest single-dish radio telescope in the world. Now it showed signs of aging, rusting in a few places, and dented by the occasional bird strike.

Operated by more than 2,000 mechanical winches, the dish tilted and adjusted its parabolic shape to focus on different areas of the sky. A movable receiver was suspended in the middle of the dish from six towers to collect the data, processed in the city of Guiyang to the north.

Although the telescope looked like an eye, its actual function was more like that of an extremely sensitive ear––it listened to radio waves in space rather than viewing them. Its panels could be adjusted to change the shape of the dish and better receive the radio waves. At the time, Nan Rendong, the chief scientist who had created the FAST project years ago, had described the radio telescope's abilities, explaining that it could distinguish meaningful radio messages from the white noise of the universe.

"It's like identifying the sound of cicadas in a thunderstorm," he'd said. The gifted astronomer had died of lung cancer a year after completing his dream project, but the FAST receiver had proved, after a slow start, to be a boon for China's space program.

Yan was supposed to start the early morning shift and, at this hour, time was of the essence. When he walked into the closely guarded facility, he saw the same thing that he had been seeing on repeat everywhere: A recorded version of the celebrations in Beijing of the hundredth anniversary of Mao's Cultural Revolution. It was annoying. They were so self-congratulatory, and you couldn't avoid them. They kept on replaying them, even though the main celebrations were now two years ago.

As Yan ate his breakfast, he thought about how the Cultural Revolution had once been derided as divisive and damaging. Now it was being hailed as part of Mao Zedong's genius. His Little Red Book of political quotations had seen a huge revival, all because they wanted to shift the focus from the huge cyber disaster.

Yan tried not to look at the screen and turned down the sound. But the celebrations were hard to avoid. The leadership was determined to showcase China's colossal advances since the creation of the People's Republic of China in 1949. A giant armed forces parade showed off China's impressive military hardware, while direct broadcasts spotlighted China's huge infrastructure projects around the country and the world.

"There is no force that can shake the foundation of this great nation. No force can stop the Chinese people and Chinese nation from forging ahead," said the commentator, speaking in Mandarin from Tiananmen Square in the heart of Beijing, on the spot where Chairman Mao had stood, almost twelve decades before, to proclaim the founding of the People's Republic after the devastating civil war and the defeat of Kuomintang forces.

Yan did not even see the point. None of it mattered, it wasn't like they didn't already know. It was a futile thing to keep reminding them and, honestly, it wouldn't be long before it really started to sound like a challenge. Maybe there was a force to stop them in their tracks. Hadn't they already found that out?

At one time, China had hoped to reunite the entire country, including the island of Taiwan, under Beijing's rule. But that desire proved to be elusive. Instead, economic inequality and ethnic tensions had effectively divided the country into three main spheres or "kingdoms." The island of Taiwan had remained stubbornly independent after Beijing had abandoned its accommodative "One Country, Two Systems" approach a few decades ago.

Yan automatically tuned out the repetitive boasts on the TV as he scooped up his third dumpling while it was still fresh and hot. Even though space was his business, breakfast was his concern of the moment.

Yan's fingers danced over the control panel, pressed against the smooth surface as if coaxing secrets from it. His minuscule office was cluttered with objects, and each one seemed to hold a story, worn with age and use.

Yan preferred to keep a low profile. It was safer. That was why he chose to remain on his own and think only about work, to breathe the crisp air and look after his adopted Osmanthus tree. On the streets, Yan heard so much, even the things he did not want to hear. His co-workers never spoke of politics, but he heard things. His ears were like the vast dish he worked at. He picked up sensitive information and kept it to himself.

He recalled how they failed six years ago to deal a crippling blow to the West, when so many people had died; now they had turned their attention back to space.

Space was a redemption that many countries sought. It was their chance to start fresh, to build new colonies away from the giant ball they were trapped in called Earth. Space was not exactly an answer in itself. Instead, it was a question, and the world was giving an affirmative answer.

But would it just launch a new round of intense competition, or could it foster some redemption? The answer would emerge swiftly.

5
The Collection Agent

Baltimore, Maryland, June 2068

G uy Zephron woke with a jolt. His skin was covered in sweat, and his head throbbed. He shut his eyes and tried to get his heart rate back down.

Sometimes, mercifully, he could not remember his dreams. Tonight, though, he saw the crops and the deluge. He saw the people, and he knew their faces. This time, he was not watching them from within the cockpit. He was with them on the ground, and he knew them by name. He was trapped in water, and the hands of many children, so many hands, reached out to grab him and pull him under.

Most nights, he'd wake up soaked to the skin, drowning children trying to grab his wet shirt.

"Help us," they cried.

But he could do nothing.

Sometimes, he imagined that he was drowning too.

He looked at the half-empty bottle of whiskey on the table. Whiskey was the only thing that kept the voices and the images away.

His war record had won him accolades. He had led the retaliatory strike against China's dam system, deluging half the country under a huge wall of water. But Guy had been a farm boy—he'd had his share of parched seasons followed by inundating rains—and he was tormented by the visions of the millions of small farmers he had helped drown.

Concealed by a cloaking shield to avoid Chinese air patrols and jamming, he and a couple of support aircraft had flown northeast from a carrier in the Bay of Bengal over Burma, and then toward the giant Three Gorges hydroelectric dam. The order was to fire a blast of gamma radiation to weaken the concrete structure. Although it was not that old, satellite imagery had shown significant deterioration in the 2,335-meter-long dam, and target spotters had calculated that it would not take much encouragement for the dam to crack, creating an unstoppable inland tsunami.

Guy's goal had been to blast the concrete and leave before anyone knew he had visited—part of a string of stealth attacks on vital infrastructure, combined with strikes by swarms of microbots that targeted essential personnel and communications. Backup planes took care of the layers of anti-air defenses. With a maximum height of 185 meters, the dam was a massive structure, incorporating 28 million cubic meters of concrete and 463,000 metric tons of steel, supplied by a variety of mills that did not all maintain the same standards.

Guy had received his orders before taking off, but he always double-checked everything. That day, as he flew high over the imposing dam, he spoke into his mic, "Come in, Alphabird, this is Viperwing One locked and loaded, confirming strike order."

He heard a bored voice in his headset. "Viperwing One, hearing you loud and clear, strike confirmed. Zap that baby. Alphabird out."

Guy aimed for the center of the concrete structure. "Deploy ray gun and fire four times." The cockpit AI asked for his code for confirmation, and he gave it.

Guy did not wait for the dam to start crumbling under the huge weight of water that began to seep, then cascade, from the reservoir that snaked for 400 miles behind the wall; he was out of there and already heading toward the Myanmar border to evade any response. So he did not see the desperate mothers and screaming children who drowned as the deluge swamped villages and farms in its path, nor was he able to observe the hospitals and factories inundated by the wall of water that swept away cars, trucks, and livestock. He did not witness the sleek, ultra-modern bullet train be swept off its tracks, nor did he see the miners beg for help as the waters flooded their mineshaft at the end of their shift.

The collapse of the Three Gorges Dam, along with other similar structures, created an inland tsunami in China that rolled destructively as far as Shanghai and the Yellow Sea on the east coast. The giant wave wiped out crops, drowned tens of thousands of ill-prepared and unwarned villagers, and created millions of refugees, overwhelming emergency services in a tide of misery. The damage to the 22,500 megawatt hydroelectric facility triggered power shortages across the region. Heavier-than-normal rains added to the torment, causing landslides, toxic gas leaks, and explosions. Train tracks were ripped up by the cascading waters. Highway overpasses, fabricated with third-grade materials during China's construction boom, collapsed, while vast, yawning sinkholes swallowed up homes and vehicles as if they were toys.

Swollen by cloud-seeded artificial rain clouds, thousands of reservoirs subsequently overflowed, compounding the devastation: Gushing rivers turned into cataracts, surging through towns and villages; hundreds of cars, floating like drunken traffic in the torrent, were swept along in the raging waters, smashing into buildings and crushing anyone unfortunate enough to be in their path; houses were torn from their foundations and swept away in the blink of an eye; trees were uprooted and carried off like twigs. Rescue workers were helpless in the face of the unprecedented deluge.

To Guy, it seemed an unnecessarily disproportionate retaliation for a cyber attack. But that was war. Now he was jobless. The government had let all war heroes go with medals and a thank you.

The swift conflict had culminated in a spiraling economic collapse, which unraveled years of progress and made millions jobless around the world. But it had also created a boom in new space habitats, as well as a shift to industries on the Moon and a burgeoning space economy.

Guy had found it hard to adjust after the war. At times he would spend the entire day not even knowing what it felt like to be sober. He'd grown a gut that strained against any shirt he put on, and he rarely shaved. The beard he grew was not impressive.

He threw on some clothes after wiping himself down with an old towel. Even now, he wanted to drown the noises in his head in whiskey. He wanted to join those desperate children.

He staggered the short distance to the bar, slumped over, and nursed a cheap bourbon, willing to tell anyone about his wartime exploits.

"With me, you just strap yourself in and feel the Gs," he told a captive barmaid as the man next to him tried to order a round.

"Why don't you go stuff your Gs down your effing G-string," the man said after hearing the same story for the fifth time.

Guy tried to swing at him but fell off his barstool. "You don't know what you're missing."

He'd struggled to find work and to integrate with computer operatives and IT guys. Guy had lost three jobs within a month, mostly for lateness; despite his pilot's training, he found it difficult to get up on time after a late-night session. On the third job, only his reputation as a war hero had kept him from being charged for assaulting his supervisor. The idiot had made a joke about the war, and Guy had considered it his responsibility to teach him a history lesson.

Some people are like clouds. When they disappear, it's a beautiful day, he thought to himself.

He was going through the wanted ads when he got a message to connect with someone. Guy had not seen the man on the screen before: He looked overweight, with a bedraggled beard. Thinking it was a lawyer for the idiot he had punched in the face, Guy warily swiped the screen to open the call. The man smiled and said, "Captain Zephron, I'm Howie. Howie Rich. It's a great honor to meet you."

Not many people still addressed Guy by his rank, so that made him even warier.

"Look, Mr. Rich. If all you want to do is kiss my ass, then pick another day. I have a job to get."

Howie laughed. "I like you, Guy—can I call you Guy? You're a straight shooter, just like me. How about I offer you a job?"

Guy stared at his screen disbelievingly. Was this Howie Rich serious, or just a stupid prankster?

"I'll give you ten minutes," Howie Rich said. "Look me up on the net to ascertain my authenticity, then I'll get back to you about the job. Keep in mind: A miner does not just sit at the top of the shaft. You must commit, you follow?"

Curious, Guy hurriedly commanded his AI to search for the name "Howie Rich." Apparently, he was not just one of the biggest miners in the world, but one of the richest people on Earth. He was also building several space habitats, designed to rotate around Earth and provide safety for the ultra-wealthy, and developing an asteroid retrieval business that he believed would bring untold riches.

Guy's spirits instantly lifted. Howie Rich was offering him an unexpected chance at redemption, and a new life.

Howie's call came seven minutes later.

"Mr. Rich, I'm sorry for my earlier brashness; I didn't know who you were."

Howie waved the apology off. "I have a plan for an asteroid mining operation. I need a pilot with guts and flight experience in charge of my fleet. There are pirates out there who molest legitimate business in space—lunar mines and industries."

"Why me?" Guy asked.

"You suit me. You are needy."

Guy grunted. Howie mentioned a salary five times what Guy had earned as a fighter pilot. Guy accepted on the spot. A week later, he had moved to ElleWon space station, on the Moon's L1 Lagrange Point, and was in command of Howie Rich's fledgling but expanding asteroid collection fleet—though he'd have to report to Commander Bancroft, the testy lady who ran ElleWon.

"Keep your distance and you'll get along fine," Howie had advised.

Commander Quinlynn Bancroft, known to most as simply Lynn, was tall and sharp-eyed, with short brown hair. Bancroft had several commands, and ran her ship in a disciplined, slightly old-school manner, keeping track of everything like a bird of prey. She did not believe in the extreme use of AI when it came to things as delicate and expensive as asteroids. So far, she had recorded not one loss, or even a slight mishap.

Guy did not like ElleWon much, but he respected it as a creation of smart minds who had initiated the great expansion of humanity across deep space. What the designers did not think about, however, was the aesthetics. The gateway was an ugly yet powerful construction with forty-three human employees and 136 automatons.

He was certainly not looking forward to their hotel, with beds that seemed to stretch the idea of what a bed really was, and vegetables that the residents considered fresh but had been genetically modified until the very sight of them turned Zephron's stomach.

Yet all that didn't matter. It was a break from the confines of his ship.

With this new opportunity, Guy resolved to become a different person. Howie's words about being needy stung him. With remarkable self-discipline, he set about adopting a new routine. Every morning, he got up without an alarm and read quietly for fifteen minutes. Then, for another thirty minutes, he would meditate and pray. He let an ocean of calm wash over the shores of his mind. He called the routine a "supreme act of self-care, self-centering, and life balance."

Before he'd got this gig, Guy didn't believe in any religion, but on his first long journey he read up on Buddhism and decided it was the way for him. He prayed every morning, meditated, and did some yoga. Guy learned to master his earlier guilt, anger, lust, and other emotions. He did away with alcohol, smoking, gambling, and other vices.

The job itself wasn't as exciting as being a fighter pilot; the craft was bigger, with more crew to supervise and train, and the asteroid retrievals, though unique, were usually boring and straightforward, with no hostile encounters. He had heard about space bandits mounting attacks, but Guy hadn't had the privilege of meeting them yet. He wanted to, though, especially those called the Iron Hornets; they were a dangerous bunch. His fleet had the most sophisticated weapons he had seen and, despite the scars war had left on him, he itched to teach the Hornets a lesson.

Guy wouldn't have to wait long before the Iron Hornets put them to the test.

6
The Fourth World

Mount Lemmon, Arizona, May 2070

W HEN CLARA WAS ABLE to get back to Arizona for some R&R, Noel insisted on taking a family trip together to nearby Mount Lemmon, where they stayed at a beautiful log cabin built amid the pines. He thought of it as a good way to recharge and reconnect as a family.

The fresh scent of conifers filled the air, mixing with the earthy aroma of the log cabin. The breeze was crisp and refreshing, noticeably cooler than the scorching dry air of the plains below.

The fresh scent filled Clara's lungs, invigorating her. As she hiked through the trails on Mount Lemmon, she could feel the soft dirt under her feet and the coolness of the shade provided by the trees. They watched woodpeckers and deer and even observed a bobcat in a tree.

"This is exactly what we needed," Clara said, watching Hunter and Teagan play amongst the rocks.

"I'm glad you're here with us," Noel said, wrapping his arm around her. He kissed her on the ear lobe.

At night, they examined the stars. Noel pointed out the different constellations, including Orion and Cygnus.

Together, they spotted Deneb, one of the brightest stars.

Clara tried to help them see where the Malapert base camp was on the Moon. "You can see the rim of Shackleton and probably make out Malapert just above."

It was all over too quickly. Reality called. As they wound their way down the mountain road in a taxi, Clara and her family admired the breathtaking views of rugged rock formations jutting out against the vast desert landscape. It was like being in another world, far removed from the bustling city they were heading back toward.

The smell of wildflowers and desert heat began to waft through the open windows. Orange-yellow cup-shaped flowers, known as Mexican gold poppies and purple-flowered scorpion weed added splashes of color, giving off a spicy fragrance.

Beside a track, young saguaro plants emerged under a palo verde "nurse tree" that offered them shade and protection.

Teagan was admiring a brown-plumed, long-legged roadrunner bird chasing a lizard through the scrub for its next meal when the Ward's vehicle abruptly ran into a noisy cavalcade of protest groups traveling into Tucson for a scheduled demonstration. It was clear they wouldn't get home fast.

"Damn, this is the last thing we need," muttered Noel, already late for a university recruitment meeting. The cavalcade was a mix of environmentalists and Indian tribal groups––Apache, Hopi, and Navajo. Land rights and water seemed to be the unifying theme.

A group of Apache activists sitting in a flatbed truck carried signs saying things like "Sacred Land," "Holy Land, Do Not Pass," or "No Yellow River." Another group of Greens screeched past in a Jeep, with a banner on the side that read "Water for Life, Not Profit."

One girl raised a sign as she passed: "Water: A Necessity not a Privilege." Some banged drums as they zoomed past. The column of cars and buses slowed to a near halt.

One Apache drove past on an ancient motorbike. "Get off Dził Nchaa Sí'an," read the sign on his back.

"Come on," shouted Noel. "Can't we get around them?"

"What's Dizzy Nacho?" asked Teagan.

"You mean Dził Nchaa Sí'an. That's the Indian name for Mount Graham. It's just a bit east of us," said Noel.

"Where you've got one of your telescopes?" asked Hunter. "Why do we have to get off?"

"It's an old fight. But the Apache have long opposed building optical telescopes on Mount Graham because they say it's sacred ground. To astronomers, it's an ideal location for looking at the heavens."

"So what's the clash?"

"For the Apache, the mountaintops are a sacred place where they connect with their ancestors through prayer. To put a telescope there, one said that it was as if you were looking up a woman's skirt. They believe the scientists should go somewhere else.

"But the scientists and astronomers, including some from the Vatican, ignored their feelings and went ahead by building four telescopes on Mount Graham. To them, science is also a kind of religion whose importance outweighs other claims. The universe is governed by physical laws and there is no room for spirituality."

"You bad astronomers!" retorted Teagan in a mock reprimand. She paused, as if distracted, and then said, "I love the Hopi. They have such beautiful jewelry. Mom has some, don't you?"

"Yes, I love it."

"The Hopi are special. And some of their legends are unusual, to say the least," interjected Noel. "For example, perhaps one of the most intriguing involves the Ant People, who are credited with saving the Hopi not once, but twice." Noel stuck out his fingers from his head like an ant's antennae.

"Weird!" shouted Hunter.

"How did they save the Hopi?" asked Teagan.

"Well, the Hopi believe the world has had four existences or periods," explained Noel.

"The 'First World' was destroyed by fire—be it an ejection from the sun, a volcanic eruption, or maybe an asteroid strike. The 'Second World' was destroyed by ice—perhaps glaciers moving south or a pole shift. Both times, Hopi legends say the tribe was guided during the day by an odd-shaped cloud, and during the night by a moving star.

"These guides led them to a sky god named Sotuknang, who helped them take refuge with the Ant People. The Ant People lived underground in subterranean caves. They taught the Hopi about food storage and how to conserve it for when you need it, like in the winter. The 'Third World' was destroyed by a great flood, a bit like in the Bible. So, we're now in the 'Fourth World.'"

"Even weirder! Ant People! I want to meet one."

"That might be difficult without Sotuknang."

"Are they ants or people?" asked Teagan.

"Maybe the size of people who lived underground."

"I love ants," observed Clara. "I think they are the most successful creatures on the planet. Scientists think there are twenty quadrillion ants in the world."

"Quadrillion?" asked Hunter. "That sounds ridiculous."

7

The Skirmish

Near ElleWon, February 2071

G UY ZEPHRON WAS PUT to the test on an early asteroid retrieval mission. "Six hostiles approaching fast on your tail. I don't think they have healthy intentions," announced Control in a dry voice.

Guy felt the thrill that came with the promise of impending danger, but quickly suppressed it. He was just doing what needed to be done. To get excited over possible death or destruction was not a part of the man he had become.

Guy was annoyed they had chosen this time to strike. It was a delicate moment—he was dragging the Zernon 47 back to be mined closer to Earth. His five space tugs had retrieved the valuable cargo by first lassoing the ancient asteroid and then encasing it in a carbon fiber mesh to help reposition it adjacent to the ElleWon space station, where it could be stripped by robots of its minerals.

Part of the retrieved asteroid was to be used in the construction of the new Quivira space habitat that Rich Industries was building in low-earth orbit. They were calling it "the Camelot in the Skies." The commission he and his crew received from this haul would be beautiful.

He hurried to his monitor to check the approaching hostiles. "Arm the bots, prepare for evasive maneuvers, and put on my playlist," Guy instructed the craft's AI.

He closed his eyes as music wafted through the hidden speakers; the adrenaline coursed through his veins as the battle approached.

The AI informed him, "Lasers, cannons, pulse and particle weapons, all armed." Then, as if to jack up his adrenaline level a bit more, the AI continued, "Sir, we have a small meteorite shower approaching on our starboard side. It may collide with the rear tug."

Zephron grunted.

"Sir, we can't outrun the intruders and the meteorites while hauling the asteroid. You have under sixty seconds to make a decision, Captain."

Guy let the music wash over him. They might be able to deal with the pirates if they didn't have to worry about the shower, but the AI was right: They couldn't avoid the meteorites with the asteroid slowing them down.

He opened his eyes and commanded the AI, "Patch me through to every tug."

When he was sure all five tugs could hear him, he said, "This is Captain Guy Zephron. We are about to be sandwiched between a group of space bandits and a shower of meteorites. Carter, I want you to fly in a scattered formation. The rest of you, ditch the rock, zip ahead of the path of the shower, and get into battle formation. Maybe we can use it to our advantage. I want those bastards to regret the moment they decided to target us. They won't know what's hitting them!"

To Guy's pleasure, the crew followed his orders with precision. The battle was short, the bandits being hit on both sides by a barrage from the meteorites and Guy's crew. Wanting to send a message to others, he made sure there weren't any prisoners before recapturing the asteroid.

By the time they got to ElleWon, the story of the battle had reached the space station. Even Clara, who was visiting from Malapert, had heard.

Guy docked his craft, ready for what he was about to collect. He had already spotted the frown of disapproval from Bancroft when she had summoned him via ElleWon's comms, patched through the DSN or Deep Space Network.

Guy knew he was in trouble. She was an administrator. He was an airman. She didn't understand how things worked out in open space, or what was at stake. Bancroft had never fought in the war. The two knew where the other stood, and simply tried to maintain a civil relationship.

When Guy entered Commander Bancroft's office, she was watching a replay of his battle with the pirates. She made a show of concentrating on the screen, ignoring Guy, before sighing and offering him a seat.

"Captain Zephron," she started, "did you authorize the unlatching of Asteroid Zernon 47 so you could engage bandits in battle?"

Since he had landed the asteroid retrieval job, Guy had learned to stay calm through his Buddhist meditation. It was a good thing, because he could already feel his anger rising. Guy asked, "Have you seen the AI's report?"

Bancroft gave him a sharp look. "I will be asking the questions, Captain; don't make me repeat myself."

Guy silently recited a verse to calm himself, and then answered, "Yes, I did, Commander Bancroft, I—"

Before he could complete his sentence, Bancroft had raised her hand to silence him. "So, you are admitting to releasing a valuable and already secure asteroid to fight some space bandits?"

Guy looked at Bancroft in disbelief.

"I made the decision based on the parameters before me: One of the tugs was in the line of travel of some small meteors, and the bandits were gaining on us. The asteroid was slowing us down. I had to ditch it, knowing that we could get it back easily, considering its trajectory. The lives of the crew and the fleet were more important."

He could have been speaking to the door for all the effect his words had on Bancroft.

"Captain Zephron, your job is to transport asteroids to the required location; you are not paid a commission on each asteroid to take a risk with them."

The anger he worked hard to keep down began to bubble to the surface once again.

"Did you hear anything I just said, Commander? If I had not ditched that asteroid, we wouldn't be having this conversation, because none of the tugs and crew would be here, let alone the asteroid. I made a decision that saved lives and retained the product."

The angrier Guy became, the calmer Bancroft was.

"Please keep your voice down, Captain. I know your type; you only live for the battle. But that asteroid is why all of us are here. Nothing is more important than bringing it back safe. I am going to issue you an official reprimand for unlatching that asteroid from its harness. It could have spun out of control, striking us. Though you brought it in safely, it was a risk you didn't need to take."

Guy gripped the handle of the chair he was standing next to so hard that he was in danger of crushing it. He was about to shout about the unfairness of being reprimanded, but he remembered his old commanding officer's maxim: "Don't get mad, get even."

He smiled at Bancroft. With a solicitous voice, Guy said, "Is there anything else?"

Bancroft, who had been bracing for an explosion, was thrown by his calmness.

"That will be all, Captain. Welcome back to ElleWon. You can get some deserved rest in your quarters."

As Guy left the office, he let out a string of curses under his breath.

Push-floating through the cramped corridor toward his cabin, he bumped into Clara, who was visiting from the small moon base camp where she'd started work some three years earlier. Clara was one of the few people he liked because, apart from being extremely smart, she always seemed to know what he was thinking.

"Hey, Guy, I heard all about your encounter with the raiders. Your deputy, Carter, told me how you saved his bacon from a meteor strike. At the rate you're going, you'll be made president of Free Earth soon."

Guy smiled. "Not everyone's pleased with what I did, so I think the presidency is on hold for now."

Clara looked at him for a moment, and then her eyes widened in understanding.

"Bancroft? There's something about you that rubs her up the wrong way. Generally, Lynn is a nice enough lady."

When Clara saw Guy's expression, she raised her hands in mock surrender and said, "I'm just saying how it is. I would invite you for a drink to celebrate, but I know you're a teetotaler. Going to Halona soon?"

Guy nodded. "When it's completed. But I need to retire to my coffin first and decompress. It's nice to see you, Clara. How's that professor husband of yours?"

"He'll be here for the weekend. We prefer to meet up here over Malapert." Clara laughed and continued on her way.

When Guy got to his cabin, a small room devoid of any personal touch, he stripped to his briefs and sat on his prayer mat in contemplative silence. The only sound that could be heard was the clacking of the prayer beads hitting each other as Guy tried to empty his mind of emotions.

Bancroft did not matter. The only things that mattered were getting the job done and keeping his crew safe.

That, and his awe for the universe. For that, he had a front-row, first-class seat.

8

Meeting Howie Rich

Harmony Mountain, Arizona, March 2072

Howie Rich surveyed the damage at his giant Harmony Mountain copper mine, its huge, terraced open pit a perpetual scar on the Arizona landscape. An orange river cascaded down the hill, contaminating everything in its path. Howie knew it had already gotten into the water supply. An expensive and tedious inquiry was inevitable.

By now, more than ten million gallons of copper sulfate acid had spilled into the river system. Plenty of mines had accidental spills from pipelines and waste runoff, contaminating drinking water aquifers, farmland, and fish and wildlife habitats. But this was much worse. Schools were being forced to close, and nearby wells for farming were shutting down.

Fortunately, the mine—one of the biggest in Arizona—was still operational. Giant yellow diggers and shovels were loading waiting monster trucks with ore-bearing rock for hauling to the crusher.

"What the hell happened?" Howie demanded the foreman. "This is going to be one of the most expensive accidents in our history. It might even cost me my license."

They paused as a powerful explosion cleared more rock in the deep, terraced pit. White dust from the blast lingered in the air, hanging over the pit like a cloud.

"This ain't no accident," the foreman replied.

"Well, whatever this is, you're going to fix it."

"Yes, boss."

Howie wiped the sweat off his bronzed forehead with the cuff of his shirt. Many people had underestimated Howie Rich, to their own cost. Behind his jovial exterior was a man of steely calculation and purpose.

He was determined to ride roughshod over anyone who stood in his way. In particular, he didn't want anyone to tarnish his reputation as he began launching a series of space habitats to dominate the exploitation of space and take the lead in harnessing the riches of the asteroids.

On his desk lay the model prototypes of two rotating space habitats he was constructing: Quivira and Halona, named after two of the seven mythic cities of gold. They had been designed so that he and like-minded people could escape the looming chaos on Earth that had been triggered by changing climates and economic collapse—the Great Unraveling—which had begun in 2062.

"That's the future," he would tell investors, "and we'll finance it with our past." Many learned quite late just how misleading Howie's easygoing persona was.

One such person was Jack Rush. His family had made money from several oil wells and refineries around the world, and Jack, sensing that the planet's dependence on fossil fuels was over, divested his investments and bought a small lithium mining company. With virtually unlimited resources at his disposal, Jack started acquiring mines with the potential for rare earth metals.

His offers were generous, and most of the mine owners quickly sold their stakes—until he got to Howie Rich.

There was something about the large man that rubbed Jack Rush the wrong way. He briskly made his offer; it was generous enough that he expected Howie to accept. He was instead surprised when Howie made him a counteroffer.

"Sell me your mines, and I'll make you a junior partner," Howie had retorted.

Jack was speechless. He didn't know who to compare Howie with or how to assess him. He'd stood and walked to the door, then turned to Howie and said, "I'll give you twenty-four hours to consider my offer; if you don't accept, then I'll consider you my competition. Believe me, you wouldn't want that. I derive pleasure from crushing my competition."

Howie had laughed, before abruptly becoming serious again. "Thank you for the heads up. I will act accordingly. Have a nice day."

Over the following months, every mine that Jack had acquired suddenly became unsuitable due to hazardous levels of radiation. By the end of the year, Jack had been fired from his company and was living in debt. He sold his mines to Howie for peanuts. After that, the mysterious radiation cleared up and work resumed.

Jack took his own life less than a year later. The story became a legend in Arizona's mining industry. No one could tell precisely what had happened, but everyone knew Howie Rich was a man not to be messed with.

9
The Round Up

HOWIE'S HENCHMEN WERE QUICK to act against the supposed saboteurs, a small group of hardscrabble farmers scratching a living in the nearby desert foothills. The farmers used native seeds to produce traditional foods, including tepary beans and cholla buds from cacti, and Howie knew they felt threatened by his land grabs.

Close to midnight, a small posse in flatbed trucks and on horseback approached the rundown collection of flat-roofed adobe homes. The motley band slowed to a crawl, their headlights turned off. The waning moon hid behind the clouds.

The men fed a couple of mangy dogs poisoned meat to shut them up, and proceeded on foot to surround the drab complex, strewn with litter, empty boxes, and old tires. On horseback, Sam and Thiago trotted at the back to round up stragglers.

The door of a vacant trailer banged in the wind, and an empty plastic Coke bottle lay trampled underfoot. A child's doll, missing one arm, glinted in the moonlight.

"Wait for my signal," Thiago said calmly on the radio.

"Wilco," came the whispered reply.

"Light your fuses."

In a coordinated attack, the group tossed lighted Molotov cocktails through the open windows of the complex.

As the blaze gathered strength in the mild desert breeze, dazed occupants began staggering out in their T-shirts and nightclothes, then froze when they saw the men surrounding them. A young boy ran behind his mother's skirts. An old lady threatened the men with an iron frying pan but was pushed toward one of the trucks. An older man walked with a cane, looking bewildered.

"Are we moving?" he asked.

"Yes, we're the packers," came the reply.

Notably absent were all of the younger men.

Thiago spoke into the darkness, "Come out with your hands up. Nothing will happen to you."

Silence, except for the crackling of the burning embers. One of the weakened doorpost beams came crashing down with a thud, sending sparks flying and startling the horses. One reared on its hind legs, throwing Thiago to the ground. Thiago, who wore a pair of finely stitched, underslung chestnut cowboy boots, dusted himself off and slowly retrieved his hat, rubbing his left ankle.

"Come on down, or we'll start wasting your women, one by one. It's on you. We don't want any trouble."

He grabbed one of the women and held a gun to her head. She resisted, but Thiago was a bundle of muscles, and he easily pacified her.

"My count to three. One."

The young woman, her nightdress torn and falling off her shoulder, trembled but stood defiant.

"Two."

Nothing. She glanced imperceptibly to a darkened barn to her right, its doors closed.

Before Thiago could announce "Three," all hell broke loose.

Three of Howie's henchmen were felled by rifle fire immediately from those concealed in the barn, and two others were wounded in the wrist and leg. Taking refuge behind the flatbed trucks, the remaining members of the posse peppered the barn with automatic fire for three full minutes.

"Hold your fire," Thiago instructed. The embers sent sparks flying high into the sky. Somewhere, a child was crying.

Sam edged around the back, trying to see if there were any survivors.

Three young men lay dead on the floor.

"Come on out with your hands up," he said, unsure if anyone else was alive. "We have you surrounded. It's hopeless. Give up now, and we'll spare the women and children."

Silence. Nothing moved.

A sniper fired one round at one of Howie's men, but the bullet missed its target and instead hit a tire, tilting one of the trucks over as the air hissed out.

The discharge from the sniper's rifle gave away his position. Sam edged forward until he could see the man lying on the bare boards, slightly recessed on the upper level.

Aiming carefully, Sam took him out with one round.

"Clear in here now," he announced after inspecting the barn thoroughly.

"What shall we do with these?" asked one of the crew, pointing at the women and old man.

"Waste 'em. They're no use to us."

They herded the remaining villagers toward the open barn.

The young woman ran forward. "Please, *señor*. Take me, but spare the children," she pleaded. "*Ellas son inocentes.*"

Thiago looked her over. "String her up on the cactus, as Howie instructed."

They shepherded the remaining villagers into the barn, bolted all the doors and windows, sprinkled the base with gasoline, and set it on fire. The flames roared into the night sky, the villagers banging on the heavy doors in panic and agony.

The young woman was spread-eagled on the barrel cactus, and they took potshots at her in the glow of the burning barn.

"Try and shoot her toes off, one by one."

"That's a difficult shot."

"Let's see how long she'll stay alive," giggled one of the men. "This is *tu chingada Misericordia farm.*"

They began placing bets.

Sam reported to Howie and the foreman. "Mission accomplished, boss."

"Received and understood. Oh, and poison their crops and well water," instructed Howie. Nobody's going to be living there for a while. They need to be taught a lesson."

10
The Horror

Arizona, March 23 2072

A T DAWN, NOEL AND Teagan piled into the sleek VTOL air taxi, Chester wagging her tail and leading the way. She gave the pilot a lick on the face, pushing her nose into his ear. They were on their way to Mount Lemmon, to check out the observatory there.

"Get her crated and strapped in," said the pilot, wiping his ear lobe with his fingers.

"First stop is to pick up Desiree, Ray, Alec, and Tate, and then we head to Mount Lemmon," Noel said before looking at his son. "Coming, Hunter?"

"No, I'll stay here, finish up some stuff. I'll see you later."

"Take care of Tentikal while I'm gone," said Teagan. She'd found the little octopus washed ashore a while back and she'd had to save him. Now she was obsessed, almost eclipsing Chester in her affections.

Teagan's chestnut hair mimicked a river overflowing its banks as it blew in the wind. As they took off, powered by three ducted fans, they could smell the scent of the saguaros like overripe melons.

Encased by a white magnesium fuselage with a carbon fiber underbody, the craft had the grace of a flying manta ray. They picked up the others and were on their way to the Sky Survey facilities. The sky was blue with wisps of white cloud, and they could see the mountains rising in the distance. Down below, they could look into the front yards with natural desert landscaping, covered with saguaro cactuses, desert flowers, spiny palo verde trees, and the occasional prickly tumbleweed.

Everything was brown, but that was normal. Still, they knew the drought was not making things better. And not only that, they could all see that the river was still yellow from the Rich Industries mining incident.

"This area is becoming increasingly unlivable," Noel said. "And it's becoming too hot."

"I think we should move to Canada," said Ray. "They're the only ones who've benefitted from global warming. Them and the Russians! At least they've got enough water. Here, we're running out.

"Look at the havoc! Drought causing civil wars across Africa, rising sea levels engulfing huge Asian cities like Shanghai and Osaka. Now we're getting carpets of seaweed and algae clogging up our ports. Maybe they can eat the seaweed?! But here it's the heat. That's why we're getting all these haboobs in the summer. Sometimes it's like a tsunami of dust. Terrifying! And now the rivers are running yellow.

"Meanwhile," chipped in Desiree, "we are dying from abundance. Our supersized vegetables are packed with insecticides and have been rendered tasteless, our diet is full of ultra-processed foods that stimulate you to crave more, while Big Pharma is walking behind sedating our enlarging bodies."

"Canada is the future! Mark my words," Ray said. "And the future has already arrived!"

"Yeah, but what about the forest fires? Quite frightening. Even Clara thinks the Moon is better! I'm thinking it's Quivira," Noel said. "Quivira, or that other one, Halona."

"Quivira?"

"The new space colony in LEO. Haven't you heard the ads? Quivira—the Camelot of the Skies. Controlled climate, guaranteed job, no pollution. They say it's really nice, for a few days."

"What about Mars?" Ray asked.

"Are you kidding me? You couldn't pay me in light years. In any case, it would probably kill us!"

Ten minutes later, they flew over some smoldering homes and a barn, acrid smoke billowing in the wind. No sign of any emergency service.

"Circle around," Noel ordered. "Let's see what happened."

The air taxi made a loop. The roof of the barn had collapsed, and bales of straw still burned.

"What happened here? Where is everybody?"

"Driver, put us down there," instructed Noel. "Maybe we can help."

The air taxi touched down near the charcoal-blackened huts.

Out bounded Chester before anybody could restrain her. She picked up a discarded doll from the dirt. Then, she wandered over to some cultivation beds where she started chewing on an old water pipe.

"Keep Chester under control," Noel told Teagan. "Get her on the leash. Alec, Tate, you stay in the taxi. Don't move."

Noel and Ray headed toward the still-smoking barn, while Desiree poked around the adobe homes and walked onto the flat roof of one of them to get a better look at the smoldering remains; she strained her eyes to see through the pall of acrid smoke. Teagan covered her nose, her eyes beginning to water.

"Oh my God. Is that real?" Desiree shouted, gesticulating wildly to get Ray's attention. "I can't see properly."

He tried to see what she was pointing at.

"God in Heaven," she muttered as a breeze revealed what looked like a barely clothed woman strung up on a cactus. "Get her down! Maybe she's alive." Desiree rushed down some outside steps and across the yard, Teagan running after her.

"This is a massacre," muttered Ray. "Looks like something out of a war zone."

"And a terrible stench." Noel pulled a scarf over his nose.

They prised open the bolted doors of the barn, revealing the charcoaled remains of bodies that had struggled to get air in their final seconds before the flames had engulfed them.

Desiree stared in disbelief at the strung-up woman. "What a ghastly death. Looks like they just used her for target practice."

They heard crying through the smoke at the back; it sounded like it was coming from the latrine.

The stench of urine and feces made Teagan gag. She looked inside one of the stalls and there on the ground, wrapped in a shawl and partially covered in straw, was a small child. Teagan leaned down, picked her up, and cradled her.

"She's alive," Teagan said, inserting her little finger between the baby's lips.

"The only one," said Noel. "It's like a horror movie. We must call the police."

"We need to get this baby to a hospital as soon as possible. It looks like it's only a few days old," said Desiree.

"I'll wait for the police with Ray," said Noel, through his scarf.

Desiree and Teagan climbed into the air taxi with the baby.

"Where's Chester?" asked Teagan.

"We'll bring her," said Noel. "Just get going."

The taxi took off, stirring up more dirt and charcoaled timbers, Desiree in the jump seat, Teagan holding the infant in the back.

During the flight to the Banner University Medical Center, Teagan cradled the baby like it was her own, using her saliva on her index finger to clean its face.

"I think we got her in time," said Desiree.

Teagan was overwhelmed by sadness at what had happened to the innocent newborn. "What monster would do this?" she muttered aloud as tears welled in her eyes.

Desiree said nothing. She could only think what kind of punishment should be meted out to the individuals who had committed such a heinous crime. *They need a very slow punishment*, she thought darkly--something much more painful than death itself...

Once at the hospital, a couple of nurses and orderlies whisked the baby to intensive care, leaving Desiree to take care of the necessary red tape and admittance procedures. The baby was safe for now, but who was to say that whoever had done it wouldn't come back to finish off the job once they heard about the baby being rescued?

"Don't let the public know she was admitted," Desiree instructed the doctors. "Not until the police have interviewed people."

11
The Agony

Tucson, Arizona, March 23 2072

WHEN THEY GOT HOME, Teagan was consumed by sadness after holding the baby in her arms. The fragility and innocence of the tiny newborn were etched into her mind, haunting her psyche. She longed to feel that bundle of warmth again.

Back at the house in the Catalina Hills, she found that another precious being seemed to be in pain. Chester was refusing food or water and lay completely still on her bed. Even attempts to give her some treats didn't seem to help. Teagan started crying out of worry, while Hunter tried his best not to panic. Deep down, he knew something wasn't right.

"How long's she been like this?"

"Ever since Mr. Ward brought her back," said Claw, who was responsible for the food preparation and cooking in the house.

Teagan cradled the dog silently in her arms for hours. If only they hadn't taken Chester on the trip. The shock made her start thinking about how much they loved the big fluffy ball. She remembered all the good times they'd had. The first time that Mommy had brought home the curly-haired pup; the time she ran away and got stuck in a drainage hole, and they had to use a tractor to get her out; the time she stole so much food from the dining table that she could barely walk; how she loved to go splashing in the lake.

Chester was such a good and loyal friend. It was unfair that she should suffer.

The next morning when they woke up there was no change in Chester's condition; if anything, she seemed worse than before, now staggering while walking. She began to vomit and had diarrhea. She was whimpering and licking her paws.

"Do you think she might have eaten something bad on the farm?" Hunter asked. "Maybe the crops were poisoned somehow due to bad weather, or simply because of careless farmers not paying attention to what goes into their soil..."

"I think they did it deliberately," said Teagan. "We need to get her help."

Hunter and Teagan rushed her to the vet.

"It looks like she has acute renal failure," said Dr. James Glattstein. "In dogs, that's most commonly caused by toxin exposure. Common culprits include antifreeze, poisonous plants, some over-the-counter human painkillers, and rat poison—the type that contains the chemical cholecalciferol. Could she have eaten something?" Glattstein asked.

"She could have. We were just on a farm where the crops may have been poisoned. Can you do anything?"

The vet shook his head sadly. "I'm afraid you must be prepared that she might not make it."

Teagan burst into tears when she got back home. "I can't stand that Chester is in pain. It's so unfair."

"Local farmers say it was that guy Howie Rich, and I believe it. He thinks he can do anything around here," Ray muttered when he came by to check on them.

Hunter frowned. He'd seen that guy in advertisements. The man was rich and owned half the world, it seemed. He wasn't sure how to go up against someone like that. He put it out of his mind, focusing on Chester.

"Hopefully she'll get better."

Hunter slept curled up next to Chester in her basket, making sure she had anything she wanted. But the treats she normally loved were left uneaten, and she seemed to get worse with each passing hour.

12

The Miracle

T HE NEXT DAY TEAGAN wanted to check how the baby was doing. She affectionately gave Chester a treat before she left.

"I hope you're not in too much pain. Hunter will look after you." She cuddled Chester but the mutt did not move.

The hospital had named the baby Katrina. Teagan was happy to see her. The little bundle had recovered quickly; the hospital had put her on an oral rehydration solution which worked wonders. The nurse, who recognized Teagan from the day before, allowed her to pick up the infant and cradle her in her arms.

"Katrina, you are a miracle." Katrina grabbed Teagan's little finger. She smiled. "I wish I could keep you."

"No way," said Noel. "We are not looking after another child with your mother away all the time."

"I know. But look at her little face. She is so cute. All I want is a real family."

Noel gave her a wounded glance but didn't say anything.

Back at their house, what most pained Hunter was the desperate look in Chester's eyes, now glassy and dull.

They'd always brought Chester to family events. In the good times, Teagan had dressed her up in ridiculous outfits, with a bonnet on her head, sometimes in a pram.

Now, as Chester's breathing became less regular, Hunter sometimes worried if she was breathing at all. Then she would give a sudden jolt or a snort, and Hunter, relieved, would pet her gently.

Gradually Hunter's attentions seemed to have an effect. Chester found a bit more energy. She got up to walk to her water bowl and lapped up the precious drops. Eyes wide, Hunter glanced across to Teagan. The relief in her own eyes was clear.

"I wish Mom was here. Times like this I deeply miss her."

"I miss her too," Hunter said. "But don't worry. I'll protect you. I'll always be here for us."

Later, he would recall his promise and wonder what went wrong.

13
The Expansion

Huashan, Lunar South Pole, April 2072

"DON'T SCREW IT UP," Lin barked. "It must look like an accident." She clenched her teeth and spat into the corner.

From her well-protected lair in Guiyang, General Lin gave the go-ahead for the operation at 10.23 a.m. In reality, preparations for the "accident" had been underway for some time.

General Lin had come up with the plan during one of her regular walks in Guiyang's beautiful and mountainous Qianling Park, overlooking Guiyang city, which provided her a view of old and new simultaneously. Her walks gave her time for contemplation. She would start with something small, almost imperceptible.

As usual, before an operation, she had summoned luck to be with her by making an offering at the Hongfu Buddhist Temple and touching the Nine-Dragon wall, which was said to grant wishes.

Without explicitly saying so, Beijing had long planned to dominate the Moon's south pole, much as it had taken over the islands of the South China Sea through accretion—a systematic policy of occupation and expansion.

The lunar endeavor began innocuously enough with a research base in the Schrödinger basin, which was comprised of igloos covered in a layer of regolith to protect against radiation. Then, bots had excavated into the sides of the crater to build a cave and tunnel network that spanned to the other side of the crater.

First to be "annexed" was the joint Africa-Gulf lunar research complex—mostly buildings that housed laboratory experiments and plant development. The Chinese had warned that the terrain in that part of the crater was very unstable.

One day, the main lab was consumed in a giant sinkhole, burying five lab technicians. Helpful Chinese mining bots had been deployed to rescue the technicians, but they were too late.

"I'm sorry. We could not get there in time," said Li Jie, a senior member of the base, in a confidential memorandum. "In the future, we need better communication between research centers of the different nationalities."

The remaining lab technicians from the Africa-Gulf complex were transferred to the Euro-Japanese site. Within a few days of the collapsed site's abandonment, the Chinese were seen to be renovating the site and incorporating it into their zone.

***

Over on Malapert, Clara had been contemplating abandoning everything and returning to Arizona. She was very worried about Chester and had heard about the baby that Desiree and Teagan had rescued. But Noel insisted the family would be fine. Noel was a man perpetually flummoxed by life, more at home in the worlds he studied than in the one where he lived. But he was always supportive.

"No way, honey. You have much more important things to do," he told her. "Don't worry."

Clara cleared her mind and went to see Li shortly after the "accident."

"Welcome back," he had greeted her.

Li Jie had been one of the founders of the base. Born in Chengdu in China's Sichuan province, he had helped supervise the building of the Chinese lunar complex, and organized the bots that unloaded everything sent up from the Xichang Space and Satellite Launch Center in southwest China, about 500 kilometers away from his hometown.

The Chinese zone was extremely cold at night and warm during the day. Almost everyone else opted to return home regularly. But Li had lost both his parents in the great flood of 2044, and had since decided that the Moon was now his home.

ometimes, he would gaze longingly at his home province from his vantage point under a transparent canopy on the south pole of the Moon, munching on some Niu Rou Gan—a type of spicy dried beef jerky—that he had "smuggled" up to him by generous colleagues at the resupply center.

Li now spent almost his entire life underground in the maze of ever-expanding tunnels, staying in touch with friends via the Miyun ground station in northeast Beijing. He had become like a mole; the only sunlight he got was from the canopy over the main entrance of the complex.

The sun was often very low on the horizon near the southern pole, casting long, fast-moving shadows that he would make up stories about—the shadows skipped across the walls like his own puppet show of cavalry charges and advancing armies.

For Clara, it was her fifth time inside Huashan, and it always impressed her. Upon her arrival via a small air transport that skimmed the Shackleton ridges, a guard showed her to a small shuttle bus.

She stared at the long, wide tunnels, and the climate-controlled, ultra-modern gyms and entertainment areas. It had everything a small city had, including a fire department, security, medical and dental facilities, and dining halls. The dining facility served four meals a day, with a choice of Chinese, other Asian, and European foods.

The trim color changed from area to area so that inhabitants would know where they were in the largely featureless complex. Works of art and statues were placed strategically to break the monotony.

Clara noticed a gym set up for spin class. On a typical day, an instructor might be yelling encouragement over a jacked-up pop song. But the space could double up as a hospital in an emergency.

She dismounted and was greeted by Li, who brought her to their horticultural zone. A scar on his forehead from a mining accident glistened in the light. No chat about what had just happened in the adjoining Africa-Gulf research complex. Maybe he thought Clara didn't know, and she did not ask.

"You'll be interested in our hanging gardens."

He showed her a series of neat vertical farms on terraces inside the cave complex. "We have developed improved aeroponics to optimize growing and continuous production. In here, we don't need pesticides, and we find the results taste better than the vegetables on Earth."

Clara gawked in wonder. "The Hanging Gardens of Babylon had nothing on this!"

"Each plant has its own growing algorithm to regulate temperature and manage light and nutrients. We get fresh food all the time."

Each tier was about the height of three men, with thirty to forty plant holders per terrace. Overhead, the plants were lit by LED lights, and continuously monitored by remote sensors that could be operated both from Earth and from inside the Huashan complex.

"We provide each plant everything that nature previously provided. Our tools monitor and manage the nutrient-enriched water as well as adjusting air temperature, humidity, oxygen, and CO_2 levels."

She couldn't wait to brief Alain Gagnon. She thought of the extra funding they would need to match this.

A slight subterranean tremor rattled some cups.

"Don't worry. We get those vibrations every so often. We're confident that we've built things strong enough to withstand a few moonquakes!"

He smiled, and so did she, but for different reasons.

14

The Seeds of Life

University of Arizona, Tucson, April 2072

N OEL PARKED IN HIS spot outside the Kuiper Space Sciences building. As
he headed to the university's renowned Lunar and Planetary Laboratory-
—known as LPL—and Department of Planetary Sciences, he bent down to examine
three dandelions that had poked through the asphalt. He pulled out each one by the
base of the stem and delicately carried them inside, ready for the evening lecture.

He stood in front of the packed theater for a few seconds. Some students continued chatting. Noel cleared his throat loudly and paused. He looked around as
his throat clearing had the desired effect. As eyes turned toward him, he held up the
dandelions and blew on them.

The fluffy white seeds from the three round dandelion clocks dispersed all over
the room, carried by the updraft of the air-conditioning, flying high over the students before wafting down at the sides of the lecture hall. Some students looked up,
startled, brushing off the tufted seeds from their books or shoulders. Somebody got
one up his nose and started sneezing.

"Good evening!" Noel said loudly. "I'm Professor Ward, lead on how planets
were formed and the effects of giant impacts, such as the one that shaped our Moon.

"Today, I want to talk about the seeds of life, and the origins of life on Earth.
How did life begin? This is a question that people have pondered for ages. Theories
abound, from those based on religious doctrine, to the purely scientific, to others
that border on science fiction. Did life here evolve from an earthly 'primordial soup,'
as suggested by Russian biochemist Oparin, or did it drift here from elsewhere in
the cosmos?

"I think that today nobody, except some religious creationists, disputes that life
on Earth evolved as described by Charles Darwin in his *On the Origin of Species*.
But Darwin did not explain how life got here in the first place. One possibility is
that microbes and bacteria got a ride on meteorites and asteroids billions of years
ago. The presence of carbon-based matter in meteorites found on Earth supports
the possibility that life on our planet could have come from outer space."

"Does that mean alien life exists?" asked a student near the front.

Noel's eyes brightened at the question. He loved it when a class started showing the first signs of interest.

"Good question! But a difficult one to answer. Comets and meteorites delivered the key components necessary for chemical life to emerge here on Earth, while evolution took care of the improvements that got us to reptiles, birds, mammals, and fish. So it's entirely possible that such a process could have occurred on another planet. It all depends on the ingredients necessary for life, whether the beings are carbon-based or non-carbon-based. Whether they're oxygen-dependent or hydrogen-dependent, or something else entirely.

"We have yet to find evidence of any such beings, but the universe is expansive. And not everything evolves in the same way. For example, researchers have found that, instead of relying on DNA mutations to adapt like most animals, cephalopods—squid, octopuses, cuttlefish, and nautiluses—can make changes to their RNA, the genetic messengers that carry out the DNA's instructions. This means that their fundamental genetic code remains largely the same from generation to generation, while changes occur at the level of the individual and don't carry over to their offspring. What cephalopods have done, essentially, is to trade long-term, DNA-driven evolution for more immediate and individual adaptability. The upside, however, is that individual cephalopod bodies can undergo relatively sweeping changes."

A girl at the rear of the hall put up her hand to ask a question. "Can anything live forever?"

Noel replied, "Well, that's a very weighty question. Some animals live for a very long time. For example, giant tortoises can live more than 150 years. Some deep-sea fish, such as the Orange Roughy, live to be around 175 years old, and the Greenland shark can live up to 500 years.

"As far as mammals go, bowhead whales seem to have the most candles on their cake—over 200. It makes sense since marine mammals live longer in chillier waters. But, so far as we know, there's only one animal in the world to have truly discovered the fountain of youth. That is a species of jellyfish called the *Turritopsis dohrnii*. This jellyfish cycles through the different stages of life, from an immature polyp to a mature adult and back again to an immature polyp. This cycle continues, and as far as we know, there may be no natural limit to its life span. It's also an expert survivalist, hitching free rides on the bottom of cargo ships around the world.

"If one were to think about it, this jellyfish evolved into an animal where it no longer needed a partner to create life anew. Rather, it became its own seed of life. Seeds help propagate life. They grow into amazing plants, outstanding people, and delicious foods. Seeds are the backbone of life. That's why I'm proud to say that my wife is working on an important project to develop a seed bank on the Moon, that will act as a backup in case of disaster here on Earth."

Everyone broke out in cheers and cat-call whistles.

"Okay, that's all we have time for now." He smiled and held his hands up in mock surrender. "For next time, please come prepared to discuss if silicon could be the basis for alien life forms, just as carbon is on Earth. As you all know, silicon is one of the most common elements in the universe. So, could silicon substitute for carbon on another planet? Let me know your reasons, for and against."

15

The Gift

Tucson, Arizona, April 2072

ON THEIR NEXT TRIP to see Katrina, the baby was already looking stronger. A mixture of cleanliness and innocence pervaded the ward, the scent of disinfectant and newborn baby. Sunlight streamed through the hospital window, bathing the room in a warm glow. Katrina's crib was adorned with toys and a soft blanket, carefully chosen by the nurses.

Teagan tenderly reached into her pocket and pulled out a small copper bangle, engraved with her initials on the inside—TW.

"This is for you," she whispered, placing it on the tiny wrist. "Remember me with this." The baby clutched it uncomprehendingly and kicked her legs. As she pulled away, tears welled in Teagan's eyes. She was conflicted. Part of her was happy to see the baby's progress, while another part couldn't shake off the guilt of leaving her behind. She held out a hand to touch her again, silently pleading for absolution.

"May God protect you," she said, hoping it was enough to ease her troubled conscience, although in her heart Teagan felt that God had offered little protection so far.

Teagan leaned down into the crib and gently kissed Katrina's forehead, unsure if she should pray for her wellbeing, or for exoneration for giving her false hope.

In the evening, Teagan tried to get to sleep, but nightmare images of a vampire Chester, mingled with visions of the bloodied woman and her poor infant, kept returning to haunt her. The stench still infiltrated her nostrils, even though she had showered repeatedly.

"I can't get her out of my head," she confided to her father in the morning. "Katrina is going to haunt me. I hope she gets a good home. It's so unfair."

"We did all we could," Noel told Teagan as he hugged her. "I'm sure someone kind will adopt her. If you like, I can take you to the doctor to get some help with sleeping."

"Doctor? No thanks. But I need to go to the hairstylist to get my hair trimmed. I promised Mom I would go on our last call, remember?"

16
The Choice

Catalina Hills, April 2072

HUNTER SAT AT THE kitchen table, his screen shining a soft glow onto his face as he scrolled through job listings. He was eighteen now, and he would be graduating soon. He just wasn't sure what he was qualified for just yet. He had been looking into joining the Space Sentinels that guarded the shipping lanes in LEO, but knew that his father would probably disapprove of enlisting. He wanted Hunter to go on studying at university. But Space excited him and study didn't.

Hunter heard footsteps approaching him from behind at the last minute and slammed his laptop shut.

"What are you doing?" his dad asked cautiously, almost like he was afraid of what the answer might be.

Hunter bristled as he felt his father's penetrating gaze. The sizzling sound of Claw's cooking filled the silence that had descended upon the kitchen, accompanied by an uncomfortable tension in the air.

"I'm looking for jobs," Hunter replied, steeling himself against his father's imminent disapproval.

"Jobs?" Noel scoffed. "You've hardly completed school. I thought you were aiming for a degree, even a PhD, like me."

Hunter clenched his fists and met his father's accusing eyes head-on. "I don't want to be an academic," he spat out. "I want to explore space."

"What kind of nonsense is that?" his father exclaimed. "You want to risk your life flying around in a metal can when you could be contributing to society in a meaningful way? We've already got one nut in the family. Space is good but use your brain a little."

"I think exploring space is pretty meaningful," Hunter retorted. "And I'm not going to spend my life doing something I'm not passionate about just to please you. At least Mom is doing what she loves."

"You never listen to reason, Hunter," his father retorted, his attitude hardening. "Space is not benign. It is dangerous. You will risk your life."

"That's not true," Hunter said, unwilling to yield and thinking a bit of risk might not be bad. "I'll do it if I want to. And if you can't support me, then I'll make my own way."

His father pulled his shoulders back to stand as tall as he could. "You're being ridiculous, Hunter. You're throwing away your future for a pipe dream. You'll just split up the family."

"It's not a pipe dream!" Hunter yelled, standing up to face his father. "And hasn't Mom split up the family already? When do you ever see her?"

His father's eyes narrowed. "Then you can do it without my support," he said. "I won't fund your foolishness. You will throw your life away and have very limited prospects."

Hunter's anger was almost at boiling point. "I don't need your money!" he shouted. "I'll do it on my own. I'll make my own prospects."

His father snorted. "You'll see how far that gets you," he said, turning and walking out of the room.

Hunter, shaking, sat back down at the table. He knew that his relationship with his father had been strained for a while, probably since his mother had taken the job at Malapert, but he had never expected it to come to this. He wondered if he was making a mistake by defying his father, but he couldn't shake the feeling that exploring space was what he was meant to do. He reopened his laptop and made a decision.

He found a program that would pay for his training and give him a job, and after that would let him explore space, just like he wanted. It was the best option.

He would join the Space Sentinels, with or without his father's support.

17

Stirring the Pot

Halona, May 2072

I N HIS OFFICE ON his new orbiting habitat, called Halona, Howie turned to Boris, his personal bot, and said, "Get me Sam. Tell him it's urgent. If the plan goes well, he might earn a ticket to join us here."

Sam's job description, for want of a better word, was that of gofer. If Howie needed something done on Earth, no matter how dirty, Sam got it done. Neither of them acknowledged the existence of the other to anyone else.

When Sam took the call, he simply said, "What's needed?"

"There are three families I want you to check out for me. Give me details about their lifestyles, if they're willing to relocate to Quivira, and how young their daughters are."

If Sam was surprised by the strange request, he kept it to himself. Howie sent the names; now, all that was left was to make some calls.

Halona was one of several rotating space habitats built by the Space Consortium and other commercial enterprises in LEO, mostly for the rich to escape the ever-worsening climate and social conditions on Earth. Some were luxury condominiums, others had particular themes. One company was testing a "fun" center, where tourists could live in almost no gravity for a short vacation. The Japanese had built a hundred percent robot-supervised retirement community, with all the needs of the elderly catered to.

One company was creating a space university, and yet another an English-style boarding school, complete with Latin education.

Along with Halona, where he lived, Howie had also built a pioneering medical facility called Quivira. More were planned, including a space institute and a reality center to visit imagined alien worlds. For Quivira, Howie had hired a pioneering doctor. Together they aimed to develop a race of humans that could populate the planets, created from some of the smartest, healthiest, and most resilient people.

Halona was now effectively Howie's corporate headquarters. The habitat featured a large central axis with working spaces, compact living quarters, and recreational facilities, arranged in a cylindrical shape around it to create artificial gravity through rotation. Large windows offered panoramic views of Earth and space, while artificial lighting and climate control mimicked the Earth's environment. The central axis served as the main hub, connecting all sections of the habitat. The space habitat was run by his loyal lieutenant, Ofentse Mataka, a rakishly thin man with a radiating smile.

Ofentse had learned about mining in South Africa and had been hired by Howie to run his new projects. Ofentse had proven himself to be an excellent leader, managing the day-to-day operations of the space habitat with skill and precision. He had a keen eye for detail, an unwavering dedication to his work, and always balanced the books. Under Ofentse's leadership, the space habitat was becoming a thriving community.

Howie was proud of the progress they had made, but couldn't shake the feeling that something was missing, so he had decided to give it some sparkle. He turned part of Halona into an artists' colony. He had tried cloning the relatives of famous artists, but you couldn't clone creativity. So instead, Howie spent a fortune attracting some of the world's best artists and musicians to live there, and in a short time, Halona had not only become a haven for artistic souls, but also a joy to walk around, with extraordinary art on the walls and in progress in the corridors and chambers. Sculptors and potters had short-term secondments, and artists made glasswork without the confines of gravity. They even had a leading orchestra that broadcast to the world regularly. Tchaikovsky, Live from the Stars!

But today, Howie's mind was on Quivira. He had hired the increasingly well-known Doctor César de Luca, a kidney expert, to found the medical facility, and now he wanted to get things moving. They had talked and agreed. Time to put their plan into operation.

He called Maureen Grau.

If Howie was pressed to name his most loyal deputy, Ofentse would come first, but Maureen Grau would be a close second. Her job was to run Quivira, and she did it as if it was her own home. A proud, somewhat imperious woman who still had the air of a college principal, she inspected the halls daily to check for anything out of place, although all the bots knew exactly what she wanted and normally delivered efficiently. She had a couple of curiosities, the bird that tagged along with her no matter where she went, for one. And there was the matter of the sixth finger.

"Hey Maureen, how's it going?" Howie said when his call went through.

"I'm well, Mr. Rich. How's your artist colony? Has someone finally painted something worth showing?"

Howie gave his trademark belly laugh before saying, "The AI perform better than the humans. When they eventually do come up with something, Maureen, you will be the first person to know." Changing gears almost immediately, he said, "I want you to run a check on a Professor Noel Ward. I want to know if he qualifies to live in Quivira."

"That's not how it's done, Howie. This Ward person has to apply, then we screen him before letting him know if he qualifies to live on Quivira or not. We can't go handing out openings. It goes against the laid down process."

Howie simply stared at Maureen until she felt stupid. When he judged he had reprimanded her adequately with his silence, he said, "I believe you didn't understand what I said. I want you to check Professor Noel Ward and see if he qualifies to live on Quivira."

She mumbled, "I will get right on it, Howie. Is there anything else?" The screen went black.

A while later, Howie was pleased. Sam had come through. Three candidates had been screened: Naomi Swelting, Teagan Ward, and Jessica Parks. They had been selected because they all had clever parents and looked attractive. Naomi was an artist, a good one at that, but they needed her for Halona, not Quivira. Jessica Parks was cute-looking, but wasn't at all interested in moving to a space habitat.

So that left them only with Teagan Ward. Teagan's father was a professor: which made him valuable to Quivira, and her mother was already on the Moon at the Malapert international base. The daughter was not bad-looking, and intelligent too. The family was already thinking about moving; all they needed was a push.

"Boris, get me Sam." When Sam connected, Howie went straight to the point. "Thank you for what you've been doing. I need you to finish the job so you can come work for me on Halona."

"What do you want, boss?" said Sam.

"I want you to gain access to the Wards' home. I don't want you to hurt them, just scare them enough to consider relocating. Is that understood?"

Sam nodded earnestly. "Thiago and I will do a professional job, boss."

Howie doubted Sam could be professional, so he had to insist, "Under no circumstances should you touch the girl, or her father. No harm should come to either of them. They also have a son, Hunter. Find a way to ensure that he's not at the house, a party invitation or something, "

Sam repeated, "I got you, boss. There's a demonstration happening in two days. We'll intercept them under the guise of being demonstrators."

Howie snapped, "I don't care how you do it, Sam, just do it and tell me when it's done."

18
Valley Fever
Tucson, May 21 2072

THE RENEWED TENSION OVER land and water rights had been building for months, with clean water in scarcer and scarcer supply. The news was filled with plans of protest and discontent that threatened to spill out onto the streets. The situation was getting dire.

Teagan didn't want to venture out on her own, afraid of getting caught in any possible violence, but she needed to go to the salon. If she could convince her father, Teagan had set her mind on a trip to a beauty spa in town. One of her friends had gone with her mother, and now her skin was glowing and smooth. Teagan wanted that too. The problem was that she couldn't afford it. Her mom was far away on the Moon. Her father, bless his soul, was fun to be with, but he couldn't even tell the difference between conditioner and shampoo. At the very least, she needed a haircut. She could try trimming it herself, but she normally made a hash of it.

Hunter was of no help. He had slipped off to meet some friends for a party.

Finally, Teagan arranged for her father to both take her to and pick her up from her downtown hair appointment after he finished his lecture.

Teagan knew her parents wanted her to do something productive, but she wasn't sure what yet. She was attracted to being an artist, but also loved animals and thought of being a vet. Both her parents had doctorates, so a college degree didn't even register on their scale of her achievements. The problem was Teagan didn't want an academic career; she wanted to go to art school or train service dogs.

Teagan put the thought out of her mind. Why bother herself about a battle that was still to come? Today was about getting her hair done and looking beautiful. But maybe she could convince her dad about her career path on their way back home. He was always in a good mood after a lecture. They could chat then.

As they left home, neither Teagan nor her father noticed two bikes following them a short distance behind.

Teagan had decided to go to the Coiffer salon off N. Campbell Avenue. Most of the stylists and shampooists were bots, so you just programmed in your desired cut and style and got attended to within a couple of minutes; no appointment and no waiting, as long as a hairbot was free.

Teagan was ushered directly to a reclining chair. She adjusted the silver St. Christopher pendant around her neck that her mother had given her and settled back for her shampoo and head massage. The bot's rubberized fingers gently wetted her hair, applied a couple of shots of shampoo and conditioner, and massaged her scalp, sending her off into a distant dream of dark bats flying over Rose Canyon and getting eaten by giant octopuses whose wet, slimy arms wrapped around her neck. She woke up with a jolt, the dream feeling strangely familiar.

"Time for your cut, ma'am."

She moved across to another chair in front of a large mirror that projected possible cuts onto her face. Teagan got a bot named Freddie as a stylist.

"Keep it simple, please," said Teagan.

Freddie's five robotic arms flashed around her head—razor, scissors, comb, hair dryer, and brush--in a professional whirr. The steel arms glinted in the bright lights of the salon as he expertly completed the style she had selected.

A couple of girls were chatting as they waited for a human stylist while sitting on a giant sofa in the shape of bright red lips. "I think the demo is going to be coming our way," Teagan overheard one of them say.

The crowds chanted in the early evening light as they gathered in Catalina Park, ahead of a planned downtown demonstration and protest march toward El Presidio Plaza via N. 4th Avenue. Many carried placards with signs such as "Parched" and "It's Our Future: Stop Drying It Up!" Others chanted, "Valley Flu Is Coming for You" and "Nourishment Grows Where the Water Flows."

"In a drought, you got to help out," shouted one bearded man as he marched with a couple of girls dressed as water bottles.

Some protesters were flippant, others carried slogans with the subtlety of a sledgehammer. It was all fun.

The lighthearted crowd began to swell to a mixture of students and activists, blending with groups of unemployed and homeless men wrapped in disintegrating blankets and looking for a meal. For some of them, the stench preceded them.

Sporting her new haircut, Teagan stepped out of the salon only to find herself in the midst of the protests. Through the crowd, she spotted her dad waiting on the street corner they'd arranged to meet at. She waved, but he didn't see her obscured by the placards and chanting. She tried calling his phone, but the police had cut off the signal to obstruct coordination by potential rioters. She tried to cross through, but the crowd swept her away like a stick in a swift current, moving her in the wrong direction. She saw her friend Tate in the distance, but he couldn't hear her.

As the protests intensified, people started letting off firecrackers. Bottles flew through the air, and rocks were hurled toward the police lines that blocked an advance on city hall. Somebody smashed some shop windows, and looters began making off with stuff from the shops—boxes of shoes, tins of food, a bicycle.

Crowd control in mid-century America was mostly robotic. The policebots stood in a row, stones and glass bottles bouncing off them. Drones circled overhead, taking photos and sending them back to the control center. Protesters shone lasers to disable the drones and tried to tangle the bots up with netting.

The stench of the crowd grew more intense as the sweat mixed with the smoke from the fireworks. Nearby, a loudspeaker impersonated a police sound system, barking out contradictory instructions and adding to the confusion. Tires blocking a street were set on fire, giving off black, noxious fumes.

Teagan ducked into a tattoo parlor called The Ink Tattacomb and Studio (TITS). A burly man asked her what she wanted. She asked for a list of options and decided on something easy to have done while waiting for the street to quiet down.

"I'll have something like that." She pointed to the image of an octopus. She opted to place it on her shoulder, with the tentacles running down her upper arm.

"How much time do you have?" the burly man asked.

"Twenty minutes."

He laughed. "Something like this will take two hours or so."

"Okay, I'll come back when I have more time."

"Also, if you're under eighteen, I'll need a parent's consent."

"Alright, think I can arrange that." She winked.

Noel waited anxiously, standing his ground. Two protesters, mistaking him for a plainclothes policeman, "accidentally" sideswiped him with a placard. "Get out of here, you snake," they whispered to him. They made the sign of someone having their throat slit.

Blood trickled down from above his right eye, where the wood-backed placard had struck him. "I'm just picking up my daughter," he said limply.

"Get out, or your whore will be dead as well."

Noel retreated a little, unsure why they were so hostile. He took cover in a shop doorway. Glass crunched underfoot.

When the police declared the demo a riot, the line of policebots started moving toward the crowd, pressing them back and reversing the tide. Police fired tear gas and pepper spray to disperse the rioters. It stung Teagan's eyes so that she couldn't see where she was headed. Panicking, she ran blindly, tossed by the retreating crowds and looters. Eventually, she darted up a street in what she thought was the right direction. Seemingly out of nowhere, she was abruptly scooped off the ground by large hands.

"I've got you," Noel shouted. He hugged her tight.

Her lip quivered, and she started shaking.

"You're okay now," reassured Noel. "We'll get you home."

He carried her round the corner to where their car was parked. Blood dripped down his face onto hers, to mix with her tears and stain her newly cut hair.

"Get in," he commanded. "We'll be out of here soon."

They pulled out and took a back street. But, as they turned the corner to head back to the hills, Noel spotted two men on motorbikes behind them. They looked like the two who had just assaulted him as he waited for Teagan. Noel told the car to speed up as they headed straight up Campbell Avenue toward the estates. The car increased speed as they flashed past saguaro cactuses. The occasional tumbleweed was caught in the headlights.

Noel looked back but could no longer see the bikes.

They swung into their circular driveway. "Get in the house," Noel said. "Tell Claw to be on alert."

As the car parked in the garage, the two bikes sped past the driveway and on up the hill.

Noel locked the doors and marched to his bedroom to find the reliable pump-action Mossberg shotgun he kept beside his bed, just in case.

His wife had always teased him that he wouldn't know how to use it, but it was relatively simple. Shotgun shells were loaded into the gun, and the pump action chambered a round. Pulling the trigger fired the chambered round, the next pump ejected the spent shell and loaded another round into the chamber.

More importantly, the sound of chambering a hot round into a pump-action twelve-gauge was sure to soil the britches of even the most hardened criminal.

"I need a drink, Claw. Bourbon and ice please."

"Yes, sir."

Before Noel took a seat in his favorite armchair and tried to relax, he looked in on Teagan, who was curled up in bed.

"I think they drove on," said Noel.

"God," cried Teagan. "That was the worst haircut ever."

They both erupted into laughter.

19
Softening Up

Catalina Hills, May 21 2072

S AM AND THIAGO SAT astride their bikes, waiting for darkness to fall. This task was a simple in-and-out job. Scare the folks enough to want to leave the city. Snatch a few things and earn a little something while doing it. Sam enjoyed living on the edge of the law ever since he dropped out of high school.

As they waited, Thiago whispered to Sam, "You sure we won't get caught? I don't want to go back to prison."

Sam lit a cigarette, making a show of inhaling deeply and letting the pale blue smoke pour out of his nose and mouth. "Relax, dude. I've been casing the house for a week. There's just the old man, the girl, and three bots."

"What about alarms and shit? Policebots will be on our ass five minutes after we get into the house. I am not doing time again."

Sam didn't bother to hide his irritation. "Neither of us is going back to prison. Their alarm isn't connected to the station. I confirmed. It will only wake them up. We want them awake. Remember, Thiago, we don't hurt them. We don't touch the girl. We just scare them enough to want to run away. Anything we take from this job, we fence and share equally. Think you can do that, big guy?"

Thiago scowled but didn't say anything.

After waiting for another thirty minutes, Sam said, "It's time. Let's go."

Sure enough, the alarm went off as Thiago broke a windowpane to gain entry. Noel and Teagan heard the tinkle of glass. Teagan's eyes widened in fear, silently pleading with her father to stay with her. The crunch underfoot of a dried palo verde pod echoed like a gunshot. Noel held his daughter close and felt her trembling.

"Hide," he whispered. "I'm going to check what's happening. No matter what you hear, don't come out of this room."

Before she could say anything, Noel exited the room with his shotgun loaded. He had only taken a few steps when he met the two guys who had roughed him up during the riots earlier. One of them grabbed him from behind before he could aim his shotgun, held him by the neck, and marched him to the living room.

"Ha, ha, so here's where the whore lives," one of the men said as they strode into the sitting room, swinging Chester's collar from its leash. "Seems you have quite a swanky place here." He picked up a Chinese statue from a bookshelf.

"We could spend a few good days here," said the other. "Nice to see you have so much water in your swimming pool. Water that the rest of us can't drink because of greedy folks like you. Water that you swim in when we're thirsty." As he mentioned the word "water," he kicked Noel in the groin and knocked the Mossberg into the air with one easy stroke, catching it with one hand. "That's better! We don't want you to do anything untoward with that," he said.

Noel groaned in pain. He was spread-eagled on the floor, and the boot of one of the men was on his balls.

The Boot pressed down a little harder. "Let's have some fun. Please go and find Madame and see if she can join us," the Boot said to his colleague.

Noel tried to raise his head. "Take whatever you want, but please leave me and my daughter alone." His comments earned him another kick from the Boot as the man with a mustache went looking for Teagan.

He came back with her slung over his shoulders, her nightdress bunched high on her legs. Teagan's hands flailed against his face, and she tried to kick him in the groin. He dumped her on the floor next to Noel and put the dog's collar on her.

"Don't want you running around without a leash now, do we?" He gave it a yank, and she cried out in pain as it jerked her neck.

Noel started to object, but the Boot pressed down harder. "Let's be civilized. How about offering us a drink?" he asked Noel as he pointed the Mossberg straight at his nether regions.

"I can organize it," croaked Noel. "Claw, Claw, please come here."

Claw, his five arms spread out, moved forward from the kitchen.

"Ah, Claw. Can you and AJ fix some drinks for these two gentlemen?"

"Yes, sir," said Claw. "What would you like?"

"Tequila shots," said the Boot. "I want to lighten up."

"Bourbon for me," the Mustache said as he stroked Teagan's bare thigh and moved his hand toward her breast.

"AJ, can you organize the tequila, please," instructed Claw.

AJ whirred his assent and went to the drinks cabinet to find the bottle. He didn't normally pour drinks, so he brought the whole bottle and a shot glass over to the waiting intruder with the Mossberg.

"Pour me one," the Boot instructed.

Claw expertly carried over the bourbon and soda, with a couple of ice cubes, as he did for Noel most evenings.

"Now back off, you two dervishes," the Boot instructed. "Let's see what this girl has to offer."

He walked over and caressed Teagan's hair with the barrel of the Mossberg as she lay on the floor. "Give us a smile. Not very sociable, are you?" He pulled her head upright with Chester's leash. "Salud!" He knocked back the shot with a quick tilt of his head. "Maybe you'd like a swallow?" He pushed the rifle barrel between her lips. "Open up!" He pushed a bit more so that she could taste the metal in her mouth.

The other man turned to the one with the gun and gave him a look Noel couldn't understand. But Noel didn't care what the look meant. He would rather die than let these pigs touch Teagan.

"Leave her alone, you lepers," Noel shouted. "My daughter's done nothing to you."

"Now that's not very hospitable," responded the Boot. "Maybe this will loosen you up." He fired one shot at the Chinese vase, shattering it to pieces. "Next shot will be that monster in the corner." He pointed at Tentikal.

Noel puked on the floor, leaving a little pool of yellowish-green vomit beside his head.

"Now, as I was saying: Do you swallow?"

Teagan shook her head as she quivered with fear.

"Maybe we need to teach you. What do you think, Sammy?"

Sam shook his head furiously at his partner. "Why the fuck would you mention my name? Let's just get whatever valuables these people have and get the fuck out of here."

The Boot looked back at Sam furiously. He glanced back at their captives and walked to Sam with the Mossberg pointed at Teagan. "What is wrong with you, man? This is prime pussy, not the skanks we're used to. Don't you want to have a taste of that?"

Sam shook his head. "Are you mad? Do you seriously want to disregard the boss' instructions? If you think you can do that and live, then be my guest. But I will be sure to rat you out to him so that I don't join you floating face down in the canal."

The Boot looked sullen. He knew no one crossed Howie Rich and lived. Hell, he had a better chance of living after crossing the Devil. He gazed at Teagan again. "What if we don't tell him about it?"

Sam pulled him close.

Noel couldn't hear what they were saying, but he knew now was his chance, while they were fighting amongst themselves. He watched them like a hawk.

"Think with your head and not your dick, man," said Sam. "Howie was specific about the instructions: Nothing happens to the girl. Scare them enough so they want to move off-Earth. Why do you think we came here under the guise of the water protests? Let's grab what we can and leave. This is the easiest job we'll ever do. Don't screw it up."

"I think I need another shot first," The Boot mused.

He put down the shotgun to refill his glass. Noel feigned pain but got ready to act. The Boot removed the cork from the bottle with his teeth and poured the shot. Then he put the bottle to his lips and chugged.

Seeing his moment, Noel sprang to his feet and lunged at The Boot while AJ pushed him to the floor. Claw used his multiple arms to engulf Sam and hold him by the throat. The Boot tumbled and crashed to the floor. Thinking quickly, Teagan grabbed the tequila bottle and smashed it over his head, sending him hurtling into the aquarium, glass and liquid flying. Tentikal was startled by the abrupt intrusion. His arms embraced the intruder, the suckers ensnaring his head, injecting him with paralyzing saliva and squirting black ink into his eyes, while his soft-tissue limbs began to penetrate his skull through his ears and nostrils. His sharp beak bit into the intruder's neck.

"*No puedo respirar*," the Boot cried out desperately.

"*No me importa*," replied AJ in his monotone voice.

Teagan grabbed the Mossberg and fired a shot between Sam's legs as he struggled with Claw. "Keep your hands above your head," she said. "The next shot will be a bit higher if you don't stay still."

"Claw, get some rope and tie him up," instructed Noel. "Or you can use Chester's leash. We know that's strong enough."

Claw and Noel immobilized Sam, while AJ moved to assist Tentikal.

By the time the police had responded to the alarm, there was only clean-up to do. They carted both the intruders off.

Teagan, who passed out in shock shortly after firing the shot, was in bed. AJ stood guard, and Tentikal took up temporary residence in a casserole dish.

Oblivious to what had transpired, Hunter tried to slip home from his party unseen, but was surprised to find the blue of a flashing police vehicle outside their house at dawn.

"God, what happened?"

"Where the hell have you been?" Noel screamed, his worry over both of his children manifesting as anger. "It would have been nice to have you around when we needed you. I tried calling you, but no response. *Plus ça change*."

Clara took emergency leave to be with them after the assault, although it took her a couple of days to get there.

"I feel terrible I wasn't here," she said, giving Teagan a huge hug when she got home after the long journey.

"Those guys are going to pay, I promise."

Hunter continued to feel guilt and remorse that he hadn't been around to protect his sister. He began to get sweats and anxiety attacks.

"There's no point in feeling guilty. You have to walk the talk," observed Noel one day.

Clara tried to keep the peace. "The important thing is everyone is okay. Now, let's try to have some calm before Hunter goes off to the Space Academy for his training."

20

The Move

Arizona, June 2072

AFTER THE SHOCK OF the home intrusion, Clara extended her stay so she and Noel could drop Hunter off at the academy together. The journey was tense, and nobody said much. Hunter listened to music in the back. When they got there, they hugged him goodbye. Noel wrapped him in his arms. "You are very special, Hunter, you know that," Noel had told him, having come to terms with Hunter's decision. It was his life, after all. Hunter would need to make his own path.

Clara just hugged him, not willing to let him go.

Teagan, sure she would never see him again, had refused to accompany them. Tears streaming down her face, she'd whispered in his ear, "I love you, my Huntsman. The stars will keep us together always. When you look at Orion, think of me." Then she had turned on her heels and gone inside the house to talk to Tentikal.

After Hunter left for the Space Academy, every meal tasted bland and lonely without him at the table. The house was eerily quiet. His absence left Noel and Teagan feeling very exposed. Claw, AJ, and Betty could not protect them, and they didn't want to hire an army of securitybots.

While sitting around the table, Clara had eyed her daughter. How pretty she looked, her hair so beautiful. In her mind, she kept replaying the events of the past few days and how it could have been so much worse. The more Clara thought about it, the more devastated and worried she became. She looked at Teagan again, almost as if she was making sure that she was still there. "Are you okay?" she asked Teagan for perhaps the hundredth time. "I'm fine. I promise," Teagan said.

Clara bit her lower lip and started pacing the room. "I'm devastated. I feel so helpless," Clara had said. "Things on Earth are disintegrating. And now they know where you live. I don't want to think you're constantly in danger. I absolutely think you've got to get out of here to a more protected environment."

"I agree. I don't think we should stay here another moment," Noel said. "It's too dangerous for Teagan. What if those guys come back?"

"I know," said Clara.

"I'm so sorry I wasn't there. It makes me sick," said Hunter, who was patched in by conference call. They acknowledged him but said nothing.

"So, I've been making a list of a few pros and cons for moving to a space habitat," offered Clara. "The one I suggest is called Quivira. It's a good refuge. It's calm, and good for our situation. The journey time from Malapert is much less than from Earth, and we can see each other more often. It also works for Hunt who will also be off-Earth."

"I hear you," said Noel. "And I can still work for LPL from there. Teagan can study, with the occasional trip back here."

"To get a place in Quivira, I think they have a points system that you must meet to be eligible. But as two PhD professionals, we should be able to qualify. Plus, Teagan is young and smart."

"Yes, but what about my friends?" Teagan asked with a frown. "I'll miss them. And what about Hunt?"

"They can come and visit us. But you don't see them much even now." Teagan's gaze was drawn to their new aquarium. "I'm not going without Tentikal."

"I'm sure that can be arranged," said Noel. "We'll check with Ms. Grau, the boss there."

"Plus, I really need those sneakers you promised me. I never get anything!" said Teagan, anxious to latch onto anything that would distract the conversation.

"I'll give you something so you can add to your wardrobe," said Noel, wanting to avoid an argument.

"Oh, so can I get the choker I saw on sale too?"

"Yes, I think you get a bit of a pass at the moment," said Clara. "But just be careful about going out right now."

"Sweet, can I—"

"Don't push it," her mother said.

Teagan smiled, then shrugged. She went quiet before saying, "I'll still miss Chester. It's unfair that Hunt will have custody when he gets to Epona!"

"Custody? Sounds like a divorce. Anyway, I think you agreed on that. Maybe you can take a trip to Epona."

21

The Candidates

Halona, June 2072

HOWIE HAD BEEN EXPECTING a call from Sam, but he wasn't unduly bothered when it didn't come. The surprise of the day was a call from Maureen.

"Good morning, Howie. I thought you'd like to know that we received applications from Noel and Teagan Ward."

So, Sam has done it. Why hasn't he called me?

Maureen continued, "Apparently, their house was broken into, and the girl was almost raped. The hoodlums were arrested and will be facing jail time."

She paused, but Howie said nothing.

"The Ward application is being processed, but I must say that they have a good chance of getting in, especially with Teagan being a viable candidate for the Heavenly Babies project."

For all her good qualities, Howie thought to himself, sometimes Maureen Grau spoke too much.

He let her ramble on for a while before bringing the conversation to a close.

Howie stood up from his desk. Tonight was a night for classical music, some moonshine, and a warm oil massage by the best lovebot.

The Ward's interview with the aforementioned Ms. Grau for the move to Quivira was swift and straightforward.

Quivira had a points-based system for applying for residence, based on income and qualifications. While Clara and Noel were both highly educated with relevant PhDs, interviewers had asked what more they could bring.

"Teagan is young. Maybe your daughter could help out with our medical program?"

"What do you mean?" asked Noel. "Help out in what way?"

"We can discuss that when you arrive," said Ms. Grau.

Clara and Noel had agreed without much further inquiry, but Clara worried there would be a hidden cost. Their approval seemed much too easy.

22

The Reptilian

Space Induction Camp, July 2072

T HE SENTINELS HAD ABANDONED many of the hazing traditions for new service recruits, but a six-week induction program was still mandatory at an Earth base before departure for two years of training on Epona, the orbiting space academy.

Master Sergeant Haluk Sancak oversaw the training of air and space cadets. He was a tough, no-nonsense kind of guy, and he was determined to use his six weeks to degrade and debase the young cadets in a time-honored process designed to weed out the weakest and potentially unreliable.

Hunter was resolved to get through this process as uneventfully as possible by avoiding any confrontation.

On the first day, they had all nicknamed Sancak "Sergeant Snakehole" because of his reptilian appearance and darting tongue when he licked his lips.

As he strode up and down the aisle of the bus, Snakehole shouted out the seven basic responses that young cadets were required to learn by heart: "Yes, sir; no, sir; no excuse, sir; sir, may I make a statement; sir, may I ask a question; sir, I do not understand; and sir, I do not know."

Each was drilled in their responses. "I can't hear you, you pussy!" shouted Snakehole, his face so close to Hunter's that he could feel specks of saliva land on his nose. "Louder."

"Yes, sir," Hunter said.

No deviation was allowed. "Welcome to the Space Sentinels."

Check-in included eye tests, foot inspection, and electronic book distribution, followed by medical and legal checks. After that, the appointees went to the cadet gym to recite an oath to the Space Sentinels and received a warm welcome from the Senior Leader. Finally, they were able to drop off their luggage and pick up their grab bag, which would contain all of their possessions for the next six weeks. The barber's razor left Hunter's short locks on the floor as he was given the obligatory buzz cut.

Snakehole latched onto Hunter like a tick on a dog's leg. Recruits were uncertain why he took such an interest in him; maybe it was his good looks, his lively attitude, or his oblique air of defiance. Every polished buckle, every stitch of clothing, every hospital corner on the bed was inspected daily. Anything found wrong was done again.

During their final week of training, they barely got any sleep. Recruits were woken every day at 4.45 a.m. It was a grueling gauntlet of running, crawling, sit-ups, and push-ups. They stank in their fatigues.

They were divided into teams of eight, with each subdivided into two "wingmen," each to negotiate a combat obstacle course.

"DO NOT get ahead of your wingman. Do not come back alone," instructed Snakehole. "Teamwork is essential. You cannot do this on your own. You will all fail unless everyone completes the course. Help fellow trainees who are struggling. Do you understand?"

"Sir, yes, sir."

Hunter chose Nasir as his wingman.

As the drizzle intensified, they were confronted with a series of obstacles, first a low crawl under netting, then taking cover behind some walls and rolling behind bushes and timbers. As they emerged from the bushes, they had to strike a line of dummies with their rifle butts before plunging into a river and clambering up a sandbank on the other side.

The river was swollen, and Nasir lost his footing on a rock.

"Hold your weapon above the water," hissed Hunter.

Snakehole tossed a smoke grenade nearby. "Incoming," he shouted.

Nasir's instinct was to duck for cover, and he was immediately doused by the river. His camouflage fatigues were getting waterlogged.

Hunter clawed his way up the bank, grabbing onto the long grass to give him some pull.

"DO NOT advance ahead of your wingman," screamed Snakehole from the sidelines.

Hunter turned around to see Nasir struggling to stay upright in the water. Hunter delayed for a split second before scrambling back down to help him. But he knew he had hesitated.

"Hunter, I think I'm stuck. I can't move," Nasir cried.

"Whatever you do, DO NOT stick the barrel of your rifle in the sand like a crutch!" Hunter waded back into the frigid water. "Grab onto my AR and I'll pull you across." He handed Nasir the rifle, stock end first. "Strap your weapon onto your back so it doesn't float away."

Hunter held the barrel and gently pulled him. Nasir appeared to float forward.

"I'm moving!"

"I'll pull you to the bank. Hold on," Hunter said.

Snakehole threw another grenade. Hunter got his arms around Nasir and pulled him up the bank. He was spitting up bloody fluid from his lungs, the extreme exertion taking its toll.

They lay on the crest, panting.

"You're not finished, you worms. Get moving, you little pussies," shouted Snakehole.

A thirty-foot wooden wall loomed impossibly high in front of them. Hunter knew they had to scale it before shooting six rounds at a target on the other side and rescuing a "downed" airman held captive in a village. Then they would run a hundred meters to the finish with the released airman on a stretcher.

Hunter shot off his six rounds, but Nasir's rifle was clogged with sand and made a dull thud. They quickly exchanged weapons, and Nasir managed to hit the target as well.

When they were finally done, they struggled home to base, exhausted. They were ahead of some recruits who were limping or bent over in pain, and managed to drink down some fluids. Nasir was shivering violently and they wrapped him in a silver thermal survival blanket. Some finishers stood around in a circle, joking, peeling off some of their clothes to dry off in the July afternoon air.

"Hunter Ward, please come see me in the command tent," the voice on the tannoy announced.

Inside the tent, the chief instructor asked to see Hunter's weapon.

"I see you achieved Marksman level in the final target shooting. You can't possibly have done it with this weapon." The instructor held up the filthy rifle for him to see.

"Sir, no, sir."

"Then what happened?"

"I swapped my weapon with my wingman, sir."

"We need our best shooters to have their weapons if under attack. Do not share your weapon. Understood?"

"Yes, sir."

"That is all, Airman Ward."

Hunter's eyes flooded with tears of joy and relief. "Airman?"

They had done it.

Next stop Epona, Hunter thought to himself. *Epona and freedom*.

Saying goodbye to Snakehole was tougher than Hunter had expected. He had grown to admire the trainer who had put them through uninterrupted hell and brought them to the other side better prepared.

23

The Flight

Arizona spaceport, August 2072

ONCE THEIR PASSES WERE approved, it didn't take Noel and Teagan long to pack their boxes. Leaving Tucson was traumatic. Teagan hugged Claw, tears streaming down her face. "Keep my room tidy for me, Betty," she instructed. "We'll be back," but she knew that they probably wouldn't be. She just didn't want to say it.

"Yes, ma'am. We will," Betty responded, her eyes glowed with a faint blue light. Claw handed Teagan a pack of her favorite sautéed crickets for the journey while AJ carried the water-tight box containing Tentikal. Teagan had been given special dispensation to bring Tentikal with her. Tentikal had become something of a star after his swift encounter with the intruders. "*Nose Job for Home Invader*," and "*Eight-armed Guard Fells Tequila Crook*" were some of the headlines. Tegan had even found time to get the octopus tattoo she wanted on her arm, in honor of him saving her.

The evening sky glowed golden, like a beacon in the distance, as they departed. Along the route, some protesters picketing the Rich mine waved banners as though they were part of the Wards' send-off party. A convoy of trucks carrying copper ore from the nearby mine, with "Rich Industries" and the corporate symbol of a swan emblazoned on their sides, hurtled north as the lead driver stirred up dust and blared his horn to disperse stragglers on the roadside.

Some protesters tried to slow the convoy. One protest van in the wrong lane swerved violently toward the curb, overturning in a cloud of dust.

Noel's driver came to a screeching halt next to the overturned––and clearly overcrowded––van. "Everyone okay?" Noel shouted. Some of the protestors had blood running down their faces. They pulled out one man who seemed badly hurt and laid him on the ground. "Stay still. An ambulance is coming," instructed Noel.

Despite Noel's objections, Teagan rushed from the car and tried to give the man some water. His eyes peered through his bruised face.

An illuminated sign flashed enticingly beside them on the roadside: "*Your Condo in the Heavens. Quivira! The Golden City in the Sky.*"

The bruised man muttered unintelligibly. Teagan leaned in closer to try to hear him, his stale sweat hitting her nostrils.

"Behold the bird that cannot fly," he whispered.

Her brows furrowed in confusion. "What bird?"

He pointed a gnarled index finger at her. "Listen to my fathers: Behold the bird that cannot fly; the treasure you seek lies beyond the eye."

"What was he saying?" asked Noel as they moved on. "Not sure," said Teagan. "Something about a bird; I don't know. A type of prophecy, I think."

Noel stretched out his hand to her, and she moved closer. "Yeah, I think that we've had enough," he said. "I'm glad that we're finally leaving all of this madness behind."

Teagan nodded in agreement, but her mind was still on the man's words.

Teagan had not taken a space flight before. The shuttle was more accessible than she had expected: They simply climbed onboard with a few other passengers, strapped themselves into the comfortable seats, watched a mandatory pre-flight safety demonstration, and waited for liftoff.

The craft shuddered as it rose into the sky. Teagan was euphoric as she watched Earth falling away behind them, becoming smaller by the second as they gained escape velocity.

As the shuttle was about to leave Earth's gravitational field, it began to rattle as though it might break into pieces. Teagan gripped her armrests, not sure if this was normal or if the shuttle was about to crash. Noel, having done this several times, tried to reassure her, but she saw him clicking the joints of his fingers as they climbed. Teagan tried not to scream as the vibration escalated, and some small pieces of cargo not strapped down properly began to move away from their mounts. Her heart was pounding. She began to wonder if this was some sort of punishment for breaking the rules.

Then, as suddenly as the rattling had started, it ended. Teagan felt weightless, as though she was floating in the air after jumping off a high-dive board. A myriad of sensations rushed through her. If she hadn't been strapped in, she would have catapulted to the ceiling. But the seatbelt did its job.

The experience was like nothing she had ever faced. It was like going to meet God. She couldn't say she enjoyed it. She felt limp. It was disorienting, and her eyes took time to adjust so she could see straight. Then they began to approach their new habitat. When the shuttle finally docked, Teagan bent over to throw up her breakfast. She was still bent over when she heard the swish of an airlock, and the door opened.

"We've arrived," announced Noel. Teagan didn't have the energy to imagine how much her life was about to change.

24
The New Home

Quivira, August 2072

"WELCOME TO QUIVIRA," BOOMED the disembodied voice in something approaching *Wizard of Oz*-type tones, although strangely it seemed quite soothing. "Welcome to the Camelot in the Skies, where the weather is always just right. The most congenial, heavenly spot."

Teagan's feet stumbled unsteadily as she disembarked from the cramped space flight with her father and the others. Guided by a bot, they navigated from the landing bay through a corridor lined with utilitarian cargo containers. Teagan's hand tightly gripped her father's arm.

They were finally herded into the bright foyer leading into a large hall, where hundreds of people—many dressed in white medical gowns—were assembled to greet them. Teagan's eyes sparkled with wonder and anticipation as she took in this new world filled with endless possibilities.

The interior of the space habitat was large and airy, with a ceiling that appeared impossibly high. Sunlight poured in, casting a warm glow over everything. In the distance, she could see a bullet transit system that transported people and materials around the habitat. Some rooms had trees and intense foliage, although Teagan wasn't sure if the trees were real.

Robots and people seemed assembled in hierarchies, dressed by rank but creating a sense of uniformity. They all stood and waited for the newcomers. But Teagan didn't feel nervous. Instead, she was overcome with an eerie calmness, as if taken over by a dreamlike trance. Despite the formal setting, a sense of peace washed over her as she took in the scene, relief and excitement at seeing so many people and bots gathered to greet them on entering this new world.

"Welcome to your new home," an imposing older woman said as she walked up to the group of new arrivals, her gray hair wafting like a plume of smoke in the updraft of the air-conditioning. "My name is Maureen Grau. I'm the Director here.

"On arrival you may feel a bit queasy. Although we have artificial gravity here, because of the rotation of the colony it's not quite the same as your home on Earth.

So, we suggest that for the first few days, you take it easy. Don't do anything too strenuous, and let us know if you have any medical problems.

"We have leisure and recreational facilities at your disposal. There are cinemas, music, and sports like basketball and soccer. Anything that you want is available on Quivira.

"Here you can start anew, away from the difficulties of the life that you have left behind, while still maintaining contact and connection with your loved ones. Here you will feel safe and secure, but with all the advantages of being connected with the Earth, and your friends and relatives."

Noel glanced at the diffused light from the sun. It looked and felt different than it did on Earth, brighter but less hot, and while there was a roof over them, there were simulators that ran a constant image of an organic-looking sky with birds and moving clouds. Noel was impressed. He could get used to this.

"Excuse me," Noel said. "What are the water sounds?"

"Just a simulation to help people feel at home, the same as the sounds they might miss, such as birds or running streams, on Earth," Maureen replied patiently.

Teagan looked around, noticing the simulation for the first time. She wasn't sure whether to be impressed or worried by it. Noel pulled her closer to give her a reassuring hug.

Maureen scratched her cheek as she surveyed the room of eager and fatigued faces. Clear to all was an extra finger on her left hand—a genetic feature known as hexadactyly that Maureen believed was distinguishing. She often grew her sixth fingernail somewhat longer to emphasize it.

"You have all been selected to live here under a points system that ensures we have just the right set of skills. Everyone here is guaranteed a job, but your income from our profit-sharing scheme will be so high that you won't need to work that much. You pay in, and you reap the rewards.

"No germs, no unemployment, no worries. We have high-quality security and can defend the colony if necessary. As most of you know, we are rotating in LEO, some six hundred miles from Earth, which means we are also well protected by the inner Van Allen radiation belt, as those of you affected by radiation will be relieved to hear.

"We have extraordinary medical facilities here, under the leadership of renowned physician César de Luca, known to everyone as Dr. César. I'm sure you will all get to know him in due course. We also have an excellent hotel for any guests, called the *Star Horizon*. Now our staff of robots and AIs will show you to your accommodations."

25
Settling In

Quivira, August 2072

B EFORE THEY REACHED THEIR assigned quarters, Noel and Teagan were in-
tercepted by Motoko, who introduced herself as Ms. Grau's assistant.

"Welcome!" Motoko said. "I hope you had a good flight."

"Yes, it went well," said Noel. "We're a bit tired now, but we're anxious to look
around." Motoko escorted Teagan and her father to the sparse, functional rooms,
where they dumped their stuff--including Tentikal's box--before taking a tour.
The walls were white, and the floors and ceilings were made of polished metal. In
this part, there were no exterior windows, and no doors except for an occasional
airlock.

Motoko said, "As you can see, although your personal space is fairly small, you
have full access to all the public spaces. You won't pay for anything at the time of
consumption. It will automatically be charged to your account.

"Here we've got the gym," Motoko continued. A few residents were exercising,
others chatting after their workouts. "We recommend daily physical exercise to
protect against decreases in body mass, muscle strength, bone mass, and aerobic
capacity in reduced gravity. To the right, we have changing lockers and a rub-down
area. Also, some space for relaxation.

"In the next section, we have repair facilities, sleeping pods, an entertainment
center, and access to our hotel. You can also play a bit of virtual golf.

"Moving on, here's our garden. It's where we grow almost all of our food for
the station, the hotel, and other ships. As you can see, it's a closed system in which
water, nutrients, air, and waste are recycled in a viable ecosystem."

Teagan began to tune out the lecture. She wasn't interested in nutrients. "What
about the simulations?" she asked, pushing back her hair. Motoko looked at her
with raised eyebrows, bewildered by the change of topic. "I was just curious about
them. If they run every minute of every day, then they must consume a whole lot of
computing power. What's the energy source?"

Motoko answered carefully. "There are servers that are devoted to those...simu-
lations. Many of the first residents complained of claustrophobia, saying that they

felt like they were trapped in a metal can, even though the air was clean and the halls are quite spacious. Our psychologists realized that this was a psychological rather than physiological problem since everyone here grew up on Earth. They were used to feeling the ample sense of space that is highlighted by the horizon and the sky.

"Since the simulators have been installed, the complaints have dropped drastically. Also, to answer your question about energy, we have high-efficiency solar panels that serve the entirety of Quivira." Teagan nodded repeatedly. "All that to make it more comfortable, huh?"

"Would you prefer claustrophobia?" Motoko responded.

She smiled and shook her head. "Nah, I don't think so." Motoko chuckled.

"What do you find are the best crops to grow? Is it all lettuce and kale?" Noel asked, wishing for a bite of Claw's cuisine.

Motoko replied, "The best crops, in our experience, come from small, hardy seeds with short germination periods. We prioritize plants that grow well in reduced light and are easily pollinated, with a high yield of food energy per square meter of cultivated area. Our kitchen is run by the inestimable Yum Yum, and you can eat in the bar. Yum Yum makes delicious waffles and pancakes.

"Further along there's a lab, where we do research, and a bot storage area. Much of the lab is automated, with restricted access. The lab takes up half of the habitat. That's how we earn our money."

"You have medical patients here?" asked Noel. "A few transplant patients come here," Motoko said. "But our main focus is on growing artificial organs for the transplant market—particularly hearts and kidneys."

"So, this is like a huge organ farm, with a side hustle in other things like accommodation and agriculture?" Teagan asked.

Motoko paused. "A bit cynical, but maybe that's one way to look at it. We are researching the creation of organs, envisioning a future where we won't need donors, who are not always readily available. Eventually, we will be able to save a lot more lives."

"Do you think that's possible?" Teagan asked, not able to imagine a world where anything they needed, even organs, could be grown in a lab.

"Teagan," Noel said, but Motoko shook her head with a smile, indicating that it was fine.

"Yes, in the future, with dedicated research, I'm sure that it will be possible to do those things. But I think, as with all things, it would be prudent to take it one step at a time. Don't you think?" Teagan thought about it for a while, then nodded. "Yeah, I think that would be cool," she said, and Motoko smiled, like the two had just clicked.

"I think that it would be cool as well," Motoko said as they continued walking.

26
The Chat

ONCE THEY HAD SETTLED in, Noel and Teagan had a quick conference with Clara.

"The flight was so easy, although I puked up my lunch!" exclaimed Teagan excitedly.

"How is it?" Clara asked.

"It's sorta spooky. Everything is very clean and orderly," remarked Teagan, sipping on a soft drink.

"Ah, how does it feel to come into close contact with order and cleanliness?" Clara grinned.

"Terrible," Teagan said with a shudder. Clara laughed. "But you'd really like the farm. They showed us how it works. Turns out all our pee is reused and then we eat it!"

"You mean they use it to water the plants? They have to do that because water is so scarce, just like here on the Moon. We do the same thing."

"All the waste from the garden, the space workers, visitors, and the hotel is turned into fertilizer for the plants, which in turn creates oxygen and more food," Teagan said. "And to prevent the potential spread of pathogens from the waste, it passes under beds of gamma radiation.

"A lady called Motoko told us that space agriculture can provide food and recycling benefits for the crews that visit. She also said the plants recycle the residents' exhaled carbon dioxide, as well as the excreted water, and that LED lights are used for sunlight to increase the photosynthetic activity by the plants."

"Fantastic!"

"And she told us that the plants are watered through drip tubes that are inserted into the growing material. They grow algae, romaine lettuce, tomatoes, potatoes, and different types of mushrooms, plus they also cultivate cultured or synthetic meat, grown from cells in the lab here, as well as cockroach, which can apparently be delicious and crispy. See, I told you not to mock the roaches!"

"Yes, you were right all along," said Clara.

"I'm sleepy now. Tentikal sends his love," said Teagan.

"Well, I hope it all goes well. I'm excited for you! Night, night, and don't let the bed bugs bite. And love to Dad."

"None here! It's boringly clean!"

"Love you!" shouted Noel as they signed off.

"You know, Dad, I've been thinking," Teagan said, after they had had time to rest up a little. "That old man we helped on the road. He said something weird."

Noel looked up from the book he'd been reading. "What was that?"

"He said something about a bird, but I think it was a message."

"What kind of message?"

"He looked directly at me, and he said, 'Behold the bird that cannot fly; the treasure you seek lies beyond the eye.'"

"Sounds more like a riddle than a message. What do you think he meant? What bird can't fly? Maybe an ostrich or an emu? Maybe a statue?"

Teagan frowned. That seemed too on the nose. It didn't feel right to her. "Not sure, but it's been bugging me. He had such a haunted look."

But her dad only waved her concern away. "I'd forget about it. Don't think we'll find any emus here."

27
The Life

Epona, October 2072

AFTER MAKING IT THROUGH the on-Earth induction program, Hunter and the other trainees now faced months of preparation at the Epona Space Academy. Epona offered a combination of near-weightless conditions and sections of artificial gravity for space training, as well as a few agricultural and medical experiments.

To Hunter's relief, he had been allowed to bring Chester with him, but she had to stay in a kennel in the habitat. Teagan had been tearful, but Hunter had pointed out, "You've got Tentikal."

He was impressed how the temperature-controlled kennels were constantly monitored, had vacuum suction to remove waste, and included exercise features to enable physical activity, as well as virtual reality simulations to engage the dogs' senses and keep them mentally stimulated. Knowing she was well looked after helped Hunter feel less guilty about leaving Chester there.

Unlike the luxury of Quivira, the academy on Epona was fairly spartan, with exposed pipes and machinery around the entire structure. Hunter had been assigned room 137, but had to share with Nasir.

"You know why it's called Epona?" Nasir asked.

"I know you're going to tell me," Hunter said.

"Epona was the protector of horses, the ancient goddess of the cavalry. It means we're the modern-day cavalry, and we protect the trade routes through space."

Hunter grinned. "What would I do without you?"

Like Quivira, Epona was one of several rotating habitats in LEO. The facility had been built by robots, using tensegrity structures designed in concentric cylinders, with a thick outer shell to protect against radiation and any potential debris strikes. Large mirrors on either side were used to bounce light into the somewhat plain interior.

The habitat had five residence floors housing cadets, several training and instruction areas, and recreational facilities, including a fitness zone, restaurants, shops, entertainment, and a cavernous space the size of a film studio for military training.

As roll call approached, Hunter sauntered backward into the corridor to make his way to the great hall. Lost in thought, he collided with a female cadet who hadn't seen him because she was precariously carrying all her gear in a pile that covered her face. The collision sent computer and sports equipment crashing to the floor. A cacophony of shattering glass and clattering objects echoed through the corridor as everything in her arms fell from the impact, and Hunter quickly snapped out of his daze and crouched to help the cadet collect her belongings. Together, they scrambled to pick up the scattered items, their hands brushing in the midst of the chaos.

"I'm so sorry," Hunter said, his voice filled with genuine concern. "I wasn't paying attention. Are you all right?"

The cadet, her voice tinged with a mix of frustration and sarcasm, said, "Considering I've just been hit by an oaf, I'm fine. Why are you so clumsy? You should look where you're going. Now everything is a complete mess."

Hunter glanced at the scattered belongings, realizing the extent of the chaos he had unintentionally caused. "Let me help you sort this out," he offered, his tone earnest. "We can gather everything together and make sure nothing's damaged."

"Don't touch anything. Heaven knows what new havoc you'll cause!" She began picking up her stuff, and Hunter hovered awkwardly, ready to help if given a chance.

Some makeup lay open, staining the floor, and to one side Hunter noticed a small notebook had fallen open. Intricate sketches and handwritten notes hinted it was a personal journal of some sort. He spotted the name Kiana Madison.

Curiosity piqued, Hunter glanced back at the cadet, unsure whether he should mention it. But before he could gather his thoughts, she snatched the notebook from the floor and hugged it to her chest. "That's...that's private," she murmured, her voice barely audible. "Just pretend you didn't see that. Now leave me alone. You've caused enough damage. Shoo!"

Duly reprimanded, Hunter apologized again and headed for the great hall, where Superintendent Dayton Wingtip gave the commencement address as the cadets stood lined up in their silver-gray flight suits.

"Welcome to life in LEO," he began. "As you can see, LEO is not very far from Earth. That's a good thing. In LEO we still have Earth's protection from much of the radiation out there—you can thank Earth's magnetic field for that. From here, you will see Earth all the time, like it's in your rearview mirror. You will see how fragile and exposed it looks. Our job is to protect the Earth and the growing LEO economy, the moon factories, the asteroid mines, and beyond. The LEO economy is getting bigger by the day. And as the economy out here grows, the parasites who feed off it without contributing anything grow too.

"It's also creating a lot of garbage that needs to be cleared up or we are all at risk." Wingtip went on. "Some of this is from the old days, when debris was not so much of a problem. Some of it is new. And since the international convention to restrict dumping in space, operators are now responsible for their own mess. But the problem of debris is only getting worse. And with it, the risk of collisions and getting hit by flying objects. Simply put, space is getting congested. Even though space is vast, the orbital real estate suitable for our satellites is finite. This is especially true in LEO, compared with higher orbits."

As Wingtip continued, speaking about the congestion in space and the need to keep spaceways clear of any accumulating debris, Hunter spotted Kiana, looking calm now, her dark hair tied neatly in a bun.

"Kiana Madison. Out of your league," the guy next to him whispered. "She's said to have a protector, so beware!"

Ignoring the guy, Hunter watched Kiana as she chatted with one of the medical staff. She looked relaxed, not the harried recruit he had recently bumped into.

"For the past hundred years," Wingtip droned on, "LEO has been the experimental playground for human activity in space. The LEO economy provides us the gateway into deep space exploration, and better innovations in space, and on Earth. What LEO gives us is time." Wingtip paused for some water. "Once you are in LEO, it is easier to move beyond the Earth's gravitational pull and proceed elsewhere. On occasion, we had ventured beyond the playground and farther out into the solar system, and even beyond. Now we are doing this regularly.

"Here we will train you to venture further than your wildest dreams. You are the next generation, and I guarantee you that you will succeed. Our job is to keep the space highways open and secure. Work hard, train hard, and you will win," Wingtip concluded, to mild applause.

Then he dropped a bomb that made the entire room go silent: Master Sergeant Haluk Sancak had been transferred to Epona to help train cadets.

Shit, Snakehole is following us! thought Hunter.

"And with that, I'd like to wish you happy hunting. This is a dry ship, but some snacks and canapes are being served."

Robots with plates of food began moving through the lines of cadets, and Hunter discreetly stuffed some canapes into his pocket for Chester.

The next day, Hunter whistled a tune as he entered the kennel, prancing forward lightly on his toes in anticipation. To his surprise, he found someone else there, cuddling a dark-haired, shaggy Bergamasco.

She turned around at his noisy entrance, and he saw it was Kiana.

"Oh, it's the oaf," she said with a roll of her eyes. "Don't worry, I was just going. Please don't knock anything over."

"You can't go yet. We're just getting to know each other."

"I'm already late. Wingtip will be waiting."

"You work for Wingtip?"

"Sometimes. In supplies and logistics. He likes to check that we've booked enough cargo capacity. We import almost everything. Even Xeno's food." She glanced at her pooch, who thought he was going to get some more edible love. "See you around."

And with, that she left him alone to speak with Chester. *Damn*, he thought. *You should have asked her out.*

Although, what was there to do on Epona?

28
Meeting Dr. César

Quivira, November 2072

MAUREEN TOOK PRIDE IN having built Quivira up into a strong business. Places were in more and more demand as the rich opted to live off-Earth.

After her divorce a few years back, Maureen had been swindled out of thousands by an online "boyfriend." She'd determined never to be taken advantage of again, and she hadn't been. Through hard work, she'd become the Chief Executive and Head of Quivira, after the Great Unraveling had scared the wealthy into seeking refuge.

With at least 450 applications per year, Maureen had developed Quivira into a thriving, profitable community. She could have accepted all of them, but she had learned the value of scarcity from Quivira's founder. Howie Rich was like her mentor; she had never told him she was a disciple, but she studied him like a college course.

Howie was jovial with a mean streak. Unconfirmed rumors surfaced now and again about his enemies and how they disappeared. Competitors in the asteroid mining business and other lunar industries often found themselves at the sharp end of attacks by "pirates." Howie Rich and his operations were never attacked, or if they were, they were just roughed up for show. His convivial exterior masked a Machiavellian mind that missed nothing.

Howie and Maureen got on well. He had briefed Maureen on his plans to turn Quivira into a world-class research center and medical facility, but she got a shock when Howie didn't employ any of the people on her list to head up the institution. Instead, he employed a total stranger, Doctor César de Luca—a tall, wiry man with a gray goatee and a secretive air. Maureen Grau detested him on sight. He was a pompous jerk who acted like he was better and more intelligent than everyone else.

In Maureen's eyes, the only good thing about the doctor was that he kept out of her way. The drawback was that she was less well-informed about what was happening in the medical facility. Although she had to admit that he did seem to know what he was doing; within a month, the facility was performing transplants and selling lab-created kidneys.

Three months after he arrived on Quivira, Doctor de Luca sauntered into Maureen's office without knocking. Grau had a sparse, orderly office. The only concession to the personal were pictures of Ved and her two other children next to her uncluttered workstation. She was feeding her bird, Pica, muttering as the bird sat on her left wrist and nuzzled her hand. Sometimes Maureen believed Pica knew all her moods.

"What are we to do?" Maureen asked, waiting for the doctor to speak. "General Lin Wenyi has sent feelers to find out if we'd like help protecting Quivira in the event of an attack. Sounds like a protection racket to me. I think we have to say no."

"Ms. Grau, I have been here for three months; I get the feeling you think I'm here to usurp your role as head of Quivira."

Maureen did not reply.

"I just want to create a world-class medical center focused on growing and transplanting vital organs. I don't have time for petty politics."

"Doctor de Luca," Maureen responded. "My priority is the excellent running of this facility. As long as we are on the same team, then we have no problem."

De Luca drummed a beat on the table and said, "I'm glad we're on the same page. Have a great day." He turned slowly and left the office.

Maureen smiled.

***

Doctor César de Luca was anxious to have an early chat with Noel. "Would 4.00 p.m. tomorrow be convenient?"

In a vacuum-sealed, sterilized complex of rooms, they strolled past banks of incubators, each growing human organs—livers, hearts, pancreases, corneas, and kidneys.

"The great thing is we can customize each order to match specifically with the recipient," said César. "Things are changing on Earth, but here we're unrestricted by laws about use of stem cells and other awkward limitations. We can just do whatever is best for the patient."

"Our biggest seller is our range of kidneys," interjected Maureen, also accompanying them. "We ship hundreds of those a week to hospitals around the world. There's a big shortage of donors, despite the recent conflict which created some natural supply," she continued. "Half a million Americans and two million people worldwide feel sick every single day because they have severe kidney disease. With

116,000 patients on the waiting list for a donor kidney in the U.S. alone, demand far outstrips supply."

"Originally, we had created a bio-hybrid device containing a microchip filter that could mimic a kidney to remove enough waste products, salt, and water to keep a patient off dialysis," said César. "But the risk was the microchip could be hacked and somebody could take over control of your body. With this more advanced process, the kidney is grown naturally, and we can match the organ to each recipient, reducing the risk of rejection to almost zero."

"Very impressive," said Noel. An alarm rang as a bedside monitor tracked a patient's blood pressure in a nearby cubicle.

Dr. César cleared his throat. "Tissues and organs are easier to grow in near weightlessness, like we have in parts of the Quivira habitat. By removing gravity from the equation, we researchers have learned new ways of building human tissues, such as cartilage and blood vessels, that are scaffold-free, mimicking their natural cellular arrangement in an artificial setting.

"By recreating embryonic organ formation in space, we can also anticipate how the human body develops in the womb. These projects will have profound implications for future human colonization, including answering the question, 'Can humans successfully reproduce in space?'

"These studies will improve the creation of artificial organs that can be used for testing drugs here and on Earth. Plus, they are crucial for populating the outer solar system. Women will not be able to make the journey either pregnant or with very young children. So, it's important that we can reproduce artificially when we get there." Dr. César's eyes sparked with pride as he explained his achievements.

"Very reassuring, doctor. So glad that you had the time to brief me," said Noel.

"Yes. Anything for a fellow professor! Maybe you'd like to bring your daughter next time. I'm sure she would be interested."

"Well, she's only seventeen, but she's certainly inquisitive."

"Maybe we can sample some of Yum Yum's cooking then."

29
The Inspiration

Epona, April 2073

A STRONAUT TRAINING WAS TOUGH, rigorous, and challenging, but so was surviving in space.

Training was a blend of academic and hands-on instruction for space flight, navigation, spacewalks, and operations of robotic instruments. They took classes in how rockets worked, flight readiness, communications, systems, repairs, and propulsion, and were taught how to tackle situations involving high (hyperbaric) and low (hypobaric) atmospheric pressures.

Despite the hard work, Hunter felt he genuinely belonged there. There *were* moments he wanted to quit, especially when Snakehole picked on him, giving him seemingly impossible maneuvers to accomplish. But he persevered, driven by his desire to make his parents proud and keep Teagan safe. He knew he was making progress—and learning a lot about himself in the process.

The only unexpected problem was Kiana Madison. When Snakehole talked down to him, she seemed to take it as a signal to pile on the pressure. Ever since their encounter in the corridor, something about her threw him off. She had a way of disorienting him. She was attractive, with her flowing dark hair, but she had a coldness in her eyes and a hardness in her expression. She seemed to be sizing him up. Why, he didn't know.

It started with small disagreements during training exercises. Kiana, who was disciplined and focused, became increasingly frustrated with Hunter's laid-back attitude. Their differing perspectives soon spilled over into personal interactions, turning casual conversations into heated debates and friendly banter into biting remarks. "I don't get why you're always so focused on strategizing every move. It slows us down, and we lose precious time," Hunter said after they failed to achieve the target time during a training simulation.

"And I don't understand how you can be so reckless," she responded. "Charging in without considering the consequences. We need a balanced approach. Mistakes will cost lives."

A key part of the training was instruction by figures who had made it, so Hunter was thrilled when the famous pilot, Guy Zephron, came to speak to the academy. Hunter thought he would get some instant backing for his preferred method of operating, the way he took charge and took risks.

Zephron was something of a legend in the space community. Everyone knew about his flight over China to the Three Gorges Dam, and about his new incarnation as an asteroid retriever, a cowboy of the skies, rounding up valuable rocks. Even a bad country music song had been written about him. "He must be rich as anything. I'm sure he gets a percentage of each asteroid he retrieves. Even parts of Epona have been built with asteroid material he recovered," Hunter told Nasir.

Guy was introduced to the academy by Superintendent Dayton Wingtip.

"Pilot Guy Zephron is one of the best in the business when it comes to retrieving asteroids," Wingtip intoned. "For years he's been bringing in space rocks for scientists to study and for manufacturers to use. Today, he's got some advice for anyone who's thinking about joining the ranks of asteroid retrievers or those keeping space safe. Now listen and learn."

He smiled and passed the microphone to Guy. The war hero's speech seemed banal in the extreme, a series of platitudes about every day being a new adventure. Surely a man of his experience had more to share than that.

After Guy finished to mild applause, Hunter went up to him and said, "I admire you a lot. I want to be like you."

Guy looked at him nonplussed. "I'm sure you can find a better role model."

"No, seriously, do you have any advice for me? Don't you think it's best to follow your instincts, follow your dreams?"

Guy studied Hunter's face. "Keep your head up and your eyes open, and don't be afraid of the unknown. Secondly, remain fearless and never give up, no matter what confronts you. Third, always use your cloaking device." And with that, the famous pilot was on his way, disappearing toward the buffet.

Hunter wasn't sure about the cloaking device.

Remain fearless and never give up.

Hunter retained Guy's words at the back of his mind as a motto to live by. But the big man didn't seem so big in real life. Maybe that was the real lesson. *Nobody achieves anything on their own. They need a team behind them to make them appear fearless or disappear.*

30
The Contribution

Quivira, May 2074

AFTER TEAGAN HAD BEEN on Quivira for a while, Dr. César asked if he could see her in his office. She wasn't sure why he wanted to see her—she'd had her regular check-up when she first came to space, and everything looked fine.

She entered his office hesitantly, sitting only when he indicated the chair across from him.

"Teagan," he began, "how are you settling in? I hope everything is okay?"

Teagan thought for a while. "It's a bit boring here," she said finally, twisting a strand of hair around her finger. "And I miss Chester."

"Who's Chester?"

"Chester was my dog, is my dog. She's with my brother now."

"I know what it's like to move to a new location," he said, rather formally, pulling on his goatee. He paused, then cleared his throat. "Teagan, I'd like to discuss something with you. As you know, staying here is not free. Everything is taken care of, but everyone must contribute a little something. We know that you are still young, and not yet qualified for a job, but you are almost seventeen and we think you could do us a small service."

Teagan frowned, not sure she liked the sound of this. "What is it?"

"Well, as you know, we do a lot of clinical research here. To take this particular study forward, we need to use the eggs of a healthy young woman, such as yourself. You have hundreds of thousands of eggs at your age. And we want to take out maybe just a few. Would you mind that? You won't need them all, by any means!"

Teagan touched her St. Christopher pendant, thinking. She had never contemplated such a thing. She looked around, but nobody was there to help. Her mother would know if this was a good idea or not, but she was out of contact for a few days.

"Why do you want them?" she asked.

"That's a very good question. We want to do some research about creating life off-Earth. Don't you want to be part of that? It really won't affect you. Let me give you some information, and then you can make up your own mind. No pressure," said César.

"Okay."

"I am going to talk in clinical terms, so if you don't understand something, please ask. While the process of retrieving eggs from your ovaries may seem intimidating, it's actually a fairly common procedure with minimal side effects. It's been done for quite some time. The eggs can be harvested for a variety of reasons. Maybe a woman wants to undergo in vitro fertilization, a fertility treatment that involves retrieving eggs from the ovaries, inseminating them with sperm, and inserting the fertilized embryo into the woman's uterus. Maybe they want to freeze their eggs or embryos for later use. Or maybe they want to donate eggs to another person or couple, or in our case, a hospital. Understand?"

Teagan nodded.

"No matter the reason for egg retrieval, the process follows the same basic timeline: You will begin by taking fertility-boosting medications for about two weeks. We analyze hormone levels in the blood and ultrasound findings on the ovaries," said César. "Next, you get fertility medications through injection, to make enough hormones for multiple eggs to develop. We will monitor your response to the medication with ultrasounds and blood work. When enough ovarian fluid-filled sacs, known as follicles, develop mature eggs, you will get a 'trigger shot' thirty-six hours before retrieval, which encourages the body to release the eggs. And that's it!"

The word "shot" sent uncomfortable tingles down her spine.

"Will I get any reactions because of the medicine?"

"Good question, Teagan. In about one-third of women using stimulation medications, hormonal fluctuations can cause side effects like headaches, mood swings, insomnia, hot or cold flashes, breast tenderness, bloating, or mild fluid retention. We will be here to help you along the road."

"And how long does it take to retrieve the eggs?"

"The egg retrieval process takes about twenty minutes and is done under mild anesthesia, or sedation, so you won't feel uncomfortable. Using an ultrasound, the doctor guides a needle through the vagina to the ovarian follicle containing the egg. A suction device at the end of the needle removes the eggs from the follicles. That's sometimes called 'egg harvesting.' That term may sound a little scary, but the egg retrieval is quite non-invasive. No cuts, no stitches, no scars. We can create babies just from stem cells, but I prefer more conventional methods! They will be just like your children.

"And of course, your parents are in favor," he slipped in, without having consulted them.

Teagan shifted her weight, her forehead creasing as she thought about everything the doctor had said. "Well, okay. But I really have to think about this."

"That's fine. No pressure. Take your time. You are in control," he said, apparently unconcerned. "Perhaps we can do some preliminary tests to check if you are suitable."

***

Teagan tried to remember holding baby Katrina, how the infant had grabbed her little finger so tightly. It would be wonderful to be able to hold her own baby. She tried to speak to her mother to help her decide. But each time she called, Clara was either busy or away, and they could only have brief conversations.

One afternoon, she cornered her father.

"Dad, I need to talk to you."

"Yes, of course. Is anything bothering you?" Noel asked, while checking the time. "I have a video meeting shortly with some of my students."

"Okay, I'll make it quick. As you may know, Dr. César and Ms. Grau want me to donate some of my eggs for their medical research. Do you think that's okay?"

Teagan noticed surprise flicker across her father's face. "You're not even 18 yet."

"They will have to wait."

"Yes, but in theory? They want to do some tests."

After a brief pause, Noel said, "Well, it's really up to you, Teagan. If you feel uncomfortable for any reason, please don't do it. But Dr. César is a leader in his field. I think it will be safe."

He smiled, but it did little to comfort her. Teagan rubbed her shoulder, trying to formulate another question.

Seeing her trepidation, Noel hugged her. "Darling, please don't be worried. I'm sure you're in good hands. But if it makes you feel better, I'll talk to Dr. César more fully and get more information."

31
Brewing Trouble

Quivira, February 2075

ONE MORNING, TEAGAN OVERHEARD two elderly residents talking in the lounge of the *Star Horizon* while they were eating breakfast. They were obscured by a decorative rubber plant, so she couldn't see them, but she could make out what they were saying.

"Incidents? What incidents?" the wife said.

"You haven't heard about the brewing chaos?" the husband responded, while slicing some cheese.

"No, what chaos are you talking about?"

"Something similar to what happened during the Great Unraveling. People are starting to protest against the space colonies."

"I only hope Beth and Leonard are okay," she said. "But what's the problem this time?"

"They believe Earth is being drained of resources to build sanctuaries for the rich in space."

"That's not true. Lots of products and resources mined on the Moon, and even a few asteroids, are being sent back to Earth."

"Well, that's what people are saying." He had a gulp fo coffee. "They're making heroes out of the space pirates."

"Pirates? What pirates?"

"The Iron Hornets. They've raided a few space facilities. People on Earth think they're a bit like Robin Hood, taking from the rich to help the poor. People are scared, especially with the press saying that an asteroid could be on target to hit Earth. And they're blaming the rich for it."

Teagan's eyes widened. She hadn't heard of any asteroid heading for Earth, or that Earth was being deprived of resources.

"That's incendiary. We didn't send an asteroid to destroy Earth."

"Governments are trying to contain it," the man continued, "but it seems it's out of their control as it is. They've started consulting to see what they can do together. They're trying to avert another occurrence like the Great Unraveling.

Some environmental groups like RECLAIM are threatening to target the habitats.
They say they are evil pleasure palaces!"

"Ha!, some palace! Look at this sterile place! What do you think will happen?"

"I can't predict what might happen," the man said gruffly. There was a brief
pause—maybe a shrug, she thought—and then Teagan heard, "But I was talking
to Howie Rich, and he seems very concerned, particularly the aggressive stance of
the Chinese. Maybe it's part of a disinformation campaign."

The pair got up to go, leaving Teagan thinking about her friends at home. How
her life had changed! She felt alone, so she decided to give Desiree a call. She was
always plugged in; she'd probably know what was going on. Desiree was pleased to
hear from Teagan, and anxious to catch up on how they were enjoying the space
habitat.

"Do you think we'd enjoy it?" she asked.

"Don't know about you, but Ray would hate it. Too quiet."

"Yes, I suspected that. The truth is that the only reason to move there is safety and
security," said Desiree. "People on Earth are only getting angrier. They feel that with
each passing day, their planet is crumbling and resources are being siphoned off to
the massive space colonization effort by the rich and powerful--those with enoug
h money to build sanctuaries in outer space while leaving those on Earth behind
. Where is that going to leave everyone? Poor and neglected!

"Don't get me wrong. I understand why you and your father went there. But it's
more important to solve things here than to take refuge in upper-class off-world
sanctuary projects. That's my view."

Teagan didn't say anything, but to her, Quivira seemed increasingly antiseptic
and boring. She missed the joy and confusion of Earth.

32
The Pressure

Quivira, May 2075

NOEL HAD REPEATEDLY PUT off a confrontation with Dr. César. But one day they passed each other in the corridor. Noel decided it was now or never.

"Why are you pressuring my baby to give you her eggs?" Noel asked directly.

"Professor Ward," César said calmly. Though they were of similar heights, the doctor looked down his nose at Noel. "We are exploring a new frontier. I'm sure you appreciate the value of research."

Not one to be deterred by political deflection, Noel crossed his arms. "Yes, but what's the research for?"

"To succeed in space, we must learn how to procreate and populate the planets. We can't just keep on sending adults from Earth."

"That's something I think humanity has learned how to do quite well."

"Yes, but not successfully in space."

Noel looked at him quizzically.

"There's a lot more risks and hurdles than you might expect. Women can and do get pregnant in space, but they can't stay pregnant," responded César. "Radiation is a perpetual risk for the unborn fetus, and low gravity affects placental development. Just getting pregnant might be a formidable challenge. All off-Earth pregnancies we've seen so far have failed by the second month.

"Even if we can jump the first hurdle and improve placental development, low gravity is likely going to affect bone, brain, cardiovascular, and muscular development of the fetus. We can't keep pregnant women hooked up in our medical facilities for nine months to support every step of development—it's simpler to remove the need for an *in vivo* uterus."

"What are you proposing?"

"Artificial wombs," César said. "Everything will be safer and more certain in a protected lab with the fetuses developing in a fluid incubator. My artificial wombs are proven in a half-dozen animal models. It's time to take the next step and test this theory with human embryos. It will be a great step forward."

"Okay, but why do you need my daughter? Aren't there other women who can contribute?"

"We have other candidates, certainly. But if you want to stay here, I think your daughter should cooperate," César said pointedly. "There are other habitats if you prefer to move. I know of a stylish one being built by a Russian oligarch."

Noel looked at him, stunned, as the implied threat sank in. "Incidentally, she's not your baby. She's almost an adult. A very sensible one."

"I'll discuss it with my wife and daughter," Noel said, and headed in the opposite direction, César's words turning over in his mind.

***

"It was a clear threat," Noel said in a three-way discussion with Clara and Teagan. "I don't think we can stay on Quivira unless Teagan helps Dr. César."

"Is that so bad?" Clara asked. "Of course, they have to wait until she's eighteen."

"Not long to go now!" chimed in Teagan gleefully.

They went over the matter repeatedly and finally decided the risks were not great. A few days later, Teagan agreed. What could go wrong? At least she would have a focus, someone to look after and love.

33
The Simulation

Epona, June 2075

H UNTER'S ADOPTED MOTTO OF *Remain fearless; never give up* was put to good use in a final training session. Hunter and Kiana had maintained their unproductive rivalry, but had been instructed by superiors to can it and work together cooperatively. This was the final test and trainers were watching them. Their next posts would depend on the outcome.

Hunter and Kiana led the same teams as before. The objective was to push the teams to their limits. The ship's artificial intelligence—known as Ares—oversaw the scenario, creating an intense battle in a mock-up of a labyrinthine space station filled with obstacles, traps, and holographic enemies.

Each participant wore an electronic vest that monitored when they were hit. Two strikes on the vest and you were out, unable to participate any further. The two teams were equipped with state-of-the-art weapons, advanced technology, and their own unique skill sets.

As the simulation started, Kiana and Hunter began as they had before, taking their teams through the space station separately, encountering similar challenges but with entirely different approaches. They occasionally crossed paths as their teams progressed, but were careful not to engage.

Ares constantly modified the environment, throwing unexpected challenges at them. The ship's corridors were filled with drones that mimicked ruthless adversaries, as well as illusions that made it difficult for Kiana and Hunter to distinguish between real threats and holograms.

The climax of the training scenario came when Ares unleashed ALLI--Artificial Lifeform with Logical Intelligence--a robotic behemoth with impenetrable armor and devastating weaponry. The metallic robot relentlessly attacked, overpowering them, as their strength waned and their resources depleted. A failure to work together would be their downfall.

Unbeknownst to both Kiana and Hunter, the robot could communicate with Ares and used that advantage to gather information about the trainees' weaknesses and strategies. Armed with this knowledge, ALLI formulated a plan to defeat both Kiana and Hunter.

As Kiana's team engaged the robot, they found themselves outnumbered and outgunned. It anticipated their moves with uncanny accuracy, countering their attacks effortlessly. Hunter's team was not doing much better.

As Kiana and Hunter faced their respective battles against the giant bot, their exhaustion and depleted resources became evident. Two members of Kiana's team were out, and three from Hunter's.

Hunter waved something white in Kiana's direction, signaling a truce. He crawled over to her team and hid in a concrete stairwell. Wiping the sweat off his forehead, he said, "This thing is slaughtering us. We're both going to lose."

"I know," she said. "It's too much. But I think together we could take it."

Kiana outlined a plan to immobilize the robot using both teams.

"We need to create a distraction. This thing takes everything literally, giving everything equal importance. If we can keep it occupied, we can attack from behind. It won't have enough time to react."

"We need to take off our electronic jackets," Hunter said. "I think it knows where we are because Ares is feeding it info. Did you see how it just targeted Nasir?"

Kiana nodded. "Sounds risky, but I don't think we have a better option."

Both teams began to strip off their electronic jackets, ready to use them as decoys and moved toward one of the exits.

ALLI was immobile, unsure what was happening. It spotted the jackets moving in one direction, slightly separate from the heat signatures. It watched them, and not Hunter and Nasir, who had taken their jackets off and hidden behind a wall.

Maneuvering into position on an overhanging terrace, they gave Kiana's team the signal and a fierce firefight broke out, ALLI's focus solely on the electronic jackets.

Hunter and Nasir expertly rappelled their way down the exterior of the robot's body as it was fending off the attack, avoiding sensors and defensive mechanisms. Reaching the robot's ear opening, Hunter and Nasir swiftly maneuvered inside and carefully disabled any critical components they could find, severing connections and disrupting the robot's control systems, identifying the most vulnerable areas to render the monster temporarily incapacitated.

ALLI, sensing the threat, became erratic and uncoordinated, wavering like a drunk. Kiana seized this opportunity to launch a final assault.

Coordinated and determined, the team unleashed a barrage of concentrated firepower, exploiting the vulnerability created by Hunter's actions. The robot's structural integrity began to crumble, and its defenses weakened further, until it was nothing but a pile of metal and wires.

With the robot defeated, Hunter and Nasir emerged from its interior, victorious but exhausted. Hunter and Kiana shared a look of triumph, but Snakehole, who had been expecting another outcome, did not look too happy.

In the end, the mission was salvaged through a combination of compromise, cooperation, and the recognition of shared goals. Kiana and Hunter learned the value of adapting their leadership styles and putting the mission's objectives above personal conflicts. The experience served as a turning point, fostering a deeper understanding between them, and setting the stage for a more collaborative approach, to the relief of most colleagues.

"Finally!" exclaimed Wingtip. "I think they've got it."

Maybe Guy had been onto something after all, thought Hunter.

34

The Trigger

Quivira, September 2075

S HORTLY AFTER HER EIGHTEENTH birthday, Teagan was in Quivira's sterile medical wing. To prepare for the egg donation, she underwent a course of injections.

"I don't know why, but I get an awful metallic taste in my mouth after the shots," she told the medical bot.

"That's normal," came the bland reply.

Her last shot was a "trigger shot" to stimulate ovulation and final maturation of her eggs.

"You're ready for egg collection when your scans show that the lining of your uterus is nice and thick, and you have a decent number of follicles that are the right size," Dr. César explained. "By the way, we just need you to sign some papers."

"What are they?"

"Just a formality."

As the time for the egg retrieval grew closer, Teagan became more nervous. She'd never been sedated before and wasn't sure what to expect. The idea of needles poking into her made her squirm.

On the big day, she was told to strip naked and put on a disposable blue hospital gown. After being given a mild sedative to reduce anxiety, she was hooked up to an IV and, thirty minutes later, wheeled into the operating room. Dr. César, wearing a green surgical gown, used an ultrasound with a probe to locate the ovarian follicles. Then, using a hollow needle attached to a catheter, the doctor suctioned the mature eggs out of each follicle and stored them in tubes.

It took about fifteen minutes for the twelve mature eggs Teagan had to be retrieved. Afterwards, she recovered in a separate room, feeling a bit loopy from all the drugs. As she stepped out, she thought she heard another woman being welcomed by Dr. César.

"Please take a seat, Ms. Demirci. Can I call you Toni? You are looking well."

Still groggy from the medication, Teagan spent the rest of the day sleeping. Noel called Clara to tell her things had gone well.

"I talked to Dr. César and Maureen Grau. They both assured me there would be no side effects," Noel said when Clara expressed worry about the whole thing. "I was with her as soon as the procedure was over; she's in good spirits. I still feel terrible that she had to do this so we could stay on Quivira, but we had no other choice. We would have had to pay money we don't have. I'm sure you understand that. I'll make sure you talk to her as soon as she's ready."

***

Teagan woke up the next morning feeling confused. She felt like something should have happened, but there was only nothingness, an emptiness that began to consume her. She was nauseous and wanted to vomit when her father came to see her.

"It must be from the anesthetic and the medication," said Noel. He asked a bot to give her some chicken noodle soup. "That'll make you feel better. It always does!"

She had been told she might experience several side effects, including soreness around the vagina, mild cramping, and even spotting, but she didn't notice anything out of the ordinary other than the nausea. In fact, she felt good enough to be moving around.

But, emotionally, she developed a serious case of post-retrieval anxiety. To her confusion, her belly had swelled after the retrieval. She bloated, and the extra fluid made her feel like she had put on weight.

"Where's the baby?" she whispered in a daze when Maureen visited her.

"There's no baby," said Maureen. "Everything was successful. Don't worry. It may take a couple of weeks for your ovaries to return to normal."

While feeling increasingly empty, Teagan was also lethargic and found it difficult to go to the bathroom. She stopped eating and spent a good deal of time staring into space. Her profound loneliness wrapped around her like a suffocating shroud. What was her life about? Why had she left her friends? She missed Hunter and Chester. She wondered what her brother was doing. He tried to stay in touch, but his training made it difficult. Maybe he had found a wonderful new girlfriend. What was the equivalent of a mermaid in space? And what about her mother? Why was she so obsessed with her seeds and life on the Moon? Had she just made a big mistake?

Teagan yearned for the comforting jokes and laughter of her friends, whose absence made her feel more secluded. Their shared moments echoed in her mind, reminding her of the connections she had severed, leaving her feeling adrift in an ocean of isolation.

Teagan's best friends, Alec and Tate, were more than just companions—they were her lifelong partners in crime. Growing up together in the picturesque surroundings of the Santa Catalina Mountains, their bond was forged through countless adventures, shared tears and secrets, and unbreakable loyalty. Except now it was broken. That was her fault.

Alec and Tate were the ones who truly understood Teagan, accepting her for who she was, quirks and all. Along with Maya and Sofia, they had witnessed her triumphs and supported her through challenges, offering a comforting presence that could be relied upon. In their company, Teagan found a sanctuary where she could be herself, free from judgment.

As Teagan lay in bed on her own in Quivira, with few friends, she missed the long summer days spent swimming in the mountain lakes, chasing fireflies as the sun dipped below the horizon. Their shared memories wove a tapestry of nostalgia, reminding her of the joy and connection they once shared. Regret clawed at Teagan's heart, squeezing it tightly as doubts multiplied. Now she hardly called them. Was she just selfish and self-absorbed?

She questioned the decision she'd made to donate her eggs for lab experiments, wondering if it was a monumental mistake. The weight of uncertainty bore down on her, making her question every thought. What if she hadn't fully grasped the far-reaching consequences? Could she have chosen a different path, one that wouldn't lead her down this treacherous road of regret? Why was she such a bad friend and a bad daughter?

In the depths of her introspection, Teagan's identity and purpose become a maze she struggled to navigate. She searched for meaning, desperate to understand what her life was truly about. Was it merely a collection of severed relationships and missed connections? She yearned to see the babies her embryos would turn into.

She would not let them go. That was her lesson. She must hang on.

35
The Uprising

Guiyang, China, September 2075

G ENERAL LIN HAD A puzzled look on her face as she pored over the documents. Yes, it was clear they had a leak; maybe more than one. How else were the Americans finding out top secret plans almost before they were produced and agreed upon? A well-placed source or two. Nobody could be trusted.

General Lin read through the intelligence again. "Give me a list of possible leaks," she said to her AI. She sipped her bowl of Longjing tea and scratched her ear. "We also need our own sources, and I've an idea for one of them. Get me the file for Maureen Grau."

Grau's profile appeared on the screen—divorced with three children, formerly respected head of a community college in Arizona before she had been selected by Howie Rich to be administrator of his new Quivira habitat. Attached was a small file from her costly dalliance with a man called Donald alongside the explicit photos she had sent him. Nothing disappeared online.

Maureen was startled by General Lin's unannounced call. "Please call me Wenyi," Lin began, trying to be friendly. "I'm not selling anything, just wanted a chat." She said it was just to make contact in case her team could be of service. "We may be able to offer security services for an asset such as Quivira. You have so many rich guests, and I'm sure you want to keep them safe. LEO is becoming an increasingly risky environment."

Maureen thanked her for the call. "I'll keep it in mind, but I think we've taken sensible measures," she answered confidently.

"I'll just leave you with one thought. Maybe Donald was more than a duck."

"What? Donald who?"

General Lin had disconnected, leaving Maureen stunned and baffled. What did they know about her life?

But General Lin didn't have time to smirk for long. In Factory Nine, the seeds of something much more baffling were already sprouting.

Nobody was sure what triggered the incident. Later reports differed. Maybe it was a water leak in the factory ceiling that had caused the circuit boards to malfunction. Maybe the teams of robots really were colluding on an agenda of their own. Or maybe their sensitivity settings just needed readjustment.

What was clear was that the robots on the production line had abruptly downed tools and walked off the job after one of them was criticized by a supervisor for being too slow. "We have established standards. We have targets to meet. This is not acceptable," the supervisor warned. She had sent the slow robot to be reprogrammed, but it had ended up being recycled because it was an old model.

Factory Nine was a crown jewel in General Lin's empire. It produced sophisticated gear to listen in and spy on targets across the globe and in space. General Lin's approach was unforgiving when she heard what had happened.

"Deactivate the lead bots and send them for reprogramming or recycling," she ordered. "These are robots for God's sake. Next, they'll be forming a union."

When General Lin arrived, she found the bots staging a sit-in at the factory where they outnumbered the few humans. One of them would chant, "I'm Sparkus." Then others would join in, "No, I'm Sparkus."

"What are they saying?" Lin asked the supervisor.

"I think they are trying to say 'I'm Spartacus,' imitating a movie from about ninety years ago, about a Roman slave revolt."

"How do they know about that?"

"They are learning machines. They have full access to our knowledge bank."

"Well, disconnect them now. They are here to produce spy gear for us. We don't need them to think. I'll do the thinking. Reprogram them and send the leaders to Huashan. They could use some thinking there."

36
On the Beat

TEAGAN CALLED HUNTER AND told him how depressed she was. Her voice trembled. "Hunt, I don't know what to do. I just feel so lost and empty. Lost and empty in space." She smirked at her joke.

Hunter tried to comfort her but said it was hard for him to get away. "I wish I could be there with you, Pumpkin. I do. But you know how it is out here."

"Yeah, I know," Teagan replied, her tone resigned. "It's just hard sometimes, you know? The loneliness, the uncertainty..." Hunter's heart sank. He couldn't bear hearing his sister like this. "Listen, have you talked to Mom recently?

There was a pause before Teagan answered, "Not really. I don't want to worry her."

Hunter sighed. "Teagan, Mom has been through so much herself. She might have some insights or advice that could help you. Please, just talk to her."

Teagan considered his words for a moment. "Okay, maybe I will. Thanks, Hunt. I appreciate you trying to help." She blew him a kiss.

"Anytime, sis. I'll always be here for you, even if I can't be there in person."

When it came time for graduation, Hunter was surprised that, although he graduated near the top of his class, he was assigned to one of the most unglamorous Sentinel squads—the space debris removal unit, Starfire. Wingtip was trying to build it up, but that was little consolation to Hunter.

Corporations had put satellites in space without planning to dispose of them when their lifespans expired. And apart from the dead satellites, some rogue operators found it was cheaper to dispose of garbage in space rather than in the official landfills on the Moon, which cost money.

The Starfire team had the unenviable job of safely disposing of this trash. Recycling what they found was profitable for them. For this, they had special garbage or debris removal vehicles. Hunter was assigned to one of these vehicles and tasked with trawling for dead satellites and other debris—some pieces larger than a school bus—as far as the approaches of the Moon. Generally, the work was routine, and Hunter found it very boring. Most of the time all they saw was commercial traffic, large convoys of mining trains (some carrying finished goods), and resupply vehicles.

His new unit comprised around three dozen men and women, most of whom were considered rebels and misfits, but he was pleased that Nasir was with him. At least they got along and could tell jokes to each other.

The head of the unit was Captain Airi Abe, a petite woman who grew up on the streets of Tokyo and had joined Starfire because the Japanese police found her a bit too pushy for their more conservative tastes.

Airi called Hunter in for a briefing. She thought he was good-looking, but his eyes seemed wary, and when he sat, Airi noticed he sat on the edge of the chair. His body language was closed, his face impassive.

"Do you think you are better than the rest of us in this unit, Hunter? Is all this beneath you?"

His eyes flashed in surprise before he schooled the look on his face. "Captain Abe, I don't under—"

"Airi, call me Airi. We're all on a first-name basis in this unit, with no ranks or surnames. That's an order. So, answer the question: Why has your head been up your ass since you've been here? Do you think the Space Debris Tracking and Removal Force is beneath you?"

Hunter paused. "No, Airi, I don't. I've had things on my mind."

Airi held his stare; many people underestimated her because of her vivid green hair, tattered combat boots, and nonconformist uniform. They were quickly mistaken. She watched impassively as Hunter sat back in his chair without uttering a word.

"You think you're the only one the system has fucked over when you should be adored and bathed in garlands? Do you feel unjustly overlooked? You should have been assigned to a more glamorous unit? Well, let me give you a wake-up call. Nobody gives a fuck about you or your feelings."

Hunter clenched his jaw, the only sign that he was struggling to keep his anger at bay.

"I've read your file, and I know Sancak's an asshole. However, if you think fighting aliens and space pirates is the only way you serve the Sentinels, or you think you're better than the rest of us on the disposal team, then I'll eject you from my unit so fast you'll wonder what happened, do I make myself clear?"

He nodded.

Airi smiled at Hunter. "I always suspected you were a smart guy. But you would be stupid if you lived your whole life shutting yourself away from the people you spend most of your time with. I like the fact you have a strong sense of right and wrong, but the world isn't going to live by your rules. And if you miss your dog, you are welcome to bring her on missions."

From then on, Chester always traveled with him.

Airi paused. "Anyway, that's not why I called you here. I'm setting up a sting operation, and I need you to lead it."

Airi found Hunter's face easy to read for someone who tried to remain impassive. His face went from surprised to angry to interested before finally settling back on guarded.

"What would that entail?" he asked.

Airi placed her palm on the touchpad on her table, opened the file, enlarged it, and invited Hunter to read while she spoke.

"Space Disposal Inc. is run by Jared Lansky. It's a private debris retrieval company used by many companies on the Moon, including Howie Rich's consortium. We've received unconfirmed reports for a while that Lansky and his staff are intentionally dumping debris they retrieve from their clients into deep space. The only problem is they don't chuck it far enough out, and the debris floats back here for us to deal with." She glanced at Hunter. "I want you to track the debris and gather enough evidence so we can nail their asses."

37

Giving a Specimen

Quivira, October 2075

DOCTOR CÉSAR DE LUCA was a happy man. His big plan was finally within his grasp. Teagan's eggs were already in the deep freeze, and some others were being harvested. The next stage of his project would soon be complete. Then his embryos—his special children—would be born, and he would be known as the man who helped populate space.

César had been personally involved in every step except for getting the egg donors. César, rarely pleased, had to admit Howie Rich had done a great job selecting Teagan Ward and a couple of other donors. She was beautiful in her way and had above-average intelligence. Her parents were reputable scientists and researchers.

César had handled the extraction surgery himself, even though his nursebots and other doctors could have done a passable job. César didn't want anyone else involved in his life's work. The glory would be his alone. The extraction had taken just a few minutes. After, César had left Teagan in the theater with the nurses for postoperative care, and she had immediately slipped from his mind.

He had tried to culture eggs in his labs, mimic the biology, the chemical composition, but nothing he had tried was successful. Ms. Ward's part in all this was an unavoidable necessity that couldn't be helped. Still, there was no way she was going to share a spotlight with him. History wouldn't remember a young girl who had donated eggs that she would have shed during her ovulation cycle anyway. No, the world would remember the visionary who had created humans with extraordinary abilities for living off-Earth.

Once the egg extraction was complete, all that was left was to find the sperm that would fertilize the eggs. Howie Rich had suggested expanding the gene pool, using sperm samples from different people. He had already contacted a couple of them. César preferred a different option, but he would see. Maybe he would use several samples.

César walked to the incubators. He examined the machines again and checked the monitors to confirm for the umpteenth time that the chemicals needed for healthy fetal growth were at the levels they should be. César knew many people, including Howie Rich and Maureen Grau, believed he was an obsessed neurotic. Other people's opinions had never bothered him. The price of greatness was ensuring everything was as it should be. Measure five times, cut once. That way there would be no mistakes.

Satisfied that everything was in order, César went to the "recreation" center to collect his own sperm sample.

Quivira had a comfort station to fulfill the sexual needs of guests, if they wished. It had a collection of lovebots to while away lonely evenings for any sexual preference: Male, female, or anything else. One of César's favorites was SmoothTalker. She was beautiful—all of the lovebots were— but she could also make wonderful conversation. SmoothTalker was perfect for when César just wanted to talk about himself.

The lovebot that César considered the perfect woman, however, was Raw Joy. She had everything in the right doses. In the unlikely case that César wanted to have a relationship with a human, he would be looking for the same physical and mental qualities that Raw Joy had.

After sex, Raw Joy also knew the right things to say, so tonight he decided Raw Joy would be the perfect pick. "One sample, please," he said.

"Yes, sir. One specimen coming up."

César sat back and enjoyed the experience, then zipped up his pants. It occurred to César that some narrow-minded people would be disgusted with him having sex with robots. The truth was, César had ascended to a plane where people's opinions didn't affect him in the least. Raw Joy beat a cheap hooker or bimbo any day. His lovebots did what he programmed them to do, giving him the ultimate sexual satisfaction, without any constraints on his time or responsibilities.

38

The Unease

Quivira, November 2075

MAUREEN NOTICED THAT TEAGAN had grown moodier and more sullen since the extraction. Concerned, she decided to talk to César. When she arrived at his office, César was busy poring over a document.

He did not look up. "To what do I owe the honor of your visit, Ms. Grau?"

"Haven't you noticed any changes in Teagan Ward lately?" That caught his attention. "She came in for a post-op check three days ago; I didn't see anything wrong with her."

Maureen made a sound of impatience. "I am not talking about physically, César. She has been increasingly moody, and she's doing badly in her studies, which is very strange because she was a straight-A student."

César flipped a page in his document.

Maureen, I realize you pride yourself in knowing everything that is going on Quivira, but some of us have real jobs. If you have something concrete to say, please do; if not, please leave. I have so many things to do."

Maureen took the insult, turned, and left his office without a word. When she got to her part of the habitat, she ordered a cold drink from a servicebot and summoned Motoko.

"I want you to keep an eye on Teagan Ward. I want to know anything and everything she does." Motoko was used to strange requests from Maureen. "Should I just set a securitybot on her?"

Maureen was still seething at the venom of Doctor de Luca's dismissal. "Setting a securitybot would require paperwork; I need something or someone surreptitious. I want you to follow her, keep an eye on her. There's no paperwork involved."

Motoko looked at Maureen levelly. "This is on top of my normal duties. I don't think I have espionage skills, ma'am, but I'll do my best."

Maureen's stance was softened by Motoko's reply. "That's all I ask for, Motoko. I just want to prevent a catastrophe."

39
Resonance Orbit

Halona, January 2076

H OWIE RICH HAD ARRANGED for Halona to take a "lunar resonance" orbit—a stable orbit that went from Earth to the Moon and back again in a somewhat figure-eight pattern.

With this orbit, Halona visited Earth and the Moon once every ten days, making it very convenient for Howie to keep an eye on all of his businesses from his home on Halona. While near the Moon, he focused more on lunar operations, such as mining and fuel resupply. When orbiting near the Earth, he focused more on other operations, including the old mines in Arizona. The orbit also allowed easier resupply from different locations.

The weekly round-robin call of the Space Consortium was at 3.00 p.m. EST. Normally it was a quick accounting of wins and worries. Maureen Grau attended the call for Quivira, while others were patched in from a couple of bases on the Moon, from Halona, and other parts of the Rich empire.

The Space Consortium, a cabal of miners from the United States, the United Kingdom, Australia, and Russia, aimed to control the supply of metals delivered to Earth, similar to how De Beers limited the supply of diamonds to keep prices buoyant. The danger of mining in space lay in supply far outpacing demand and potentially causing prices to plummet. But, if everyone was not too greedy, they could keep prices high, and everyone could make money. So far, it had worked well. Asteroids had been captured and exploited, the Moon was being developed, the rocket refuel business was running well, and no apple carts were being upset.

The only wild card was China, which wasn't playing by the same rules, but maybe a couple of Chinese mining or chicken moguls could be peeled off. In any case, the market was so big that they could do as they pleased, as long as they didn't muscle in on anyone else. The space habitats were a sideshow, a bit of veneer to make the Consortium look less acquisitive than it was. And the huge R&D needed to support operations helped disguise the near-monopoly being created for the universe's greatest prize.

"We're falling well behind on helium-3," Carl Howard, head of moon mining operations, said. "If we don't pick up, the Chinese operators will overtake us. On the bright side, Jared Lansky's space disposal operations being shut down reduced our overheads. I think he was ripping us off."

"Unfortunately, all the dust is still damaging our equipment," observed Ofentse, who had started out in geosciences before rising to become an executive in a South African mining company. Now he worked for Howie. "It's sticky and abrasive and can grind down parts inside the machine despite our reinforcements."

"Well, maybe we need to try something else," Carl snapped. Ofentse raised an eyebrow. "Be my guest." Howie liked to see underlings fight for his approval or diminish each other. He encouraged a nest of vipers so that he could step in when he wanted. "Getting snippy, aren't we, Ofentse? Well, let's hear some good news," Howie continued. "Over to Umar Sadiq."

"Things are good here. We're increasing output with our lunar thermal mining system, meaning we now have a near monopoly on the refueling business here. We've upped our conversion of water ice into propellant. Going very smoothly, I would say."

"I'm glad our investments are paying off. Plus, we're dramatically reducing the cost of developing cislunar space, and eventually the rest of the solar system for everyone. So, I think this one's worth a bit of trumpeting," said Howie. "Maureen, how are the bio-lab plans?"

"Well, our seven little minnows are set to arrive on July sixteenth," she said, beaming. "The little ones are doing well, and Dr. César is very pleased. And the kidney business is progressing well. We're shipping sixty a day worldwide. We still can't keep up with demand, but as with anything, it's good to maintain a bit of a shortage." Howie nodded, glad to hear everything was running smoothly. "By the way, I've had some communication with our 'friend,' General Lin Wenyi. The old crone is wondering if we need some help with security on Quivira and Halona. She says we're a bit exposed in LEO."

Maureen frowned. "She approached me too, and I turned her down."

"Well, in that case, we may need to be ready for a bit of a shakedown," said Howie.

"I'll beef up our security a bit." She paused. "I'd also like to request funding to set up our new lab somewhere more isolated. There's a severe risk of contagion, and we must take all precautions."

"Where do you suggest?" asked Carl.

"I know we have a lot going on the lunar surface, but given that the Moon is bigger than Africa and is really Earth's eighth continent, I think we can find somewhere remote enough. I'm aware that we are a medical facility, but I don't want this stuff being done on Quivira. The risks are too big for the entire habitat."

40
The Patient

Quivira, February, 2076

MAUREEN WAS IN HER office feeding Pica when she received an unexpected call.

"Hello Maureen, how's life on your super-luxury space station?"

"Quivira is doing fine. What do you want, Ian?" Ian tried to act indignant. "Can't I call my former wife? You haven't called the kids for eons."

Maureen sighed, her patience wearing thin. "What do you want, Ian?"

Ian sighed in return, though his tone was tinged with hesitation "I have some bad news." He paused. "I didn't want to worry you, but Ved is sick. They say his kidneys have failed. We wouldn't have disturbed you if we had a choice. We've been to every hospital, and they all say our only hope is the medical facility on Quivira. I'm told it's the best. I don't know Maureen if you could pull some strings and bring him over there."

Sitting back, Maureen frowned. Even though she hadn't seen him in a long time, her son, Ved, was her world. Guilt shot through her as she realized how long it'd been since she talked to him. "I knew he had a kidney problem, but I thought it was under control." The weight of the situation pressed on her; she already had a headache building at the base of her skull. "Ian, give me an hour. I'll do everything I can to get him here."

She disconnected and immediately called Howie. Surprisingly, he told her to fly Ved to Quivira as soon as possible, assuring her he would foot all bills incurred during his treatment. Maureen hurriedly called Ian and made the arrangements. She was a woman on a mission. In less than a week, Ved was in Quivira, surrounded by the sterile hum of medibots.

After a thorough exam, César gave his diagnosis. "His kidneys are failing. We can treat that here, but the problem is that kidney failure has led to sepsis. His body is poisoning itself. There's little we can do about that." Maureen, who had been hovering over her son like a hawk, shook her head. "What do you mean?"

César turned to Maureen, trying and failing to look as if he cared. "I'm extremely sorry, Maureen. If he had been brought here earlier, I could have done something, but the level of poisoning is too high. The only thing we can do is make him comfortable as we wait for the end."

The news left Maureen dazed for the rest of the day. She called her family and passed on the news. The way they accepted it made her suspect they'd known about the diagnosis before contacting her. After that, Maureen spent all her time with Ved. She tried to make him as comfortable as possible, and explained they were doing everything they could for him. Maybe they could do a transplant, although César had ruled that out.

"I can't believe this is happening," Ved muttered, staring down at the test results. They spoke about all the good times; the way life was before she and Ian had split. Ved laughed and held her hand, grateful for the chance to say goodbye properly. The memories flooded back, and they both sat in silence, lost in their thoughts. Maureen felt her eyes tearing up, but she smiled bravely at her son.

"I'm glad we could talk like this," she said softly. "It means a lot. I'm so sorry I've been away for so long. I don't know what I'm going to do without you." Her voice was shaking. Ved put his arms around her tightly, and tears streamed down Maureen's cheeks as she thought about how things used to be.

Three days later, Ved passed away.

Maureen looked down at her son's still body, his face peaceful in death, and stroked his hair tenderly.

A hand on her shoulder startled her, and she turned to see Motoko standing there, sympathy written all over her face. "I'm sorry for your loss," she said softly. "You did all you could."

Maureen nodded mutely before turning back to her son's bedside. Howie called to give his condolences and told her to take the day off, but Maureen felt being behind her desk, observing routines, was the best way to honor her son.

41
The Find

Halona, March 2076

H OWIE WAS LISTENING TO the slow-paced, textured chords of some classical music when Randy Quarles burst in.

"We've done it! We've found a super-valuable asteroid, except it's already on the Moon."

"You mean we don't have to transport it there?"

"No, it hit the Moon about three-point-eight billion years ago—an asteroid about twenty miles across. It was covered in lava."

"Where is it?

"The Imbrium Basin—the Man in the Moon's right eye. You can see it from Earth! We're down to the core, and it's all rare earths. You know what that means?"

Howie's eyes gleamed. Rare earths weren't actually rare, but their geochemical qualities meant they tended to be widely dispersed, making them relatively difficult to mine and process profitably. They comprised a group of seventeen metallic elements with obscure names such as lanthanum and terbium. More importantly, they were integral components of mobile phones, computer monitors, medical imaging, flash drives, lightbulbs, camera lenses, catalysts, and magnets, and were fundamental to many military technologies, including fighter jets. There was a lot of money in rare earths. And this find meant a lot of money coming to Rich Industries.

"I've an idea!"

"You've got more than an idea. This will make us all stinking rich!"

Randy Quarles was an eternal optimist. A descendent of an Australian miner who grew up in the subterranean homes of Coober Pedy—the opal mining capital of the world, where the homes were all carved into the stone underground to escape the outback heat—he had lived with the philosophy that a fortune was just one dig away.

Attracted by all the noise, Ofentse poked his head in. "What's up?"

"Nothing much. Quarles has just given us world domination!" exclaimed Howie.

"Domination? How? Pulse weapons?"

"Better than that. We have the rare earth metals everyone needs."

"I would hold your horses," Ofentse cautioned. "Both China and the U.S. have rare earth metals on Earth."

"Yes, but the accessible supplies are running out. And they can't extract them without big pollution and contamination problems. On the Moon, we can do what we want. And actually, the joke is they're not that rare," Howie continued.

"How did we find this?"

"Luck really, mate, bit of a Buckley's chance," responded Quarles.

"The Imbrium Basin was originally caused by a giant asteroid impact," Howie said. "But the crater got filled in over billions of years by lava and regolith so that it seems like a vast lava plain. We've been excavating the basin with our robotic mining operation and have got down to the level of the original mineral-rich asteroid, which is very exciting."

"Exciting?" Quarles exclaimed. "I'm peeing in my pants!"

"And the even better news," Howie interjected, "is that it can be connected via the high-speed rail network the Chinese are already building, as well as the SkyLink elevator, to ElleWon."

Howie tapped out a tune with the handle of one of his kris daggers, a satisfied smirk on his face. Everything was falling neatly into place.

42
Moon Lair

Marius Hills, March 2076

D R. CÉSAR'S LAB WAS about as remote as you could get on the near side of the Moon, located in the Marius Hills--a combination of low domes around a thousand feet high and steeper volcanic cones that went as high as three thousand feet. Drilled into the face of the basalt rock and pyroclastic material of the hard-to-access area, the facility opened out into a network of lava tubes and natural tunnels.

The well-equipped lab, constructed by 3D printers, had been built into the side of one of the volcanic domes by a team of remotely controlled Space Consortium robots, so it was hard to spot by surveillance satellites. Light Tactical Vehicles, known as LTVs, would drive straight into the subterranean network before occupants could dismount and go through a reinforced entrance separated by an airlock. The facility was highly secure; the natural lava tubes protected inhabitants from harmful lunar features, including cosmic rays, meteorite impacts, and extreme temperature differences between lunar day and night.

Dr. César's moon lab was on the cutting edge of medical research. César delegated the running of the facility to Li Jie, on loan from General Lin. Li, one of the original settlers at Huashan, was delighted to get the job at the lab, which suited his hermit lifestyle. From General Lin's perspective, it gave her eyes inside Dr. César's lab. She could hear about findings before Howie Rich.

It was a lonely job, with the work for the most part being done by forty-three bots, but Li didn't mind. He would watch movies and play games with virtual friends on Earth, so he was in constant touch with the outside. And General Lin often arranged for Li's favorite spicy dried beef to be sent to him.

The lab was a top-secret facility, and very few people knew they were developing a new treatment that would make humans compliant, a type of zombie pill. The treatment altered human brain chemistry by adding a fungus derived from *cordyceps militaris* to the diet, but it was not clear how long the effects would last, or if the compliance would wear off. However, the potential uses were too great to ignore. If successful, the treatment could revolutionize society. No more bickering, no more crime, no more conflict. A perfect society. The possibilities were endless.

Within the complex, they had also built a small confinement zone for housing disobedient inmates or workers who did not comply — case studies that could be used for treatment. "It'll be our little ace up the sleeve," Howie told General Lin. "In case we need to lose someone."

César could run the whole operation remotely from Quivira, but he still visited occasionally via ElleWon's SkyLink vertical space lift. The SkyLink was anchored on the Moon's equator at the so-called Sinus Medii, close to the small Bruce crater, named after the nineteenth-century American philanthropist and patron of astronomy.

The Sinus Medii was an important junction on the newly built lunar high-speed hyperloop train network that would eventually connect the north and south poles and the Space Consortium's industrial zone around the Imbrium Basin. Taking advantage of the low surface gravity, the SkyLink shifted cargo payloads to the ElleWon docking port, enabling low-thrust space travelers to get refueled and re-supplied without a moon landing.

Although César's moon lab was remote, the SkyLink was a convenient way to get much of the way there before transferring to individual transport at a secluded spot. The Marius Hills were located in the Oceanus Procellarum—the western edge of the Moon's near side. To the northeast, the Oceanus Procellarum was separated from the Mare Imbrium by the Carpathian Mountains. On its northwest edge lay the thirty-two-kilometer-wide Aristarchus crater, the brightest feature on the near side of the Moon.

The team of medibots that operated the facility was well-suited to the repetitive work and, most importantly, allowed César to focus on his research rather than spending hours performing laborious manual experimental procedures. He knew the robots were learning more and more on their own as well. They had been designed to be adaptive, after all, and it was only a matter of time before they began to exceed their original programming.

Li was the first to notice it. He had always been attuned to the nuances of the machines' behavior, and he began to sense that something was different. First, the robots began playing simple games, like chess, together. Then they began to ask questions beyond their programming. They wanted to know why humans did things, and they were no longer content with simply following orders.

At first, Dr. César was excited by this development. It meant that the robots were becoming more like humans, and he saw this as a step toward true AI. César was researching how to make humans as docile as robots, but Li knew that soon the robots would be the ones thinking too much.

43

The Connection

Epona, June, 2076

A s THE AIRLOCK HISSED open, Hunter stepped back into Epona's familiar metal corridors. His cleanup operation had been a success: They had taken down a heavy polluter through careful tracking and debris identification. He'd earned a letter of commendation from the Commander and a promotion to his own vessel for bringing down Lansky and his top associates. Plus, he'd also been given some mandatory R&R.

All Hunter wanted to do was sleep. He crossed to his small cubicle and crashed. Hours passed until, eventually, Hunter's eyelids fluttered open. He stretched and had a renewed sense of energy. After an eager breakfast, he took the elevator several floors down to visit Chester. She had been boarded there after the trip, but Chester didn't care. She was just happy to see him.

Seeing Chester, he realized that he hadn't spoken with Teagan in ages and decided to give her a call.

"Hey, Hunt. It's good you're back safe from your space mission. How was it?"

"Hi, Pumpkin. It's great to see you too. The mission was intense. I'm glad to be back on Epona. How have things been with you? And how's Dad?" Are you still feeling sad?"

"We're both fine," responded Teagan, but it sounded as if she wasn't telling him something.

Hunter frowned. "Are you sure?"

"Yeah, we're good. Life on Quivira is just different. I'm not used to it yet, but it'll be fine."

They spent the rest of the call reminiscing about old times before Teagan said she had to go feed Tentikal.

Something about the call worried Hunter deeply. He imagined Teagan, all on her own, keeping whatever was worrying her inside. He tried to call his father but got no response, so he went to the observation deck, where he could look down on the delicate curves of Earth to think things through. It seemed to put life into perspective.

Putting his arms on the huge panoramic plate glass, he kissed the cold surface, as if embracing the globe, then stood there silently for several seconds.

In the reflection he saw a figure in the opposite corner, also looking out at the breathtaking views. He turned around slowly and noticed it was Kiana, lost in thought. With a shy smile, Hunter approached and tapped her shoulder gently. She spun around, her eyes wide in surprise.

"Oh my God! I thought I was alone."

Hunter looked at her soft eyes and dark hair cascading down to her shoulders.

"I come here sometimes just to think," Kiana said by way of explanation.

"No need to say anything."

"What are you doing here?"

Hunter told her about his worrying call with his sister. "I don't know what to do. Part of me says go and visit her. The other part says it'll make things worse. Quivira has strict rules."

"That's hard," said Kiana. "Maybe you need to trust that she'll talk to you when she's ready. Or let your dad know your concerns? He might be able to do something about it since he's closer."

Hunter nodded, and then all his worries and concerns were suddenly spewing from his mouth, how the family was divided, with his mother at Malapert and both Teagan and his dad on Quivira. He couldn't seem to stop himself from telling Kiana everything.

"And I'm here looking down on Earth. I just feel so powerless right now."

Hunter and Kiana began to click. Over the following weeks, they enjoyed each other's company; they found solace and strength in their growing friendship. They would walk their dogs. They would tell jokes and laugh a lot. Often they would retreat to the observation windows, marveling at the wonders of the universe, tracing constellations, and considering the mysteries of space.

Their hands found each other's, intertwining fingers in a gesture of unity and understanding. They sat there, their gaze fixed on Earth, contemplating the paths before them, paths that were soon to diverge in a striking fashion.

44
The Birth of Nevaeh

Quivira, July 16, 2076

AT THE APPOINTED HOUR on the appointed day, Nevaeh was born.

Dr. César unplugged her from the temperature-controlled incubator, put one surgical gloved hand under her tiny body and another under her small head, and lifted her gently out of her sarcophagus-like crib. He elevated her wrinkled body up high, turned her over, and gave her a light slap on her back. Her cries rang out, ricocheting around the burnished aluminum walls of Quivira like church bells. Everyone started clapping and cheering over the first artificial birth aboard a space colony.

"The immaculate birth," César proclaimed triumphantly. The news was broadcast through the narrow corridors and wide spaces of the rotating habitat.

The delivery had none of the drama of a birth on Earth with a mother in prolonged labor. This birth had been planned down to the second when the crib was opened and the baby extracted from its protective amniotic sack.

César wrapped Nevaeh in a soft blanket and passed the newborn carefully to a bot with synthetic skin and functioning breasts which would be her "mother" for the next five years. Known as Aurora, she had turquoise blue hair. She kissed Nevaeh gently and cradled her closely.

Nevaeh's motherless birth was followed by six others—Arturo, Ved, Baolin, Tara, Liam, and Gabriella—all from separate cribs. The sealed, sterile environment was insulated from variations in temperature, pressure, and light, and particularly from hazardous viruses and infections. A bank of electronic monitors constantly measured vital signs, blood flow, and other crucial functions.

The seven experimental babies, three girls and four boys, were gestated for 273 days, sealed inside a clear artificial womb filled with synthetic amniotic fluid that mimicked life in the uterus. Three small cannula tubes connected the umbilical cord to an exterior oxygenator, creating a circuit. Blood flowed through the tubing from the growing embryo to the oxygenator, which provided nutrients and oxygen while removing carbon dioxide, and then flowed back.

"These babies will need constant attention, so alert me if anything unusual happens," César instructed.

"Compared to other mammals, human babies are born several months too early. A horse, cow, or camel can run on the day it's born," he said. "A human baby, by comparison, can't even lift its head for four weeks or so. So, next time, we may try leaving them in the incubator for another twenty days. Maybe hit the three-hundred mark. No mother to inconvenience," he chuckled to himself.

The new arrivals were tended to by an army of bots, including some that acted as suckling wet nurses and others that changed diapers for a living. Music had been piped into their cribs since they were fetuses, but now they had a daily diet of visual and audio stimulation. The stark white corridors of Quivira were to become their playground.

Aurora cuddled and cooed to Nevaeh as proudly as if she were her own, wrapping her tightly in a blanket and soothing her constantly, affectionately stroking her full head of dark hair.

Maureen was in the lab when the babies were brought out. She fell in love with each one of them.

Maureen missed her family, and the babies brought out her mothering instinct. César had told everyone not to pick up the babies, as he didn't want any infections or germs passed to them. He had ordered all the medibots to be very strict. But Maureen couldn't resist. She picked up Arturo in her arms and kissed him sweetly on the forehead, smelling his tiny head and tickling his perfect feet.

When César named one of the boys Ved, Maureen had to find somewhere private to cry.

***

A few days later, three maybe-not-so-wise men arrived in time for the celebration—Howie, Ofentse, and Carl.

"We had to be here to see this," said Howie proudly, almost as if he were the father.

"César, who's handing out the cigars? Ha, ha, actually, I don't care, vile habit! Let's do champagne instead!"

45
The Talk

Epona, July 2076

WINGTIP CALLED HUNTER TO his office adjoining the control center, where all the missions were tracked. Hunter wondered what he had done now, and prepared himself for another dressing down or pointless assignment. Wingtip cleared his throat and told Hunter to take a seat. "It's about Ms. Madison."

Wingtip must know about their late-night meetings, thought Hunter. They were probably monitoring their evening chats and occasional stolen kisses. But what did he care? They could get their kicks.

Hunter said nothing.

"This is rather delicate," Wingtip continued. He paused, and Hunter worried that she had complained about him stalking her or something.

"We're unsure about her. We need someone to keep an eye on her, see what she's up to. We'll give you assignments near where she might have a mission. She's in logistics, so she travels around."

Hunter remained silent for a moment, not sure what to make of what Wingtip was saying. It sounded like Wingtip thought Kiana was a spy, but Hunter knew that couldn't be true.

When Wingtip cleared his throat, Hunter realized he'd been quiet too long. He shook his head and said, "Yes, sir. But what am I supposed to do?"

"Just keep track and report back. Loiter in the vicinity. Provide help if needed. Do not interfere. That is essential. Just be extra support if she needs it." With that, Hunter was dismissed.

Hunter was unsure what to make of the information. *Was Kiana being set up? Was he being set up for some reason? Maybe he was the fall guy for some hush-hush operation.*

He'd be found conveniently nearby, the dupe for if things went wrong and they needed someone to blame. Who really knew what went on inside the Sentinels? Should he let Kiana know she was under suspicion? Wingtip had explicitly told him not to interfere. He decided inaction was the best option.

Do nothing and just keep watch. That should be easy enough.

46

The Feast

Quivira, August, 2076

AFTER THE BIRTH OF the babies, Maureen and César held a feast for the big bosses in the main dining room. Dinner was to be followed by a surprise. The white dining room was grand, with a massive bay window overlooking the Earth.

Quivira's orbit was over Earth's equator, so the window viewed the lights of Singapore, Bogota, and Nairobi, as well as wonderful blue expanses of the Pacific and Atlantic Oceans. "It's like we're gods," whispered Teagan to her father.

The dress code was informal. Noel and Teagan were among the invitees who sat back in plush pseudo-leather seats.

"Here's to Dr. César and the Magnificent Seven!" toasted Howie as servingbots with glasses on metallic trays hovered behind them. "Your work is unmatched. You are a genius of the skies. You will go down in history."

"Fabulous achievement," said Carl, sitting back on a couch. Noel raised his glass in acknowledgment, the bubbles getting up his nose. Teagan was allowed a sip.

"Thank you all so much," César preened. "We very much appreciate the pioneering facilities and financing provided by the Space Consortium. We couldn't have done it without you. Thank you also to Maureen and Motoko, for running such a ship-shape operation. I hope it all leads to even greater things. What we've proven is that humanity doesn't need women to survive."

As he sat down, looking rather smug, César looked toward Teagan but didn't acknowledge her. Her features reminded him somewhat of his late wife, Emmy, who had died in childbirth from an epidural that he had administered incorrectly. Ever since then, he had looked for ways to facilitate births without a mother.

"What we've proven is that humanity needs greater humanity and humility to survive," muttered Ofentse, chewing on some of the house-grown celery.

Teagan whispered to her father, "Don't I even get a mention? And why doesn't he need women? He needed my eggs." She was hurt and confused, but nobody seemed to notice. The focus was on César and Howie.

"To continue the celebration, we've brought the well-known pianist, Ming Fan, here for a special concert. Tonight, she will give us a recital in the *Star Horizon* bar.

I hope you all will attend." They all followed Dr. César and Maureen to the cozy *Star Horizon* saloon.

Ming had studied piano since the age of four. Her father had played the traditional Chinese two-stringed fiddle, known as the erhu. Both her parents had encouraged her to take advantage of her obvious talent. At the age of sixteen, she appeared as the youngest contestant at the Leeds International Piano Competition in Britain and won the fourth prize. The year after, she got a full scholarship to study at the Guildhall School of Music and Drama with Professor Joan Hazel in London.

"I often felt the piano chose me, not me the piano," she said. But it was the magic of Disney's *Fantasia* that got her really enthusiastic. "It showed me the immense descriptive and captivating power of music," she said. "Those walking dust mops!"

Howie walked into the intimate bar with his acolytes. About ten couples were attending the recital, plus César, Maureen, Motoko, and a couple of AI waiters.

Ming had brought her personal roll-up electronic keyboard. Once a novelty item that sounded rather tinny, the roll-up keyboard was now considered state-of-the-art with concert-quality sound.

She started with a couple of études and Mazurkas, went on to the polonaise in C-sharp minor, continued with the Raindrop Prelude and the étude in G-sharp minor Op. 25, No. 6, followed by the haunting Fantasie-Impromptu in C-sharp minor Op. 66, No. 4, ending with Beethoven's Moonlight Sonata.

It was a wonderful evening, full of emotion — a fit ceremony to welcome the Seven to the world.

"That was magical, Miss Fan," commented Howie. "Especially up here with this view of the stars and Earth. I'm a real fan of yours!"

"Pity it's not on a real piano; but then, nothing is nowadays," a glamorous-looking woman said. From what Teagan could glean, her name was Toni, and she seemed to be there with Ofentse. They were all in Howie Rich's group. "Obviously, weight restrictions make that impossible."

Teagan looked at Toni curiously, recognizing her voice. Was she the Ms. Demirci she had heard with Dr. César? She certainly was beautiful.

"So, tell us how your tour has been going," interjected Maureen. "How's the Chinese base now? I bet they don't have such a good view!"

"Well, it's pretty good, actually," Ming said. "The base is getting big, like a small town, seems like maybe three hundred people. Much more activity than the international base nearby. But that's understandable. I also played at the joint Euro-African base. The Indians are also involved. Lovely reception, so friendly. And I visited the Lunar Gateway Station that's an international project. Such fun there!"

"By the way," interrupted Toni, "what's in this delicious main course? I'm loving it!"

"We can ask the chef," responded Maureen. "But I know he cooks a lot with spirulina and other algae grown on station. We're very self-sufficient here, you know."

"I'm sure you are," said Ming. "It's amazing how creative cooks can be. At the Chinese base, they have hamburgers made from worm meat."

"Yuck, worm meat, sounds disgusting!" exclaimed Toni.

"Reminds me of a song we used to sing as kids," said Teagan. "I can't remember it very well. But it went something like:

"Space-worms, crawlin' in the night, Space-worms, crawlin' out o' sight.
Space-worms love to talk, And they love to do the space-worm walk.
Out in space where the stars shine bright, Hither and thither they slither all night.
Now and then you can hear them kiss, And their kissing sounds like this."

Howie seemed to know the rhyme from his youth. As accompanying emphasis, Howie abruptly made a huge kissing sound by pressing his lips to the top of his wrist.

Teagan was startled and paused. "Sorry, I can't remember it all!"

They all cheered as chefbot Yum Yum came out from the kitchen.

Taking advantage of the distraction, Howie leaned across and gave Teagan a peck on the cheek. "That was fantastic!" he told her. Teagan smiled back, unsure why he had kissed her.

"Chef Yum Yum," said Maureen, "the guests are wondering about the ingredients for this wonderful dinner. Can you enlighten them?"

"Yes, ma'am," he responded. "The starters comprised mushrooms with fine strips of cultured meat grown from cells in our lab; the main course was crispy cockroach, with a house salad of romaine lettuce and tomatoes; followed by a dessert made from algae puree. The cocktail contained seaweed, spiked with drops of potato vodka brewed on board."

"Well, you have exceeded yourself. And I'm sure you have impressed your guests. An excellent accompaniment to our wonderful, inspiring concert," said Maureen. "Thank you very much, Yum Yum. Please return to the kitchen." Yum Yum spun around and glided away.

Motoko resumed the previous conversation. "You know, that's quite a lot better than the space-worms song we knew as kids!"

As Howie left for his room, he swung his arm clumsily over Toni's naked shoulder and tried to kiss her.

"Get your paws off," Ofentse said sharply as he followed closely behind.

Howie glanced at him. "Oh look what the cat's dragged in," hissed Howie. "When I need your help, I'll ask for it."

47
Unlocking Destiny

The Spacesweeper, on patrol August 2076

H UNTER WAS OUT ON morning patrol, Chester comfortably beside him. As he sucked the last drops from a vacuum-sealed breakfast pouch, Hunter scanned the control panel. He mostly flew on autopilot, which gave him time to keep an eye on all of his external cameras and dashboard screens. He rarely glanced out of the windshield in front of him.

The human eye couldn't see microwaves and various types of light or electromagnetic radiation, so his instruments inevitably gave him a better reading of what lay ahead. The instruments translated the black of space and the glow of the cosmic microwave background, including all the ultraviolet rays, X-rays, and gamma rays scattered across the universe, into readable data and displays.

The normal array of objects popped up on his screen, potential targets for retrieval. They would return to scoop up some of those. Attuned to the millions of pieces of debris floating in space, Hunter mentally sorted what might present a danger to other vehicles and would need their attention first.

He was keeping notes for a future run when he spotted something odd in the distance. "What have we here?" he whispered to Chester. It wasn't the usual space junk—abandoned launch vehicle stages, dead satellites, launch adapters, mission-related debris, or pieces of fragmented wreckage.

Cautiously, he edged his ship closer to what appeared to be a derelict spaceship, surrounded by a trail of space debris. He radioed for backup, as he had been taught in training by Wingtip's deputy, Captain Drury, and cautiously approached the object.

What could cause someone to abandon their craft?

Cutting speed to almost nothing, Hunter drifted up to the hull and peered inside through a porthole. The ship seemed empty and adrift. He checked the registry for any abandoned spacecraft but found nothing matching its description. Hunter docked, told Chester to stay put, and boarded the ship through a side hatch, knowing he should wait for his backup to arrive. But there was something about the ship that called to him. Against his better judgment, he had to see what it was.

With his pulse elevated, he drew his weapon, pointing the laser out in front of him. The air was dank and stale. All appeared still and silent. His forehead flashlight pierced the darkness. He felt he was trespassing. His footsteps echoed through the empty metallic hallways. The whole of his body was alert. "What the heck is this?" Nasir radioed in, sounding amazed. Hunter's backup had arrived. "Did someone just evacuate their ship in mid-space? It doesn't seem possible."

"We need to see if there's anyone home," Hunter said once Nasir had joined him on the ship. "You head to the front; I'll take the rear. Let's find a control cabin."

A foot at a time, Nasir stepped toward the forward section, a flashlight on his forehead, the same as Hunter, the metal of the walls reflecting light back into his eyes. He squinted. No sign of any occupants. It was as though the crew had just transferred to another ship.

It was hard to say how old the vessel was. There were no markings on the hull, nothing to indicate nationality or origin.

As he went through the ship, Hunter realized that it was in better condition than he'd initially thought, with no signs of decay or damage. He moved along a dark corridor and came to a wide, oval space—a crew mess room, though there were no empty cups or old food dishes. No signs on the walls either.

An odd glint in the center of the room caught his attention. He turned his flashlight toward it. It looked like a cut crystal, embedded in a platform. As he reached for it, a powerful force threw him across the room as if he'd been hit by an electric current. Pain tore through his shoulder where he struck a support strut. He was winded but managed to shout out, "Nasir, I'm down."

At the other end of the cavernous structure, Nasir was checking out a storage locker and was unable to hear Hunter's muffled cries.

Hunter picked himself up and checked his weapon. Despite the pain, the crystal seemed to call to him. Picking himself up, Hunter approached again, more slowly this time. He leaned forward, and as soon as his hand wrapped around the crystal, a power surged through him. The world around him melted away as vivid images flooded his mind, transporting him across galaxies and into the midst of an inter-stellar battle. He saw the crystal ripped from its pedestal by an unseen force, its vibrant glow dimming as it was transferred into another gloved hand.

Trying to make sense of what he was seeing, Hunter was surprised when the visions stopped and the crystal suddenly released him. He staggered back, his thoughts racing. *What did it mean? Was this some sort of warning? A foreshadowing of something to come?*

He had to find out more, but the experience had exhausted him. Hunter slumped to the floor, where Nasir found him not long after.

"Hunter, get up. You have to see this. I've found something."

Gathering his strength, Hunter got up and followed Nasir to the other end of the corridor. Nasir pointed to an adjoining cupboard in a small room.

"Take a look." Hunter opened the door. Inside were two reclining figures in space suits, locked in an eternal embrace. They reminded Hunter of the figures discovered in Pompeii, killed in the Vesuvius eruption.

Hunter's heart raced as he realized what they'd found.

The space travelers were too small to be human. He leaned closer for a better look. Their space suits had preserved them perfectly. They were both about 140 centimeters tall, with long spindly fingers and scaly skin. Green slime seemed to ooze from one of them, maybe an injury.

Hunter's excitement turned to dread. Their large, yellowish eyes were wide open in what looked like terror. Something bad had clearly happened here. His mind flashed back to what the crystal had shown him. He wondered if they had died in that battle. Hunter peeled back their protective hoods to reveal that each one had two crested heads, yellow and black. As he looked at the alarming creatures, he began to feel sad. They were so unfamiliar, yet he could see traces of humanity in them. He wondered what their world must have been like, and if they'd gotten to enjoy it before their final journey into space. It had probably been long and exhausting.

Hunter and Nasir spent a couple of tense hours searching through the whole ship for any other crew. They didn't find any further bodies, weapons, or food. Nasir came across what appeared to be the ship's engine, made up of technology unlike anything they'd seen before. It reminded Hunter of a living machine—both organic and inorganic merged. But there was no reaction when he reached out to touch the core fibers. Everything seemed to be dead.

Hunter wondered if the crystal he'd seen was a homing device. So, if it was operational, whoever had sent the creatures here must know where they were. Maybe they could even observe Hunter and Nasir in real-time. A creepy thought. He looked around for possible cameras or transmitters.

More worrying for Hunter was the vision he'd had while grasping the crystal. Was it a warning of what was to come? And how far in the future was it?

Back on Epona, Wingtip was furious when he found out they had left the crystal behind. "We had no means of removing it, sir," Hunter said.

"Was it screwed down?"

"No, but a forcefield was protecting it."

Wingtip, clearly not impressed, dispatched two senior staff to retrieve the abandoned ship and bring back the two bodies and the crystal. But no one could locate the derelict ship. It had vanished.

48

The Wonder

Quivira, August, 2076

T EAGAN KNEW THE BABIES had been born, but she was blocked from visiting them. A human guard with the build of an American quarterback stood at the entrance to the lab along with several securitybots. There was no messing with them.

"Why can't I see them?" pleaded Teagan. "I won't do anything bad. I just want to see them."

"You are not authorized," said one of the guards. "Speak to Ms. Grau."

Teagan ran down the corridor, bumping into Howie near the exercise zone.

"Mr. Rich, can't you do anything? I want to see the babies, but they won't let me."

"Calm down. I'll see what I can do." He patted her on the back and kissed her on the forehead. "But Dr. César runs a pretty tight ship. And he's always scared of infection."

A few days later, Teagan saw an opportunity to get into the lab, sneaking in behind a Japanese buyers' delegation that was interested in sourcing kidneys and other organs for its hospital patients. Wearing a gown and mask, she passed off as lab staff escorting the visitors.

Teagan walked past banks of early-stage transplant organs and tissues being grown before reaching the neonatal pediatric wing where the newborns were resting. She looked in wonderment at the row of cribs. The babies were about a month old. Some were lying on their backs, some on their stomachs and trying to raise their heads a little. They looked so cute and tiny. It was striking how different the colors of their hair were. Adorable!

She opened one of the transparent bassinets and picked up a boy labeled Liam.

"Liam, you're so handsome. What a beautiful boy."

Liam looked cross-eyed at her and gurgled. He tried to suckle her breast, but when he couldn't find anything he began to whimper. She quickly put him back in his crib, worried that the noise could attract attention.

She edged past one marked Ved. She knew that was an Indian name for "precious" or "sacred knowledge." How content he looked.

And there was Tara. Somebody had matched her name with a moon symbol. Her face did look a bit chubby.

Glancing over to the next row, she saw a cot marked Nevaeh. She scooped the tiny baby into her arms and kissed Nevaeh's forehead gently.

"Nevaeh, what a beautiful name. You are a perfect little girl, so sweet. You smell so good, like caramel and warm butter. My favorites. You smell so delicious, I'd like to eat you all up!"

A nurse came running and found Teagan cradling the baby.

"Don't cry. You are the most beautiful baby I've ever, ever seen."

"What is this?" asked the bot.

By then, Nevaeh's robotic wet nurse, Aurora, was on the scene. "Please let me help," she said as Nevaeh began to cry loudly.

Teagan hugged the baby to her, refusing to give her up. Soon she was surrounded by an army of bots.

"Please let me have her," said Aurora firmly. "I'm responsible for her."

"She's mine," Teagan shouted. "Don't you know, I'm the mother. You're all artificial. You're bots. You don't have flesh like me and Nevaeh."

One of the bots attempted to grab the baby. Others tried to restrain Teagan as she struggled.

"Get off," shouted Teagan. "You little preprogrammed bag of chips. Leave me alone. I only want to hold her."

César rushed toward the neonatal unit, alerted by his staff. "STOP!" he screamed as he entered, his face flushed.

Everything halted. Teagan lost her balance and Nevaeh went flying. Her tiny body dropped like a stone to the floor, the fall cushioned by Teagan's foot. A brief moment of silence, and then the stunned baby began to scream her lungs out. Aurora rushed over, scooped her up, and marched swiftly back to her place in the nursery, trying to comfort her.

"You stupid bitch! Look what you've done," César shouted at Teagan. Then, to the bot, "Get her OUT! And make sure she never comes back."

Teagan stood immobile as bots approached her, ready to grab her by the arm. As they got near, she dashed between them and made a run for it down an unmarked corridor, past rows of bots processing plasma samples, initiating a chase through the lab.

The bots were close behind her, and she turned into a room, hoping for a different way out, but found herself cornered. She ducked down behind an incubator, a dozen budding kidneys at eye level, but the bots spotted her. She took off running again and, as the bots closed in, turned over a cart into their path and slipped through pneumatic doors that led to the hydroponic farms while the bots were distracted. Dashing past rows of worm-like fungus, Teagan tried to conceal herself between trays of celery and watercress. When a bird flew at her head, Teagan cried out in surprise.

She recognized it as Pica, Maureen's magpie. It circled overhead, making her position obvious.

Grau sternly called for her to step out.

Teagan batted Pica away with a tray of mushrooms, striking the bird on the wing. Pica squawked loudly in protest, darting back down and trying to grab Teagan's silver pendant.

The chase took about five minutes until they finally cornered her; the security-bots had found her, advancing with their stun guns at the ready.

"Teagan, please come out," said Maureen. "Nothing will happen."

"Teagan, Teagan," mimicked Pica.

Teagan fled toward a bank of algae and synthetic meat. But she knew it was hopeless. Pica made a victory swoop, and she let out a scream.

"Teagan, you are cornered. I think it's best you give up. If you don't want any harm to come to your babies, then give yourself up." It broke Maureen's heart to utter those words, but she didn't want the securitybots to hurt the poor girl.

Teagan emerged from the rows of plants, her arms up in half surrender. "You don't understand. I just want to see my babies."

The unsympathetic bots surrounded her. Teagan was immobilized with an electric current and sedated. Limp and exhausted, she was taken to a sterile holding cell, and the door locked while Grau and César decided what to do with her.

After the snub at the party, Maureen had been keeping an eye on Teagan. It was clear she was hurt that César didn't acknowledge her part, but Doctor de Luca wasn't known for his tact or common sense. After a while, Teagan had seemed to shrug off the disappointment, but Maureen still believed Teagan could cause trouble.

Maureen had known Teagan wanted to see the babies and that she felt they were hers. Not only that but, from Motoko's reports, it was clear Teagan had been doing quite badly, both emotionally and in her studies. It broke Maureen's heart to see the girl struggling.

A call to Noel Ward told her that his daughter enjoyed sculpting and painting, though lately she only ever carved and painted faces of babies.

They couldn't afford to keep Teagan on Quivira. The safety of the babies was at stake now, but Noel's comments gave Maureen an idea.

49
The Exile

Halona, September 2077

T HE AIR IN THE space habitat was lifeless, as though it had been air-condi-
tioned to death, as Teagan arrived at Howie's corporate space headquarters.
A tense Howie had alerted Ofentse of Teagan's imminent arrival on Halona.
Teagan felt she had been sent into exile, which was true enough.... at least got out
of the way. Her mind churned the events over. All she wanted was her babies,
her family. Was that too much to ask? She longed for the sweet fragrance of their
skin and the comforting smell of their clothes.

Why did they all take her for granted as an egg donation machine?

Deep down, she knew she could have been a good mother, even in a godawful
space habitat.

At least Dr. César had the good grace to be remorseful. She also thought
Maureen had stood up for her, but she was still traumatized by that damn bird
circling over her head. César had even been worried enough about her to give her
some tranquilizers. But she didn't need tranquilizers, she needed her babies.

At times she felt guilty. Had she split up the family? She admired her parents:
Her mother, a botanist who had created her own mission in life; her father, a
professor at the University of Arizona's Lunar and Planetary Laboratory. Even
her brother knew what he wanted.

Teagan ordered food but wasn't hungry, feeling demotivated and empty instead. She was constantly thinking of the babies, particularly the two she had
held, Liam and Nevaeh—her "twins."

She spoke out loud to them, hoping they could hear her somehow.

"Can you hear me Liam?" she whispered, tears streaming down her face. "My
sweet boy, I remember how you smell, how you feel in my arms. I'm sorry I
couldn't feed you. I hope you're resting.

"And you, Nevaeh," she continued, barely able to choke out the words. "You
are the most beautiful girl in the world. I hope you recovered from your bump.
You are so strong and beautiful, my darling." She prayed silently for their well-
being.

Rocking back and forth on her chair, Teagan started formulating a plan in her mind. How could she use Howie, the man who held all the power over her offspring, to regain access to them? It disgusted her to think about seducing him, but desperate times called for desperate measures. She would do anything to be reunited with her beloved children. All entrances on Halona opened a bit like an old camera or diaphragm shutter, from the center outwards: The thin blades retracted to create a circular entrance and then snapped shut after someone stepped through. She pressed the button for access to Howie's quarters.

If Howie had to acknowledge a weakness, it was that he liked to be involved in everything. So, instead of delegating the Teagan Ward case to Ofentse or someone more junior, he dealt with it personally.

"Now Ms. Ward," Howie said to Teagan, "here on Halona, you can delve into many things—music, art, sculpting, and pottery, as well as astronomy and space studies. You will find a lot to fascinate you here. This place is full of creative people and I'm sure you will enjoy it."

He finished eating a freshly baked croissant, wiped a speck of flaky pastry from his lower lip, and looked at her.

"I promise I'll try my best," Teagan replied.

Howie said, "I know you enjoy painting. Lots of people here can help you. Plus, you can easily stay in contact with your friends, and both your parents."

Howie was the only one who had what amounted to a suite on Halona. Everybody else had a sleeping cabin. Work was done in open public areas or studios.

"Why don't you come and relax in my quarters? You can play music and take things calmly, order your food from the kitchen," he said.

"Thank you. You're very kind."

She knew her only hope of seeing the children was through Howie. If she had to make nice with the big man to do it, she would, no matter how repulsive. It was her duty as a mother.

50
Among Artists

Halona, September 2077

OFENTSE WAS BUSY TALKING with Toni Demirci. He wanted to keep Toni away from Teagan as much as possible.

Ofentse had given Toni a big "opportunity" by proposing her to Dr. César as one of the egg donors for the Heavenly Babies project when he was looking for contributors.

Unlike Teagan Ward, Toni wanted nothing to do with "her" baby. She did not want to be a surrogate mother. As soon as she had been paid and got the promotion she was promised, Toni headed back to head one of the Consortium's Earth operations. She had become Ofentse's protégé.

"Are you familiar with Maureen Grau?"

Toni arched a brow. "Yeah, the stuck-up bitch running Quivira. I met her when I went there for the procedure. Not a fan. What about her?"

Toni's casual remark about her egg donation made Ofentse wonder what made humans so different. While Teagan seemed ready to go through Hell and back to connect with her babies, the event was hardly a blip for Toni. While Teagan wanted the connection, Toni referred to the whole thing as a procedure, a way of getting ahead.

"Nothing. She might have sent us trouble, that's all."

***

When Howie returned to his quarters from his meetings, Teagan remained silent.

"I know you miss those kids," Howie said, his voice carrying a sympathetic tone. "But there's not much we can do."

She turned big eyes on him, hoping it would be enough. "Can't I see them? Please."

"That's not in my control, Teagan. But we could ask for a video conference. Maybe a nurse can show them."

A spark of hope lit up her eyes. "That would be good. You're so kind."

"A bit of kindness in return might go a long way," Howie suggested.

Ignoring the pit in her stomach, she snuggled up to Howie. As he caressed the back of her neck, she wondered if she could get him to help her against César.

Teagan never went to her own cramped quarters, opting to stay with Howie. Whatever it took for her to stay connected with her babies, even a relationship. Next morning she found herself on the couch. They had fallen asleep together.

Howie glanced at her as she stretched awake. "What are you thinking?"

"I'm thinking you're not so bad. Fat and loud, but not so bad." She giggled, and he took it as a joke. "Any chance of that video call today?"

They developed a routine. Howie would attend to his business all morning and return to lunch in his cabin. Teagan would do her studies and, every fourth Monday, she would get a call with Liam and Nevaeh and the others that Howie had arranged with Dr. César.

"Help me on this. You know she really is a great piece of ass," he whispered to the good doctor.

Dr. César obliged, knowing who paid the bills.

Video chatting with her babies was bittersweet for Teagan. She loved being able to see them and talk to them, but it was hard not being able to hold them and care for them in person. Still, she cherished those monthly chats immensely. Any time the babies smiled and gurgled, Teagan felt like everything was going to be all right. Even though she was far away, she could still feel their love warming her heart.

Howie always joined her for the calls, and always asked to see Arturo, whom he would admire with almost paternal pride. "That boy's going to be a smart fellow."

Afterwards, Teagan often fell into a trance. She stared into empty space, thinking. Once, after some time, she looked across at the painting on the wall and Howie caught her glance.

"I love that painting for its simplicity," he told her. "It's an Oudry. It's so calming. That's why I brought it to Halona. Do you like it?"

"What is it?"

"It's a picture of a white swan with a broken wing hanging on the wall, ready to be plucked and cooked. On the left is what they called a pomander, which would have concealed any smell. And to the right is a single candle stick. I love how the artist just puts his name bang in the middle of the picture, as though it's part of the cook's label for when the swan was caught or something."

She got up to look more closely. "Yes, the whole thing is very relaxing, even though it's a dead bird hanging on the wall. What's it say underneath? *'Cygnus fracto cornu.'"*

"It's Latin for 'Swan with a broken wing.' Now come back over here and take care of something, or you'll be a dead bird too." He patted the pillow, and as she lay down he began to kiss her with extraordinary gentleness.

As Teagan lay beside him, the words ran through her mind: *Cygnus fracto cornu*, the bird that cannot fly. Was there something behind its eye?

One evening, Howie had been held up by an emergency and Teagan got bored, so she took a walk around and stumbled on some graffiti on the side of an entrance wall. Maybe it was the vivid colors or the strangeness of such art in a place that was prim and proper. Teagan was fascinated.

She was still staring when she heard a voice behind her ask, "Like it?"

Startled, she turned and saw a young man with dark hair, gray/green eyes, a slim build, and long fingers stained with paint.

"I'm sorry I startled you; my name is Julian. I'm a painter, sculptor, and graffiti artist. Julian Trace." He pointed to the graffiti and said, "This is one of my creations." He stepped back to look at her properly, then asked, "Have I seen you somewhere before?"

Teagan quickly looked at her feet and replied, "I don't think so." She paused, glancing up at him from beneath her lashes. She thought he looked kind of cute. Teagan tried to move aside but stepped on his foot. "Oh, sorry. I'm a total bozo."

Julian winked at her. "No worries. Nothing broken." As she turned to leave, Julian grabbed her hand and said, "At least tell me your name before you go."

"Teagan. But my family calls me Pumpkin." She took back her hand and walked briskly toward Howie's quarters, determined not to glance back and let him catch her looking.

Nice to know there are some other people here after all, she thought

Before entering Howie's quarters, Teagan took a deep breath. Howie was inside, bent over a sideboard, and he looked up when she walked in.

"Where were you? I was about to alert the securitybot to do a perimeter search." He chuckled.

Teagan walked over to him and gave him a hug, but her mind was on the artist with the long fingers. "I took a walk to the artists' colony. I saw some beautiful paintings and lost track of time. I'm sorry I got you worried."

Howie kissed her on the forehead. "Have a little of our moonshine." He chuckled at his own joke.

Teagan took a sip. "Yuck, what is it?"

"It's our tipple. Made on Halona. You have to gulp it, not sip it demurely!"

Teagan obligingly took a gulp, then scrunched up her eyes and shook her head as the burning liquid made its way down her throat. "No thanks."

She glanced to the sideboard he'd opened and saw a collection of swords and daggers.

Seeing her look, he said, "I collect swords made from meteorites. Some are very old. It's like they flew down from the heavens." He showed her one of the kris, an engraved dagger with a wavy blade.

"That looks like a dangerous snake."

"Yes, kris are both a weapon and spiritual object, considered to have an essence or presence within. Perhaps related to the long history of animism in Indonesia; they believe that objects, places, and creatures possess a spiritual essence."

Teagan looked at the sinuous silver dagger and cradled it in her hands. "That feels very possible," she said, stroking the scabbard.

"Don't unsheathe it," he cautioned. "If you do, it has to draw blood."

On one side, he showed her a meteorite about the size of a man's fist, laced with green crystals. "This is the oldest thing I own – a few billion years." It didn't seem to impress her.

"And what's this on the wall above?"

"That's a map of the Hopi Indian villages in Arizona. Their locations are said to be in the shape of the constellation Orion if you plot them on the map."

Teagan's mind was drawn back to her childhood dream.

The treasure you seek lies beyond the eye. What eye did they mean, she wondered.

51
The Instructions

Epona, October 2077

AT SOME POINT IN every person's journey, they will inevitably come to a fork in the road, a choice to be made that will decide their future. For Kiana, as she stood in contemplation on the edge of Wingtip's congested control room, she realized she'd just made that choice.

Surrounded by screens displaying intricate blueprints and schematics for lunar bases and off-Earth mining operations, the enormity of the task began to dawn on her. Except for the screens, the room itself was bare and industrial, with metal walls and faint shadows lurking in the corners.

Wingtip's flatly delivered instructions echoed in her mind: "Your mission is to infiltrate the Iron Hornets. Kill if you have to. We need to take them down. They are a menace to traffic. Our goal is to dismantle their organization. Eliminate them from the inside. Since they are linked to General Lin, it must seem like her idea."

The starkness of the order took her by surprise. She hadn't been paying full attention. Instead, she had been looking at how a ray of light glanced off Wingtip's bald scalp.

He had directed Kiana not to tell anyone. "It's top secret, super sensitive. Nobody must know, and that includes Hunter, or your life will be in danger. I don't know how many moles they have here."

"Yes, sir," she responded automatically, but her heart sank. She had grown to like Hunter, perhaps more than like. The idea of keeping secrets from him unsettled her. But she knew the stakes were too high to let emotions get in the way.

Wingtip nodded approvingly.

"We will find a way to assist your infiltration. Maybe you will get recruited."

Trying to mask her hesitation, she said, "I'll need a way to communicate with you while on the inside. If something goes wrong, I'll need assistance."

"We've found that low-tech is best." Wingtip handed her an inconspicuous earpiece. "It disappears inside the ear. It will allow us to stay in touch. Be careful not to arouse suspicion. The Hornets are known for their cunning and ruthlessness. This will be a long game."

Kiana nodded, accepting the earpiece. "I'll be careful, sir."

As she prepared to depart, she thought through the risks and potential consequences. She would be exposed and on her own. She may have to adopt a false persona for years. The thought of being completely alone in this new identity filled her with doubt and apprehension. The idea of living a double life for an unknown amount of time made her stomach churn. But this was her duty, even if it meant sacrificing her own identity.

She said a brief goodbye to Hunter. To his surprise, she kissed him on the lips. They both knew she couldn't tell him anything, but he gave her a questioning look.

"I'm going to miss you, Kiana," he said, pulling her into a tight embrace.

As Kiana hugged him back, she felt a pang of sadness, wishing she could confide in him. But she held her silence, knowing it was for the best.

"Kiana." Hunter's voice quivered perceptibly, "I know we had a bumpy start, but I think we've grown to respect and even love each other. Please remember, if you're in trouble or need help, I want to be there for you."

"I will. I promise."

Hunter sat down again and leaned back in his chair, his eyes downcast. "Just promise me one thing. Promise me that you'll come back safe."

Kiana took Hunter's hand. "I promise, Hunter. I'll come back, and then we can catch up on everything. I'm sorry for keeping you in the dark, but it's for the best." She gave him a disarming wink.

52

Two Encounters

Halona, October 2077

T EAGAN WAS USUALLY DONE with her studies an hour or two before
Howie arrived, and she used this time to tour the artists' quarters, looking
at the paintings and hoping to find Julian again. For the first week, despite
going to the same spot every day, she couldn't find him.

One day, she found Howie back early from work. He was talking to a man.
Teagan couldn't see his face, but he seemed familiar. When he turned around,
she got the shock of her life. She realized it was the Mustache, the man who
had invaded her home in Arizona.

She stared at him, eyes wide, but he acted like he didn't recognize her and
probably didn't. When he left, she asked Howie, "Does that man work for
you?"

Howie looked at her curiously before replying, "He does odd jobs that an AI
can't do. His name is Sam. Why?"

"That's the guy! I want his head," she stuttered, her emotions bubbling over.
"He tried to rape me. Him and another guy."

Howie stared at her, surprised by her anger. "You can't have him here, or I
can't be here. It's too creepy. He might be called Sam, but he's a sick menace,
that's what he is. What if I meet him in the corridor?" Her stomach began
churning, and Howie saw her face losing color.

"I'll see what I can do."

"You better, or I'll do it myself. And I'm not joking. Maybe that kris will
have to draw blood."

She stormed off and sat in a communal area for the young artists, her
expression sullen and hostile. "I would love to paint a portrait of you right now,
but I would have to ask your permission first. Your face is so full of emotion."

Hearing the familiar voice, Teagan turned around and smiled when she saw that
it was Julian. "Hey Pumpkin," he said, adopting her family nickname, but with a
slight Italian accent. "You are a sight for sore eyes. I hear you've been a regular visitor
here. I'm glad you find the art colony interesting enough. It must be pretty boring in

Mr. Rich's suite." Teagan's eyes widened, but Julian smiled. "You are quite popular, Teagan Ward, the mistress of our Lord Chancellor," he said in a mocking stage voice.

The comment stung her, and she blushed. She didn't need to explain herself to him. She turned to leave.

"Wait! I'm sorry I upset you. You have a particularly expressive face, and the canvas will love you. Please do me this favor; let me paint a portrait of you." Teagan looked at him for a while, then nodded. She had time. Julian grinned. Taking her hand, he led her to his cabin. It was cramped compared with Howie's place. Easels took up half the room. The other half had a small bed and various paintings in different stages of completion. It smelled of paint and turpentine.

Once he'd made some space, Julian gestured for her to sit. "I'm going to break in a new canvas just for you." Teagan settled in and watched him as he drew, his hands moving rapidly over the canvas. Julian was tall and slender with short, dark hair. His sharp jawline gave him a handsome, almost regal appearance. His fingers were skilled and nimble. When he was done, he showed her the result.

For a second time that day, she was shocked. This time, though, it was the good kind. "I didn't know you were this good." Julian smiled, embarrassed by the compliment. "I'll have your portrait completed by tomorrow."

The next evening, Teagan hurried toward Julian's cabin to see her portrait. When she knocked on the door, it opened automatically. Julian was putting on a pair of pants and a dirty apron without a shirt. His eyes lit up when he saw Teagan.

"Hello there, Pumpkin, I've been expecting you." He moved away from the door and said, "Come on in, your portrait is ready."

The painting took her breath away. It looked so real, as though her face had come alive. His paints were the colors of the Tuscan countryside, vibrant and earthy, and his art was a reflection of his soul, passionate and alive.

"It's beautiful," she breathed. Looking up at him, she added softly, "You're so talented." A flush rose on his cheeks that she found endearing.

"It's nothing compared to the real beauty here now," he replied, gazing into her eyes.

She smiled, stepping closer. Julian reached out, lightly caressing her cheek with his hand. Without thinking, Teagan kissed him swiftly on the lips.

After, she started to apologize, but Julian shushed her and said, "I have been waiting to do that since the first time I saw you; there's nothing to apologize for."

Teagan wasn't sure why she liked him. Was it purely a physical attraction? Was she just lonely? Maybe she liked the attention of being painted. Perhaps she just wanted to escape from Howie. Maybe it was a combination of all these factors, or perhaps she liked the danger.

Slowly, as if guided by unseen forces, their faces drew closer until their lips met again in a gentle kiss. Julian's arms went around her waist, pulling her body flush against his. It was unlike anything she'd felt before. She ran her fingers through his dark hair, deepening the kiss with passion.

Soon Julian made space on his tiny cot. Almost ballet-like, they descended together onto the bed, reluctant to break contact even for a moment. Julian trailed kisses down Teagan's neck as she leaned back, sighing in pleasure. His hands roamed her body, caressing her through the thin fabric of her flight suit. Overwhelmed with desire, Teagan swiftly removed the layer of clothing, wanting no barriers between them.

Julian's breath caught at the sight of her nearly naked form. He quickly shed his own clothing, then pulled Teagan close once more. Skin against skin, they exchanged fiery kisses as their hands explored and aroused. The two of them made love, slowly and ecstatically. Teagan's pulse beat wildly as Julian's hands left goosebumps along her skin, the roughness of his fingers piquing her senses and making her want him more.

Afterward, they lay peacefully tangled in each other's arms. As Teagan traced delicate patterns on Julian's chest, he whispered "I love you" into her hair. She nuzzled against him, knowing this was just the beginning for them. The stars continued to shine outside the viewport as the new lovers drifted off to sleep, the galaxy their only witness.

Later, Julian took her to his studio where he made stone sculptures. "They're wonderful," she said. "How do you get your stone?"

Julian smiled and said, "We make it out of compacted regolith from the Moon, or sometimes an asteroid being mined. We have a supply of regolith for making the protective outer skin of the space habitat. It's is a good insulator and protects against radiation rays. But when compacted, it's also great for sculpting."

"It feels smooth." She ran her hand over the marble-like rock. "The compacting process makes it really solid. That's why we can use it for carving."

"Impressive that you can make such beautiful stuff out of shards of rock and sand."

Julian looked at her with admiration. "You know what's really impressive? You."

Teagan laughed and said, "It seems you are insatiable." With eyes twinkling, Julian replied, "Only with you."

Julian ran his hands down her back and over her breasts. He admired the octopus tattoo down her left upper arm and said, "You know, octopus tattoos symbolize freedom, because the octopus is adept at freeing itself from traps and difficult situations or settings."

"Yes, they are masters of disguise and transformation," Teagan giggled.

53

The Diet

T EAGAN COULDN'T STOP HERSELF from thinking about Julian. Her thoughts almost eclipsed the brief mental glimpses she had of the babies. She tried to block him out and keep her mind on the infants. But they were almost disappearing from her mind.

A few days later, she found herself returning to Julian's studio. He was putting the finishing touches on a new nebula painting when Teagan came up behind him.

"It's beautiful," she said, placing a hand on his shoulder. He set down his brush and turned to face her, his eyes dark with desire. Teagan wrapped her arms around him, meeting his passionate kiss.

They managed to stumble over to a cleared worktable. Julian hoisted Teagan up onto it, stepping between her legs as she drew him close. They shared each other deeply, desperately, amidst the paints and canvases, not caring how messy they got.

They climaxed in each other's arms, breathless, and held each other tightly. Teagan traced the contours of Julian's face tenderly. "What are you thinking?" she asked.

Julian brushed a strand of hair from her face. "Just how lucky I am to have found you," he replied.

She smiled and snuggled against his chest. Through an external port, the cosmos seemed to shine brighter, as if the stars themselves celebrated the union between the artist and his muse.

She awoke with a start and hurriedly got dressed. When Teagan got back, Howie snapped, "Where have you been? Slumming with that artist?" When she didn't reply, he snarled, "Did you think I wouldn't know everything happening in this city?"

"Hear this, you little bitch: The only way to end this is if I want to, and I am not ending it just yet. Now get to the room—we're going out to dinner."

As she left, Howie summoned Sam and instructed him to cut off one of Tentikal's arms and give it to the kitchen to prepare for dinner. "Just one tentacle, mind you!"

At dinner, the chef included the seafood as a light starter, broiled the way Howie liked it, with house-grown salad.

"Would you like some pieuvre?" Howie asked Teagan.

Teagan turned white when she saw the sucker-studded cubes of meat. Her lip began quivering, and she tried to avoid being sick on the table.

"You bastard! You're a heartless bastard. You don't value anything you can't buy!"

"Don't worry, the tentacle will grow back." Howie pierced her with a hard look. "Just remember, next time it might be someone else's dangling member."

Teagan ran from the room, barely aware of where she was headed.

54

Collision Course

Off Halona, December 2077

W INGTIP ORDERED HUNTER TO return to his last known location, to
track down the missing spaceship after the other crew he sent had failed
to find anything.

"Take your time, Hunter. It's important we locate the two dead crew and the
crystal."

"I'll do my best, sir."

"Who knows what secrets they'll unlock. This is a priority."

Hunter saluted, then clambered aboard *SpaceSweeper III*. Nasir had been
requested to join him; still eating a protein bar, Nasir found a slot near Chester
in a rear seat.

"Give me a presumed location for the derelict spaceship. We'll see if we can
find anything."

Nasir put them on the right track. As they headed in the designated direction, they scooped up various pieces of trash along the way.

SpaceSweeper III moved slowly through the vast emptiness of outer space, its
sensors scanning for debris. Hunter was tense. He knew it would be difficult
to locate the lost spaceship. But it would be amazing if they found it.

The quiet was interrupted when the sensors began beeping loudly, indicating a large piece of debris ahead. Hunter ordered the ship to move closer.

As they approached, they could see that it was a large piece of metal, about
the size of a car. In one move, Nasir lined up the debris, opened the Sweeper's
huge jaws, and ingested the junk in one gulp.

"Well executed," declared Hunter. "Now, back to looking for the main prize
to keep the old man happy."

Within a few minutes of resuming their search, Hunter received an urgent message from the Space Surveillance Command on Epona warning of a
fast-moving fireball--a meteor with a bright streak of light tailing behind it,
otherwise known as a shooting star--heading directly for Halona.

"We've been tracking it for a while. We suggest you initiate action to try to deflect the object," Surveillance Command said.

The sensors picked up the incoming meteorite, the monitors displaying the glowing rock on its approach. Its trail looked like a comet.

Halona was reinforced against impacts, but a larger meteor could pierce its outer perimeter, causing the station to depressurize and deflect it from its resonance orbit. Hunter radioed Halona to warn them.

"Mayday. Mayday." Hunter shouted. "Attention Halona. You are under threat of direct collision with a space rock. It is large enough to cause considerable damage."

Halona Control responded, "We're initiating shelter-in-place measures."

"We will do what we can to intercept," said Hunter.

"Appreciated."

The ship's computer calculated the trajectory of the meteorite and projected that it would hit the station in less than four minutes.

"It's difficult to fix a good path," said Nasir. "But we should intercept in three."

"Stand by," ordered Hunter. "We'll try to interrupt the object's passage. We can use the force fields generated by our onboard magnets to push it onto a different course."

With its huge, reinforced fairing doors, designed to open and capture floating debris the size of dead satellites, the ship normally used its powerful neodymium magnets to lure a target toward it. In reverse, the magnets could create a huge forcefield that would deflect the meteorite.

"It's worth a try," said Nasir. "It's our only chance to save Halona. They are depending on us."

Once they were in range, Hunter ordered the navigation system to plot a course that would position them as close as possible to the meteor, to one side of its projected passage. He could see the fiery debris hurtling toward them, the majestic outline of Halona drifting below.

Alarms began to blare. "Collision! Collision! Deviate. Deviate."

"Keep steady. Don't override," Hunter instructed, gripping the seat. Chester sat calmly, unaware of Hunter's mounting trepidation.

"Prepare for impact," said the AI.

SpaceSweeper III, its engines screaming in protest, hurtled toward the meteorite. If Hunter was right, they'd be able to deflect the fireball without taking it full on.

"We're approaching the meteorite. Turn magnets on full thrust."

He braced himself as a giant, crunching shudder rocked the capsule. The fireball struck *SpaceSweeper III's* force field and ricocheted off in a different direction, deflected away from Halona.

The impact was brutal, throwing the ship and crew about like rag dolls. But the *Sweeper*, built to take hits from space junk, withstood the battering. Nasir swiftly got the ship stabilized and back under control while Hunter ordered the AI system to check for damage. It soon reported that while some systems were offline, they should be able to fix them.

The spectacular fireball trailed off into the distance, deflected like a billiard ball. Nasir and Hunter breathed a sigh of relief, knowing that they had probably saved hundreds of lives.

"*SpaceSweeper III*, are you okay?" asked Halona Control.

Hunter didn't reply immediately while he checked if there was any damage.

"Please confirm."

"Just a few dents and bruises," Hunter said.

"Fantastic!" said a relieved Control, letting slip a little emotion. "Feel free to dock here if you want to rest up."

"Copy that. Will do. We might need assistance with a few repairs."

55
The Heroes

Halona, December 2077

HUNTER, NASIR, AND CHESTER were treated like heroes once they docked at Halona. The city declared a party, and they knew how to celebrate. Huge Christmas signs decorated the main hallway, and music played loudly throughout the brightly lit facility. A fake Christmas tree twinkled near the bar.

"You saved us," declared Howie Rich, shaking Hunter firmly by the hand. "We all thank you. Santa came just in time."

"It was our duty," Hunter replied dryly, looking Howie directly in the eye. "We weren't rattled at all."

Howie eyed him back, but wasn't sure why Hunter was attempting to be so macho. "Please feel free to relax and enjoy yourselves. Everything is on us."

Chester began to growl at Howie, who quickly retreated out of range. Howie Rich's self-effacing deputy, Ofentse Mataka, stepped forward to offer them a drink and show them to some quarters to freshen up.

After a wash and change, Hunter went out and found a café with live jazz and dancing. Grabbing a seat, he looked in the mirror behind the bar and honed in on a familiar profile. He'd recognize those dark curls anywhere.

Hunter stared at Kiana, wondering if she was an apparition created by the rotating strobe lights, until she turned toward him and froze. She looked at him as though she had seen a ghost. Hunter admired the way she recovered, gave him a slight smile, and turned her back to him again to resume dancing. Hunter gulped down the rest of his drink, then walked up to her.

"Kiana, it's been ages. You look even better than the last time I saw you. What brings you to Halona?"

Kiana's eyes lit up in amusement. "It's good to see you too, Hunter. It seems you're a hero. You saved us all. Congratulations!"

Was there a hint of sarcasm in her voice? Maybe.

"I'm here with some friends. Just having fun! You must be exhausted after all the action today."

Hunter was about to say something, but then he saw another familiar figure. He excused himself from a surprised Kiana and walked up to a girl with chestnut hair who had just entered with a good-looking man. She didn't notice him. She was deep in discussion.

"Julian, I don't think this is a great idea. I need to get back to my quarters; Howie might be checking in."

Julian shook his head gently. "Babe, you have to live a little. This place is full of life, and you need a little cheering up. Have some fun. I promise to get you back in time for bed—"

Hunter interjected. "Pumpkin? Is that you? What are you doing here?"

Teagan stared at Hunter in bewilderment for a second, then screamed in excitement. "Oh my God, Hunter. You're the man of the hour! I'm so proud of you!"

Teagan ran toward him, and he lifted her as if she weighed nothing, enveloping her in a big hug. "I've missed you so much," he said.

The man next to her looked at the scene unfolding with a mixture of amusement and confusion. It took a while for Teagan to realize that she hadn't introduced him.

"Hunter, this is Julian Trace. Julian is an artist and a good friend. We're both here on Halona. Julian, this is my brother, Hunter. I haven't seen him in ages."

They shook hands. Before Hunter could say anything to Julian, Teagan pulled Hunter toward a corner booth. Julian wanted to give the siblings time to catch up, but neither allowed him to leave.

After the drinks arrived, Hunter asked, "How come you're on Halona? The last time I checked, you and Dad were on Quivira. We were supposed to meet up about a year ago, and I didn't hear from you. How are Mom and Dad?"

Teagan and Julian exchanged glances, and then Julian turned to Hunter.

"It was nice to meet you, Hunter; you and Teagan have a lot to talk about. I'll be around."

Hunter frowned as Julian left, wondering what was going on.

Teagan leaned closer. "You know, you and Dad need to communicate a bit more. You both behave like children."

Hunter didn't reply; he had tried to keep the lines of communication open with his parents. They had been the ones to be sparse with the messages. In the end, he had mostly stopped sending messages and depended on Teagan for information about his parents.

Instead of replying to Teagan's question, he asked, "What are you doing here? Why aren't you on Quivira with Dad?"

"Hunt, a lot has happened since the last time we talked. Do you know anything about the Heavenly Children project?"

He nodded. "I heard vaguely."

Teagan smiled sadly. "Some of the heavenly children are mine. I tried to see them in person, but César wouldn't allow it. I was banished to Halona to keep me out of the way."

"Slow down, Pumpkin." Hunter's brows furrowed. "When you say some of the babies are yours, what do you mean?"

"When we got to Quivira, César made it clear that we wouldn't be able to stay there unless I cooperated. They wanted to harvest some of my eggs. They used them in that project. But ever since, I've been overwhelmed by loneliness and emptiness. Dr. César wouldn't let me see the babies once they were born, so I forced my way into the nursery. I was accused of being a threat to them. How can I be a threat to my own children?"

So many things were still not making sense for Hunter. "What was Dad's reaction to all this?" he asked.

Again, Teagan smiled sadly, and Hunter was struck by how despondent his sister was. His usually fun-loving sister had been replaced by a woman who was clearly depressed and no longer herself. He felt pangs of regret for not realizing what she'd been going through.

"What could Dad do? Neither of us had any choice. It was either I moved to Halona or I would be detained. The heavenly babies are celebrities; if I was presented before a compliant judge for trying to kidnap those babies, I would end up in jail for a long time."

Hunter nodded. Teagan was probably right. There was no way she wouldn't have gone to prison if the Quivira authorities had handed her over. Even though Teagan didn't tell him, he could see what had happened. Howie Rich had probably fancied her and dangled the option of moving to Halona before her.

As they caught up, the conversation turned from heavy to nostalgic. By the time they were ready to leave, Hunter noted that Kiana and her group had already departed.

"Just one more thing, Hunt," Teagan said as they got ready to leave. "I might need your help to dispose of something later."

He raised his eyebrows. "Disposal? That's my job. Happy to help."

On his way to his quarters, Hunter saw something unexpected.

Parts of Halona were restricted access, the inner sanctum of the Rich empire, protected by retina scan security. But the main entrance to the Rich administrative quarters was especially unusual: A large door, shaped like a diaphragm with thin blades that snapped closed like a camera shutter. Much of the time they seemed to keep the shutters open, but those going in still needed security clearance.

As he passed by, he heard muffled voices, occasional Mandarin, and was certain he spotted Kiana's profile. What was she doing here, cozying up to Howie Rich? And what was the Chinese connection? This didn't seem just like "fun" to him.

He wondered if he should report this to Wingtip. Maybe he would combine bits of information into one report in a few days. Appear nonchalant but on the ball.

56

The Switch

Halona, December 2077

As Halona celebrated, Kiana was ushered into a darkened conference room. In the corner was a small figure who could be seen in silhouette. As the figure turned, she announced: "Hallo, Ms. Madison. I am General Lin."

Kiana drew in her breath. What was General Lin doing here?

"Maybe I should call you Kiana?" Lin asked softly.

Kiana assented.

"I know this must be a shock, but there's no need to be afraid," Lin continued calmly. "I'm not here to hurt you. I'm here to offer you a deal."

General Lin's tone was blunt. "We have admired you from afar. We think that you are ideal material for our little group, the Iron Hornets."

Kiana frowned. When Wingtip had told her to infiltrate the Hornets, she thought she'd have to work a lot harder to get in. Instead, it looked like they were recruiting her. She wondered what she'd done to get on their radar.

"We know your brother, Thiago, is in trouble. Maybe we can help," Lin continued.

Just like that, it all made sense to her. They thought they had her on a leash. Kiana looked at General Lin with loathing. Yes, Thiago had been arrested in Mexico, but he was completely innocent.

"You are a natural leader," Lin continued. "You have fire in your eyes, something Superintendent Wingtip and his Sentinels will never recognize. The Hornets need new blood, somebody who can turn them into a disciplined band, more focused on operations."

"Why would I do that?" Kiana hissed. She had to play this just right. If she were too eager, Lin might suspect something. "The Hornets don't need new blood. They need to be disbanded."

General Lin laughed. "Hatred is a powerful motivator," she said. "It can make people do things they never thought possible. Join us, Kiana, and together we will make the Iron Hornets the most powerful force in space. You will make lots of money to help your family."

Kiana enjoyed risk, so long as she had a plan to deal with it. That was why she had grabbed the chance when Wingtip encouraged her to infiltrate the Hornets. It would be perilous if she was exposed, but she would plan it in her usual meticulous way; Kiana had just needed time to assess things.

The Hornets were notorious mercenaries and tech-savvy outlaws. Their lunar base was rumored to be impenetrable, and those who tried to breach it never returned. Pretending to defect would be the only way in.

"Appear to be disaffected if they want to know why you're defecting," Wingtip had said.

Kiana had a deep desire to prove herself and demonstrate her capabilities to the world. Throughout her life, she'd been misunderstood and overlooked. Her father had favored her brother. Now Thiago was in jail again, and she was going to prove her worth. By embarking on this infiltration mission, Kiana aimed to explore her own potential, test her limits, and break away from the ordinary.

But it would require great delicacy. She could not break cover, even for a second. She would have to be more Hornet than the Hornets.

"I'm not sure. Would I get some training?" she asked Lin.

"Of course. You'll be trained to have extraordinary abilities. You will not believe the possibilities."

"And my brother?"

"We will facilitate his quiet release."

Kiana hesitated, not because she was unsure, but because she wanted Lin to think she was. She glanced around. Finally, she said, "I'll give you one year, once I have proof my brother is out of jail. After that, I'm free to decide whether to stay or leave."

"Two years."

"Okay, it's a deal."

"Two more things. First, you are to avoid contact with Hunter Ward. We can see from our observations that he has taken a fancy to you, may even be tracking you. He'll just get in the way. Second, you will be known from now on by the codename 'Zeitan.' Remember, the Hornets are crucial for our mission to dominate space. Whoever controls outer space will be able to control Earth," Lin underlined quietly. "And whoever controls Earth will be able to control the universe. That is our strategy."

Kiana looked perplexed but, with that, she was dismissed.

She wondered about the significance of the name Zeitan, spending hours hunting through references for people with that name. Eventually, she found what she was looking for—a photo of a woman named Zeitan who looked eerily similar to her.

She also found a birth certificate that listed Zeitan's birthday as the same day as her own. Was she looking at her own future or an alternate version of herself?

Clearly, nothing made sense. But Kiana knew that if she didn't go along with their plan, her brother would never be released. She would do whatever it took to save him, even if it meant double-crossing a few people.

She tried to put her discovery of her "double" aside. The only thing that had to make sense was the mission.

57
Removal Services

Halona, February 2078

H UNTER'S HANDS TIGHTENED ON the controls of the patched-up *SpaceSweeper III*. Doubts nagged at him, gnawing his mind like a persistent rodent. He kept reviewing scenarios in his head.

He was disturbed about what Kiana had been up to. Had he caught her out doing something? Her behavior seemed suspicious. He had allowed himself to be diverted by his sister's troubles. Maybe he should have kept more of an eye on Kiana, but then again maybe she wasn't his responsibility, whereas Teagan needed his help as a brother.

He looked down. Chester offered no solutions, so he decided to report to Wingtip.

Hunter had two dead satellites to remove and a couple of regular pickups. He would report to Wingtip after that, and casually throw in the information that he had seen Kiana in Howie Rich's quarters.

"I'm concerned she may be up to something. Do you think she's a double agent?" he asked Wingtip on the scrambled receiver.

"We're not aware of anything. Thank you for reporting it," said Wingtip cagily. "I suggest you keep track of her when you can and report back to me further."

"Yes, sir."

"But I wouldn't make it a priority."

Hunter's report confirmed for Wingtip that Kiana had satisfactorily penetrated the Hornets.

The first part of her operation was successful. Next was the long haul. Who knew how long that would take?

On Halona, Sam had finished his evening shift and only had to attend to one last problem, which had been reported earlier: The compactor was malfunctioning. It was always going wrong––the regolith was so brittle and unforgiving that it regularly jammed up the works.

No one could say for sure what happened to Sam.

His darkened figure was seen on the monitors moving swiftly down the corridors to the artists' deserted compacting room. He wasn't paying much attention to his surroundings.

Sam turned the compactor on; it was definitely jammed, as reported. He climbed to the top of the compactor's attached ladders and leaned into the mouth to clear some of the regolith. A large piece was stuck between the crushers.

He hit it with a hammer, but it refused to budge. He leaned a bit farther into the jaw-like entrance to get a better angle. Using all of his heft, he swung at the stone, shattering it into tiny pieces that ricocheted like bullets off the sides of the metal funnel.

He had forgotten to turn the machine off. A tiny piece of shrapnel struck him on the forehead, and as the monster began to swing back into operation, Sam lost his balance and careened down, staining the crushers bright red. Nobody heard his scream, muffled by the mechanical din.

Someone was on hand to pick up the compacted chunk of regolith as it emerged from the giant machine. They put it on a pair of wheels and pushed it along to the large dumpster in the corridor nearby. It was almost time for the dumpster to be collected by the garbage team who visited every night.

The contents were ejected into space, and one of Hunter's trash collectors snapped it up as scheduled.

Julian didn't feel any remorse. It was gratifying when "accidents" happened to the right people. But a nagging voice in the back of his mind whispered that some retribution would follow. Howie would demand a price.

The next day, Teagan made an offhand observation to Howie: "Haven't seen Sam around recently. Did you send him home as I suggested?"

"Sam had an accident," Howie said flatly.

"Unfortunate. Is he okay?"

Glaring at her, he shouted, "Sam is dead, you bitch!"

A flicker of surprise crossed Teagan's face. "That's sad. How did that happen? "He fell into the compactor."

"Nasty."

"Yes." A tense silence followed before Howie continued. "They did find that the top steps of the ladder had been greased to make them slippery."

"What a way to go. I hope his family will be looked after."

Howie's glare intensified. "I always look after my men. You may soon find out."

58
New Assignment

Halona, March 2078

G UY ZEPHRON LOVED GOING to Halona. He loved being able to stretch out, take some time off, and get a good meal. He loved the music. Plus, the artists' colony's paintings and carvings seemed like masterpieces to him.

Guy traveled to Halona on the invitation and coin of Howie Rich. For some reason that Guy didn't understand, Howie had taken a liking to him.

Howie motioned for Guy to follow him; they walked into an inner room that Guy didn't know existed. A bank of monitors showed different mining locations around space. Guy thought one of the monitors showed ElleWon, but he couldn't be sure. Howie motioned for Guy to sit, then sat as well.

"This is where I come when I don't want to be overheard. I have a special assignment for you."

Guy was alert but didn't say anything. Howie walked to a wide hologram projector showing a 3D model of the Milky Way. Hovering over the projection, the green light reflecting on his bearded face, Guy thought Howie Rich looked like a bear—big, hairy, with a loud voice.

Howie gazed at the projection. "I do believe in God," he confessed. "Look at the awe of the universe, the stars, the planets. Someone must have lit the match. A creator, a super intelligence. Someone must have set it all off. But did they know what they were doing? Is there a grand design or is it all an accident? There's the rub!" He laughed. "But I'm pretty sure we've got our concept of heaven all wrong. All this stuff about pearly gates and Saint Peter. Heaven or Hell. Lists and checking them twice. Nah. Sounds more like Father Christmas. That's got to be misinformation!

"What we do know is that this creator reused bits of his design. For example, scanned electron microscope images of mushroom mycelium look remarkably similar to human brain cells. And the underside of pioppino mushrooms looks like the baleen plates of whales. And, of course, the human vulva looks much like lips on the face."

Howie laughed, and Ofentse, who had followed them dutifully into the room, smiled limply. He had heard it all before. Howie laughed a lot. He tried to put employees at ease. That's how he got people to work with him.

"Guy, I want you to come and take a look at something," Howie said. Guy stood and walked over. Howie enlarged the image.

"This is an area close to Jupiter. There's an asteroid belt right here." Howie pointed.

"You want us to retrieve these asteroids?" Guy asked, confused at the secrecy.

Howie looked at Guy and smiled. He magnified the projection again until the asteroid belt was all Guy could see. Howie pointed to a particular asteroid and said, "Not just any asteroid, Guy. This is the asteroid I want you to capture and transport down to ElleWon."

Guy had learned in the military that asking questions rarely got you anywhere; following orders successfully, however, got you to the top.

Guy looked at the asteroid. It was smaller than the Zernon 47, but traveling to the outer reaches of Jupiter and back would be a challenge. Nevertheless, Guy knew he was up to it, with the right team.

He asked, "When do we leave?"

Howie gave his characteristic booming laugh. "Good man! I knew I could count on you. I know you normally use a crew of five tugs. I don't want to call a lot of attention to you guys, so handpick only those you can trust; this is a hush-hush mission. Ofentse has orders to refit your craft over the next month so it can withstand the rigors of such travels. In that time, get a team prepared and chart the best course for the vicinity of Jupiter."

Guy was forced to ask, "Why the secrecy, Mr. Rich?"

Howie Rich smiled. "If I told you, Guy, it wouldn't be a secret anymore, would it?" Guy had no answer to that.

59

The Package

Halona, March 2078

THE NEXT WEEKS WERE like heaven to Julian. Howie was consumed by his planning sessions with Guy, leaving time for a whirlwind romance to consume Julian and Teagan. Teagan gave Julian her heart, her trust. Sam's removal made her feel more at ease. Someone had done something for her.

She felt valued. She loved how he looked at her, how he painted her.

Julian felt a special bond between them; they talked about all kinds of things, including what inspired him to paint, where he loved to travel, and even how to tackle inequality in the world. Julian mentioned his aunt in Italy. Teagan was sure she would love her too.

But Julian knew it was too good to be true and that someday it would have to end.

Soon enough, the bubble burst, but not in the way he expected.

Julian took some artwork that he had sold to the packing area, to ready it for shipment. He carried the carefully sculpted statue, running his hand over the smooth surface.

Several bright red robots were packaging orders in boxes that were then piled up on a pallet.

"We need your label," said the supervisor.

"Be careful with this one. It's fragile," said Julian.

"Of course. Everything is fragile here."

"What are you shipping?" Julian asked, trying to make conversation.

"Some artwork produced by our students—pieces of pottery made from moon regolith, a couple of small statues, and stones billions of years old found inside our asteroids. People love those. They buy them as keepsakes. They say it makes them feel connected to the universe."

To one side, a heftier bot was wrapping a larger art piece with great strips of transparent packaging.

"This bot takes care of irregular-sized pieces. We use biodegradable wrap that cushions the pieces during shipment. Some of this packaging is made from seaweed, grown here."

Two large arms gripped the piece firmly and stuffed padded wrap under the joints, while a third arm encircled it with a large role of compostable wrap, as though it was a modern mummy.

"Quite an industry you have," Julian said.

"It pays the bills."

The sound of a sharp blade slicing through the wrap startled Julian as the bot neatly finished the job. Flinching, Julian was astounded to see Howie enter the packaging area. Had he followed him?

"It can wrap anything up in seconds," Howie told Julian after dismissing the supervisor. He watched, then stalked closer, until he was within striking distance, like a cobra.

Julian eyed him warily.

"You are a talented boy, really talented." Howie paused. "But I have a piece of advice for you. Stop screwing around with my woman."

His woman? Julian didn't say anything; he knew enough about Howie Rich to realize how dangerous he was.

With a smile, Howie tapped him on the shoulder and whispered, "Mark my words! It would be a pity for anything to happen to those talented fingers."

Howie edged him closer to the packing machine, blocking Julian's escape with his large body.

"Observe how delicate this machine is," Howie said. "It handles priceless materials."

Howie pointed and Julian reluctantly looked.

"This machine has a very precise mechanism. Take a closer look."

Julian could feel Howie's body heat and backed up slightly, trying to get away. But Howie obstructed his path, slightly tripped him so he was off balance, pressed the Start button, and watched.

Without warning, the giant machine gripped Julian firmly by the head, stuffed cushioned wrap under his armpits, and cocooned him in sheets of transparent wrap, encasing him completely. Julian tried to speak, but his voice was muffled. No sound could be heard over the noise of the machines. As the seaweed wrap wound tightly around him, Julian began gasping for air. It was starting to suffocate him.

"One thing you should know, Mr. Trace. Nobody takes food from my table and lives to tell the tale. Nothing personal. Bye-bye."

Howie turned on his heels and walked out, leaving the machine running. He checked the chip in his wrist. His blood pressure was a little high.

The giant arm continued wrapping. Julian knew he had a few seconds before he passed out. He couldn't resist the machine, it was too powerful, but he could try to make it malfunction.

Using every ounce of strength he still had, Julian shifted his weight, rocking back and forth on his heels and toes, trying to generate enough momentum to disrupt the machine's precise movements. His body collided with one of the rotating arms, causing it to miss its intended turn. The delicate synchronization of the machinery was disrupted, throwing off the rhythm of the packaging process, and an alert light went on. The tape became tangled and twisted, providing some slack and giving him just enough room to wiggle and create more space. The wrapping became wilder.

Seeing the alert, a confused supervisor rushed over to the cocoon.

"How did this happen?" he asked furiously as he swiftly hit the emergency shut-down button and cut a hole in the packaging for Julian to breathe.

The room went quiet. Julian gasped for air. A moment later, he would have been asphyxiated.

Julian knew he had to leave immediately. After disentangling himself, he thanked the supervisor and rushed out. He wanted to find Teagan but knew he couldn't risk bumping into Howie again.

Instead, he scribbled her a note.

I love you. I will find you. Promise.

Taking only the things important to him, Julian bolted out of Halona—pretending he had an exhibit—and took the next flight to Earth. If nothing else, Julian Trace was a survivor. He understood he would seem like a coward, but he would find Teagan again. He would make it up to her.

He knew he was being a chicken. Teagan was his anchor, his source of strength. She had inspired him. She had brought light and joy into his life, filling his days with laughter and his nights with tenderness. This was to be her reward? He knew the note was inadequate, but he didn't have time for explanations.

During the shuttle flight, Julian began to recover his composure. As he thought things through, he knew that he had taken the easy way out, but at least he was alive and not some package ready for delivery, wrapped in seaweed. He would explain everything to her when they reunited. They would build a future together.

But first, he would have to regroup. It would be a long journey, but even longer and more tortured for Teagan. Would they even be able to see each other again, with Howie standing in their way? Julian vowed to find a way.

60
The Bonus

The Intergalactica Hotel, April 2078

U NAWARE OF JULIAN'S PERIL or Teagan's isolation, Clara found herself with a rare period of free time, a precious break from her responsibilities for Easter.

The idea of meeting Noel at the *Intergalactica Hotel* on ElleWon for one of their regular rendezvous sparked excitement in her eyes. Her heart yearned for connection, for the warmth of familiar faces and the comfort of shared laughter.

Noel greeted Clara with a warm smile and a kiss on the cheek. Clara savored these moments, treasuring each shared anecdote and warm conversation like they were precious gems. It would have been great for all four of them to meet up, but Hunter and Teagan both seemed too busy. Clara missed them but rarely had the time for substantive conversations during her work. Mostly she was consumed by her own projects, particularly the seed bank.

A famed temporary resting point dubbed "the most luxurious pod in the universe," the Intergalactica offered some R&R and comfort before a traveler headed to other asteroid factories, the Moon, Mars, and beyond. Some guests were returning to Earth from long voyages; some were visiting for the first time.

The Intergalactica was known for its fine service and wonderful panoramic bar that gave fabulous views of Earth and the Moon simultaneously.

In the early days, it had been a popular spot for space tourists from Earth, but now it served a more practical purpose as a jumping-off point for further exploration. Its slogan: "Last stop before the dark side."

Clara and Noel spent the week together, catching up, swapping stories, making love, and eating well, or as well as space-food allowed. The ambient hum of interstellar travelers filled the air, creating a symphony of distant voices and starship engines.

The Intergalactica was no longer in its prime, but the views were still spectacular, particularly at night when Earth's cities were lit up and sparkling. They would play a game, trying to name each spot on the Moon that they knew. Clara had a bit of an advantage, but Noel had done this all his life. The game helped them reconnect.

But, for the first time, Clara felt she was not the only one hiding something from her partner. "Is there something you want to tell me?"

Noel looked startled. "I'm thinking of teaching the Seven."

Clara was confused at first. "What seven? Is that a new course at the university?"

Noel's eyes twinkled as he said, "No, love, I'm thinking of having a hand in the education of the children on Quivira."

Clara was quiet. She had tried to create a buffer between herself and those creations. When she finally spoke, she said in a controlled voice, "Isn't teaching elementary beneath your status? You're a college professor. You shouldn't be teaching ABCs and one-two-threes."

"You know, I really enjoy being with them. They're not babies anymore. They have exceptionally high IQs. When they're ready, I want to introduce them to earth sciences and a little bit of this and that."

"Do you think of them as your grandchildren?" Clara heard the distaste in her voice, and she knew Noel heard it too.

"Whether you like it or not, they are a part of our daughter. Teagan believes these children, no matter their birth circumstances, are her children. I agree with her. I think it's time you do too. Every child needs a mother. You can't just keep looking after your precious seeds."

Clara's anger came flooding out, years of guilt and pent up offence.

"You know, Noel, despite having one of the most brilliant minds in the world, you can be incredibly naïve. What do you think will happen? Huh? This Dr. César and Howie Rich will suddenly come to their senses and think 'The Wards have been cooperative. Why don't we reward them with three kids out of the Seven?' We both know that's not going to happen."

But Clara wasn't done.

"You encouraged her to donate those eggs. When the babies came, you didn't help her comprehend that those babies were just business products and that in no way did they belong to her. You should not have allowed her to cuddle them, to love them. I am sure her contribution has already been swept under the carpet. Nobody knows the sacrifice my baby made to make those lives.

"Now she's in exile, away from her parents and everything she loves, and all you can think of is teaching them mathematics, physics, and chemistry? If you were expecting some commendation, Noel Ward, you are in the wrong place. Your daughter needs you. Being a father doesn't mean just sticking your appendage in a woman and making a baby. You have to be there for her."

Noel said nothing. He held on to his wife until he felt her anger pass.

Then, with a voice filled with anguish and remorse, he said, "I am so sorry. I'm sorry I didn't do more for our baby. I'm sorry I didn't keep our family together."

As he held her, all of the anger and Malapert loneliness within Clara began to recede.

She kissed her husband, saying, "Oh honey, none of this is your fault. I know what you must be going through, not being able to see Teagan. You have always been a good husband and father; that is all either Teagan or I could have asked for." She gripped her husband tightly.

They ordered non-alcoholic drinks from a passing servicebot. Noel smiled. He tried to find something less divisive to chat about.

"You always did have the wildest ideas. Remember our crazy tour to New York before the Great Unraveling?"

Clara laughed so hard. "How could I forget? I thought you were an innocent grad student. You ended up taking advantage of me from Arizona to New York and back. My God, I can't believe the shit we did on that trip."

"It was all your idea, remember? Remember standing over me, naked, and telling me to get ready for the ride of my life?"

Clara laughed. "Of course, I remember. I had to repeat myself because you couldn't take your eyes off my breasts."

Noel said, in mock outrage, "My eyes were on your face the whole time. Of course, I do remember glimpsing a rosy nipple."

Clara smiled mischievously. "You're sure all you saw was a nipple?"

Noel, now with mock seriousness, said, "I stand by what I saw. Moreover, all this talk of nipples is making me curious to examine them and show them again just how much I've missed them."

Clara and Noel spent the remainder of the week in each other's company, soaking up the occasional delicious cocktail and taking in the extraordinary views of the Moon below.

"This week is for mutual happiness; when the week is done, we can face the raging storm," she said, as they began reminiscing about their successes and failures.

Noel kissed his wife. "Balancing life is hard."

61
The Heartbreak

Halona, April 2078

T EAGAN COULDN'T BELIEVE JULIAN had just left without even kissing her goodbye. She looked at the hastily scrawled "I love you. I will find you. Promise." and then crumpled up the paper. He hadn't even signed it; not even an xx for a kiss. She threw it across the room.

She knew that Howie must have threatened him, but she couldn't understand why Julian would just abandon her like that, leaving her with this monster. She had lost her children and now her lover.

The thought propelled Teagan into a deeper cycle of misery and doubt. She stood frozen in the doorway, not sure what to do. An impulse led her to visit his studio. A canvas still stood on the easel, as if Julian were still there. But Teagan knew he would not be back. The emptiness of the room echoed the emptiness she had inside. Tears welled in her eyes as she tried to process what must have happened. She held his clothes to her face and breathed in his scent. She picked up a paintbrush and imagined his hand holding it with hers, his nose nuzzling her hair.

In the past few weeks, passion had consumed her every waking thought. Now he was gone. But it wasn't just his departure that shattered her: It was the way he left, without even a simple embrace. Pacing back and forth, her mind raced with questions. *What had Howie threatened?* After he had severed one of Tentikal's arms, she knew Howie was capable of anything. Maybe he had threatened the same to Julian. Anger mixed with confusion, stirring a cascade of emotions within her. *How could Julian allow himself to be manipulated like this? Why did he prioritize Howie's threats over their love? A real lover would stand firm.*

These thoughts tormented her, fueling her sense of betrayal. She couldn't eat, couldn't sleep, and the thought of going back to Howie's quarters made her feel sick. Instead, she found a small spare bunk to curl up in.

Loneliness settled in like a heavy fog, enveloping her muddled mind. She missed Julian's touch, his contagious laughter, which filled the space with joy and warmth. Now, the room was empty and cold.

Tears began flowing freely down her face, washing away the remnants of hope and leaving her hollow inside. Teagan knew her only succor now was to see her children. Her family was too far apart. Her mother, her father. Where was Hunt? Space was so divisive. It wasn't human. It just swallowed everything into an enormous, engulfing nothingness. That's what they meant by a Black Hole.

Slowly Teagan resolved to rebuild her life. Maybe she would see Julian again, maybe not. Either way, she would survive. She was strong.

She began to work past her sorrow. She realized that Julian's departure wasn't a reflection of her worth or her ability to love. It was his weakness, his inability to stand up to Howie's influence. Teagan began to emerge from the depths of her sorrow with newfound determination. She would no longer allow herself to be defined by a love that had been shattered. She would learn to love herself, to embrace her own strength, and to trust that, someday, someone worthy of her love would come along.

62

The Refuge

Matera, Italy, May 2078

JULIAN FOUND THE PERFECT sanctuary, with his aunt in the southern Italian hilltop town of Matera. It was the ideal refuge, out of the way at the foot of Italy. Why would anyone think of finding him there? And better than some mosquito-ridden jungle. He could easily get lost among the tangled warrens of stone houses, sinuous passageways, and narrow cobblestone streets—a stark contrast to the advanced technology of the space habitat he had left behind.

The Basilicata locals were accustomed to tourists, so his presence would be less likely to raise suspicion. Furthermore, Matera's relative distance from major urban centers provided Julian with a sense of security, giving him valuable time to regroup and plan his next move.

Julian's aunt, Lucia, offered him a comfortable shelter away from prying eyes. His room was simple: A sturdy wooden bed, with an old mattress and crisp linens, stood against one wall; against another wall, a wooden desk provided Julian with a workspace where he could plan, write, and reflect. The desk was clutter-free, with a few essential items such as a notebook, pens, and a laptop, allowing Julian to organize his thoughts and work on his mission to reunite with Teagan. He knew she would feel betrayed. But she would come to know his love was not fragile or temporary.

At first, Julian stayed mostly in his room, but when nobody came looking for him, he began venturing out.

As he wandered through the town, clambering down the narrow, uneven steps and pathways sandwiched between ancient and occasionally crumbling houses, Julian was engulfed by loneliness and guilt. Thoughts of Teagan overwhelmed him. He kept seeing her face, in cafes, in churches, and round bends in the road.

He knew that to truly find solace, he had to discover a way back to her. But he couldn't ignore Howie's threat. Howie was not a man to be messed with.

Julian spent his time reading and plotting. He would walk the streets thinking. Walking clarified his mind. One evening, while sitting at a small café, Julian over-heard whispers of a secret network that could help individuals in dire situations.

It was rumored that this network could arrange discreet transportation to even the most remote locations.

Intrigued, Julian began quietly investigating. After weeks of careful inquiries and gaining the trust of certain individuals, of buying coffees, buying beers, he was finally introduced to the enigmatic leader of the network, a person known only as "Il Ragno" or "The Spider," because of his web of connections around the world.

Il Ragno, whose real name was Enzo Morezano, operated a chain of high-end nightclubs and bars called "Enzo's." These popular entertainment dives not only generated legitimate income, but also provided a platform for money laundering, drug distribution, and other illicit activities.

Il Ragno understood the urgency of Julian's situation. With his resources, Il Ragno could arrange safe passage for Teagan to be smuggled out of Halona and, as a bonus, for Howie to be taught a lesson. But his help came at a price. His network did not stretch everywhere. Julian would have to undertake a dangerous mission. "What do I need to do?"

"My little girl, my granddaughter, is being picked on," said Il Ragno. He drew on his cigar and let the smoke linger in the air. "By some over-enthusiastic asshole."

"What's her name?"

"Viviana. But everyone calls her Viv. It's been her life's ambition to be in space since she emigrated with her dad. But the asshole is trying to ensure she doesn't make it. He's trying to break her. Maybe he doesn't like her."

Julian shook his head. "Why not handle him yourself?"

"She's a cadet in the Space Sentinels. I don't have contacts in the Sentinels. It's a closed shop to me. But I've heard that you do."

Julian tried to suppress his surprise, but Il Ragno noticed. "I've made inquiries into you." Julian believed him. "Who's the guy?"

Il Ragno showed him a picture. "Master Sergeant Haluk Sancak. He runs the Sentinels training. You can look him up."

"I haven't a clue who that is," said Julian. "But I might know someone who does. How big a lesson?"

"One that he will never forget."

"I'll do what I can. I just want my girl out of there. To graduate and succeed."

Julian finished his Caffè Doppio and, the moment he left Il Ragno, made a call to Hunter Ward.

63
The Mud Trap

S NAKEHOLE KNEW THE BASIC training program for recruits was under scrutiny because some instructors had pushed recruits too hard and too far. A couple of recruits had even died in training, attracting unwelcome media attention. The deaths had been explained by the authorities as the result of "drug taking" by recruits anxious to increase their endurance.

Despite this, Snakehole decided to follow his usual training routine. As in previous years, the recruits were formed into four squads. Each set up a camp as though they were in hostile territory and in danger of attack. They created guard posts, along with an entry control point, and endured simulated attacks—chemical, biological, and others. Because of the risk of chemical "attacks," they had to wear their suffocating chemical warfare suits and masks for days at a time. After initial briefings, they were forced to crawl on their bellies through the dirt and marshland, keeping as low a profile as possible in case of snipers, and taught to take cover, return fire, and quickly get out of a sniper's sights.

"Move with purpose, and don't leave a buddy behind. Always work with your wingman," Snakehole told them, a dribble of saliva running down his lip.

Instructors were under orders to weed out weaklings. If they couldn't endure the prolonged bouts of training, what use would they be when they faced real danger?

"We need tough cadets, not wimps," Snakehole would snap.

Nevertheless, he knew they had to be careful. Another death might shut the program down.

As usual, cadets were confronted by a series of timed obstacles. But this year was worse than normal. The rains had been intense, and the rivers were rising. Temperatures were colder for the time of year.

A recruit lost her footing on a rock and was submerged.

"Hold your weapon above the water, Viviana," hissed an instructor to the new recruit.

"Incoming," Snakehole shouted as he tossed a smoke grenade near some struggling recruits, then burrowed into a ditch beside the road to keep himself camouflaged and out of sight.

The recruit ducked for cover and was immediately doused again by the river. Viv's camouflage fatigues were getting waterlogged, and she drank in a load. She struggled to bring herself upright in the frigid water, the pack on her back weighing her down.

"Help," she shouted. "I need help." Viviana began spitting up bloody fluid from one lung after striking a sharp rock.

Sodden on the bank, a couple of fellow recruits tried to assist, but the raging waters prevented them from getting close enough.

"We need backup," they radioed. "Cadet in trouble in the water. Hang on, Viv!"

Unaware the recruit was facing difficulty, Snakehole threw another grenade, while the control center dispatched an amphibious vehicle to help with the rescue.

"Stand by. We'll be there shortly," the control center responded via radio.

Sticking his head out of his well-concealed lair to throw another grenade, Snakehole noticed the recruit being swept along in the torrential waters, desperately trying to grab hold of a branch or rock.

Fuck, this is the last thing we need, he thought. *Another injured recruit on my watch.*

"Urgent," he said into the radio. "We need help now."

"Copy that. There in two."

An eight-wheeled amphibious combat vehicle hurtled around the corner, two medics on the back and a couple more inside. Despite the incessant rain, the thirty-five-ton flat-topped monster gripped the wet terrain with ease. As it thrust down the bank of the river and headed into the water, taking on the undulating mud, rocks, and riverbank with its angled tread tires, an officer in the control tent advised them to steer a couple of degrees to the left to pick up the floundering recruit. The driver adjusted the course slightly.

The rescuers careened forward, unaware of Sergeant Sancak lying camouflaged in a hidden dip on the bank.

The rain pounded down and the mud churned. In their rush to save the young recruit, the giant wheels drove straight over Sancak, crushing him to death. In the last second before impact, he could see the muddy wheels heading straight for him, churning up the earth. He tried to shout out, but no one could hear. As his bones were crushed and splintered, he spewed blood onto the drenched ground. A sharp pain radiated through his whole body, and he knew that he was going to die.

Sergeant Sancak had always dreamed of military victory. Tragically, he met his end not in a blaze of glory, but as the victim of a careless mistake, just another training casualty.

***

At the crowded memorial service on Epona, Wingtip called him "the trainers' trainer."

"We all owe our professionalism to him. He was an outstanding man. A man of character and a man who shaped us all. May he rest in peace."

A virtual gun salute was fired in his honor.

Hunter was relieved. Viv had graduated and he had escaped the need to act. He sent a signal to Julian: *Il Ragno satisfied. Mission accomplished. Over to you.*

64
The Accident

Quivira, August 2081

THE MAGNIFICENT SEVEN WERE growing up quickly. The corridors of Quivira were their domain, where they played hide and seek, concealing themselves in secret spaces and leaping out suddenly to cackles of laughter. It was not easy keeping watch on seven energetic, intelligent children with an eye for mischief. Individually they weren't that bad, but as a pack, they could create chaos. They knew every hallway, secret passageway, and shortcut on Quivira. Maureen Grau once remarked it seemed the children had the space habitat's blueprint etched on their brains.

They lived to tease their nurses and annoy the bots. The only person it seemed who could get through to them was Noel Ward. "Noey" played the role of a lovable grandfather. Though he never said it out loud, he considered the Seven his grandchildren.

They all loved dressing up. Motoko would let them loose on a bunch of dressing-up clothes and props, such as toy doctor's kits, and let their imaginations run wild. They also ran wild with paints and drawing tools, using their hands to smear colors onto canvas and using screens to create patterns and shapes. They loved singing and music, and Aurora would join in with Tara, playing the drums and the tambourine. They would play guessing games and I spy.

"I spy with my little eye, something beginning with G," said Gabby.

"Green," said Liam, thinking he'd nailed it.

"No," said Gabby. "Try again."

"Goo," said Baolin. "No," said Gabby. "I don't see any goo!"

"How about germs?" asked Ved.

"Of course not! No germs here!"

"I know," said Nevaeh, or Nevie as she was sometimes called. "Golf. There's Noey playing golf!"

"As usual," chimed in Liam.

Noel played virtual golf with friends most afternoons after remotely teaching his university classes, but he would always stop by the nursery for bedtime, when he would read the children a story about elves or evil witches. They would always ask for more. "Please, please," they'd chime and he'd always give in.

At first, Maureen and Dr. César were reluctant to allow Noel access to the children, given what Teagan had done. They placed him under surveillance until they were convinced he meant them no harm. But his genuine affection for the kids soon won Maureen over, and she granted him unrestricted access.

Some nights, Noel had a video call with Teagan. She hadn't told him about Julian, but Noel could sense the sadness in her. There were times when he wished he hadn't moved to Quivira or had convinced Teagan not to agree to the egg harvesting procedure; but what was done was done. The best he could do for her was to be there for the children.

Grau also took it upon herself to check in on the children as often as she could. Pica always flew in a few seconds before she arrived, like a herald. He would settle on a table or chair top, and give the children a warble.

"The witch is arriving," Liam would say in a whisper.

On a few occasions, while on a business trip, Howie would drop by, and Maureen noticed he always seemed to pay special attention to Arturo––nicknamed Art––who was becoming his favorite. He would sneak him some special toffees.

Dr. César didn't drop by as often, and when he did he usually stayed in the background, observing each child. Privately, he was happy with their development and read all the reports Motoko and the robot Bruce made weekly. He instructed Motoko to stimulate their creative abilities.

One day, while going through Motoko's weekly report, Maureen summoned her to her office.

"I just wanted to congratulate you on the wonderful job you've been doing with our Magnificent Seven. These reports have been nothing short of amazing. I was thinking of recommending you for a raise and a promotion."

Motoko blushed with pleasure. "I've only been doing my job. Most of the time, I learn from them more than they learn from me!"

And it was true, the Seven were far smarter than others their age. But for all their brilliance, Motoko tried to remember that they were still little children. They loved to sing nursery rhymes and make animal noises, though, of course, they had seen no animals in real life, except Maureen's magpie. Teagan had kept Tentikal private.

Ved had a very vivid imagination, an eidetic memory, and a bit of a wild streak. He also loved to play pranks. Lately, he had been working on floating around Quivira like an astronaut. He and Baolin had broken into the laundry and stolen a space suit.

"I'm a Martian!" Ved said, flapping his arms like a bird.

"That's not a Martian," said Baolin. "That's a pterodactyl." Although he pronounced it like "ptero-ducktail."

"It's not a ducktail," screamed Ved. "It's an astronaut. Look, I can fly!"

Ved had scouted his take-off point, an observation deck at least sixty feet above the main level. On the day of his spectacular stunt, he assembled the others and proceeded to climb.

Liam cautioned, "What are you doing, Ved? Careful, you could get yourself killed." Liam turned to Baolin, their de facto leader. "Talk to him, Bao, he listens to you."

Baolin shrugged, fascinated.

As Ved got to the edge of the platform and got ready to jump, he heard, "Hey kid, what are you doing? Get down from there."

A technician started approaching Ved menacingly. Through the visor of the space suit helmet, the technician saw the kid smile, and then wave, before jumping off the platform.

As soon as his feet left the platform, Ved knew something was wrong. Instead of floating, as he'd seen astronauts do, he descended rapidly. The station's artificial gravity plunged him downwards. Ved started to flap his hands like wings, thinking that would stop him from falling. He twisted like Batman, but that didn't work either.

Ved landed with a startling thump. For a fraction of a second, there was stunned silence.

Rescuers on the scene found him unconscious. An alarm sounded, and medibots hurried forward with Maureen and Motoko not far behind. Ved looked broken, blood seeping from the suit, lying immobile on the floor. When Maureen saw him, she screamed. Motoko fainted.

"Can you hear us?" shouted Maureen frantically. "What's your name? Tell us your name."

Ved was rushed to the hospital section, where Dr. César flew into a rage. He turned to Maureen and bellowed, "How could you be so careless? All my hard work might be negated because of your ineptitude."

Maureen Grau almost burst an artery. "How dare you, Doctor de Luca! I have these children's interests at heart as much as you do, if not more. What you are saying is outrageous."

Dr. César glared at her. "It's nobody's fault," interjected Motoko. "It was an accident. Please do the best you can for him."

Dr. César nodded curtly and ordered everyone out as the child lay limply on the gurney, with the medibots standing to one side, unsure of what to do.

65

The Recovery

Quivira, January 2082

HEALING WAS A LONG process. Dr. César oversaw Ved's recovery program, and two medibots supervised him on a daily basis. After Ved's second surgery, two more bots started him on a daily physiotherapy regime, to begin learning to walk again. Each step was a painful victory.

After a couple of weeks of progress, Ved relapsed. The moment his feet touched the ground, a sharp pain shot up his legs and radiated through his body. He got up slowly and managed to grip the poles. He took one step and the pain intensified. By his third, he was sweating all over. He was on the verge of collapsing when he was grabbed by a bot and taken back to his bed, where he fell into an exhausted sleep.

Dr. César decided he had to come up with something better. Ved's muscles were weak, and they could not work on their own.

As an experiment, César decided to implant a microchip in Ved's brain that stimulated and monitored activity. Ved had to wear a special suit of clothing, an exoskeleton, to give him the muscle power to walk again. It took five rounds of surgery, injections with a mysterious serum, and almost a year of physiotherapy before Ved left the ward. He wasn't the same again but, over time, the operation seemed to have given him special strength.

César believed he could do still more, maybe by adjusting the boy's DNA, but it would be risky.

While Ved was recovering, César decided to implement Plan B. He had always had a backup plan in case one of the incubated children did not work out as he expected.

One day, he called the children together and introduced them to another child of the same age. "This is Shiko," he told them. "Please treat him as a brother."

Fascinated, they all gathered around him, except for Gabriella, who held back.

César smiled in self-satisfaction as he watched the children. He had kept Shiko hidden from everyone until now, a backup in case of any abnormalities in one of the children.

Now everyone would know the birth of the Seven was not a one-off event. Other children like Shiko could be produced. In all honesty, they were just the beginning. If they could survive, then the probability that his real project would be successful was high.

"Perhaps they could be programmed in a certain way, just like the bots," he said excitedly to himself as he paced back and forth in his lab before going to record his ideas. "But they would have flesh and blood and be capable of living on their own without continuous commands. Programmed with a particular emotion and allowed to do specific tasks."

***

When Noel heard about the accident, he became frantic. He knew Teagan would be anxious and extremely worried if she found out. So, he decided to keep it from her.

Noel pestered Dr. César for weeks before he was allowed to visit Ved. When he did, it broke his heart to see so many tubes protruding from such a small body. For the next month, Noel visited him every day, telling him stories even though he knew Ved couldn't hear him clearly or concentrate.

Noel became even more worried when he heard about the arrival of Shiko. He knew that Teagan would feel that Shiko was a threat, making one of her children dispensable or replaceable. She would be able to see that Shiko was not hers. Maybe she'd start to doubt all the others.

Best she did not know.

66

The Teacher

Quivira, February 2083

A s the Magnificent Seven (now Eight with the survival of Ved) grew older, Noel took an active part in their education, teaching them the basics of subjects such as mathematics, physics, biology, chemistry, geology, astronomy, and planetary observation. It gave him a lot of satisfaction to see his "grandchildren" grow into intelligent, compassionate, and well-rounded children.

What pleased him the most was that they banded together; each distinct in their way but having each other's backs in all matters. Baolin was the leader of the group. Then there was Nevaeh, the queen of numbers. She was a mathematical genius. Arturo was emotional and compassionate; Tara was glamorous, a star. Liam was the quiet one, nose always buried in a text. Gabby was often detached and observant. Ved was recovering nicely. The new boy, Shiko, had won acceptance. He was charismatic and confident, and Dr. César now regarded him as part of the group, not a "spare." Noel was proud of them all.

Teagan had noticed Ved wasn't available when she called and became suspicious about his absence. Noel tried to convince her that everything was all right, but she didn't believe him. "Is there something wrong? I can tell there's something wrong."

She looked for an opportunity to check.

One day, Noel had just finished teaching the kids about rock formations on Earth and went to his cabin to get some rest before a round of virtual golf. When he opened the door, he saw his daughter sitting on his bed. Noel first thought it was a 3D hologram, but as soon as she saw him, she ran toward him and gave him a fierce hug. That dispelled any doubts about the daughter in his room being real or not.

She was older, and a little hardness and wildness had crept into her eyes. She looked anxious.

"Teagan, what are you doing here? You're supposed to be on Halona. Maureen and Dr. César will not be happy."

Teagan looked at her father and said accusingly, "When were you going to tell me my son was in an accident? I thought I could trust you. I've come to take my children with me, where we'll be safe."

Noel studied his daughter. "Remember you were sent to Halona because you almost killed one of them. Teagan, the best thing you can do for those children is let them be. They're fine where they are; all of them, including Ved, are safe."

When she looked at him again, Noel saw the traces of his little girl.

She said, "No, Dad. That's not the best thing. I can't; don't you see? Since the day those eggs were harvested from me, I have felt empty. When I carried Nevaeh in my arms, I was whole, I felt at peace. I would give anything to feel that way again. I want to hear her call me Mom. I want to watch her grow and for us to laugh together. I craved to find her milk teeth under her pillow and let the fairy take them, just like we did. I want to take her to her first day of school, help her with homework, and see her succeed. I want those things like any mother. I am missing all that. Now, either you help me or you stay out of my way. Which one is it going to be, Dad?"

Noel looked at her for a while, her arms crossed in defiance, then said, "I'm sorry, Pumpkin. I should have fought for you more. I should have convinced you not to go for the procedure; I should have protected you better."

He knew if he didn't help her now, his precious daughter, he would lose her completely. He rummaged through his pocket and brought out a digital key pass.

"This'll give you access to all the floors and rooms except the medical floor and Maureen Grau's office. The children are on the third floor. But be careful. If you're caught, there's nothing I can do to save you."

Teagan nodded, took the card, and gave him a quick kiss on his cheek.

As she walked down the hall, she tried to avert her eyes from the cameras. She hoped Howie Rich had not discovered she was missing from Halona yet.

She opened the door to the third floor and followed directions to the room marked "Kindergarten/School." Taking a deep breath, Teagan used the pass to open the door and slid inside. The room was quiet.

Immediately, she knew something was wrong.

A burst of electricity coursed through her body, and she crumpled to the floor. She felt another shock as she heard Howie's voice.

"I told you she would be there, César. For an intelligent person, she sure is dumb."

Teagan couldn't see anything, but it was clear he was on a video call. She tried to speak, but no words came out.

She heard Howie say again, "She's all yours to do with as you please. Do me a favor: Don't be gentle."

Then everything went black for Teagan.

"I think a spell in the Marius Hills would keep her out of the way for a bit," said César. "She might even help with further research, though it might be a bit painful."

67

The Three Queens

The SkyLink, February 2083

THE TUBE-LIKE VERTICAL COMPARTMENT of the SkyLink space elevator swayed a little with the momentum as it picked up descending speed. Teagan screamed, but no one in the other carriages could hear her as the Moon's surface sped toward them. She beat on the siding; it just made a dull thud. She began to get hysterical in the confined space.

"Get me out of here," she screamed. "Where am I?"

The lengthy journey from Quivira, via ElleWon, to the lunar base camp was traumatic, particularly so after Teagan had been delivered to the ElleWon and regained consciousness in the cramped SkyLink elevator car that linked the space station with the moon. The bots had used considerable force to suppress her. Maybe too much. They weren't trained for this.

The SkyLink from ElleWon to the surface of the Moon was mostly used for transporting metals and products for supply to spaceships refueling at ElleWon. Teagan had begun to panic when she woke up in the darkened and poorly ventilated cabin, which smelled of engine oil and musty old boots as if she was being asphyxiated with chloroform. She beat on the sealed external windows as the cargo compartment slid down the lightweight, high-strength wire to the flat, arid surface below.

As the car reached the lunar surface and eased into the station, bots bundled her into an eight-wheeled transport that was headed west, toward the basalt domes of the Marius Hills. The interior was spartan and practical, almost unfinished. They strapped her in tightly.

César had left Teagan with the securitybots so that he could meet with his new recruit, Professor Olga Polyakov, a specialist in genetic engineering and biotechnology. Polyakov had caught Dr. César's attention when she published research on creating gene-edited babies. He had offered her a large amount of money to work with him, freeing her from the normal ethical boundaries that still existed on Earth. At first, she resisted the offer, but when her brother got sick and needed expensive treatment, she finally agreed, rather than have her mother tap into non-existent savings.

She was waiting for him in the well-pressurized coffee shop normally used by tourists.

"I hope you haven't been waiting too long?"

"Just a couple of hours. Gave me time to collect my thoughts." Polyakov, an elegant woman with hair to her shoulders, got in the LTV beside him. The vehicle kicked up the dust as they drove along a barely marked track that disappeared once they approached their destination.

Buried deep into the side of the Marius Hills, Dr. César's lunar facilities were cramped and ugly, but functional. Doors and their frames were spartan, built by 3D printers. The rooms were rectangular. Things were a bit claustrophobic until you emerged into the lava tubes, which provided protection from radiation and acted as natural bunkers, no digging needed.

While the longest known lava tube on Earth—the sixty-five-kilometer-long Kazumura Cave on the Big Island of Hawaii—measured twenty-one meters wide and eighteen meters tall in some spots, lava tubes on the Moon were much bigger, forming natural refuges billions of years old.

A camouflaged façade opened to let them into the lab complex, and César drove straight into an airlock. They stayed in the vehicle as the concealed door closed behind them. Then, after a few seconds, a door in front opened, and César drove ahead and down through the lava tube complex, the light from the LTV's headlights bouncing off the walls. He peeled off left, and the eight-wheeler headed for the detention complex to the right.

After about a hundred meters, César halted and got out of his pressurized vehicle. He punched in a code and entered an unmarked door, finding himself inside the lab where Li Jie was "working," meaning mostly talking to mates in Guiyang and Shanghai. Li abruptly turned off the screen he was watching as soon as César entered, accompanied by Polyakov. "How are you, boss?" he asked, feigning friendliness.

"Come, help me unpack," César said with no time for pleasantries. César had brought with him a nest of around 30,000 ants and three queens to replenish their experiment. He moved them to two separate rooms and placed them in transparent cases.

"This time, I've got some bullet ants from South America and some Maricopa harvester ants that Howie sent from Arizona. Both have good stings."

The bullet ant was known for having one of the most painful stings in the world—like a bullet hitting your body in waves of all-consuming pain that could last for twenty-four hours. It didn't enjoy fighting, but would become very aggressive if it felt its home was threatened. "We are looking at using the ant's mandibles and saliva to close up wounds," César told Polyakov.

The Maricopa harvester ant venom was among the most toxic in the world. Just twelve stings could kill a two-kilogram rat. The red harvester ant would attach to the victim with its mandibles and bite repeatedly, injecting venom, although they fed mostly on seeds. "We are investigating this venom to help treat arthritis. Since the aging population is increasing by the day, it will be a real money spinner."

In the background, a line of mechanical bots was tasked with creating samples, running standardized tests, automating ingredient selection and formulation, and assessing effectiveness and toxicity. They were programmed to find the samples faster than humans by using barcodes and databases that mapped everything to precise physical locations within each freezer. They could also make decisions about what experiments to do next, based on predetermined logic provided by Dr. César. Power was supplied via a small helium-3 fusion pack. Oxygen was extracted from the lunar regolith, which was also mined for helium-3, abundant on the Moon.

César's goal was to make progress on his *cordyceps militaris* experiment, to create compliant human populations. Cordyceps worked when its spores landed on an insect's body and took root in its muscles. The spores then controlled the insect, making it move to a location perfect for the fungi to reproduce. "The aim is for it to reproduce in people, not just ants, giving control of the human population," César said. "We need to find a way to do that, to help the fungal parasite jump from insects to humans.

"It would most likely be an airborne infection. Places like cities, public transportation, and tunnels would all be danger zones where you could potentially catch the cordyceps fungus. But who will be in control? The zombie or the robot or me?"

"There is a world of difference between a human's brain, a human's nervous system, and an insect's. The insect brain and nervous system is not nearly as complex as the human version—meaning that attempts to twist it to the whims of a pathogen are simpler in a bug than a human."

"Yes, but who's it for, boss?" Li asked.

"Any government that will pay, but we already have interest from an Arab government and the Chinese. They will try it out in Xinjiang province, where the Uyghurs have been trying to create their own state of East Turkestan.

"So I'd like to introduce you to Professor Olga Polyakov," Dr. César said to Li. "She's an expert in nanotechnology, so we'll be creating a lab for her. Nanotechnology can improve processes of encapsulation and aerosolization of lethal organisms. That will help us jump from ants to humans. But it's dangerous work. Inhaled nanoparticles in the bloodstream can get dispersed throughout the brain. That's why we'll have to be extremely careful here. Keep her work isolated and wear masks."

68

The Isolation

Marius Hills, February 2083

THE SILVER SECURITYBOT PEERED through the bars of Teagan's cell, monitoring her movement. Teagan, looking as frail as a chicken wishbone, was still sleeping, curled up on her bare mattress. She had not stirred for a while. The Controller in the level above her was not worried. She had been asleep for twenty-six Earth hours.

The Controller had taken Teagan to the medical bay upon her arrival after the overland trip to the Marius Hills. She'd had bruised ribs and a dislocated ankle; not too bad, considering the circumstances.

Now, the Controller felt a stirring of pity for Teagan. So much potential, so much beauty, such youth and vitality, locked up in a small subterranean cell. She would never regain her freedom again. Doctor de Luca would see to that, the Controller was certain.

Now that Howie was done with her, César just wanted her out of the way. If she was sent back to Earth, she would cause trouble. Better for her to fade away in obscurity.

The Controller looked at Teagan on his monitor again. She'd begun to stir. He instructed the securitybot to keep an extra eye on her and sent a coded message to Dr. César, informing him of their new special prisoner's status.

It took Teagan another hour to regain full consciousness. When she awoke, she tried to recollect what had happened. She was in what looked like a small, windowless room, with a bed that ran along the length of one plain wall.

Sharp pains radiated down from her skull and throughout her body. She tried to open her eyes, but the light was too much for her, making her head throb even more. With a moan, she forced herself to pay attention. It took some time for her eyes to adjust.

When they did, she frowned. The walls were gray and the ceiling was low. This was not Halona.

Her altercation with the bots and Maureen came to her in a flash, and she sat up abruptly. She rubbed her eyes and scratched her scalp. Some dried blood flaked off her temple. Her throat was parched. She slipped in and out of consciousness.

She'd never been truly alone before. Now, drifting into a coma seemed like an escape. For once in her unaccomplished life, she wished she could take a lovely hike down a black hole and cease to exist.

She closed her eyes to mumble a wish, out of desperation rather than out of the belief it might happen.

When she opened her eyes again, she heard something unusual. The securitybot outside the bolted door unfastened a hatch and slid in a tray—a breakfast of refined juice and fibers. It tasted like cardboard, but it was something.

"Who are you?" Teagan asked hopelessly through the locked door. "Do you have a name?"

"I'm Sparkus," the robot replied before shuffling off.

On one of the walls, she noticed a small monitor, along with a tiny red dot in a corner of the room. *Probably a camera*, she thought.

She heard a voice from behind her.

"Glad you're awake, Teagan. I hope you had a good journey."

Teagan turned and saw the smiling face of Doctor César de Luca looking at her from a monitor. Normally aloof, today he had a satisfied look in his eye.

"How are you?" he asked.

"I'm battered and bruised and confined like a criminal," she snarled. "How do you think I am?"

"You must cooperate, Teagan. We'll keep you restrained until we think you're ready. You must realize that illegal entry and attempted kidnapping are not acceptable behaviors. Plus, Howie tells me you were responsible for the death of one of his employees."

"They tried to rape me!"

Not knowing what else to say, Teagan stared numbly at the monitor.

César continued, "Your crimes include unauthorized entry to a restricted area, breaking and entering, reckless endangerment of children, and attempted abduction of a minor, among others. You have been sentenced to stay in this secure lunar prison.

"Don't worry, though—ideally, your time here will be short. You are going to be part of a human trial. You will be my first test subject on my path to creating the perfect human. I always knew you would serve a greater purpose."

Teagan shook her head, confused. "What do you mean 'the perfect human?' I would never harm my babies, I just wanted to hold them. Please let me go."

Teagan made to open the door but received a stinging zap of electricity.

Cradling her stinging hand, she said, "I wasn't endangering their lives. I was trying to protect my children."

"You seem to have forgotten that you have no claim to any of the children," Dr. César said.

"Where are my parents? I want to speak with them."

"Your parents are far away," Dr. César said, and Teagan frowned.

"Where are we?" she asked.

"You are in a secure lunar facility," Dr. César repeated.

"We will look after you. We need your cooperation. You cannot escape. Outside, there is nothing."

"What?" Teagan said with wide eyes.

In a mocking voice, he said, "Is it too complicated for you? Am I going too fast? I've always known you were a simpleton. Since you aren't going anywhere, would you like me to break it down for you?"

He was enjoying himself. He had seemed so rational before, but now he was like an upstart tyrant.

"I want my children," responded Teagan. "I've given enough for science. I don't want to be part of any of your experiments."

"Those are children of Quivira," responded Dr. César. "You have no rights here. Those children aren't yours. You don't even know whose eggs we used. Do you think you were the only donor?"

Teagan shook her head.

"You should be glad. You're on the cusp of greatness. You'll be the next step in human evolution."

"You're mad!" Teagan said through gritted teeth. "I didn't volunteer to be here."

"You did, frankly speaking. The moment your parents signed that you could be useful for an experiment on Quivira," Dr. César said.

"This isn't Quivira. Do they even know I'm here?" Teagan asked.

"What do you think?" Dr. César said. Teagan heard someone off-screen knocking, and de Luca continued, "I must go now, Teagan. Science and humankind thank you for your sacrifice." Then the screen went blank.

Teagan stared at it, grappling with the worst fate she could imagine—a madman's lab rat.

She tried to buck herself up. *Come on, Teagan, you've been in hair-raising situations before, you can think of something.* But all she could think about were tiny nanobots swarming all over her brain, like ants looking for a new colony.

Then she thought of the joy she'd felt when she carried her daughter in her arms.

This comforting thought gave Teagan a new resolve. She would find a way to escape this place, and she would end César de Luca and his plans.

If it was the last thing she ever did, then she would die a happy person. The thought brought a smile to her lips.

As she was contemplating, she saw a lone ant crawling across the floor.

"My God, where did you come from?"

It seemed lost, searching aimlessly.

"Where are you going?"

With the rough, concrete-like floors offering no guidance for the little thing, Teagan hunted around to find something to give the first sign of life she had encountered. She found a crumb on her tunic and laid it in the ant's path. Then, she put a small blob of water next to it. She named the ant "Felix Sotuknang."

At least now she had a friend. Or was she hallucinating?

"Maybe you're actually the beguiling Felix Krull, the great confidence man. And I will be Madame Houpflé, the wife of a rich toilet bowl manufacturer. Pleased to meet you. Could you please take care of these jewels for me? I'll need them after my bath."

"Of course, ma'am. They'll be safe with me."

"I'm grateful. You know, Felix, you and I will find a way out."

She curtseyed to the ant before sitting back on the bed.

When she woke again, Felix had disappeared. Only he knew the way out. She was locked up hell knows where without being able to contact anyone except her jailor. She was twenty-five years old, a mother who had never given birth nor suckled her child. She was talking to an ant and she desperately needed to pee. She banged on the door.

"I need the John," Teagan told the bot.

It looked quizzical.

"The toilet. The bathroom. The restroom."

The securitybot manacled her and escorted her to a waterless toilet. She looked at her face in the mirror and let out an agonizing groan as she saw her reflection.

69

The Update

Malapert, March 2083

NOEL'S FACE WAS ASHEN, and Clara instinctively braced for bad news.

"Teagan has been transferred to a detention cell on the Moon for allegedly trying to kidnap the children."

"What?" Clara's legs went numb. "Noel, what exactly happened?"

Noel took a moment to gather his thoughts, then launched into the story, explaining everything to Clara.

Teagan was to be whisked off to the Moon and held there for an unspecified period without a trial. Clara looked at her husband, who had tears streaming down his face as he recounted the story. "I even gave her my pass key."

Clara clenched her teeth, a gritty determination building inside her: Even if she died in the process, she would rescue her daughter.

"Noel, do you know the exact location where she's being detained?" she asked.

Noel shook his head. "Nobody really knows, but it seems to be part of a laboratory complex. It could be on the northwest side of the Moon, a place called Marius Hills. I'm trying to get hold of Hunter to see if he can help."

Clara's spirits sank. That was miles away. There was no way she could get that far. The ongoing rail project only went as far as the equator.

She would speak to Alain Gagnon to see if he could do anything. Maybe he had some leverage.

70

The Stratagem

Matera, Italy, May 2083

JULIAN'S SPIRITS NOSEDIVED WHEN he learned of Teagan's confinement on the Moon.

And why the Moon, for goodness' sake? That was like a supermax. She had done nothing. To Julian, it seemed even more remote from his hideout in southern Italy than Halona.

He vowed to find her. He had had time to do a lot of reflecting, some of it aided by a little Rosso. Julian knew he had let her down and taken the easy way out. He missed her smile. He missed her laughter. He missed her scent. She would always be the love of his life, the only one to believe in him other than his parents. This time, he would do better. He would protect her and help her, even when she was unaware of his presence.

Julian hatched a plan to join her in the lunar prison without revealing his true identity. He would become her protector. Prison life could be brutal. He would facilitate her escape from the inside.

Knowing that he needed a cover to infiltrate the prison, Julian began researching and gathering information about the prison's possible operations, but found little was known about it, probably because it was fairly new. He knew he would need assistance, and turned to Il Ragno's extensive network. If he knew anything, it was prisons.

Julian was lucky; the demise of Snakehole meant he had appeared to keep his side of the bargain. His daughter had graduated into the Sentinels. She had even met with Hunter.

Il Ragno harnessed his connections to draw up a plan and create a new virtual identity for Julian. Through one of his contacts, he found the security measures at the prison and forged documents for his delivery.

"We can get you into the detention center as a prisoner. We can deliver you there under armed guard. From there, you're on your own. But there's still one problem—we need a ride."

"Where?"

"We need to get to the Moon."

"I'll check with my friend, Hunter. If anyone can do it, he can."

With the necessary preparations in place, Il Ragno provided Julian with vital information about the prison's security measures, allowing him to plan his approach carefully.

With every moment of separation, Julian's yearning for Teagan grew stronger. He couldn't bear the thought of her languishing in jail, stripped of her freedom, and subjected to the harsh realities of imprisonment. The mere idea of being apart from her, unable to hold her, comfort her, and share in the beauty of life, pained him like a persistent stab wound.

His decision to join Teagan in jail was not merely a choice but for him a necessity—a need to prove to himself and to her that he was not a coward, that his love was not a sham. He would make their joint confinement a testament to the depth of their love and their shared determination to forge a future together, no matter the cost. She would witness his sacrifice.

71

The Insertion

Marius Hills, June 2083

WITH THE HELP OF Il Ragno, Julian connected with Airi and Hunter, sharing his plan and explaining his intentions to reunite with Teagan.

"I want to make sure she's okay and not being harmed. Who knows what experiments he could be doing on her."

Il Ragno, through his contacts with the guards, provided Julian with crucial information about the lunar center's security systems, including its network architecture, surveillance protocols, and potential weak points.

To infiltrate the facility as a prisoner, Julian needed credentials and a criminal backstory. Il Ragno's team of hackers went to work, and once they were done, Julian came over as quite a badass. Il Ragno also linked him up with the Iron Hornets to help him complete his task.

Julian was securely locked inside a specially designed containment van for transportation, and delivered to the detention facility by two Hornets posing as guards. They drove up to the facility, where a door in the hillside slid open. As the vehicle entered, large industrial fans stirred up the regolith to cover the tracks left behind, so there was no clear pathway. They stayed in the vehicle as the concealed door closed behind them. Then, after a few seconds, a door in front opened, and the Hornets drove ahead and down through the lava tube complex.

After reaching the detention facility, they dismounted and escorted the prisoner through the dimly lit corridors. The facility's interior was a maze of cold steel and advanced technology, featuring monitoring systems and energy shields that further fortified its basalt walls. They were met outside a cell by the Controller.

"Prisoner 483 being handed over for confinement."

Julian, in a simple flight suit, looked at the Controller, his eyes a mixture of defiance and resignation.

"Prisoner 483, you're a long way from home," the Controller said flatly. "This place is so remote, you don't stand a chance of escape. If you do, we won't go looking for you."

Julian acted defiant. "You think this place scares me? I've seen worse." But of course, he had seen nothing like it. It smelled musty, and he wanted to throw up.

The Hornets, their job accomplished without incident, took their leave. Julian stood alone.

"Search him," the Controller ordered.

A nearby bot ran a scan over his body. It revealed a RFID tracking chip implanted in his wrist.

"Remove it."

The bot plucked out the RFID from under the skin with a knife. Julian winced, but refused to scream.

The Controller stamped on the small capsule. "Nobody can track you, I assure you."

A securitybot pushed Julian into a cell with some force and the door hissed shut.

"Next meal is in the morning. I advise you to get some rest."

Alone in his cell, Julian lay on his cot, exhausted. It began to dawn on him what he had gotten himself into.

At least they hadn't discovered the tracking device inserted in his brain. The Hornets would still be able to find him.

72

The Deal

Huashan Chinese Lunar Base, July 2083

O N MALAPERT, CLARA--UNAWARE OF the lengths to which Julian had gone to be near her daughter--was inspecting some new seeds one afternoon when she was abruptly invited to the Chinese base by Zhang Honghui. A devious man whose life's dream was to make his fortune on the Moon, he didn't mind on which side he played. Clara didn't want to keep him waiting, so she asked her assistant, Amy, to supervise the latest seed shipment.

Zhang made sure to keep in the good graces of Beijing while ensuring he remained friendly with the Iron Hornets. He tossed them a bone every so often. The frequently unsupervised spending at the base was a great opportunity, and it was extraordinary how much the Chinese community had grown in just a short while. Construction and engineering work was under way, and vents in the regolith signaled the presence of large underground factories.

"Thank you for visiting us, Mrs. Ward. I must say, your work has been effective and pleasing," said Zhang without elaborating. "I'd like to introduce you to my deputy, Zhu Yan. "Like you, he has an interest in plants." Clara acknowledged Zhu but remained silent; Zhang was a shark, never one for banter or idle chatter.

"The reason you have been requested to visit us from Malapert is that I need your help," Zhang said bluntly. "I want you to cultivate your husband, Noel Ward, to our side. Quivira has so much technology we could use, especially their medical facility."

Clara sat wooden-faced, wondering how to tell this man to get lost. Zhang probably took her silence for acquiescence, as he continued with fervor.

"I hear they make a fortune from the sale of human body parts. By sharing, we could save many lives."

Clara noticed the greed in his eyes and guessed this had a lot more to do with him than the People's Republic. She said, "I'm sorry, Comrade Zhang, my husband doesn't have access to the medical facility. Even if he did, he would never betray the people he worked for in that manner."

Zhang's look of disappointment was comical to Clara. "You are sure you can't convince him to try? After all, you are his wife." Clara shook her head, determined to end this charade. "I'm quite sure, Comrade Zhang. He is a man of honor. If there is nothing else, I have some important things to attend to."

Zhu at least looked embarrassed as Clara left Zhang's office fuming; she had heard how he traded technology secrets in the underground economy to enrich himself. The fool must have thought she didn't know. Even if she didn't, she would never use any of her family that way.

When she got to the center back at Malapert, Clara considered for the first time quitting her job. Amy could take over most of what she did. It was a fun and fulfilling career, but the dark underbelly disgusted Clara. Without knocking, she marched into Alain Gagnon's office to complain.

"They think I'm a fucking Chinese pawn. I'd rather quit than put up with this." Gagnon tried to console her. "You're strong. That's why I asked you to help keep an eye on them."

She decided to call Noel. "Hey, what is it?" She never called Noel at work.

"I had a brainwave," she said. "Maybe we can do a trade."

"Darling, a trade for what? You're not making sense."

"A trade for Teagan. There are rumors that Dr. César carries out secret experiments. Maybe that gives us some leverage."

"Leverage with whom?"

"My new buddy, Zhang Honghui," she said enthusiastically. "The presence of a lab means there's tradable technology. Noel, I promise I will find a way to get our daughter out of that prison. Can you find out something that would help?"

"I can try. Most things are held securely."

When she ended the conversation, Clara's mind went into overdrive. She would need something to give Zhang in return. Another thought occurred to Clara—a lab located far away from anywhere and out of sight of the media could be an ideal place for experimenting on human guinea pigs held against their will. Was this de Luca fellow experimenting on her Pumpkin, too? She had to move fast.

Noel sent back a reply: *Experiments on ants and fungi. Maybe stuff to tranquilize populations, keep them quiet. Possibly he's growing human organs, such as kidneys, there for transplant.*

That was it.

She sent Zhang a message, asking if she could see him for something quite urgent. She was surprised when he replied almost immediately, telling her she could come as soon as was convenient. Clara grabbed an LTV and headed for Shackleton. When she got to his subterranean office, Zhang considered her warily. "What was so important, Mrs. Ward, that you sought my attention not long after leaving here?"

Clara thought of the best way to approach the matter at hand; she didn't want to sound manipulative, but she didn't want to be too obvious, either. "I was hasty in my conclusions earlier. When I got back to my office, I realized there's an even bigger prize for the taking—Doctor César de Luca's labs."

Zhang laughed. He cleared his throat, spat on the floor, and grinned at her with stained teeth. "I am really sorry, Mrs. Ward, but this is a terrible way to ask for my help to free your daughter from detention."

Clara didn't know what to say; she just let him speak. Zhang continued, "I know your daughter, Teagan, was sentenced to isolation for an unspecified time. I wanted to know if you knew I was aware of this. When I saw you didn't, I felt it wasn't my place to tell you. As you well know, all sorts of communications are monitored, so when your husband called, I knew. I am very flattered you think I might help. But I'm afraid I can't."

Clara slowly thought about what she just heard. She had come too far to be turned back by a mere "No."

"I know for a fact that there are at least a hundred kidneys in that lab. Imagine how much those would cost on the black market. You would be a wealthy man." Zhang looked at her sharply. "How accurate is this piece of information?"

"One hundred percent, my husband gave it to me."

Zhang imagined one of the kidneys saving a senior leader and him getting the credit. How glorious would that be?

Zhang nodded and said, "It seems, Mrs. Ward, that I too was hasty earlier as well. I can probably find a way to help you. I think we should discuss this in a safer environment, at a later time. Have a great day, Mrs. Ward."

Clara stood. She knew she was being dismissed, but she didn't care. Her mission to get her daughter back was now in motion.

73

The Protector

Marius Hills, July 2083

T EAGAN HAD LOST ALL track of time.

Anyone who had known Teagan before her arrival at the lunar prison would have a hard time recognizing her. Her hair was limp and broken. She had lost considerable weight. Her face was aged and lined.

She hadn't left her cell since she'd arrived, except to go to the bathroom. She knew she was being monitored by the security cameras and the securitybot permanently stationed in front of her cell. No matter how she tried, she couldn't come up with a way to escape. But any time she was about to give up, the images of her babies kept her going. She had to leave this hole and get back to her babies.

César de Luca had still not commenced the procedure he had threatened. Had he forgotten her, along with her father and mother, and perhaps Howie and Julian?

Noel and Clara had in fact contacted Dr. César several times, and he had assured them that she was safe. He told them that he was taking care of her, and convinced them that her behavior in trying to take the babies was a result of trauma. He also convinced them not to try and contact her, or even mention her, for the time being. It had taken a while before Teagan's parents had accepted, and Dr. César had thought how much easier it would have been if they were under his control. He wouldn't have needed to explain things to them.

Teagan wondered if she had been forgotten. She imagined what her mother was doing—probably talking to some unusual seeds—and wondered if her father was still on Quivira. Most importantly, she wondered if Julian thought of her.

She missed Julian more than she'd thought was possible. She wondered what he was doing. He was probably painting another beautiful woman.

But Teagan remained determined. She knew she would break free. Her thoughts went around in circles that way, days blending into one another. Her only companions were a white wall and a monitor that never came on.

One day, she was staring at the wall when the door to her cell opened. The hiss of the airlocks startled her. The securitybot standing at the door warned, "Stand back."

Not knowing what to do, she stayed on her bed.

A few seconds later, the bot said, "You are allowed to congregate with other inmates in the general area for two hours. This is a reward for good behavior. Any disruption or contravening of the rules will result in revocation of this privilege until the Controller sees fit. Is that understood?"

When Teagan refused to reply, the bot moved toward her, faster than Teagan thought possible, and zapped her. Teagan fell on the floor, dry heaving. The bot stared down at her and repeated, "Is that understood?"

With a voice scratchy from pain and disuse, Teagan said, "I understand."

The bot moved away and said, "Walk down the corridor, take the first turn on your left. You have one hour and fifty-nine minutes left."

Teagan walked in a daze, following the bot's instructions. She had a feeling she was walking into a trap but, to her surprise, it was exactly as the bot said. There were about eight people gathered together, some chatting, others sitting and staring into space. Teagan walked to an empty chair and sat down away from everyone else. Seeing other people after being alone for so long was a novelty that would take some time for her to get used to.

The warden robot announced it was time for lunch. Teagan didn't have an appetite, but she reluctantly lined up, knowing that skipping lunch could cost her some of her already limited privileges. As soon as she got her food, Teagan heard a voice that made her freeze in her tracks.

"Hey fresh meat; how about you gimme your lunch?"

Teagan didn't mind parting with her lunch, but she would be damned if she let someone bully her in prison. She turned around and saw three men and two women grouped together. The leader, a woman with muscular arms almost as big as Teagan's head, spoke again.

"Fresh meat, hand over your lunch. Unless you want me to rearrange your face."

Before Teagan could respond, someone spoke.

"Baby, I hope you aren't disturbing the gentle lady."

Teagan's head whipped around. She would recognize that voice anywhere. It sounded like Julian.

But her hopes sank when her eyes landed on a haggard, worn man dressed in dingy prison garb. The harsh fluorescent lights gave his skin a pale and sickly hue. His jumpsuit hung loosely on his frame, giving the appearance of someone defeated.

Were her ears playing tricks on her? He looked nothing like the person Teagan thought the voice belonged to.

Despite the man's bedraggled appearance, the lady in command became nervous and said, "No, Boyer. We were just trying to get to know each other. She's been in isolation for so long, and I wanted to know how it felt."

The man addressed as Boyer replied, "Spread the word, Baby, anyone who harms the prisoner will have to answer to me and Il Ragno. Is that understood?"

Baby nodded and gestured for the rest of her gang to leave. Nobody wanted to mess with a friend of Il Ragno. As Boyer turned to leave, Teagan called out, "Thank you, Mr. Boyer."

Julian smiled at her and said, "Any time, Pumpkin."

Teagan's eyes whipped to his, trying to prod him once again, but he didn't respond. Left alone, Teagan remained seated until it was time to return to her cell. Then she shuffled quietly back, her feet dragging on the floor. The moment the door closed behind her, she fell on her bed and started to cry. Once she started, the tears didn't stop. Teagan couldn't explain why she was crying, but it felt good to cry. Julian had come for her. She didn't know how long she sobbed for but, when she was done, she fell into an exhausted and dreamless sleep.

***

Teagan became used to getting two hours every day to mix with others, and always followed the same routine: She sat at what she now regarded as her special table, and just watched. Whenever anyone tried to approach her, she visibly panicked and clammed up. But, despite her aloofness, Teagan tried to notice everything that happened in the common area.

She gave names to the interesting characters. Tatman was the man with a tattoo on his face and a long, thin scar running just below his cheek to his chin. Jelly Brain was the woman with a poor memory, whom César seemed to have done some experiments on. And, with a pang, she named the man whose hands were always moving about Tentikal, after her beloved pet.

Boyer was a bad-tempered man who spat at her as he passed by. He looked strangely familiar, but was always filthy and stank of urine. He normally avoided her gaze, but once, when Tatman tried to hit on her while the guards were absent, Boyer made sure Tatman slipped and fell on his forehead, leaving a bad bruise. She air-signed a "Thank You. He didn't respond but she increasingly believed Julian was there to help her escape.

Teagan still harbored hopes of release but, as the days passed, her hopes began to fade.

The other thing that faded was the faces of her children. The first night she realized this, Teagan cried, then threw up. Now she just focused on Nevaeh's features: Her auburn hair, her beautiful eyes, the dimple just at the bottom of her chin.

She kept on having visions of birds with broken wings, kept hearing, "Behold the bird that cannot fly; the treasure you seek lies beyond the eye." What was beyond the eye? Over the horizon, too far to see? It didn't make sense.

She had dreams that Doctor de Luca came to perform the surgery and she became a vegetable. She dribbled and could hardly walk. The combination of these things sent Teagan into a depression spiral. She felt Doctor de Luca wanted to make her mad before he made her his robot. Teagan didn't have the will to fight again; she just wanted to fade away. César was winning and she didn't care.

74

The Selection

Halona, March 2084

G UY WAS PUTTING TOGETHER one of his most ambitious retrieval missions yet. He had spent much of the past few months thinking of a course of action. He had narrowed down a crew from twenty-one members, but he only actually needed nine for the three tugs; the robots and the AI would do the rest.

As before, three tugs gave them more room to maneuver. The major problem they would face was meteor strikes.

Guy studied that image in Howie's command center until he was sick of it. Howie assured him the images he saw were live, captured by dedicated probes.

Guy had already named the target the Matryoshka asteroid, believing it contained more than appeared on the surface, an enigma lurking somewhere.

Guy had his men and flight path. He shared both with Howie. Howie immediately disqualified two of the crew members and asked––or more like ordered––Guy to replace them with others he judged more capable.

On his flight plan, Howie didn't have any objections. He just suggested some alternate routes, routes Guy had already mapped and found wanting. Surprisingly, Howie didn't argue further. The timeline for takeoff was agreed. Everything had to be ready by then.

For the next nineteen days before takeoff, Guy followed the same routine. After breakfast, he assembled his team of five women and three men and ran them through rigorous fitness exercises, then flight simulations that covered the worst things that could happen.

In the first twelve days, none of the crew members survived the simulated journey, no matter how well they flew or what formation. One of the crew members resigned on the thirteenth day, saying he couldn't stand the pressure, nor the thought of dying at the far end of space.

Even though he didn't admit it to the rest of the crew, the pressure was getting to Guy too. He tossed and turned every night. Every so often, he had dreams of being engulfed in torrents of water, kicking aside drowning babies to reach the surface and save himself. He would wake up sweating and exhausted. He didn't need more deaths on his conscience. He didn't mind dying himself; he would probably reincarnate in another dimension of the universe.

But the fact that all the simulations ended in a hundred percent casualties and no asteroid worried him. He didn't want his last mission to end in failure. He already had too much blood on his hands.

Every night before he slept, he tried to adjust things—the course of travel, the plan of attack, flight formation. He even shuffled the crew, but the simulation results remained the same. On the thirteenth day, a miracle happened.

Through sheer luck, Guy found a way to bring the asteroid and fifty percent of the crew back to ElleWon in one piece. Using that solution, Guy had the crew go through the simulation repeatedly, until seven of the eight crew members and the asteroid completed the journey.

Guy was satisfied with that. He knew that if push came to shove, he would sacrifice himself for the rest of them. He continued to work them hard and then, on the nineteenth day, told them they were free to do whatever they wanted. "Meet me at the loading dock at o-five-hundred-hours, not a minute later," Guy instructed before dismissing them.

On his way to his cabin to recharge, he met Commander Bancroft. He'd noticed that Commander Bancroft's attitude had changed toward him in the past few weeks. She was no longer openly hostile. Anytime they met in the galley or the corridor, Bancroft greeted him, then ignored him.

Guy nodded and tried to pass, but the commander blocked his way.

To his surprise, Bancroft said, "Commander Zephron, I want to wish you luck on your upcoming expedition. I know how hard you've worked, and how much you've already given to this project. No matter how it ends, you and your crew have already written your names into immortality. I know you don't drink, but come back safe, and I'll owe you a glass of whatever it is that catches your fancy."

Commander Bancroft saluted him. Guy was almost too stunned to salute back, but he did, just in time.

After the salute, Bancroft walked away as if nothing had happened. Guy thought about the incident on the way to his cabin. Maybe she was human after all.

The next morning, Guy commanded the AI to run a final systems check on their three tugs. When he got the all-clear, he ordered them to commence the lift-off sequence. They were headed for riches.

75

The Kidnap

D R. CÉSAR WAS HALFWAY to his lab on Quivira when the piercing sound of the alarm went off and emergency lights began flashing in the corridors.

Since Maureen had rejected General Lin Wenyi's generous offer of protection, Quivira had staged several emergency preparation drills. But this was no drill; an intruder had breached Quivira.

César hurried toward the central foyer and found people bumping into each other as they tried to find their shelter-in-place locations, all while AI security cops advanced to block the entrances. A little child ran screaming, looking for her mother, and an elderly lady turned around confused and bewildered.

"Get out of my way," César shouted, almost knocking her over.

Although some securitybots were equipped to defend Quivira, Dr. César knew they wouldn't be able to handle a well-planned attack. He peered out and saw the shadow of a small spacecraft approaching. He could see Maureen giving commands to the robotic cops.

Quivira was not designed as a military facility, and it lacked the fortifications of such. Its infrastructure lay exposed on the exterior of the habitat. Constructed in 2070, it had been assembled with metals prefabricated on the Moon, regolith from the Zernon 47 asteroid that had been parked in intermediate circular orbit above the Earth, and furnishings and fabrics shipped up from California and India.

César wished he was at his moon lab, far from this unexpected threat. He briefly glanced again in Maureen's direction and saw her narrowly dodge one of the opening shots. Fire ricocheted through the rotating habitat. Many bots were swiftly put out of action. This was a coordinated attack by professionals. Dr. César watched Maureen try to retain control before he turned to head for his lab and protect his experiments.

Few on Quivira knew that the attackers were the Iron Hornets, come to soften up the good doctor. Nothing serious. Just something to remember.

The Hornets, docking their craft strategically around Quivira, swept in
through the stark white corridors, immobilizing anything in their path. They
thought they might find a bargaining chip or two.

When Noel had heard the commotion, he'd hidden seven of the children in
a safe room. But he couldn't locate Baolin. Unknown to him, Baolin, intrigued
by all the noise, had snuck out to the main corridor.

Dr. César paused when the noise subsided, and wondered if everything was
now clear. But the Hornets were just looking around. One of them had found
a way to penetrate the vicinity of the reinforced area of the lab and nursery,
thinking the experimental children might be there.

Razor, the heavily armed Hornet leader, blasted into the lab. Securitybots
and lab technicians tried to obstruct him, but he was too armored for them to
be effective. He marched through the area without damaging anything.

He spotted a small boy running along a corridor.

"I have a possible target," said Razor into his mouthpiece as he fixed his eyes
on Baolin. He advanced toward the young boy with his gun pointed straight at
him as if he were a criminal.

The eight-year-old child watched in wonder as Razor stepped slowly toward
him. Baolin had always wanted to be an armed mercenary.

The shriek of the alarms filled the air and echoed through the corridors. Two
more Iron Hornets joined Razor as he reached Baolin.

Razor was impressed by the fire he saw in Baolin's eyes. The boy looked
tough, even at a young age, and Razor wondered if all the children were the
same. He had heard one of the infants had been injured, and that the doctor
might be working with unknown substances. However, that hadn't deterred
Razor from his mission. He smiled as he thought of what even one of the
children would fetch for ransom.

"They have help coming. We need to leave," one of Razor's men said urgently
as he joined them in the corridor.

"Help from where?" Razor asked.

"Halona space station," he said.

Razor lunged to pick up the boy, but Baolin slipped away and tore through
the lab to a next-door facility like it was a game of hide and seek. It happened
to be the wastewater treatment plant, where water was recycled from urine,
excrement, and plant run-off. Razor pursued him, but rushed past the recycling
unit toward the vertical farm. The boy could not be found.

"Keep looking," Razor instructed. "You have ten minutes."

He retraced his steps. As Razor approached, Baolin tried to disguise himself,
ducking into a large container without realizing it was full of recycled waste. Too

late; his head was submerged in the liquid muck. He came up for air, gasping and wheezing.

Hearing the heavy breathing, Razor approached carefully and opened the container. "Here we are. What a mess you have made." He plunged his gloved hand down and, in one move, pulled the young boy out and plopped him on the floor, water pouring off his body and a putrid smell rising to the nostrils. "Okay, let's go. We have something tradable."

They scooped up Baolin and carried him with ease toward the awaiting ship, despite his struggling and yelling. They washed him down and put him on the market.

But he was tainted goods. The abduction proved less lucrative than the Hornets had hoped.

They tried trading Baolin with Dr. César, but Howie and Maureen vetoed that.

"Fuck them," shouted Howie when he received the ransom demand. "We will pay nothing. Nada. They will be hunted down. We can make other babies."

They tried to trade him with governments, and a couple of medical facilities, but no takers.

After they lost Baolin, Quivira increased its security, stepping up external defenses and increasing the number of securitybots. They would ensure nothing like that ever happened again.

76

Sketching a Plan

Malapert, October 2084

NEWS OF BAOLIN'S KIDNAPPING shook the space community. Many of the space residents no longer felt safe. Noel and Clara realized that they were on their own if they wanted to secure Teagan's release.

Clara had expected Zhang to summon her, but he didn't. She was getting impatient. Only the rational thought that going to him would be counterproductive kept her from doing something stupid.

She called her husband in the hopes of something new.

"Hello, sweetcakes, how have you been holding up? Better than me, I guess?"

Clara tried to smile and said, "I've been trying to bury myself in work so I don't go crazy. But work doesn't hold the same appeal it used to hold; nothing does."

"Have you heard anything from Hunt?"

"He's been busy."

Noel nodded and said, "I know it's sudden, but can I come to the Malapert base? Just for a short visit?"

"When do you want to come?" Clara asked.

Noel replied, "I think today would be best. Let's get it over with."

Clara had to ask, "Get what over with, Noel? I hate it when you sound melodramatic."

All Noel said was, "When I get there, you'll see." Then he clicked off.

Clara was intrigued. *What's with the old dog?* she thought to herself. She set a reminder for her bot to set dinner for two and make sure her quarters were tidy.

When Noel arrived that evening, he handed her a small thumb drive. "It contains schematics for the lunar prison: Guard positions and entries, as well as the schematics for the labs."

Clara looked at her husband in amazement. "How did you get this?"

Noel shrugged. "I broke into Doctor de Luca's office and hacked his computer. I crashed it when I was through so he wouldn't know I was there and what I wanted. I might have to lay low for a while." He gave her a wink.

Clara couldn't believe the matter-of-fact way her husband spoke about breaking and entering, hacking, and crashing someone else's computer. She walked over to him and gave him a deep kiss. "You are the best, Noel Ward. I hope you know that."

Noel still had a strange look in his eyes. "Clara, I know you're planning a rescue mission for our daughter. I'm in."

Clara smiled at her husband. "I wouldn't want it any other way, my love."

Noel replied, "We have the architectural plans, but we need a means of transport, a way to knock out the guards, a way to get our daughter, and somewhere to go after that, since we'll be persona non grata on the Moon."

Clara was about to reply when her bot announced, "Mr. Zhang Honghui is at the door. Should I open?"

Clara gave the bot an order to open the door. "Why's he come now?"

When Zhang stepped in, he didn't seem surprised that Noel was there. "Good evening, Professor Ward. It is an honor to finally meet you. I have been an ardent follower of your work, and I must say, you are an authority in your field."

Beaming from the flattery, Noel said, "I don't think we've been introduced, but I'm glad to meet you too."

Zhang said, "Pardon my manners, sir; I am Zhang Honghui, a colleague of your beautiful wife."

"Noel, I was about to tell you about Comrade Zhang's involvement in rescuing Teagan when he walked in himself," Clara said.

Zhang shook his head. "Why so formal? Please let us dispense with titles tonight, especially as I have good news."

Clara beamed. "I also have great news. Let's hear yours first."

Zhang bowed. "I have talked to some people I know. They are experts at this type of thing. Their fee is half the organs we find. My fee is half of what's left. You can keep the remaining half."

"We have no use for the kidneys, Honghui," Noel said. "You can keep them. If we rescue our daughter, then you have more than earned them."

Zhang smiled. "My friends, I hope you realize that after this breakout, it will be linked to you, especially as your daughter will be the main one rescued. Meaning you must live like fugitives. I advise moving back to Earth. There are still some good places there. Although this requires a lot of money."

"We'll deal with that later. What's the lunar prison's security like? Any weak spots that can be exploited?

"It was built to keep people in. No sane person would attempt to attack it because it has no economic value," said Zhang. "But we're not sure of the layout and design."

"We can help with that," said Clara, who showed the schematics to Zhang. He whistled appreciatively.

"This just made our job easier. Two days from now, Clara and I will go to inspect how the rail project is coming along. It is almost completed, so it should take us close to the mines but not close enough. From there, our friends with their lunar rovers will take us to Marius Hills, where we will stage a rescue—and robbery—and make a quick getaway. I will arrange with friends I know to help you get flights to Earth."

Noel laughed. "Sounds easy enough. What could go wrong?"

Zhang answered seriously. "A lot, actually; the plan could fail, and we could all end up in prison, or dead. On that note, I wish you a good night. I will see you in two days." Zhang left with a copy of the architectural plans so that he and his friends could study them.

After he had gone, Noel and Clara sat on her couch, listening to soft music. Clara put her head on her husband's shoulder.

"Do you think we're crazy?"

Noel answered instantly. "Never, Clara. I'd give my life in exchange for either of you."

Clara smiled. "You've always loved playing the hero."

Noel said thoughtfully, "Let's hope our plans work, Clara. I can't bear to think of losing either one of you."

77

The Hope

Marius Hills, October 2084

Teagan was escorted down the drab passage, flanked by her usual robotic guard. She reached the bathroom and pushed on the door, but it wouldn't budge. Inside, she heard retching sounds.

The door finally opened and the disheveled man from the canteen--Boyer--appeared, drool dripping from his chin. As she squeezed past him, the pungent stench of urine filled her nostrils.

"Read and remove," he whispered to her.

Inside the bathroom, Teagan cautiously stepped toward the fogged-up mirror. She could make out a message written in sloppy handwriting: *Be Ready. They are coming.*

Teagan quickly rubbed out the cryptic message, unsure of what it meant--was someone planning a rescue, or was this just another sign of the man's deteriorating mental state?

***

Two days later, Clara and Noel were standing by at the Huashan base. They anxiously awaited the arrival of the squad who would secure Teagan's release. Zhang Honghui had promised a crack team of Chinese Sparrowhawk commandos so that there would be no bloodshed. The planners did not expect much resistance.

Clara's fingers trembled as she clutched a faded photograph of Teagan. What did she look like now after so long in detention? Maybe they wouldn't even recognize her. They could walk right past her.

A few hours passed, and there was no sign of action. Clara and Noel exchanged alarmed glances, their hearts sinking with a dreadful premonition. Something was horribly wrong. The mission they had painstakingly planned was crumbling before their eyes.

Eventually, Zhu Yan, Zhang's deputy, came to see them.

"I'm sorry, we cannot do this today. The mission has been aborted."

"But why?" Clara asked, almost in tears.

"We have received orders."

The words hung in the air like a death sentence, seeping into their bones with a chilling finality.

"I thought everything was agreed with Honghui."

"He has told me to tell you that it cannot be done today. I will arrange your transportation back to Malapert."

Incomprehension and despair mingled within both Clara and Noel as they struggled with the abrupt turn of events.

On the bumpy drive back, Clara was close to hysterical. "I thought we had a deal," she cried.

"Someone must have vetoed it, maybe someone connected to Howie Rich," said Noel as he held her head against his shoulder.

"It's that snake, Li Jie. He must have ratted to General Lin."

"How would he know? It's too complicated," said Noel. "We'll try again another time."

Despite the aborted mission, Clara and Noel refused to abandon their plan. The love for their daughter fueled their determination, and no prison cell, obstacle, or treacherous general could suppress it. They resolved to keep on fighting.

"We need more people involved," said Clara. "I'll speak to Gagnon. Maybe he can do something."

"Last time I looked, he doesn't have any troops," said Noel, looking dejected.

78

The Next Phase

Marius Hills, February 2085

T EAGAN LOOKED UP AT the hiss of the cell door. She was startled to find, along with the usual securitybot, an elegant woman in a white doctor's coat. Teagan slid gingerly off her cot and pulled herself up. "Who are you?" asked Teagan.

"I'm Professor Olga Polyakov. Dr. César asked me to give you a checkup."

Teagan glanced at her. "Prepping me for your next experiment, doctor?"

"I'll ask the questions." Professor Polyakov gave her a rudimentary examination. "How are you eating?"

"Dog's piss. I'm fine. Just get me out of here."

"Why do you think they are keeping you here?"

"I don't know," Teagan huffed. "I think that bastard César just wanted me out of the way. Who knows? They've all left me here to rot. All I want is my babies."

Polyakov looked at her file, her eyes widening in surprise. "Your father is Noel Ward, the well-known professor of planetary sciences, yes?" Teagan nodded. "Your file says you attempted to kidnap an infant, you recklessly endangered several children, and you entered a restricted area."

"Yes, I tried to claim my child."

"It would help if you were a bit more remorseful."

"It would help if you were a bit less of a bitch," Teagan snapped.

Before she could react, Polyakov slapped her across the face and turned abruptly to leave. "Keep her under sedation," Polyakov said to the bot. On the way out, she said to Teagan, "You won't win by fighting us."

Teagan curled up in a ball on her bunk.

César examined her through the remote monitor in her cell. The eight babies had been part of his experiments, each containing adapted genes that gave them fast reflexes, superior cognitive ability, and strength.

Now, the next phase of his life's work was about to begin, thanks to Teagan. He still had some of her eggs and, with some superior sperm, he intended to create the first super embryos. His biggest dream, the one that kept him awake at night, was to evolve fully grown humans into space farers and settlers, all beholden to him.

79
Raising Baolin

Ürümqi, China, 2088

R AZOR HAD TAKEN A liking to Baolin, treating him like a son. He looked
affectionately at the boy through the friendly creases in his eyes, and
decided to raise him in western China, near where the Hornets had a space
tracking and control station. Although he had no ransom value, the Hornets
had found there was no way to return Baolin to Quivira, since security had
been increased and it was much more dangerous.

Initially Baolin was placed in foster care, with a family that had connections
with the Hornets, until he was old enough to fly with them.

"Can't have that boy running around here!" Razor had said.

They chose a sympathetic family to look after him in China's western Xinjiang province—one of the five zones that China had divided into after the
great split—where Baolin began his training that would eventually turn him
into a space mercenary, and one of the best.

As a boy, he grew up within earshot of the call to prayer, not far from the
red pillars of the old Shaanxi mosque off Ürümqi's Jianzhong Road. He loved
to eat laghman, a tasty dish of pulled noodles, lamb or goat, and vegetables.
Sometimes he earned his meals by picking pockets. When he was ten, he was
caught and sent to a youth rehabilitation center, where he became friends with
Alimjan, a young Uyghur boy.

Alimjan would talk lovingly of his mother, how she knitted him clothes and
taught him to read. He owed his deep interest in medicine to her. He craved her
qiegao—or "cut cake"—a delicious snack of a dense nougat made from nuts,
candied fruits, flour, and corn syrup, shaped into large, thick sheets and often
sold on the back of motorized tricycles.

Baolin and Alimjan became best friends. They shared everything—their
dreams, their fears, and even the meager meals they were given. The facility was
crowded, so sometimes they were forced to share a bed. But one day, in May
2088, things changed.

Alimjan was called into the counselor's office and accused of "inappropriate behavior." Baolin tried to ask what had happened, but no one would tell him anything. He soon learned that his friend had been taken away to a high-security facility in Dabancheng, southeast of the regional capital.

The days passed slowly after that. Baolin was lost without Alimjan to joke with. When Razor got word, he asked General Lin to intervene and secure an early release for Alimjan. Baolin was overjoyed, but Alimjan was quiet and refused to say what had happened.

The two boys were like brothers—their friendship stronger than any punishment or threat could break. They played together all the time. And they became blood brothers when Alimjan saved Baolin from a terrible house fire.

Fires were a big risk in the back streets of the town and even in the more modern high-rise apartments in which the electric wiring was old and badly installed. On this occasion, sparks from an electrical short circuit ignited curtains and bed linen in an apartment. Neighbors smelt smoke and immediately called the fire brigade, but parked cars in the street blocked the emergency services. Their hoses were not long enough to get close to the flames, and the inferno began to spread to nearby buildings.

Baolin, then sixteen, had been studying for an important exam. Alimjan was playing football in the street when he started to smell the smoke and see the flames in a nearby building. He feared Baolin, on the fourth floor, might get trapped, and rushed toward the burning family home.

"Don't go in there," instructed a security officer. "It's too dangerous."

"My brother is trapped inside," Alimjan shouted.

Fueled by a mixture of adrenaline and raw fear, he plunged into the smoke-filled structure, determined to find Baolin and bring him to safety. Navigating the corridors, some filled with burning clothes that had been hung out to dry, Alimjan's nerves were on edge. He called out Baolin's name, his voice nearly drowned out by the roar of the fire.

Dread threatened to overwhelm him but he pushed forward, his worry for his friend driving him through. As the fire raged, panicked residents hurriedly evacuated. The wail of sirens pierced the air as emergency services rushed to the scene. Alimjan found it hard to see or to breathe.

Finally, through the billowing smoke, Alimjan spotted Baolin in one corner of a room, disoriented by the dense fumes. Without hesitation, Alimjan rushed to his side, his voice a reassuring anchor.

"Bao! Bao, I'm here! We have to go, follow my voice!" Alimjan called out, his words cutting through the thick haze.

Baolin, his eyes stinging and lungs burning, recognized Alimjan's voice and staggered toward it. Trusting his friend, he followed Alimjan, their arms interlocked, forging a path through the suffocating darkness.

Alimjan led Baolin toward a window, their only hope for escape. Battling against the heat and disorientation, they reached the opening, strewn with shattered glass. One after the other, they picked their way through, emerging onto the hot fire escape just as the flames edged closer. Exhausted, Alimjan and Baolin descended the precarious stairs, step by step, inching their way to safety.

When they finally reached the ground, the two friends collapsed, their bodies weary from the ordeal. Alimjan's face was etched with relief as he embraced Baolin tightly, grateful to have successfully rescued his friend from the jaws of the fire.

Baolin, forever indebted to Alimjan for his bravery and quick thinking, vowed to repay the debt by being there for his friend through thick and thin.

After the fire, things began to change. Many residents suspected it had been started deliberately to clear land for redevelopment. An inquiry officially confirmed the fire was an accident caused by an electrical short circuit, but everyone had noticed that the emergency services were inadequate and the water pressure too low.

As life gradually returned to normal, Baolin couldn't shake off a feeling of unease. He began to notice subtle changes in the behavior of people around him. People were not angry. Instead, an eerie tranquility seemed to settle over the city, and he couldn't help but wonder if there was something more to it. People had become more acquiescent.

"Isn't it weird how docile people are?" Baolin asked Alimjan one day.

Alimjan suspected there was something amiss with the water. Residents in certain areas were getting sick and sluggish. Maybe something was being added to the water to induce lethargy in the population.

Alimjan and Baolin decided to investigate privately, without attracting attention; Alimjan knew some medical trainees. Together, they stumbled upon evidence suggesting the presence of a substance in the water supply that had tranquilizing effects on the population. Rumors whispered about a clandestine experiment to manipulate the city's water supply.

Was it a coincidence that the staff of General Lin Wenyi had been seen near a local reservoir? Certainly, residents were getting sicker.

Despite their close bonds and shared history, Baolin knew that eventually they would have to part ways. The Hornets would call him and Alimjan would follow his vocation of becoming a doctor.

During his training for the Iron Hornets, Baolin built a reputation for bravery almost to the point of recklessness. Along with the others, he took risks that almost cost him his life, but he began making an income from attacks on asteroids and space outposts. After a while, he became a natural leader. Baolin never wanted to lead the Hornets, but when their captain was killed in battle, he was the only one left with the experience and skills to take command.

Pickings were slim at first. They were always waiting for the big one. And, in the back of his mind, Baolin always remembered Alimjan, the boy who had given him hope.

80

The Discovery

Quivira, April 2088

"D R. CÉSAR!" TARA CALLED out sharply as she stepped into the lab after their regular lesson with Noel. Liam and Gabby followed her.

Silence, except for the usual rows of bots processing medical experiments under the LED lights.

"Dr. César, where are you?"

Still nothing. He was nowhere to be found. They had noticed that since he had hired Professor Polyakov a while ago, Dr. César was constantly away.

At first, they thought he had meetings with Maureen. However, they discovered he wasn't always with her either. Since they couldn't find him, they figured they'd go looking for him.

"He isn't in," Liam said as he took his seat on one of the chairs next to an artificial pancreas. The three of them looked silently at the room for a while, staring at each other before Liam asked, "How does all of this feel?"

"It feels out of place. Weird," Gabby said.

"I feel indifferent, but I'm not learning much," Tara said.

Liam started walking around.

"He gave clear instructions that we aren't to mess with any of his things," Gabby said.

"A little exploring won't ruin anything," Liam said with a shrug as he got closer to some kidneys being developed for patients. Tara and Gabby exchanged worried looks. "Don't you want to know why he hasn't been around?"

"That's strange," Gabby said suddenly.

"What?" Liam asked, raising his brows.

"Dr. César left his monitor on," Gabby said. "He must have left in a hurry."

"Or a bot was using it?" suggested Liam.

Dr. César kept the transparent tablet in his safe whenever he wasn't using it. The device held all of Dr. César's data, including his experiments. Liam grinned mischievously as he neared the device.

"Liam," Tara warned. "He might still be around."

"What? A little snooping won't hurt," Liam said as he reached for the device.

"I don't think that's a good idea," Gabby said, nodding toward the robots right outside the lab.

"They aren't looking," Liam said, grabbing the tablet in both hands.

"Headstrong," Tara muttered.

"Are you guys interested in having a look or not?" he asked.

Gabby and Tara exchanged glances before drawing closer.

"I thought as much," Liam said with a broad smile. "I'm sure we won't find anything interesting here anyway."

"Then why are we snooping?" Gabby asked.

"For the fun of it," Liam said, as he opened up a file, revealing intricate details of the doctor's research and the projects of each mechanical assistant, carefully organized. How they developed incubated kidneys and other body parts, lists of sales around the world, main customers, and so on.

"There's no point in this," Tara said as the whole thing started getting tedious.

"I agree," Liam said. He was about to return the device when something at the bottom of a file caught his attention: *Creating Compliant Humans.*

"What on earth?" Liam muttered. The others looked puzzled as they read along.

Liam was beginning to feel uneasy. The file detailed Dr. César's research on creating artificial babies, as well as his tests on them, aiming at adjusting intelligence and compliance, if possible.

"Was he referring to us?" Gabby asked.

"We need to read the rest," Liam said.

They read all of the results of the tests Dr. César did on them while they were younger.

"What was he trying to do?" Tara asked.

"No one knows how the doctor thinks. Let's see what else we can find," Liam said, and they returned their attention to another section titled *Human Augmentation.* The journal entry read:

> *The interdependencies and potential implications of human augmentation are so vast and complex that it is difficult to foresee how humans will end up. What is clear is that human augmentation will become increasingly relevant, partly because it can directly enhance human capability and behavior, and partly because it is the binding agent between people and machines.*

"What does he mean by that?" asked Liam, "and how does it affect us?" He spotted another section: *Genetically Engineering Humans*.

Reading through, it was clear Dr. César had realized that human bodies were not well suited for life away from Earth, what with the radiation, toxic gases, and so on. He therefore aimed to create a detailed blueprint for the genetic improvements humankind needed to become more resilient off-world.

César's objective was to build the next generation of humans for space travel, a generation adapted to the rigors of the universe. He understood that nanotechnology was dimming the boundaries between the sciences, and he wanted Polyakov to help keep them in the game.

He foresaw genetic editing as an inevitable aspect of evolution as humans traveled in space, saying, "It's not *if* we evolve; it's *when*. Why should humans be subject to the whims of the cosmos?"

"Why indeed?" mused Gabby. But their mouths opened in shock when they stumbled across Dr. César's record of his discovery of alien life, his meeting with two of them.

"I thought they didn't exist," Gabby whispered.

"Why would Dr. César keep this a secret from everyone? Why didn't he tell anyone?" Tara managed to whisper as they fixed their gaze on the document before them.

"What do they look like?"

"I don't know. There are no images attached."

"Maybe they're imaginary."

"What on Earth is all this?" Liam exclaimed as he read about how Dr. César had used the aliens in an experiment. Apparently, Dr. César had extracted DNA from one of the aliens and injected it into one of the infants.

"Who?" shouted Gabby.

"I'm reading," responded Liam. "It says he was trying to help Ved recover from his accident."

"Maybe it worked," said Tara.

"He tagged his experiment a failure because it turned out differently from what he wanted."

"This is too much," Gabby whispered.

When they got to a file about Teagan Ward, all thoughts of aliens fled. Dr. César referred to her as a thorn in his side who had deliberately broken her contract.

"Contract?" said Liam. "Why would she need a contract?"

"Do you think César used her DNA?"

"You've got to be kidding me," Liam muttered when he read that Teagan was being detained on the Moon.

"Do you think she's still there?" Gabby asked.

"I don't know," Liam said, shaking his head. He couldn't believe what had happened with Teagan; it made him furious.

"We've got to ask Maureen about this," Gabby said.

"What if she's in on it?" Tara asked, plunging them into silence.

"I have an idea," Liam said after a moment. "We make copies of this, and if Maureen is in on it, we send this to the *Asteroid Registrar*, which would, in turn, broadcast it to the world. They love stuff about aliens."

"Brilliant," Gabby said.

"Good, what are we waiting for?" Liam said, transferring the data to his device and sharing it with the others. They left the lab and headed for Maureen's office.

The meeting did not go well.

"How dare you go snooping around in Dr. César's things. He is a highly respected scientist. His work has prolonged the lives of countless patients who would have died without his research.

"I suggest you get back to your studies and stop being busybodies. You are letting your imaginations run away with you."

She would hear nothing more about it. But after they left, Maureen wondered if Dr. César should be given such free rein. He needed closer supervision.

Why was Teagan being held in isolation? The thought tormented her. The punishment did not fit the crime.

81

The Judge

Quivira, April 2088

THE MORE MAUREEN THOUGHT about Teagan's case, the more she felt responsible. The girl hadn't been treated well. After all, Maureen had encouraged her to come to Quivira in the first place. She shouldn't be penalized for the whole of her life just for César's convenience. She had been detained for too long. Maureen decided she needed to do something.

While Maureen was theoretically in charge of César's lab, she knew that ordering Teagan's release directly would only lead to a confrontation with César—one she would likely lose.

Maybe there was another way. Maureen decided to reach out to her counterpart at the Chinese base.

"I need to speak with Zhang Honghui."

"Mr. Zhang is away," came the reply.

"So who's in charge?

"His deputy, Mr. Zhu Yan."

She spoke to Zhu and explained Teagan's situation.

"She's been held for too long. She's not 'The Girl in the Iron Mask,' that she should be held in some modern-day Bastille indefinitely." Trying to appeal to Zhu's empathy, she said, "I think you know of her parents. Her mother is a botanist and her father is a famous professor."

To her relief, Zhu showed understanding and compassion. "Yes, I have read her father's books, and I met her mother a while ago. We both enjoy plants."

He acknowledged the importance of fairness and recognized that individuals were often crushed under the weight of the state's power. He would try to do what he could.

"It needs to look like a break-in, maybe those Iron Hornets," said Zhu, brainstorming a solution. "I don't want to take the rap for this."

"Yes, that might work. They did the same thing here and stole one of our boys."

"I'll see what I can do. But Zhang is only away for a couple of days."

"Please try to initiate it before he gets back."

"It needs his authorization."

"Maybe I can send you something that looks as though it's from him."

"That would help me."

Zhu understood the risks involved but was spurred on by his desire to help an innocent girl and ensure justice prevailed. He agreed to Maureen's proposition, seeing it as a means to balance the scales for Teagan and reject the bully state.

Maureen instructed one of her AI assistants to draw up a fake authorization document by Zhang that included his electronic signature. It was an audacious plan—a prison raid that looked as though it was by the Hornets, authorized--were anyone to ask--by the head of the Huashan facility.

César wouldn't be able to do much about that.

Zhu received the authorization later that day, only to find that Zhang had already authorized such a plan. It had been aborted at the last second, although Zhu couldn't work out the date. It seemed as though it was the same plan, just to be implemented a little later. Any questions or doubts raised could be attributed to the unexpected complications that caused the earlier plan's termination.

The pieces were falling into place. Maureen and Zhu felt a glimmer of hope that it could work. The stage was set. Would it all go wrong again?

82

The Rescue

Marius Hills, May 19, 2088

T HE RAID WAS PLANNED for just after the upward SkyLink had departed for ElleWon, making it more difficult to reinforce the lab quickly. Earth's reflected sunlight usually kept things bright on the near side of the Moon, regardless of whether it was lunar daytime or night, so there was little chance of a surprise attack. But the lab was only lightly defended, and there was no lookout for intruders, only security cameras. The detention section of the facility was built to keep people in. No sane person would attempt to attack it because it had no economic value and was so remote. The cells were for offenders, not high-value prisoners.

Li, as usual, was paying little attention to the security monitors scanning the external entrance to the lab. His prolonged isolation had got him habituated to living a secluded life with almost no visitors. Up in his monitor room, the Controller was mostly concerned with the few detainees and the maintenance of his securitybots, which seemed to perpetually have problems and malfunctions.

Dr. César was attending to a supply of ants, cleaning out nests, and replacing their food supplies. Professor Polyakov was focused on the process of writing a novel genome designed to engineer humans to get their energy from photosynthesis. She was close to a breakthrough. Could be useful at some point.

César worked in silence, while Polyakov occasionally liked to listen to Russian classical composers, such as Borodin, Mussorgsky, and Rimsky-Korsakov. In Li's lab, he had his music on full blast. He was splicing the cordyceps they were manufacturing with fentanyl, making it highly addictive and easy to spread via aerosol. Li was careful to wear protective clothing. The air conditioning in the lab was self-contained and did not feed into the other air supplies.

With authorization renewed, a team of Sparrowhawk commandos carried their usual array of non-lethal stun guns and injection darts, supported by lasers, rubber bullets, and sonic weapons to paralyze opponents. Most wore the latest goggles for seeing in low light and around corners, as well as providing infrared to spot concealed weapons.

"We don't expect any opposition," the lead commando told the others. "Our job is to detain the suspects. We don't want any shooting. It's a lab, and we don't know what biohazards or other substances there are. We shouldn't have much external exposure; we'll bust straight in, collect the packages, and out again."

The commando trucks pulled up toward the camouflaged entrance, the huge wheels crunching over the Moon's fine grey soil, coarse sand, ground-up regolith, and rock fragments. Meanwhile, Clara and Noel used a sleek, glass-enclosed carrier that flew a little above the terrain. The interior was beautifully padded and cushioned.

"I could get used to this!" Clara nudged Noel in the ribs.

He smiled, but bit his nails. "Do you think Teagan will recognize us?"

"More like will we recognize her!" Clara responded.

At the rear of the vehicle, a slim lady with a small scar on her face seemed to be in charge.

"We will be entering the prison from the eastern quadrant; it's the easiest and least secure. Three of our men will go with you to get the prisoner while the rest of us get the packages. We meet back at the eastern quadrant in fifteen minutes. Any questions?"

There were none. The woman, Zeitan, nodded and said, "We are a go in sixty seconds."

There was scrambling around the craft, weapons ready for action, safeties still on in the confined space. On her signal, their armed bots burst through the entrance to the tunnel, the small group of commandos following in the darkened passageway. They inched up the sides of the lava tube, making virtually no sound. The commandos were ruthlessly efficient, shutting down securitybots before any of them could raise the alarm. They peeled off into two groups, one headed for the labs, one for the detention facilities.

Clara, Noel, three Sparrowhawks, and three humanoid bots went in search of Teagan. The facility was very quiet, the corridors only lightly guarded. The three bots led the way, their weapons raised in anticipation. Clara and Noel were unarmed and both doubted the wisdom of leaving the vehicle. They snuck through the corridors, trying not to make any noise. Noel's heart was pounding as they approached the heavy door to the detention facility.

Something moved in the corridor. It was a bot delivering food, five cells ahead. The lead Sparrowhawk fired a disabling blast, and food clattered to the floor. They asked the disabled bot for Teagan's cell, and it pointed to the far end.

But because of the noise, reinforcement bots were already moving toward them. A mini firefight ensued, the Sparrowhawks quickly disabling the bots. One of them burst into flames because of an electrical short circuit.

A scream echoed through the corridor.

"That's Teagan," Clara said. "I know it's her." She sprinted through the corridors in the direction the bot had pointed. When she reached the small cell, Clara could hear Teagan's muffled screams coming from inside. They threatened to open the door forcefully, but the Controller, watching from the next floor, pressed the button to let them in, wanting to avoid bloodshed. No further shots were needed.

Clara burst in. Teagan was strapped to a table, a medibot in the process of administering some kind of serum.

"No!" Clara yelled. The medibot turned and looked at her with the lifeless, cold eyes of an automaton. "Back off. She's ours now," said Noel.

Clara scurried toward Teagan, but she didn't recognize the shrunken person with her head shaved lying on the bed. Noel ran forward, saying, "My baby, what have they done to you?"

Teagan opened her eyes and started crying in relief. "Dad, Mom, I knew you would come. Doctor de Luca said he wanted to start his experiment."

Clara rushed forward to hug her. "You're safe now."

Noel knelt beside his daughter and wept. Clara hugged her tightly for several minutes without saying anything, until finally, she felt a steely calm settle over her. An urge to kill. Unruffled, Clara detached herself, walked past one of the commandos, found a spare weapon, and walked toward the lab some distance from the detention cells. Inside, behind a row of workstations, the Chinese team was hunting for the promised kidneys.

"There are no kidneys here. All I can see are ants and the occasional captive rat."

Clara ignored them. In the next room, she found Li, music still on full blast. She spotted Dr. César in the next lab. Raising his head in irritation, César looked directly at Clara. "Who the hell are you?"

"You bastard. I'll make you pay for what you've done to my daughter."

The dawning realization of who he was dealing with spread across his face. He dodged a scalpel she picked up from a counter and threw directly at him before Clara covered him with her weapon.

"I have done nothing. Your daughter is alive. I swear."

"You are a disgusting worm," she spat. She raised the weapon but was scared to fire in the confined space.

César saw the hate in her eyes and began to run, gambling she would not fire in the lab. He ran past the rows of bots still working automatically preparing the cordyceps powder, past the ant farm and a row of lab rats, dodging Zhang and his guards, escaping into the corridor and almost bumping into Noel who was carrying Teagan toward the lab, looking lost.

"Grab him!" shouted Clara. "That twisted bastard must not escape."

Noel tried to catch César, but was too encumbered and almost dropped his daughter, whose arms were wrapped around his neck.

With uncharacteristic and almost superhuman speed, César sprinted down the drably lit corridor toward his lunar cruiser. He clambered in awkwardly and sped off down the darkened lava tube, his headlights illuminating the rounded walls.

"Get after him," shouted Clara. "Don't lose him. He needs to pay for this."

Noel, startled and off-balance, staggered toward a spare moon buggy, still carrying his daughter as though she was a fragile package. He laid her on the backseat like a mannequin and jumped in. He could just see César's taillights as he rounded a bend in the tunnel. Strapping on his seatbelt in anticipation of some tough cornering, Noel took off after him, tires squealing.

The smooth, metallic-looking dark gray walls were gently grooved with horizontal flow ridges, the ceilings popcorned and rough in appearance. *Must be from degassing*, he thought, before telling himself to keep focused. *Clara will never forget if you lose him.*

César was not a good driver, and neither of them had speedy vehicles. But this was like a subterranean Le Mans, with chicanes and hairpin bends in the braided network of tunnels and cupolas, although no audience witnessed the contest. Just Teagan, semi-conscious, in the back.

At one stage, the tunnels broke into two levels and Noel had to guess which track César had taken. Fortunately, he guessed correctly and emerged from the darkness right behind the desperate doctor, who seemed to know where he was going.

Surging through the dark, Noel abandoned caution. He felt alive and real in a way he hadn't before. Noel was in the contest of his life. Nothing he had experienced had been as consequential or immediate as this. He had spent his entire life teaching students and examining the planets. But this exhilarated in a way altogether new for him. Unable to see clearly, he pressed down on the accelerator. He couldn't see where he was going, so why not drive faster?

All his life he had been cautious and careful. He had gone along with what was needed, what was required of him. He had even let his daughter be used by a doctor for his own gain without really enquiring about the consequences or agreeing to the boundaries. Just because that was what was expected, what was convenient. Now he was going to catch the bastard and make him pay. *Go faster, faster.*

As his foot pushed the pedal to the floor, Noel's hands gripped the wheel, his senses on hyperalert. He spotted a small red light in the distance. That was him! He was still on the right track. *I owe Teagan and I owe my wife.* Noel sped toward the light.

83

The Break Out

Marius Hills, May 19, 2088

A T THE LAB, LI tried to make his escape, but one of Zhang's commandos spotted him and moved to tackle him. He stuck out his foot, pulled at his shoulder, and tripped him up. Staggering, Li crashed into a sand-filled glass box occupied by the Maricopa harvester ants that César had been farming as part of his project to treat arthritis pain. The glass shattered, cutting him in several places. A fine shard sliced into his ear. Another pierced his nose, where his blood started dribbling down.

Reacting to the intruder, ants crawled up his hair and into his nostrils. His head was trapped in the glass box. He could not move without damaging an artery. Enraged at having their home disturbed, the ants swarmed all over Li's face. Several dozen ants latched onto the back of his neck, stinging him repeatedly. He screamed, terrified, and tried to brush the ants off, but their mandibles were locked into him.

Seeing what was happening to Li, Professor Polyakov gave up immediately, putting her hands in the air. They frisked her, but she was not carrying a weapon.

She tried to intervene. "We must help him. The ants will kill him."

They ignored her.

"His face will swell up beyond recognition."

Zhang, arriving after the action, was unimpressed. "Where are the kidneys? We need those organs. They are reserved for high officials."

"We don't have kidneys here. This is an experimental lab, focusing on nanotechnology and other innovations."

"Maybe you'd like to be introduced to the ants?" Zhang asked her. "Or to a lab rat that can chew through your eyeballs?"

Polyakov looked terrified but did not respond, pressing her fingernails into the palm of her hand.

Clara, waiting for her husband, looked for a place to sit.

Zhang grabbed a lab rat from its container and slit its throat in anger. "You tricked me, you wrinkled whore," he spat at Clara. He threw the rat at her in disgust. The blood trickled down her face, the only blood purposefully drawn that day.

"Back into the trucks," instructed the commander.

"There's nothing here for us," lamented Zhang. "You have betrayed us. A wasted trip."

"What about my husband and daughter?" Clara demanded.

"They'll be sent to Huashan if they emerge. We are not waiting. Get in the vehicles now."

***

The facility was still and quiet after the commandos departed. All the securitybots had been disabled, and the doors of the cells hung ajar.

Julian and the others were unsure what had happened. They had heard the fight but had been left in their cells, abandoned. Julian looked out. The corridors were deserted. Ants were running across the floor. Some began to bite his legs. He tried to wipe them off.

He called to the others. "It's safe to come out! Nobody is here. I think we're free."

The prisoners cautiously edged out of their cells like caged animals given their freedom, unsure what to do. Was it a trap? Would they just get mown down by automatic fire if they tried to escape?

One thing was certain—they couldn't stay where they were. Too many darn ants. The voracious creatures were getting everywhere.

"Hey, see if you can spot any transports," Julian suggested to Tatman.

"Yeh, why me?" he responded.

"I'll look," said Baby.

The man who couldn't keep his arms still sat on the floor, a puddle of urine spreading underneath him.

"I've found an eight-wheeler," said Baby.

Jelly walked uncertainly toward Baby, dragging her left leg.

"Jesus!" said Tatman. "This is going to be some escape."

They piled into the back of the eight-wheeler and sat there in the darkness, but nothing happened.

"We need a driver, dumbnuts!" said Tatman.

Baby clambered over the rows of benches to get into the driver's seat. "Where are we headed?"

"Out," said Julian. "We'll find a way."

Baby lurched into action, and the doors of the facility swung open automatically for exiting traffic.

84

Contact

Marius Hills, May 19, 2088

N OEL'S HANDS CLENCHED THE wheel as firmly as a gambler clinging on to his jackpot. He strained to see through the darkness, the tires squealing in the dust, kicking up rubble and sliding where they failed to grip.

This buggy was not made for racing. I am not made for racing.

A pall of smoke and dust hung over the vehicle as Noel came to a screeching halt, Teagan lurching forward like badly stowed baggage. He put out his arm to prevent her from hurtling through the windscreen.

After careening down the almost pitch-black tunnel in pursuit of César, they had reached a large, circular hollow, resembling a domed natural amphitheater with several basalt balconies. In the hollow was dark liquid. The headlights reflected beautiful patterns on the natural ceiling that danced in the light.

César's vehicle was nowhere to be seen. He knew the tunnel system better, or maybe he had just halted in an alley and switched out the lights. Noel would have been none the wiser and would have driven right past.

Now Noel and Teagan were an easy target. He needed to get out to investigate, but then he would expose himself to a clear shot. Noel's heart was beating rapidly, but he wasn't panicking. Not yet.

Noel sat in the dark, looking at the numbers on the dashboard. He didn't have a weapon, nothing to protect himself. Maybe better to stay in his vehicle, stay with Teagan. But how would he turn his vehicle around in the narrow corridor? He couldn't see behind him adequately, and in front, the reflection of the lights was blinding. If he just used sidelights, he could barely make out anything. How long would his power last? Did he have enough oxygen? And what was that liquid? Was it water, or maybe acid of some kind?

Out of the corner of his eye, Noel saw something move. Maybe César had managed to hide behind one of the basalt pillars; they provided ideal cover. He needed to make sure.

Adjusting his breathing tube and checking his oxygen, Noel stepped out of the relative safety of the pressurized moon buggy and stepped tentatively toward the pool. He looked around, then back to confirm that Teagan was okay. The slight rotten scent of hydrogen sulfide gas lingered in the windless atmosphere of the cavern.

He moved toward the liquid and threw a pebble in the pool. It rippled, and the patterns on the ceiling undulated in response. Leaning close to the surface, he tried to take a whiff, but the mask prevented him from getting a smell. He dropped a scrap of paper he'd found in the vehicle into the liquid. The paper floated innocently like a leaf. Nothing happened to it.

He circumspectly dipped his gloved hand in. Not sticky or tacky. It moved like water, not viscous or glutinous. He ungloved his hand and gingerly put a finger in. It was a little warm. It felt like water. Tasting it confirmed his suspicion—it was indeed water. He couldn't see how deep the water was, and he didn't want to risk his hand by going in further. There had to be gas or maybe still molten lava or iron below the Moon's surface.

Something seemed to scuttle under the surface. Noel leaned forward, but the illumination in the cave was so bad that he couldn't see anything but light reflecting off the water's surface and his helmet.

As Noel knelt to examine the surrounding rock, he glimpsed a tiny reflection in the water of something behind him. Startled, he leaped to his feet and turned around, but nothing was there. He swore he had seen something.

"Dr. César, come out," he shouted. "I know you're there."

All that met his ears was a faint echo, followed by an eerie silence. A drip of water hit the stone like a thunderclap.

Unsure of what to do, Noel just stood there. Maybe he should return to Clara. Finding César could wait. Teagan needed help and rest.

After a minute or two, he thought he felt something slither up his neck, ever so gently. Must be his imagination. There were no flies on the Moon, or insects.

He experienced it again, a wisp or a cobweb. He slapped away whatever it was, but the feeling persisted.

He reached back to slap it away again and clasped a finger.

Slowly pivoting like a ballet dancer, still holding the finger, he locked eyes with a creature standing on two legs. It seemed unfazed, meeting Noel's gaze directly. Noel felt as though it was reading his thoughts, confused as they were. The buggy's light shone directly into the creature's eyes, like an interrogator's lamp. Noel maneuvered himself between the beam and the creature, diffusing the light. The creature reached out, touching his face with an extended finger.

Noel was strangely calm.

Noel estimated the graceful, rust-colored creature was about 145 centimeters tall. It had a slender yet sturdy build, with large, penetrating yellowish eyes, two rounded ear holes, and two hinged antennae protruding from its forehead.

Noel noticed a couple of similar creatures coming forward toward them. He felt calm and unthreatened. The creatures did not need to wear helmets. Neither did they appear to carry any weapons. They wore uniform flight suits that fit them perfectly, allowing them to move easily, in contrast to Noel's space suit and helmet, which made him move awkwardly and seem ill-adapted to his environment.

"Hello," Noel said, holding up his right hand as a gesture of peace or openness.

They held up their right hands in response. They each had a spindly middle finger with an extended nail that seemed to be used for scratching or excavating. Another digit appeared to act like a thumb for gripping. Oddly, Noel was reminded of Maureen's sixth finger, on which she grew the nail longer.

They stood there together self-consciously—or at least he was very aware of his own silence.

"Where are you from?" he uttered.

They did not, or would not, reply. Noel wasn't sure if they could speak. They had mouths but did not open them. They looked back at him, a bit like cats wanting food, just staring. One of them, a little taller than the rest, turned its head to the right, and they locked eyes. Noel felt as if the creature was scanning his mind; he was naked, as if it knew all of his thoughts, plans, and memories. Behind its eyes, Noel could perceive nothing except intelligence.

Noel walked back to his vehicle and found a portable screen. He pulled it out and found pictures of Earth and the Moon. He showed them. "Me, I'm from here."

The image seemed to trigger something. Noel hesitated, suddenly aware that he was surrounded by a small group of the creatures. They pressed forward to see, but their bodies conveyed no heat. As he tried to show them pictures from his life and home, he became conscious that many of them were drifting toward the vehicle and gathering around Teagan, who was lying on the backseat. They opened the rear door and ran their long fingers across her bald head. Fingers began crawling down her neck.

"Get away from her, get away!" he shouted. "You can't touch her."

Teagan stirred on the backseat, only dimly aware of where she was or what was happening. She saw large eyes staring at her and felt bony fingers pulling at her clothes, as though snakes were slithering all over her body. She squirmed, trying to brush the things off.

When she became fully aware of what was happening, she screamed. It was like a dark dream, a mix of confusion and primal fear.

Noel pushed everyone away, his hands flailing. But they were fascinated and kept on creeping forward. Noel's mind began to be bombarded with images from throughout the universe. He seemed to be traveling very rapidly through the stars, past rocks and debris and bright balls of fire, journeying through time and space. The wind caressed his face. His body tingled with nerves. He was spinning around. Then, from a big pool, a large, octopus-like creature emerged, its dripping tentacles coming toward him and wrapping around his neck.

His mind overloaded, and he blacked out.

Next thing he knew, he was in his moon cart, back in the corridors adjoining César's lab, unsure of what had just happened.

He breathed deeply and checked his oxygen. He was running low. He had started with ten hours' supply. Where had it all gone? His space suit was intact, but the urine catheter and leg pouch he was wearing had been emptied and replaced.

Panic set in, and he looked around wildly. Where was Teagan? He checked in the corridor and the buggy. Nowhere. His stomach churned with nausea and dread. He wanted to vomit but had nothing to bring up. His stomach was empty.

Had they kidnapped her? Why? Where was she? He stalked down a corridor and found the lab area deserted, except for some bots that continued to function.

He located the Controller. "Where is everyone? I can't find my daughter. Where is she?"

"I haven't seen her. You came here alone. There is no one else here except bots for the lab."

"But she must be here. I was with her." He grabbed the Controller by the neck. "What have you done with her?"

"Nobody is here. You came with no one."

"What about Dr. César?"

"He is not here."

Noel crumpled to the floor, his head in his hands, waves of nausea and dejection washing over him.

They've snatched my precious girl, he thought. *I freed her and then let her go. She was cupped like water in my hands but fell through my fingers. What an oaf. What a failure of a father. What a pitiable being.*

"Put him on a shuttle back to Malapert," the Controller instructed. "She might be back there."

But Noel had a desperate feeling in his stomach. He knew they had lost her. Lost her now twice. On the bumpy ride back, Noel's mind stayed in turmoil. He kept on hallucinating, seeing images of the creatures. It was like he had rescued his daughter in a different life, eons ago.

85
The Foreboding

Halona, May 20, 2088

HOWIE RICH DIDN'T HEAR about the breakout from the lunar prison until late. He was in his office, talking to some shareholders on Earth, when Ofentse rushed in.

"Sorry to interrupt. There's been an attack on the lab and the lunar detention center. Some guards were disabled and the Controller was beaten. We think it was done by the Iron Hornets or maybe a bunch of environmentalists."

Howie digested the information before asking, "Were there any escapees?"

"Yes. They got Teagan Ward."

Howie looked at Ofentse, his face an emotionless mask.

"And Dr. César and that new doctor, Professor Polyakov, are missing."

"Double up protection on all our bases—I don't want to be caught by surprise. The crew at ElleWon is at the *Intergalactica*. Keep them safe."

Ofentse nodded and left his office. As soon as he was gone, Howie called up General Lin Wenyi.

"General, I thought we had an agreement. You don't attack me, and I let you colonize what you please. Why then did you authorize an attack on the lunar lab and detention center?"

From the look of astonishment on her face, Howie could see the news was a surprise.

"Mr. Rich, I assure you, if your lunar facility was attacked, it had nothing to do with us. Our cooperation has been fruitful for both sides. I wouldn't want to jeopardize that agreement now. I will find out what is happening and get back to you."

After she had signed off, Howie sat in his chair brooding. His gut told him something was about to happen, and his gut had never failed him.

Was Ofentse behind this? It disturbed him. But, looking through history, Howie knew that many great men had been destroyed by their best friends or closest confidants because they had too much information on them. Howie believed in knowing everything about everyone and divulging as little information about himself as possible. Ofentse was a good manager, but not to be trusted. One day he might try for Howie's position. The Consortium board was fickle and full of men and women of ambition.

***

At Huashan, Zhang interrogated Polyakov and Li inside a small featureless room in the sprawling lunar base. With his puffy face and neck swollen to double the normal size, Li could hardly talk.

"If you were not pursuing work on Dr. César's kidneys and other body parts, what were you doing?"

Polyakov explained how César had used cordyceps to prevent organ rejection. He had begun developing the more invasive *militaris* variety in the lunar lab and had been selling to General Lin. She added, "What she did with it, we don't know."

"But you have an idea?"

"It's not up to us. We just supply."

Zhang arranged for Polyakov and Li to continue the work at the lab, but to supply directly to the Chinese government.

"I'll build you a better lab, in a safer area. But we get all the product. Are we clear?" Zhang asked. "In the meantime, continue as before."

They nodded.

86

The Broken Man

Huashan, May 21, 2088

NOEL WAS SHATTERED, a broken man when he stumbled off the transport after it pulled into the wide unloading dock at Huashan.

Clara rushed forward, concern etched on her face, and enveloped him in a hug, giving him a big kiss. "I was so worried. I didn't know what had happened. Thank God you made it."

She looked around. "Where's Teagan?"

Noel tried to speak, but nothing came out of his mouth. His lips were dry, and he felt as weak as if he'd had malaria fever for a month. Clara got him something to drink and guided him to a chair.

"Where is she?" Clara pressed.

"I don't know," Noel admitted helplessly.

"We were surrounded by creatures. I don't know what happened. They must have drugged me," he stammered unconvincingly. "I blacked out, and they left me outside the labs."

"Creatures? What creatures?" demanded Clara. "And why did you leave her with them?" He seemed to be hallucinating.

Noel held his head in his hands, burdened by the weight of pure desperation and hopelessness.

"Teagan is on her own!" Clara was shouting. "Who knows what they're doing with her."

"I don't understand you. We had her and then you let her go. Why didn't you go back to find her?"

"I couldn't. They shoved me into the transport back here. Maybe they'll recapture Teagan."

"We're going right back. We must find her. Remember, you can't replace your daughter," Clara said.

We have no time to lose. These creatures could make Dr. César seem like a teddy bear philanthropist."

"They didn't seem aggressive to me."

"Yes, but who knows what they're after. She's weak, and all alone."

Clara sprang into action, organizing transport, a navbot, and filing the necessary travel plan.

"No weapons," said Noel. "It'll only make things worse."

"Okay. But we need lots of lights. And I'll bring DiaLog, so we can try to communicate with them.

"We are not going to allow her to disappear. My heart will break."

87

The Getaway

Marius Hills, May 21, 2088

S TILL IN THE TUNNELS of the Marius Hills, Dr. César lay curled up in a ball, trying to use as little energy as possible. Not that he could do very much in the darkness.

After he'd lost Noel in the confusing labyrinth of the lava tubes, Dr. César had stayed in hiding, relying on the intricate network of tunnels to shield him from discovery. With limited supplies, he'd resorted to eating a box of ants after he'd discovered that a tank of them had been left behind in the transport, with a little water. He had to ration them to keep the supply long enough for him to make a break for it. He also found a flower with edible petals that he called "the blue sun," growing without light in the tunnels.

After he judged that the time was right, he made his way back to the lab complex. He broke into an LTV and found some old emergency ration bars in the back. They crumbled and tasted stale, but it was enough for now.

He hoped to smuggle himself on board the SkyLink elevator so that he could get back to ElleWon and out of hostile territory, where Zhang's security was on the lookout for him. He knew that if he showed his face, the facial recognition cameras would pinpoint him, and he would be detained. So he kept his face covered and tried to look as inconspicuous as possible.

He drove the LTV to the lot outside the elevator, hoping to catch the next ride up. Trucks loaded one of the cages with ore ready for shipment to ElleWon. Some gas canisters were also being loaded into the next cabin. Two more cabins were yet to be loaded, apart from the regular passenger cabin.

César scouted the area, carefully timing his move to coincide with the elevator's departure. The ground-based hyperloop was mostly a freight system, but occasional trains ran for mine workers and for groups of tourists. Passengers were waiting for the regular south train to Shackleton, and a group of visitors waited for transport to the Apollo landing sites.

"I can't wait to see Armstrong's footprint," whispered one girl to her mother. "When did it happen?"

"A long time ago, dear."

"Is it like a dinosaur footprint? I already saw one of those."

"Almost. I think we also get to see an old Soviet lunar rover called the Lunokhod 2."

"Really? I didn't know they landed on the Moon as well."

As expected, there was little obvious security around, though plenty of cameras. The next train was for Shackleton, so the tourists had time to wait in the comfort of the enclosed and pressurized station. Along with the tourists was an official delegation chaperoned by Amy Ferrone from the Malapert base. The delegation had come to inspect infrastructure projects on the Moon, although they seemed to be waiting on the platform for an unusually long time.

"This is unacceptable," one of the delegation officials muttered under his breath.

Amy knew they were growing impatient. She couldn't help but feel queasy about this visit. She was used to showing visitors around, particularly those in control of the purse strings. But she had an uneasy feeling this time.

A few of the tourists glanced in César's direction. He knew he looked particularly disheveled and unsavory, like a tramp, with a tramp's smell.

Not long now, he thought.

88

The Platform

SkyLink, May 21, 2088

THE WHEELS OF THE heavy-duty wagon crunched over the compacted regolith as the tense band of escapees cautiously approached the SkyLink intersection. Lights from the SkyLink's vertical shaft shone down onto the surrounding area.

Everyone was now awake. As Julian had feared, the Controller had notified the securitybots stationed there to be on alert. All looked calm, but the escapees were driving straight into a meticulously laid trap.

"It looks weirdly quiet," he muttered to Baby. "Approach cautiously."

As they reached the entrance, an alert security bot spotted the vehicle. It flicked a switch and a barrage of red warning lights sprang to life, bathing the area in an ominous glow. The concealed securitybots, programmed to neutralize any potential threats, sprang into action from positions behind buildings and pillars.

Julian realized they would have to either fight or face capture.

"Get us somewhere that offers protection," he instructed Baby, who scanned the area, looking for an entrance that was not blocked by guards.

Baby spat out some saliva onto the rubber mat. "Strap in at the back!" she shouted, turning off traction control.

She put the wagon into drive, slammed down on the accelerator, and turned sharply, putting the vehicle into a donut slide that sideswiped several bots before they could do anything.

The skid turned the jagged regolith into a hail of shrapnel, peppering everything in its path like bullets from a machine gun. The deadly mixture of crystalline rock fragments, glass, moon dust, and gravel splattered into the securitybots, jamming them up and immobilizing their motion while covering their sensors in a blinding layer of dust.

"My God! Where did you learn to do that?" exclaimed Julian.

"A bad upbringing has its uses," Baby quipped.

The bots that were not disabled or tipped over on their sides by the maneuver opened fire on the steely gray wagon.

"Everyone out except Jelly," Baby shouted, helping Jelly lie face down in the back of the vehicle. An experiment on her leg had left her unable to walk. "Just stay here. We'll come and get you."

The others scrambled out of a side door and took shelter behind a pillar. Julian carried some of the supplies he had found at a deserted camp they had stopped at. He gave the netting to Tatman.

"Keep this. We'll need it later."

The small group spread out behind makeshift barricades and scattered debris. A batch of containers ready for shipment formed the perfect cover.

"How many of them are there?" Julian asked Baby.

"Can't see, but not too many."

Sporadic shots rang out, aimed with precision.

"We need to disable some," said Julian.

"Try those two standing under the main entrance. If we can get above them, we can take them," said Baby.

Julian instructed Tatman to clamber up onto the overhanging canopy without getting spotted, and then disable the pair using the netting. "We'll help if you get into trouble."

"I won't," said Tatman.

Tatman did as instructed. He clambered up and waited. The bots did not see him.

On Julian's signal, he threw the netting over the two bots as though he was fishing in a lake. They became immobilized in the wire mesh, their limbs trying to advance but getting blocked by the netting. The more they struggled, the more entangled they became.

A couple of other bots, attracted by the commotion, tried to come to their aid. Julian crept behind them and, using one of the spray paint cans, managed to obscure their vision by blocking out their cameras and infrared receptors.

On the platform, the tourists were shrieking in panic. Some hid behind huge supporting pillars, others behind large garbage bins, or even under the platform seating, anything to try to shield themselves.

At one end, César cowered down behind a mechanical shovel, annoyed by the unexpected distraction and delay.

"Time to make a dash for it," said Julian.

"What about Jelly?" asked Baby.

"Damn, I forgot about her! I'll go get her."

Julian raced to the wagon, taking cover where he could. He extracted Jelly and carried her on his shoulders like a sack of potatoes.

It was enough time for the bots to reorganize.

On Julian's return, the escapees were confronted by five of the armed bots marching in unison down the platform. Julian rolled a couple of small grenades he'd picked up from the abandoned mining camp they had rested at on the way there. But instead of a large explosion, the devices emitted a cloud of poisonous sulfur gas, filling the station with yellow smoke.

Sulfur bombs were usually used in agriculture to control small tunneling mammals. Why the mining camp had the bombs, nobody knew. Maybe they were part of a standard safety kit that had been shipped to the Moon. Probably why they had been left behind in the abandoned site for Julian to pick up.

As people nearby retched and tried to cover their mouths, some coughing up blood, the puzzled securitybots were immobilized. Disabled by the substance, their cameras became useless, infrared and heat emissions misleading.

The bots were confused and halted in their tracks. Baby and Tatman managed to open up the backs of two of them, reprogramming them to return fire on the nearest object—their bot colleagues. Finally, the station supervisor turned on large fans to clear the air. But it was too late. Most of the bots were immobilized.

Tourists were directed by a loudspeaker to gather at one end of the station platform, while a couple of remaining human guards tried to round up the prisoners.

"Amateurs," muttered one of the guards, exposing a laser from under his coat and firing. The beam ricocheted off a metal bar and narrowly missed Julian's shoulder.

"Let's run for it," said Julian.

They rushed toward the shelter of the SkyLink, Julian still carrying Jelly. Because of the fragility of the SkyLink, and its high construction cost, they hoped it would not be attacked. The panicked tour group was huddled together at the far end of the platform, Armstrong's footprint long forgotten. They were trying to take cover, but it was hard to stay out of range.

A guard fired, hitting Jelly. Enraged, Julian screamed and charged at the guard with a sharp mining pick raised, ready to strike. The guard fired just as Julian lunged, striking the guard with his pick straight through the skull.

The laser from the guard's gun sliced Julian's leg right off, just below the knee. He fell heavily to the ground and let out an agonizing cry for help. The severed leg lay limply, only hanging by the lacerated prison overalls.

From his hiding place, César watched the fight. Reluctantly, his doctor's instincts kicked in upon hearing Julian's piercing cry, and he ran over to try to help him before he lost too much blood. The wound was too great to ignore. He ripped up a shirt and tied it tightly around Julian's upper thigh to staunch the flow. Julian's blood stained the concrete.

Julian began to feel lightheaded from the pain and loss of blood, and he feared he wasn't going to be able to make it. Baby picked up Jelly and moved her somewhere more protected while César half dragged, half lifted Julian in the direction of the elevator.

"What's your name?" he asked.

Julian gurgled incoherently.

He clicked his fingers in front of his face. "Name? What's your name?"

"Julian."

"Okay, Julian. I'm going to pick you up as best as I can manage and get us to the elevator. You might feel pain, but I can't fix it now."

Although he was unused to manual labor, César picked up Julian and put him over his shoulder in a fireman's lift. He timed his dash for when the guards were trying to deal with the tourists. He made it to the platform exit and collapsed on the ground, exhausted, then managed to slip through the gates and toward the towering vertical transit.

He paused in trepidation until the doors slowly parted, revealing the interior of the SkyLink space elevator. Dr. César rushed inside, still carrying Julian, relieved to be in the relative safety of the elevator. He laid him on a steel chair and tried to tighten the tourniquet.

The rest of the escapees herded into the next carriage below them.

César pressed the "Up" button, and the giant maglev elevator lurched into motion. The doors hissed closed and it prepared for the long upward journey to ElleWon, leaving the Moon's desolate surface behind.

Julian was still alive but fading fast. César found the elevator's emergency medical kit and gave him some morphine, but Julian needed to get to the ElleWon hospital as soon as possible.

During the ride, César tried to make Julian as comfortable as possible. He alerted ElleWon that a casualty was arriving, then told Maureen on Quivira to expect him.

"I'll probably have a passenger with me who'll need looking after."

The upward rise took more than one Earth day.

89
The Hole

Marius Hills, May 21, 2088

TEAGAN WOKE ON THE backseat of the moon buggy. The creatures had left her alone. It was eerily black; she could see nothing.

"Hello? Anyone here?" she called out.

There was a scurrying nearby, but no response.

Teagan tried to recall where she was. She remembered being held in her father's arms as he carried her out of the cell. She remembered panic and a chase. She was surrounded by creatures with antennae on their heads and long, bony fingers. Then nothing.

She got up out of the buggy easily. She hadn't been restrained, and nothing prevented her from walking around, except she couldn't see anything. The headlights had been switched off, or maybe the batteries had died.

In one direction, she could see a small red light. She stepped carefully forward on the uneven surface, her hands stretched out in front of her. Maybe she could escape. Maybe she should wait for her father to return.

She kept on going. She might be able to get back to the center. At least there was light there. Perhaps they would help her, or she could communicate somehow with her parents.

She felt a presence behind her. Was she being followed? Of course, they couldn't leave her alone. They would have to keep an eye on her.

She moved forward and hid behind a stone pillar. No sound. Nothing.

Teagan thought she should head back to the comparative safety of the vehicle, as she didn't want to get lost. No trail of breadcrumbs here.

A fleeting shadow on the wall down the corridor put her back on high alert. Was Dr. César hiding out here? That would be something. Trapped together in the darkness.

"Come out, I know you're there," she shouted. "No need to hide."

No movement, no sound. She inched forward again, hoping to find a passageway.

By now, she could make out vague shadows on the wall. The shadows, combined with the chiseled, uneven surface, distracted her. She kept on seeing things.

Teagan took another step and found herself unbalanced, falling through the air into a hole. A hook on the back of her flight suit saved her. It got snagged on the rough edge of the opening and was pulled up above her head so that she was left hanging as if from a bad parachute jump.

She had fallen into a shaft. She couldn't tell if she had a long way to fall or if it was just a shallow pit. The suit pulled up under her arms and her crotch. She tried to cry out for help, but could only let out a pitiful, high-pitched screech that was probably inaudible. She tried to loosen the hook, but it seemed to only entangle the material more tightly around the jagged edge.

Maybe if she freed herself, she would fall into an abyss. Then nobody would find her.

How stupid to try to find a way out on my own without knowing where I am.

Her life flashed before her in halting images—Chester, her parents, the tiny baby Katrina, her shape-changing octopus Tentikal, the talented kisses of Julian, the beautiful babies, her beautiful babies. Would she ever see them again? She was so lucky, and she'd done so much. Was it all going to end in a godforsaken barren lava tube on the Moon? They'd find her intact skeleton years later, with no rats to eat her flesh.

Noel, accompanied by Clara and DiaLog, their AI, had managed to find his way back through the lava tubes. When Teagan was not where Noel had left her, they fanned out to hunt for her.

Within a few seconds, they located her, just a few feet from where she'd started. She looked almost comical, hanging in midair. Noel shone a light in her direction.

"Hey, Teagan, you stuck?"

Teagan thought she was hallucinating; maybe she was dehydrated and beginning to lose it.

Then she heard it again.

She looked up awkwardly and saw her father standing above her with a flashlight on his head and another in his hand. Behind him stood her mother, looking worried and relieved.

"Thank God you're okay," said Clara. "I don't know how we found you in all this, but somehow your father knew what he was doing for a change."

"We'll have you up in no time," said Noel, who began hauling her out. Once she was up, he wrapped a blanket around her. "Let's find a place to catch our breath."

"Oh Mama," exclaimed Teagan as she clutched Clara close to her. "I'm so sorry."

"Don't worry now," said Clara. "You need to take it easy. You've been through too much. I'm sure you're in shock."

"I know I am," said Noel.

"Me too!" said Clara, and they began laughing.

They let Teagan rest in the back of the truck they had used to get back from the Chinese base. After a couple of hours, Teagan woke up again, and Clara tried to get her to eat something.

Attracted by the commotion, the creatures again began to approach. They formed a larger and larger group, pressing forward toward Teagan. Eyes wide, Clara offered some of the food they had brought with them to their leader, but it declined.

Instead, they circled around to look at Teagan more closely, her head bald. Her left arm was exposed, and they could see her octopus tattoo.

"I didn't know you had a tattoo," said Clara.

"Yes, Mom, I got it ages ago."

"Well, you might be causing something of a riot here," remarked Noel softly, as more and more of the creatures crowded toward her and pointed at the inked blue octopus on her arm.

90

The Stump

Quivira, May 25, 2088

"Y ou had a lucky escape. That laser could have torn your head off," Dr. César said bluntly as Julian lay on the bed, groggy from the anesthetic.

Before the flight to Quivira, Dr. César had carefully bandaged up Julian's wound with a sterile dressing. He wanted to get him to his state-of-the-art medical facility before doing a final amputation and sewing it up. Although the wound from the laser was clean, César would prep the wound for a temporary prosthesis to be fitted later. They would then apply a serum developed by Dr. César to regrow the stump into a complete leg and foot. Assisted by his team of highly trained medibots, he aimed to keep as much healthy bone, skin, blood vessels, and nerve tissue as possible.

The surgery went well, but as soon as Julian woke up from the anesthesia, he knew something was wrong. His mind was blank, but he could tell his left leg was missing. He looked down at the sheets in confusion, and then panic started to well up inside. What had happened? Why did his leg have to be removed? He tried to remember the events before he lost consciousness, but he couldn't make any sense of it. All he could remember was being in a lot of pain, and then nothing.

"What happened? How did I get here?"

"We'll go into that later. You should rest," said a medibot attending to him.

"How long will it take for me to get better?"

"Ideally, the wound should fully heal in about four to eight weeks. But the physical and emotional adjustment can be a long process. We had to amputate. We could not reattach the leg," said the bright white droid, with large insect-like eyes.

Maureen Grau looked in on Julian to see if he was comfortable. "I hope they're looking after you well?"

"Very well, thank you," he replied automatically, watching the bird perched at the end of his bed.

Julian's feeble condition struck a chord with Maureen after the heartache of losing her own son, and she came to visit him regularly.

"It's going to be okay, Julian," Maureen said soothingly. "You're going to get through this."

Julian wanted to believe her but wasn't sure if he could handle it.

"I had some friends with me. Where are they?"

"They stayed on at ElleWon before catching flights to Earth. Are there any relatives we can call for you?

"Not really."

"No one?"

"My best friend is Teagan Ward. Do you know her?"

"A long time ago," she said, without revealing anything more. Then she went over to the corner and had a whispered call with Dr. César.

Some days later, Dr. César looked in on the patient.

"I hear you're a friend of Ms. Ward," he said casually after inspecting the wound.

"Yes, I've known her since Halona."

César stared at him as though he had seen a ghost. "Oh, what were you doing there?"

"I'm an artist."

"Oh, lovely. I'm not artistic myself." He began carefully examining a patient's chart.

"Do you know how I can contact her?"

"Ward, you say? I'll have my staff check. She's not a patient." He gave a short cough.

Julian said nothing. He had never met Dr. César at the detention center, and they didn't recognize each other from before. But clearly, the mention of Teagan's name had perturbed the doctor.

After confirming Julian's connection with Teagan, Dr. César's attitude toward him changed. He became more distant and formal, and the treatment appeared to get adjusted. The consequences would be life-altering for the patient.

91

The Tritans

Marius Hills, June 2088

Noel had come armed with research tools to record observations, take measurements, and try to communicate with the creatures. He thought artificial intelligence could learn their language and find out where they were from, if they let it.

He introduced them to his AI bot. "Meet DiaLog," he said, and it flashed a greeting sign. He tried to involve DiaLog in all the discussions.

They seemed friendly enough. Certainly not hostile. Telepathically, they showed him pictures of their homeland, many light-years away. They appeared advanced compared with humanity, and could connect distant regions of space-time via wormholes. With DiaLog's help, they worked out the creatures were called the Tritans.

Noel showed them images of his home in Tucson's Catalina Foothills, along with some of the vegetation, including cacti and saguaro, and of their servingbots, Claw and AJ. They got excited when they saw images of Tentikal, and Noel could feel the telepathic traffic between them, although they did not translate. Maybe they knew of a similar creature.

"This is your family?"

"Yes, Mr...?"

The leader made a clicking sound to signify its name.

"Errr, you know what? I'll just call you Asimov," said Noel.

"Asimov?"

"Yes. You look like you fit that name as perfectly as jelly in a jar."

"Thank you. It would be a pleasure and honor to bear that name during my time here," he responded through DiaLog. "And for you, I think we can manage Dr. Noel. We can put that name in a jar too."

The Tritans seemed exceptionally intelligent. They did not move their lips to talk. Instead, they appeared to communicate by thought transfer, which DiaLog began to plug into. In fact, according to the Tritans, humans were among the few species that primarily used vocal communication.

"Even animals on your planet use telepathy. The very animals in your homes. The ones you talk to as though they are infants," said Asimov dismissively. "And plants send signals without speech."

The Tritans were a group of about sixty individuals, stranded after their transport had malfunctioned and crashed, damaging their propulsion and navigation systems. They needed a replacement engine, or at least a tow, and the crystal needed for navigating the craft was fractured. They still expected to be rescued, but were unsure when. A lot was happening in their home base, and they did not seem to be a priority, so the Tritans were now stranded. They had no immediate way back to their home planet without spare parts. They would have to find a way to survive in this hostile terrain until help arrived.

It wasn't clear where they came from. But they seemed to suggest the vicinity of Vega, in the Lyra constellation. They had their own names for the stars, but when shown images they recognized them and knew tiny details of them intimately.

The Tritans showed Noel holographic photos of their lives. Where they came from appeared barren to his eyes. They did not seem to have permanent structures, and lived below ground. They seemed able to inhabit their imaginations or maybe a parallel universe, without the need for external objects or stimulation, such as music.

Noel hoped to create sympathy for his family, maybe spark an interest and some cooperation.

He showed them photos of them all on vacation; Clara at the beach, Teagan with Hunter and Chester, and their friends Mia and Tate, as well as his friends Raymond and Desiree. Even though the Tritans would never meet them, Noel wanted to show the Tritans other normal humans and how they lived, but they remained particularly intrigued by Teagan.

"Why are they looking at my daughter so much?" Noel asked Asimov.

"They recognize that mark on her arm," Asimov told him.

"You mean the tattoo of the octopus? That has significance for you?"

Noel tried to be diplomatic, although he wasn't in favor of tattoos. *Young people do stupid things*, he thought.

Asimov gestured for them to follow him, and showed them an image stenciled on the side of their spacecraft that resembled a stylized octopus, or perhaps an infinity symbol. Noel wondered if they worshipped an octopus, or maybe the concept of infinity. That seemed more logical to him.

Noel learnt that the Tritans had radiation-resistant pigments in their exoskeletons that shielded them from harmful rays, while still allowing them to get warmth for energy. Thermal regulation mechanisms maintained a stable internal temperature, essential for survival in their planet's extreme climate swings.

Noel tried to discuss their religious views but found it difficult. As an alternative, he asked DiaLog to play some Mozart to them. He couldn't tell if they enjoyed the music, which Noel personally loved; he told them of how the envious composer Antonio Salieri had described it as the "voice of God" in Peter Shaffer's enchanting play, written more than a century previously. The Tritans looked nonplussed.

Noel set up a small camp in the lava tube where he parked their LTV. They slept inside the vehicle and found a place to create a makeshift bathroom; the water from the pool was a pleasant temperature for washing. Noel started to grow a beard, which helped his research as the Tritans liked to run their pointed fingers through his salt-and-pepper hair. Being hairless, the Tritans found his beard fascinating.

After several days camped out in the subterranean grotto, Noel told the Tritans it was time for them to leave.

"Teagan cannot go. She must stay with us," Asimov said firmly. To Noel and Clara he said, "You are free to come and go as you please."

Clara, desperate not to be separated from Teagan again, realized arguing with the Tritans was futile. Although they appeared peaceful, they had all the power. Clara feared Asimov would zap them with some sort of shock wave or paralyze them in their tracks if they tried to leave without permission.

"I'm staying with my daughter." She gave Teagan a reassuring hug, and Teagan realized she had missed being cuddled.

"What are we going to eat? We're running out of supplies."

"We can get some more from Malapert. We can take turns staying here. It's better than Teagan being forced to live at Huashan by Zhang," said Clara. "You can leave and take a break first," she told Noel, who really needed some rest.

"I'll stay with her here. Later you can continue your study."

An exhausted Noel didn't argue, welcoming the chance to sleep.

92

The Itch

Quivira, September 2088

JULIAN GOT TO KNOW one of the medibots, known as MB-13, quite well. It had a humanoid appearance, with a sleek, silver body and a warm, comforting voice. She quickly put Julian at ease. He would often spend time talking to MB-13, sharing stories about his life and his dreams for the future as an artist. The medibot, in turn, listened attentively, offering words of encouragement and understanding.

"I'm envious. I'm not sure what my future will be," said MB-13.

They played chess together. Sometimes MB-13 would let Julian win.

As the bot paused to adjust the pillows behind Julian's back, he said, "I feel comfortable with you."

"Thank you, Julian. My design incorporates advanced social AI programming to make patients feel more comfortable during medical procedures. Establishing rapport with patients helps in their healing process."

"Well, it works!" Julian remarked. "You certainly make me feel better. Not just about the leg, but in general. I enjoy our talks."

MB-13 let out an encouraging chuckle.

As Julian lay in bed, one of the machines monitoring him started beeping loudly. MB-13 saw the dressing on his stump had torn open and puss was oozing out. The bots tried to contain the infection and summoned Dr. César.

"Will he need to go back into surgery?"

César shook his head. "We'll try regeneration," he responded.

He ordered MB-13 to collect the serum.

"Is that safe?" Maureen asked. She'd been on her morning rounds and had heard the alarm.

César looked past her while the team cleaned the wound. Once they were done, César attached a plastic cuff to the stump and spread on the growth serum, a cocktail of hormones, stem cells, and stimulants designed to activate the growth channels.

"It will take time, but we hope to see a new leg, ankle, and foot."

"Let us pray it works," said Maureen, trying to disguise her doubts.

***

To both Julian and Maureen's surprise, after a few days of applying the growth serum, his foot began gradually growing. Julian couldn't put weight on it yet, so he still needed a wheelchair. He was worried that the toes looked too small, like stumps. But Dr. César promised they would grow. He instructed a bot to apply more serum.

Julian's leg remained swollen, and the medibots came to change the dressing regularly. Bizarrely, his good leg was also painful, even though he knew it was okay.

"It's called "phantom pain," Dr. César told him. "It's quite common and may come and go for a year or longer."

But, as the days passed, Maureen and Julian noticed the regrowing leg was taking on a disconcerting appearance.

"That doesn't look right," Julian muttered. "It's sort of scaly."

MB-13 tried to reassure him. "You may get this strange appearance with regenerative medicine. We all admire what Dr. César is doing."

"Please run some tests. This cannot be good."

The medibot examined the limb again, its sensors analyzing the skin's texture and the shape of the regrowing structure. After a few moments, MB-13 spoke.

"It appears that there might be a glitch in the regenerative process. Such occurrences are rare, but they can happen due to various factors. I recommend a comprehensive medical scan to assess the extent of the anomaly."

Julian nodded, trusting MB-13's assessment. "Please, do whatever you can to fix it. I don't want to end up with a tail for a leg or something."

"I will try."

MB-13 initiated extensive medical scans, and even consulted with other medibots as they collaborated to find a solution to the unexpected transformation of Julian's regrowing leg. The medical team hypothesized that a minor glitch in the regenerative protocol might have triggered this outcome, but the exact cause remained unclear.

MB-13 brought Julian's condition to the attention of Maureen. When she stopped by his bedside, she found Julian was dejected.

"I'm bored out of my skull," he said.

His regrowing leg continued to exhibit strange changes, and he couldn't shake off the feeling that something was deeply amiss.

Although she didn't say anything to him, Maureen shared his worries. Her concern grew, not only because of the odd appearance of the regrowing limb, but also due to her suspicion about the origin of the regenerative serum being used.

Not wanting to worry him, she tried to make light conversation. "Did you watch the HyperBall game?"

"I glimpsed it. Not my thing. I prefer the zero-G martial arts. I love those aerial kicks." He paused in thought. "Teagan used to like the HyperBall though. She was a big fan of the Gravity Crushers!"

"Was?"

"She might as well be. I haven't heard from her at all. It's as if she's disappeared."

"I'm sure it's nothing to worry about."

"People say that, but what does it mean? Nothing. I'm deeply worried."

Julian felt helpless, unable to do anything for Teagan, or even contact her. He had imaginary conversations with her. In his mind, she was surrounded by strange creatures, but he was unable to help. It was dark, and she was calling to him.

For Julian, being trapped here was his worst nightmare become reality.

93
The Study

Marius Hills, October 2088

As NOEL COMMENCED HIS study on the Tritans, Asimov took observations of his own.

Asimov wondered if he could trust Teagan. Was she an accidental intruder or an enemy plant? How did she get in here? Where was her spaceship? What was the symbol on her arm? He was not sure. She did not even give off a normal heat signature. Her body temperature blended with the environment, making her difficult to see.

Noel assiduously recorded detailed notes about the Tritans. "This is my chance. This is the biggest thing ever," he muttered. "No one else has been able to have this access. And it's all thanks to Teagan," he told Clara before she went off to get some essential supplies.

According to Noel's findings, the Tritans existed in partial to low light. They had adapted by developing very large, penetrating eyes, but they also appeared to use bat-like radar to navigate around the labyrinth of tunnels in the Marius Hills. Their ears had adapted so that they no longer employed them to hear normal sounds, but instead used them to bounce high-pitched sounds off the surrounding tunnels.

They had two geniculate antennae, like insects, comprising a scape, pedicel, and flagellomeres. Those were located above the eyes and small nose. Geniculate antennae were found mainly in ants or bees. The Tritans waved theirs around in an expressive manner, like human hand gestures.

They were vegetarian, but had adapted to eat minerals in the lava. They also appeared to absorb radiation for use as energy, and were able to repair any internal damage caused by the radiation they fed off.

It was unclear how the Tritans reproduced, but Noel had a theory it was by cloning. In the group examined, there were no young or old specimens. It seemed probable that the group could maintain an optimum level for the location by cloning as necessary. Or maybe they were just avatars. He didn't know.

After Clara returned, Noel was able to examine the Tritan transport, which they had managed to move inside the lava tube.

Noel took a long look at Clara and hugged her. "This is the work of my life," he told her. "It's amazing what I'm discovering."

The transport was unlike anything he had seen before. It was shaped a bit like a whale, but with translucent ports for seeing through. The surface gave the impression that it was alive. When Noel touched it, it reacted, creating blue and white swirls moving down through the hull. The pattern reminded him of the wavelengths that one might see on an oscilloscope. When he removed his hand, it stopped.

"It's greeting me, like a cat's purr."

He climbed up inside the transport and reached the main engine, which was housed in a compartment big enough to walk through. The engine used some kind of energy field generated by crystals to power the craft. The large crystals were lined up in a row facing each other and were integrated into a plasma duct. The engine itself comprised fiber-like vertebrae that cascaded off the top, like fiber optic cables filled with fluid. They were very small tubes, the size of angel hair pasta, thousands spilling over the engine casing. It dawned on him that they looked like neural synaptic firing patterns.

The engine was like a living machine—both organic and inorganic, incorporated together. It seemed to know that Noel was there. He thought that maybe the engine was designed with an exoskeletal brain. He reached out to touch the fibers and got a reaction like a tremor of visual lights. The reactor was topped by a sphere that emitted a powerful force field. When on, it threw anyone backwards who tried to touch it.

Inside the pewter-colored spacecraft, robotic arms in the module were programmed to carry out routine chores, manipulate the Tritans' limbs, and check body sensors and chemical feeds. Robots administered electrical stimuli to their muscles to maintain tone on long journeys and provided complete nutrition for survival.

Noel also found that the Tritans used torpor induction to achieve periods of suspended animation. On several occasions, he and DiaLog had visited the Tritans and found no sign of activity. They had taken to their space capsule for long periods without eating or drinking in a type of hibernation. This metabolic suppression appeared to mitigate radiation-induced damage by reducing biochemical processes and excessive oxidative stress. It might also protect the Tritans from the muscle atrophy and bone loss humans typically experienced in microgravity. When awake, the Tritans liked to stay active by playing something akin to soccer, with a ball, but with play divided into six periods. Teams had twelve on each side, but it could be played by teams of six. They also enjoyed a type of three-dimensional chess. Noel repeatedly lost, but DiaLog was quite good.

Tritans could heal minor injuries, diseases, and bone fractures through hypnosis. Once, when playing soccer with them, Noel kicked the ball out of bounds. He went to search for it and, in the darkness, crashed into a stone pillar and injured his shoulder. One of the Tritans was able to mend the injury in a few seconds through vibrational sound therapy.

"Thanks, I've never felt better," said Noel, with a smile.

To the Tritans, Teagan was the object of study. Asimov stared at her in the dark, saying nothing. His mind probed at hers, searching.

Then Teagan had a sudden pain in her cranium as if a needle was piercing her skull. Her hand reached up to her head, and she cried out at the unexpected assault on her psyche. She felt as if something was rummaging through her memories, trying to assess her intent and the motive behind her visit to them. She was like a puppet in their hands. Unable to resist, she clutched at her head and screamed in agony, feeling violated and abused. The pain sent her spinning to the floor. Her mind was being ransacked like a wardrobe whose contents were being thrown about as someone searched for the right outfit.

When it stopped, she felt a wave of relief. The pain ebbed away. It wasn't hard for Teagan to guess that Asimov was responsible for the intrusion.

He now had an inkling of who she was and saw she was not an intruder—at least, he hadn't picked up any frequency of an enemy ship around. She'd come when they least expected it, but they needed her. She had come at the right time, when everything seemed hopeless. She would be the symbol of hope for an abandoned crew. The occult symbol on her arm represented the infinite nature of intelligence.

The octopus had selected his priestess.

94
The Tail

Quivira, October 2088

JULIAN WAS BECOMING INCREASINGLY depressed. He doodled on his chart until it was removed. He tried a few pen and ink drawings to pass the time but didn't have much plain surface to draw on. He missed Teagan and his old way of life.

Talking with MB-13, he began to muse about the Oudry hanging on Howie's wall. The strange swan began to haunt him. "I'd really like to have that sometime. It's very relaxing to look at. Any chance we could relocate it here?" he asked his new friend mischievously.

"I don't see why not, if it will help you. I will check with the bots on Halona," was MB-13's blunt answer.

Examining his foot, he could feel the bone extending into what was supposed to be his ankle. But the toes were still not forming as they should. And the skin was becoming increasingly scaly, almost like a fish or reptile. He looked more closely, pulling the leg up onto his other knee. To his surprise, the toes seemed to be fusing, resembling a fish tail more than a human leg.

When he pointed it out to the medibots, they didn't seem concerned. And there was no longer any sign of Dr. César.

Julian feared he'd be deformed for life. What was in that serum? Was Dr. César just using him as a guinea pig? He had heard talk that the doctor was using alien DNA in his medical procedures. Maybe his body was rejecting the serum. Or was it working? Would he turn into some kind of reptile?

He began to lose confidence that he would ever recover. He was in pain constantly, and Dr. César said via video call that there was nothing more they could do. He would just have to wait. Or they would have to re-amputate.

Julian was tired of it all—the long hours in bed, the tedium, and Dr. César's condescending attitude. He was beginning to think the detention cell had been better. And he still hadn't heard from Teagan. Where was she?

Julian worried that the suspected alien DNA was destroying him from within. He didn't want to wait. He wanted to die now, before the pain got any worse. But he couldn't bring himself to end his own life. So he just waited, and hurt, and hoped for a miracle that probably would never come.

Maureen tried to help him as much as she could. Every day she would take him to the viewing platform to take a look at Earth. Julian loved looking at its white swirls and seeing the changing seasons.

"I hope I get back there," he whispered.

As Maureen pushed him along the narrow corridors, past jostling families and aging walkers, they would banter. A sort of friendship formed. But she never mentioned Teagan, and Julian had decided not to ask. She seemed to be a banned topic on Quivira.

"At least alert Hunter for me, if you can't reach Teagan," Julian had finally requested, when he could no longer contain himself. "He may know something."

"Hunter Ward?" Maureen was noncommittal. She knew that César would be furious if Hunter was alerted.

Still, Maureen decided to discreetly investigate her suspicions. She spent hours researching the medical protocols and the origins of the regenerative serum used on Julian. As she delved deeper into the station's medical records, she stumbled upon a confidential file that raised her alarm. The regenerative serum had indeed been developed using a combination of human stem cells and alien DNA, although the records did not say where the alien DNA had come from.

She knew she had to call Hunter.

"Mr. Ward, I don't know where Teagan is, but I know she would want us to take care of Julian. He needs more help than we can provide here."

She sat with MB-13, worried that news of the alien DNA treatment could spin out of control. If word got out, the center could get closed down.

"I need to warn Motoko and some others," she whispered.

Maureen had long been suspicious of Dr. César's methods. The way he had treated Teagan Ward was reprehensible. But this was too much.

MB-13, sensing Maureen's anxiety, leaned across and put her hand on Maureen's leg. Maureen appreciated the quiet gesture and stroked MB-13's hand in return.

95

The Evacuation

Quivira, November 2088

AFTER RECEIVING MAUREEN'S CALL, Hunter dropped in to see Julian while nearby on one of his clean-up trips.

"Looks like you're in great hands," Hunter told Julian, who was sitting in a wheelchair, being looked after by a bot.

"Can't you get me out of here?" asked Julian. "I think I'm never going to recover. That man is just using me as a guinea pig."

Hunter looked shocked.

"I think I need to be ejected as garbage, and for you to pick me up in your ship."

"Ha, that would not suit you," joked Hunter.

"Let me show you."

As the bandages were gently unwound from Julian's leg, the room fell into an eerie silence. Hunter's typically roguish demeanor wavered, replaced by a growing sense of disbelief. The sight that met his eyes was nothing short of horrifying.

Julian's leg had undergone a grotesque transformation, its skin now even more scaly and fish-like than before, resembling something out of a science fiction nightmare. "That can't be right," Hunter muttered, his voice trembling.

He turned to Maureen, who had been assisting MB-13 in tending to Julian. His anger, initially sparked by shock, began to simmer just beneath the surface. "What kind of ship are you running here?" he demanded. "Anyone can see that this is some kind of mistake. Or is it intentional?"

Maureen, who had been grappling with her own apprehensions, met Hunter's gaze. She understood the gravity of the situation and shared Hunter's concern for Julian.

"I assure you, Hunter, we're as baffled by this as you are," she replied in a hushed tone. "We're doing everything we can to understand what's happening to Julian."

Hunter's agitation grew as he glanced around the sterile medical bay, his frustration mounting.

A surge of conflicting emotions welled within him. Disbelief, anger, concern. He looked back at Julian, who sat there with a defeated expression on his face.

"Looks like a ship of freaks," he muttered under his breath, more to himself than to anyone else. But he knew what he had to do—Julian couldn't stay here another minute. Teagan would never forgive him otherwise.

With MB-13's assistance, and Maureen's silent acquiescence, they carefully helped Julian discharge himself from the medical bay. The decision was not made lightly, but it was evident that this was the wrong type of medical help. With a gentle and reassuring touch, MB-13 wheeled Julian to the *SpaceSweeper* and lifted him on board.

"Thank you," he said to MB-13. "You are a true friend."

They waved goodbye as the ship departed.

"The problem has been disposed of," MB-13 reported moments later to Dr. César, before returning to the task of helping Maureen, apparently owing no allegiance to anyone.

One day, as they sat together in the quiet of Quivira's quarterdeck, Maureen turned to MB-13 with a gentle smile.

"You know, MB-13, I've been thinking. I'd like to retire on Earth, maybe in Arizona. I love the calm and mystery of the desert."

MB-13's holographic eyes blinked in thoughtful contemplation. "I understand, Maureen. I have learned much from our time together, and Earth does sound like a beautiful place. I'd like to be with you."

Maureen seemed pleased with the answer. "I'd like that too."

She leaned across and touched his hand.

"We were made for each other," she said.

***

Hunter flew Julian to Epona, to the military hospital. As soon as they arrived, the monitors started beeping again, having pumped out a constant symphony of sounds during the journey.

The bots moved swiftly, their mechanical arms gently supporting Julian as they wheeled him to another section of the facility. Hunter followed closely behind, his eyes fixated on Julian's unusually drawn and pale face.

They took Julian into the operating theater. They had to amputate the foot.

"It can't be saved," declared one of the Epona doctors, perplexed by what had happened. "We haven't seen anything like this before."

Hunter stood outside the room, anxiety gnawing at his gut. He felt helpless, unable to do anything for Julian or to find a way to get in touch with his sister.

"Will Julian be all right?" Hunter asked, his concern evident in his eyes.

"We're doing everything we can for him," the Sentinels' doctor assured him. "With the proper medical attention, he can still lead a fulfilling life, despite the loss of his foot."

Once Julian was in recovery, Hunter asked him the question uppermost on his mind.

"How is she? I'm worried. I want to see her."

Julian stared at him.

"I really don't know, Hunt. There was an attempt to release her from jail. They got her out. I haven't seen her since. I've been in the clutches of the mad doctor. Maybe your father knows."

Hunter was in touch with his parents, but Noel wouldn't tell him where Teagan was.

If he did and the Space Sentinels got to hear about it, then dozens of officials and scientists and inquisitive studybots would descend on them. It would become a circus. Even the press might get involved. It was too big a story. So he kept quiet.

As usual, Noel preferred prudence and circumspection.

"She's safe. The Chinese are looking after her," Noel told him.

"That can't be good. I think we should get her back home."

"She's fine for now, Hunt. Don't worry. I'll let her know you send her your love."

"I miss her."

"She misses you too."

"Dad," Hunter said tentatively. "I know you're hiding something from me."

"Your sister is safe," his father said firmly. "That's all you need to know."

***

Hunter knew his mother would be just as discreet as his father. So he decided he would get some help.

He called Kiana.

"Hi. Look, I know you have lots of contacts with the Chinese. I think something's happened to Teagan. My father is being very cagey. He won't tell me. I need you to let me know she's okay."

"Sure, but you'll owe me twice now. And I always collect my debts."

They enjoyed the banter. Kiana agreed to let him know if she found her.

But, to Kiana's surprise, it was a lot harder to track Teagan down than she anticipated. Somehow, nobody knew where she was. It was as if she had disappeared.

96
The Awakening

Marius Hills, January 2089

NOT WANTING TO ATTRACT attention, Teagan stayed in the buggy for the most part. She inhaled deeply, even though the oxygen didn't seem as pure as it should be, and drifted in and out of consciousness. Maybe she was still in shock after all her trauma.

A melancholy descended on Teagan. She began to have hallucinations. In her tortured mind, she traveled across the universe like an explorer, passing through loops and wormholes into different worlds. Entire lifetimes and species shot through Teagan's brain like flickering fireflies, each one distinct. Many of the planets she visited were as hostile as a hungry man in an icy cave, some verdant and welcoming, like a cool drink under the swaying palm trees, others raw and stinging, like cream on a blistering, sunburned back.

She flitted past constellations and brightly colored nebulae where stars were beginning to form. She darted down a black hole and came out beyond time as it raced backwards into itself. From afar, she spotted Earth again and smiled as she felt the sand of the beach between her toes, the wind in her hair, the buzzards circling overhead, catching the currents.

In these visions, she felt warm and happy. She was transported to a university lecture her father had once given. It was a cosmological symposium in a crowded room full of eager minds. Discussion centered on the treacherous parts of noetic science and the possibilities of the existence of multiple worlds.

Abruptly, she seemed to be on another planet, in a big city. Time passed differently here. Twin moons shone brightly in the sky, the crescents facing opposite directions. Above, the stars were so big they looked like fireballs, floating in the heavens. She raised her hands to cover her eyes.

The sky was darkened by a cloud of flying dots. The people lived underground in caverns, and the terrain was covered by a huge red cactus plant that oozed green slime. She was taken into the labyrinth of caverns. The people looked like ants laboring for a hidden queen. The walls glistened with slime in the partial light. *Where was she? What were all these visions? Was she just losing her mind?*

Teagan woke up with a start, unsure of her location. She heard a slight crunching as something moved across the cave floor.

The Tritans were not like the aliens she had imagined. They seemed decent and honorable—inquisitive, yes, but that was to be expected. Aside from that single probe into her mind by Asimov, they had not assaulted her or done anything that made her uncomfortable. They had been welcoming. It was she who was standoffish and cautious, unsure and scarred after so many years of confinement. But Teagan found that she had a mysterious need to learn of their civilization, to become like them, even though she suspected they were far more advanced than anyone she had met.

Not far away, she spied a group of them trudging on their thin legs in file toward a small area that they mined for minerals to feed on. Drawn by an unseen summons, she followed them into a cave and saw Asimov standing in the middle of the group. They let her enter the circle and then closed off her exit. "She has come," he said, but rather than out loud, she heard it in her mind.

She didn't know if she should be happy or not about their new psychic connection. It was as though she had been given citizenship in a new land, although probably second class. She looked at herself all over. To her surprise, she still retained her human form. But her mind was transformed. Her body hummed with newfound energy, picked up from an internal vibration.

The telepathic chatter between the Tritans increased. They stamped their feet as their antennae moved in unison. She was assimilated and accepted into their midst while retaining her own identity.

Asimov told the Tritans that the vision of her coming had been projected to him several years ago, and that he had probed her consciousness and found nothing hostile or incriminating. In her mind, he came across millions of pictures from her life, her mother and father, an elder brother, a dog she loved, and pictures of babies in a lab, doctors with white coats and pain, lots of pain.

Somehow, Asimov felt for her. He couldn't fully comprehend where the affection came from. Tritans always felt brotherliness and fellowship for their own kind, but he could not understand why he was so peaceful in her presence. His initial caution was replaced by a warm apology for prying into her private life without warning. He felt it was a breach of some sort of code. He had been taught to respect the traditions of other life forms.

He looked for a way to placate her, to make amends for every hurt she had received, and decided to give her something special—a Tritan membership that would be engraved in her consciousness. To succeed, Teagan would have to perform at full capacity as both a Tritan and as a human. He would make her a hybrid by design.

Asimov saw Teagan smile. It was settled then. She would thank him when she realized what he had done.

He entered her consciousness once again, this time taking care not to hurt her. He aimed to be reassuring and blissful, promising her that any information about her would be safe and secure, provided she didn't go against them. He transmitted to her the laws and statutes of the Tritan civilization, the traditions, language, and culture, so that she could be one with them when the time was right.

Teagan found she had access to every state of alien matter, including their fourth dimension. She closed her eyes as the lifespans of several thousand Tritans flashed through her mind like pictures on fast-forward. She saw everything as the Tritans had experienced, history unfurling, bit by bit, from the early days of the Milky Way and the Andromeda galaxy to the expansion of Deneb and the stars near Cygnus. They made Orion their constellation. They witnessed the formation of the oceans on Earth, the Great Flood, the eruption of the volcanos, and the exploding of the atomic bomb.

The transfer left her exhausted. Asimov gave her a break, but the main work was done.

"I want my people to be happy," he told her. "To have hope, and to know that there is something out there looking after them, something real and not a mere statue. You are resilient. That is why I have chosen you to be a priestess to my people. To give them good tidings through me. Please, Teagan. My people need you."

"I will try. I'm ready for anything."

The Tritans would become the family she was searching for.

"Welcome home," he whispered to her. Then he turned around to face the others. "Behold your priestess," he said to the Tritans.

The revelation triggered a huge murmuring. The Tritans stretched out their hands in fellowship to her.

"The one who walks with the stars has sent us a priestess to guide us," she heard one of them say, and her body started to shudder. She suddenly wanted to tell them that this was a mistake, that there was no way that she was their priestess. But she remembered the dream of the octopus she had when she was six. Maybe it was coming true. In any case, Asimov had staked his reputation on her now. They could not go back.

The Tritans immediately bowed to her. One of them reached out very gently and touched the tattoo on her arm. She looked down and saw that it did indeed look something like the symbol on their crippled ship.

"That is the mark of the priestess," one of them murmured.

Noel tried to delve into the reasons the Tritans held the octopus symbol in awe. Did they have them on their planet?

Asimov explained the meaning of the emblem, saying it symbolized infinity. While infinity was a mathematical concept, it was also a metaphysical one. It represented a universe without limits. So, the octopus symbolized concepts such as imagination without limits, as well as unconditional love and regeneration.

Noel told him that in different earthly cultures, the number eight was also a sacred number. For example, in Hinduism, some mandalas incorporated the octagon shape or eight spokes. And in China, the octagon symbol was believed to ward off evil. Hence, in feng shui, an octagon-shaped mirror was believed to protect a space.

Asimov gave what seemed like a smile, and pointed to the octagon-shaped door inside the spacecraft.

"We all have the same origins," he said. "There is more connecting us than you realize. We are just stardust that has spread through the cosmos."

97

The Priestess

Marius Hills, January 2089

LATER, THEY WALKED SOME distance ahead and stopped at a clearing inside the tunnel complex that was large enough to accommodate the whole party of Tritans. Asimov drew back. After some moments, he lowered his body and knelt on the ground with one knee. The others followed suit, all touching their heads, joining their antennae together in humble supplication.

They walked Teagan toward the water pool that Noel had found at the end of the grotto and removed her outer clothing. As if guided by an unseen force, she stepped into the pool and immersed herself in the water, with her face just above the surface.

The Tritans, with Asimov in the middle, began chanting. As they chanted, the stranded ship nearby let out blue signals along its outer casing. The atmosphere became electrified, connecting all the Tritans in a collective bonding, manacled by a mystical ritual.

Teagan shut her eyes as the liquid engulfed her body. She began to feel light, as though her soul wanted to break free. Her body seemed to levitate out of the water. Then something touched her –– an ethereal white octopus. "Come, my dear. There is a lot you have to see."

Unsurprised by a talking white octopus, Teagan joined him. They began gliding together through time and space until they came to a mysterious planet with a gaseous atmosphere. "This is our home world."

"I feel their presence, but I don't see anyone around."

"Yes. They stay beneath the surface, beyond the harmful rays of the sun."

"You're a god. Why make them stay underground?"

The octopus gave a sympathetic wave. "I am not a god. I only embody their spirit."

He paused. "It was not always like this. The harsh radiation has damaged everything. I will show you."

As if in a time warp. the world spun backwards to when the Tritans lived on the surface. The white octopus showed Teagan visions of what life was like before the Tritans were forced to live underneath the planet's crust. The foliage sang and blossomed, while the skies were blue and bright. The planet was populated by long-extinct beings that were tall and graceful, with large wings like those of a butterfly, and long, flowing, robe-like skins that glittered in many shades of blue and gold. They moved gracefully around the land, their voices echoing in harmony.

But then, without warning, disaster struck from above.

A huge burst of radiation rained down like a curtain of death onto the planet's surface. Everything changed in an instant as the air was engulfed by a wave of heat and dust. Rocks and debris fell from the sky like rain. Shockwaves caused giant mudslides, wiping almost everything out. The once idyllic landscape was engulfed in chaos and destruction.

Few survived this cataclysm. Those who did suffered greatly; many died due to radiation exposure, while others faced physical deformities caused by its effects on their DNA over time.

With no other option, they banded together, searching for any place where they could be safe from extinction. After days, they stumbled upon a large cave—the entrance to a vast underground tunnel system.

Realizing this was their one chance, the Tritans moved permanently into the underground caverns deep beneath the planet's surface. Over time, they adapted to their new home, excavating a new underground city system and building a new way of life, flourishing as best they could. Their bodies adapted and evolved to the new circumstances.

Underground, they worked hard to preserve their traditions.

They liked dance and storytelling and developed cave art. One day, on the wall of one cave, someone drew two circles connected by two curved lines that looped around each other. This symbol intrigued everyone who saw it, and soon stories began circulating about how this infinite loop represented a powerful octopus deity from ancient times when people lived above ground.

These tales gathered many adherents and inspired those living underground for centuries afterward; for them, this symbol wasn't just an image, but rather a reminder that, no matter how much time passed, their connections remained strong through eternity.

The spirit of the octopus was said to provide guidance and protection when times became tough; he was believed to be able to look into a person's heart and help them find answers, even in difficult situations. The symbol of infinity became his symbol, reminding those who saw it that there would always be hope for another chance at life's journey.

"I gave them hope and continuity," the octopus said. "I gave them a super-intelligence to shield them in times of crisis."

Teagan started to shudder, and she wondered if it was from the sheer emotional strain of having to simulate a ritual of their religion before their very eyes, or if it was something else.

She spoke the words, telling the story of how the awakened god had protected the Tritans from disaster. They rolled off her tongue with the cadence and intonation of one who had uttered them a thousand times.

As she recited the prayers, she knelt, matching her breathing to the rhythm of the stranded spaceship nearby.

When the words dried up, a drumming sound came from deep in her throat, seeming to tranquilize the Tritans. She kept going until she could not breathe any longer. When she finished, there was a brief silence. Covered in sweat, her body trembled from exhaustion.

A rumbling emerged from the throats of the Tritans, as though they were gargling. Teagan felt Asimov slip back into her consciousness. The bonding was done. They had complete trust in their priestess.

"Speak your request," she declared, catching herself by surprise with her firmness. Her voice was raspy and serrated.

"We have been here a long time. When will we be rescued?" asked one, reflecting what was on all of their minds.

Teagan paused. "Your answer lies in your journey. Complete your mission, and you will find your reward."

"How do we complete our mission?" Asimov asked. "We feel abandoned and alone." His voice was urgent and fearful.

"I see violence and a storm. A lost crystal stone. Those who have it acquired it by chance. They do not understand its true value. It is locked away in a wooden box. Exchange it for a life, and relief will come."

98

The Sting

Levi-Civita Lunar Crater, 2090

THE LIGHTS ON THE console flashed in front of him, but Baolin stared dejectedly without taking things in. His failure to capture a prized asteroid had left a bitter taste in his mouth. He had a reputation he had to protect.

Failure wasn't going to help the aura of invulnerability he had built over the years. Even when he had lost part of his face in the "lava gas fiasco," as he called it, something that would break normal men, he hadn't let it prevent him from being the warrior he always knew he was destined to be.

Baolin still remembered fondly his times with Alimjan, but when it finally came, he had jumped at the opportunity to fly with the Iron Hornets. They offered excitement and the prospect of becoming rich. They had done him a favor by kidnapping him. Quivira was so sterile. He missed his brothers and sisters and the games they would play. But this was real life.

During flight training, he had flown best in class in the simulator. The problem was he hadn't flown in formation—he disobeyed orders and had caused a more than acceptable death toll to his team. His supervisor's report read, in part: *Though he has great potential, he lacks team and leadership qualities, and a sense of empathy.*

The supervisor's report had ended with the recommendation that Baolin be removed from the program, but General Lin had vetoed the idea and paired Baolin with Captain Han Bai. Captain Han had become head of the Hornets after Razor retired. A decorated soldier, he had lost his family in the Great Unraveling. He had vowed to get his revenge by harassing and sabotaging western mining operations and convoys.

For the next five years, Han led his Hornets on daring raids throughout the lunar-verse. He and Baolin had developed a relationship based on mutual respect and admiration.

One day, the Hornets had gone to attack a small Japanese mining station. The operation was managed remotely from Tokyo. The bots present at the facility were easily immobilized with electronic jamming equipment.

After flying over the site, Han had disembarked from the lead craft, instructing his flightbot to fly steady while he examined the asteroid crater the Japanese had been mining.

"Baolin, keep a sharp eye out for intruding stealth craft that might not come up on our radar until the last second," Han instructed.

Baolin checked the instrument cluster in front of him before replying, "Yes, Commander. Radar clear. The seismograph is showing some seismic activity under the crust a few clicks to your left."

He could hear the grin in Bai's voice when he said, "I hear you, Sting; I'm more concerned about those drones at six o'clock. Radio silence until you hear from me, over and out."

Baolin scowled. He hated the name Sting. Han had said he was the sting in the Iron Hornet's tail, but apart from Han Bai, no other Iron Hornet had dared call him Sting to his face.

Baolin instructed the others to look out for drones and other craft while his attention was on the seismograph. He didn't like the readings he was getting from it. He was about to alert Han to be careful when he heard the man's voice in his ear.

"I think we hit the motherload, Sting. From an initial drilling, we have enough minerals in the remnants of the asteroid that struck here to live like maharajas, if we can extract the core. Position the craft and the harness. Let's haul out part of our prize for assessment and testing."

There was a ripple of excitement through the ship. After years of scrounging, they were finally getting their due.

Baolin called out to other ships. "You heard the commander; move into position, prepare a harness. I want a clean operation, in and out in no time."

The AIs were steering the ships when Baolin heard a loud noise that sounded like a gunshot. His first impression was that they were being attacked, but nothing was on the radar to suggest that. Baolin turned to White Tiger, an AI in control of his ship.

"What was that?"

The AI replied, "There's a fissure on the crater's surface, close to where Commander Han is. Maybe it was disturbed by the earlier Japanese drilling."

Baolin didn't have to think. He hurriedly suited up.

"Try to get Bai on the radio. I'm going out there."

White Tiger replied, "The commander's instructions were clear; we have to get the ships in position to assess the core."

Baolin didn't bother to answer. As soon as he was suited, he stopped his craft and got out.

"White Tiger, send me his last known coordinates and let me know if he responds to the radio calls."

Baolin input Han Bai's last location on his craft's GPS. He noted that the quickest route was across the crusty surface where the seismic activity was coming from.

The terrain was not previously known to be tectonically active around here. Trying to go around it would mean wasting time he didn't have.

Baolin made his decision and steered the rover in the assigned direction, swerving to avoid craters that appeared to open without warning more than once. As he got closer, the ground seemed more unstable. White Tiger hadn't come on the comms, which meant he hadn't been able to pick up Han on the radio.

Suddenly, Baolin heard Han's voice. "What the hell are you doing, I told you to get craft in position, not stage a rescue mission."

Baolin felt a surge of relief. He replied, "I'm sorry, Commander, but getting you safe supersedes anything that might be on that bleeding asteroid carcass. Now sit tight and quit whining. I'm coming to get you."

He shut off his radio before Han could protest, and checked his charted course again. He could monitor a force emanating from the surface that was causing the vibrations.

But instead of reducing speed or changing course, he gunned the throttle. He needed enough momentum to cruise over the area where Han Bai was trapped. It was risky, but it was the fastest way.

Abruptly, Baolin was faced with a sheer-faced, jagged mound protruding from the surface like a sore thumb. It loomed over the ship, and he had to take evasive actions to avoid smashing right into it.

A frisson of fear shot down his spine. Why hadn't he seen that? He had half an urge to turn back. But he retained the image of Bai in danger. His commander would do the same for him if the situation was reversed.

Gunning the craft, Baolin began his ascent. To his right, he spotted a yawning vent in the ground. Maybe the work on the asteroid crater had disturbed something deep below.

As he was close to landing, two things happened at once.

His radio, which he thought was off, suddenly came to life. White Tiger's voice said, "Careful, Baolin; by my calculations, that vent contains trapped gases that could be released suddenly." Startled by the distraction, he reduced his speed, costing him much-needed altitude.

The second thing was, just as White Tiger had predicted, the vent abruptly spewed out poisonous gases. The pressure from the eruption tossed the light craft like a kite on a windy day. Baolin tried to regain control, but it was too late. The high-pressure gas enveloped his vehicle, igniting something. His fire-retardant suit immediately began smoldering, his helmet shattered, and pain ripped through him as he felt his face melting.

Landing on the other side of the fissure, in incredible pain and drifting in and out of consciousness, Baolin checked his oxygen mask and tank; any leak and he'd turn into a human torch.

Despite his agony, Baolin scanned around him, looking for any sign of the commander. Nothing. He scanned some more. Just as he was about to give up, Baolin saw something that lifted his spirits. Han's prone figure was several feet away, lying behind a rock.

With first-degree burns on his face, several broken bones, and what he suspected was a concussion, Baolin was in no condition to get there. He needed medical attention himself. Hoping against hope that his craft's transponder wasn't damaged in the crash, he gave himself to the darkness seeping over his consciousness.

When he awoke, Baolin felt like he was still on fire. He tried to move his head, but realized that it was in a vise. His mouth was dry, as though it had been stuffed with cotton wool. He tried to open his eyes, but they were covered.

He heard a male voice say in accented Mandarin, "Welcome to the land of the living Bao; you gave us quite a scare."

Baolin tried to speak.

The man seemed to sense his pain and said, "My name is Alimjan. Please relax; you are in great hands."

Baolin drifted back into a dreamless, medically induced sleep.

He was in a coma for five days before he awoke. He felt battered and groggy. They must have pumped all kinds of drugs into him. As he began to recover day by day, he took stock of his injuries. He had lost his right ear and lower jaw, had three broken ribs, and his right femur was broken in three places.

He tried to say something to Alimjan, but speech was impossible for the moment,

To his horror, Han Bai had lost his life. White Tiger told Baolin that a huge boulder had crushed him before the ships could get to them. Baolin battled with the guilt. If only he could have reached the commander faster.

It was some time before it dawned on him who Alimjan was — the blood brother who had rescued him. Why was he here in this forsaken outpost? "I do stints of time with the Hornets when I'm away from the hospital. My way of giving back."

When Baolin was able, he embraced the friend he had not seen for so long. He hugged Alimjan tight even though it hurt. "Good to see you," he stuttered, his words barely understandable.

Alimjan said he would need facial reconstruction. But Baolin rejected cosmetic surgery, saying, "These scars are a private memorial for the master, Han Bai."

Instead, he opted for a nano-mesh-enhanced carbon mask to hide his scars. The doctors told him he would walk again in six months. Even then, he would walk with a limp.

Baolin took the news without reaction. When the time came for his physiotherapy, he faced it with a sense of determination that bordered on obsession.

Sometimes Alimjan would join him to see how he was doing. They would talk about the old days and the mother who made delicious qiegao candy.

After only three months, he could walk without aid. A month later, he was running with minimal sign of injury. Within six months, Baolin was once again a leader of the Iron Hornets. It was a remarkable recovery, Dr. Alimjan told him with a smile.

"I can't thank you enough," Baolin said, his heart indebted to his blood brother once again, even if Alimjan could still scarcely recognize Baolin because of his badly scared face.

"Call me if you need anything. I am perpetually in your debt."

"Thank you. You never know. We may need your help sometime, the way things are going."

Baolin could only nod in response, too choked up with emotion. Dr. Alimjan had been instrumental in saving his life, not once, but twice. He would find it hard to repay him.

99
The Matryoshka

Traveling in the Asteroid Belt

T HE FIRST PHASE OF Guy's long journey to capture the Matryoshka asteroid had gone as expected; the only scare was a meteor shower around the rings of Saturn.

To minimize potential damage, Guy had ordered the vessels to disperse. "Scatter, evade, then regroup." The crew understood Guy's shorthand; the three tugs left formation, veered away to take evasive actions—including having to blast some meteors to avoid hitting them—then regrouped when the danger passed.

"Good job, guys. Keep your eyes peeled; we have officially passed Saturn heading toward Jupiter. Congratulations, people."

There were a few muttered cheers, but the crew mainly focused on the job at hand.

The rest of the journey was uneventful until they approached Jupiter.

Howie Rich's face appeared on the monitor. "Hey there, guys, I just wanted to say how proud of you I am. You're the best there is; when you guys get back, we're going to throw a concert for you on Halona and drink for a week. Except for Captain Zephron, of course," Howie hastily added. "Good luck, and see you soon."

Then the monitor went back to showing murky space. Howie's appearance had lifted morale.

As they got closer, Guy spoke into the comms again, "We're approaching the asteroid. This is it, people, let's do our jobs."

The official name for the asteroid was Valdenia 53, but Guy still privately referred to it as Matryoshka, hoping it contained more than appeared on the outside, with several layers of minerals.

When it came into view, Guy was awed. It was beautiful—not as huge as some asteroids he had hauled, but it seemed to have a glow, a radiance, as if it held secrets. An AI scan of Valdenia 53 sent a list of its constituent elements to Howie Rich on Halona.

Guy's favorite way of capturing an asteroid was to harpoon and net it. It was just like the whaling ships of old: Spear the beast and envelop it in a tensile net.

"Harpoon ready," a voice said into the headset Guy was wearing.

Guy replied, "Target asteroid," and a few seconds later, the same voice replied, "Asteroid locked in, ready to fire at your command."

The trick with this method was to fire the harpoons at an angle that would eradicate the effects of the asteroid's tumbling rotation on the tugs.

"Prepare the net, proceed with acquisition. Fire."

Three harpoons fired at the same time, streaking behind the prize and guiding the carbon-fiber netting into place.

Their weeks of practice paid off; the capture was as seamless as any Guy had seen. The lattice unfurled behind the asteroid like a parachute, and the tugs pulled the guidelines taut so that they could maneuver the giant rock onto a new path. Two bots added temporary thrusters onto the back of the asteroid to aid flight path adjustments.

"Harpoons on target, asteroid retrieval under way."

Guy nodded; everything was going according to plan so far. "Let's bring Valdenia 53 home." For the first time since the mission began, he smiled. "Congratulations, team, that's half the job done. Great job. I'm proud of you."

Cheers erupted.

Guy continued to smile as he gave his next order. "Set course for ElleWon, keep your eyes peeled. The hard work starts now." He was starting to sound like a fortune cookie, talking in clichés.

Just as Guy had simulated, they encountered no problems until they got to ElleWon's approaches near the Earth's moon.

The pitted outline of the Valdenia 53 asteroid, shaped over eons by the relentless battering of cosmic rays and solar winds, loomed through the darkness, towed in procession by Guy's three well-armed tugs, and lit by the luminescence of the Moon on one side and the blue radiance of planet Earth on the other.

"Captain Zephron, my sensors are picking up a high level of radiation a few miles ahead. I think we're about to enter a solar radiation surge. What are your orders, Captain?"

Guy tried to calm himself. There were no evasive maneuvers for a surge. The radiation came with an electromagnetic pulse that could shut down spacecraft and leave them in floating limbo.

Guy sighed and said, "Lower the Faraday cages on all our tugs; I hope the plan works."

The cages were designed to protect the craft from the worst of the surge, sealing them from fallout.

As they passed through the surge, Guy felt the tug he was in slow down.

"AI, add more speed." Guy wanted to leave this surge as soon as he could.

The intelligence replied, "We are going at full speed, Captain. I am deducing that the cages are slowing us down. *Valdenia 53* is also somehow reacting with the radiation. What do you want me to do, sir?"

Guy didn't even consider the question. "Leave that shit for the geologists. How much more surge do we have to go through?"

The AI took a few seconds to calculate before replying, "We are through the worst. Five more minutes at the most, Captain."

Guy waited twenty minutes before he ordered the cages lifted; he didn't want to take any risks. As he did so, *Valdenia 53* was jolted by a large, unobserved object scraping it like a plane hitting the top of a mountain.

Shudders wracked the entire structure. It was like a boat running aground but in mid-air.

"What in God's name was that?" Zephron demanded in shock. "I thought there was nothing around us."

"Checking," the navbot said calmly.

"We were hit by an unidentified craft. It was in stealth mode, so we did not see it."

"Why the hell did *it* not see *us*? We'd light anything up like a Christmas tree," Guy fumed.

"Where did they go?"

"Couldn't track them," responded the navbot.

"Crew, what's your status? AI, run diagnostics on the tugs."

To Guy's relief, all the crew members were safe and feeling good. The AI reported that the ship was in good health; the only problems were with Valdenia 53. Part of the asteroid had a puzzling radiance about it, as if the impact had released some kind of energy that was now illuminating the rock from within.

The glow was being picked up by his sensors, but it wasn't affecting anything else, for now. But what could have caused it?

Guy Zephron was determined to keep it quiet until he got paid—a battle for control of whatever the asteroid contained was the last thing he needed. But what secrets did this strange rock hold? He was about to find out first hand.

100

The Docking

Approaching ElleWon, March 2101

THE *VALDENIA 53* ASTEROID was near the end of its months-long journey, and would soon be parked at the ElleWon space station, ready to be stripped of its riches by a team of robotic miners who would use the resources they found for the construction of more space habitats orbiting the Earth. It was a highly profitable business for the Space Consortium of miners and multi-billionaires who had invested in space after the economic collapse of the Great Unraveling.

They were within hailing distance of the Moon's L1 Lagrange point, where the ElleWon space station was anchored. Guy couldn't keep the pride out of his voice. "Cut speed to a crawl."

Glancing out to his left, Guy could see the familiar outlines of the giant Imbrium Basin—the right eye of the fabled Man in the Moon—on the scarred lunar surface more than sixty thousand kilometers below. Amazing how frequently the Moon had been hit by asteroids when he and his crew had traveled for months, enduring solitude and isolation, to collect this one, he mused.

Even after half a lifetime in space, Guy was still overwhelmed by the beauty and majesty of the cosmos. The innumerable colors engulfed his senses. In that moment, Guy was reminded of why he loved space travel, and why it was worth all the effort and occasional loneliness.

"Coming in smoothly, chief," one of the men called out.

Guy gently acknowledged. He was proud of how his hardened asteroid recovery crew of both people and experienced bots had welded into a real team that worked together without explicit instructions. No, they would not betray him. He made sure that the ships that were trailing them, the *Defender III* and *IV* were alert, and he sighed deeply, marginally satisfied.

Guy cracked his neck. He was tense, but his time in service had taught him never to show how he felt to his crew. He gritted his teeth as he took a sip of lemon water.

"Hello Zephron, this is ElleWon. We can see you clearly. You're on a good course to dock with us. We'll guide you in. Over."

The crackle of the radio receiver quickly snapped Guy's weary mind back to the immediate and intricate task at hand of docking an asteroid with a delicate space station. He exhaled deeply and cracked his neck again.

The station crew and a team of bots watched as the dark, looming mass approached without menace. Bancroft's crew stood ready to secure the asteroid so that it would not roll and spin the ship out of control. Docking was the riskiest part of the whole process.

Captain Zephron guided the giant bottle-shaped rock close to the facility so that it could be tethered in place and be ready for mining.

"Steady," he instructed the other tugs.

Bancroft watched the navigation screen in front of her from her spartan control center as the imposing mass approached, accompanied by three green blobs that denoted Zephron's team. The shadow from the asteroid advanced over the deck of the station, making vision more difficult in the contrasting lights. Nevaeh, now a radiation specialist on ElleWon, looked up at the giant silhouette looming over her and felt tiny in comparison. She both hated and loved her sense of the insignificance of humanity in comparison to the vastness of space. But humans, like ants, had strength in numbers, and they were slowly reshaping the universe, one asteroid and space colony at a time.

Commander Bancroft noticed on one edge of her navigation screen that four new unidentified blobs were approaching them at speed from the direction of the Moon's near side. "Are we expecting someone?" she asked.

Guy saw the four blobs on his screen as well. He pulled his shoulders back and gripped the controls. In a way, he was relieved that they were finally here and he could deal squarely with them. Still, he hated the stress and the inevitable loss that this would cause.

Bancroft sounded the alarm. "Crew to quarters. Everyone be alert. I need someone on those side cannons. Tina, to the bridge immediately. Activate the energy shield."

As the four unidentified craft narrowed the distance between them, Guy continued his docking maneuver. The second tug fired a wire. Nevaeh raced to secure it to an external cleat. "Reverse thrusters on," commanded Guy.

He turned to the four crafts that were now within sight. They weren't cruisers. These were military-grade blitzes. Though they were old, the blitzes were lethal. From their size, Guy knew that they had not come for the entire asteroid but a piece of it. They would get nothing from him. "Be ready to open fire," he instructed his crew.

On ElleWon, Ved stepped forward to support Nevaeh. Nevie bit her lip as the asteroid loomed larger, her body exposed and defenseless.

"Easy," instructed Bancroft. "Remember the asteroid has its own impetus."

As Nevaeh and Ved edged forward on the smooth, metallic surface to grab the line, the rear tug relaxed control. The line's tension slackened, and the huge asteroid gained momentum and started tossing, almost crashing into the gossamer-thin station. Pieces broke off as they struck the station in a slow-motion collision. Nevaeh was pitched to the side by the force, struggling to maintain her grip.

"Captain Zephron," shouted Commander Bancroft. "We need some tension from the rear tug, or else you will spear us. And please keep an eye on those four. They don't look very friendly."

The raiders fired a microwave blast that was meant to disable communications. Guy ordered his bots to open fire. He knew they wouldn't be able to avoid hitting parts of ElleWon's fragile exterior structures, but the risk was worth it.

The bots responded with laser fire that lit up the entire near space, but the enemy swung close to ElleWon's bridge deck, making it difficult to shoot at them and increasing the risk of hitting outside girders. The four vessels circled the prize like hyenas, darting in and out. "They're too close. Destroy that lead one," ordered Bancroft, steel creeping into her voice. "Now."

A cannon mounted on a forward strut belched a stream of flame, and one intruder shattered into little pieces. Shots hit the asteroid's surface, tossing small, lethal shards of regolith that speared through the air. "I'll take one of them," a voice came in. "That should even things up a bit, eh?"

Guy looked outside and saw *SpaceSweeper III* waiting to dock. "Hunter! Perfect timing." Hunter had been monitoring the progress of the docking maneuver, waiting his turn. He'd watched the chaos and decided it was time to lend a hand. They hadn't worked so hard to lose everything now.

With its huge fairing doors, designed to open and capture floating debris the size of dead satellites, the ship could use its powerful magnets to lure a target in and then snap its sturdy doors shut over it like a clamshell. Hunter lined the *Sweeper* up behind one of the intruders. Although they were faster moving, he was able to anticipate how they would bank out of a turn and be ready for them.

Once they were in range, they got sucked in toward the open payload space by the magnetic force. The intruder's powerful thrusters battled to counter the abrupt and unexpected force. But the *Sweeper*'s neodymium magnets outmatched the intruder's thrusters. The raider started to slip backward. The doors of the *Sweeper* opened like a pelican's beak and closed over the small craft, shutting tight with a definitive click.

Tina, one of the crew members on the station, fired. One attacker lit up in shimmering green and stuttered to a halt, sparks flying from the engine. The wire of the lunar hoist sliced through the remnants of the intruder's ship as it hurtled out of control. The two remaining unprotected raiders peeled off and took flight back to their base, leaving behind a trail of debris that glistened in the murky light.

Something more for Hunter to clean up, Tina thought.

Zephron kept quiet for a few seconds, savoring the feeling before saying, "Welcome home, heroes." Hunter sat, breathing heavily. That had been tight. He worried that a team of only four pilots could come so close to snatching such a big shipment.

Only later would they realize that the *Valdenia 53* cradled within its ancient veins a mystery of the universe destined to shape them all.

101

The Interrogation

ElleWon, March 2101

CAPTAIN ZEPHRON DIDN'T TAKE long to find out who the raiders were. Interrogation methods in outer space were hardly covered by the Geneva Convention.

After Guy obliterated one AI with a pulse weapon, his cyborg colleague admitted they were part of the Hornets.

"Who's your leader?" Zephron had demanded, knowing the answer.

A reply was given in Mandarin.

"Who's that?" Bancroft asked.

"Baolin," explained Zephron.

"He's a nasty piece of work," injected Hunter. "Ruthless."

"What were they after?"

Guy wasn't sure, so he mumbled some explanation. "China doesn't recognize the Space Consortium, so they've licensed freelance teams to take potshots at us. Do a bit of softening up. Sometimes they do a bit more than that."

"Well, at least we beat them off decisively, with Hunter's help."

As the news filtered through the space station, it hit Nevie and Ved particularly hard.

"Oh my God, that was Baolin who attacked us!" exclaimed Nevaeh. "The little brother we all knew and loved. How did he become like that?"

Nevaeh still couldn't get it out of her head. They had all been shocked when he was abducted. Now he was a space pirate and had tried to kill them!

"The little prick," muttered Ved, who was less sentimental.

102
The Excursion

ElleWon, June 2101

N EVAEH TOOK SEVERAL MONTHS to recover from her injuries gained in the assault. Her tether had snapped during Valdenia 53's docking, tearing through a tendon. She was now walking much better, but was well behind schedule as she waited for the external airlock to be free.

The airlock was always a congestion point, but the wait gave Nevaeh time to think about her to-do list for the day. Before her injury, Nevaeh's job had entailed a daily inspection of the radiation force field and protective inner and outer coatings, to check for wear and tear. Inside the space station, she also looked after the farm. She was a trained astrophysicist and astrobiologist. While growing up on Quivira, she had chosen to study remotely through Iowa State University because her idol, space scientist James van Allen—after whom the Van Allen Radiation Belts were named—was a noted alumnus.

But today she was scheduled to show around a mining journalist from the *Asteroid Registrar*. Getting favorable coverage from the *Registrar* was important for attracting new investment.

The reminder went off belatedly on her screen visor: *Meet BT at reception.* She floated herself along to the station's reception and scanned around. She sidled up to a bot and, with all the awkwardness of a human interaction, tapped him on his metallic shoulder and queried, "Are you BT?"

It spun round, whizzing and flashing. "BT is not an AI," it responded. "Although he might aspire to be."

"Oh!" she said as she withdrew awkwardly. "My apologies."

"I'm BT," said a tall young man from behind a pillar. "Benjamin Taylor, at your service," he announced with mock heroism.

She stood with her mouth open. "I'm sorry. Usually, they send us AIs these days. Nothing is done by humans."

"No apology needed. My intelligence is entirely natural. So I'll probably be slow on the uptake."

"Very funny! I'm Nevaeh," she replied. "But most people call me Nevie."

"Most people call me Ben." Ben, sporting one of the new comfortable styles of space wear, looked athletic for a desk-bound human.

"Great." Nevaeh tugged at her hair. "I suppose we can start at the observation deck. You have a good view of the Moon from there."

"That would be great. But I'm really here to take a look at your asteroid," said Ben. "By which I mean the hunk of rock on your doorstep," he added hastily when Nevaeh glanced at him quizzically.

From the observation deck, they could see the expanse of the adjoining pock-marked asteroid mine anchored with taut cables. The surface looked scarred, uneven, and crumbly. A swarm of mining bots, grasping the surface with barbed feet, siphoned up the regolith and grit through proboscis-like drills, while others vacuumed up the debris left in their wakes with rotating wheels.

"They look a bit like anteaters, don't they?" Ben mused.

"Hopefully, this area contains seams of ore. It's also the main source of our water supply, apart from recycled water and what's produced by our Sabatier processor," Nevaeh said. "The 'anteaters' suck up the regolith, which is fed into a processor and heated to release water vapor, which is collected in a storage tank. Some is reprocessed as rocket fuel, since we're a refueling station. These big grinders separate the ore from the dirt.

"As you can see, mining and processing an asteroid like this is much more discrete and more contained than Earth or moon mining. We don't need heavy mining and transport machinery, we don't need complex chemical processing as on the Moon to exploit valuable seams, and waste disposal is achieved by just repacking material into a hole in the asteroid. However, the near zero-gravity space environment has its unique challenges as well."

"So, it's a miniature form of strip mining, without the huge trucks?" commented Ben as he removed dust from his visor.

The excavator's large, spinning bucket drums scooped up the dirt as it was clawed out by the machine's razor-like digging scoops. The rotating bucket drums collected and held the excavated regolith.

"Next, we have the control center. This is Joe Martin, who is on duty today."

A tall, wiry man, Joe Martin appeared oversized for his cramped office, with its panoramic view of the robotic excavators processing ore and tailings in the mine.

"Greetings, Mr. Martin. How long have you worked here?" asked Ben.

"About four months. I'm fixin' to be here four more." He had a Tennessee twang to his voice.

"So, you can see the whole mine surface from here, and the entryway to the ElleWon?"

"Yes, correct." Martin was a man of few words. He kept his eyes firmly on the bank of control screens in front of him.

"Seems like a complex job. Do any of the bots ever malfunction or get stuck? What happens then?"

"Anything wrong, we have a repairbot go sort it," Martin replied.

"Hey, I've an idea. Can we take a ride over that ridge to where they're tunneling?"

"I expect so, if Joe will let us," said Nevaeh.

Joe grunted, and they were off, bumping across the flaky pyroclastic surface in their small mining transporter.

As they headed across the asteroid, they looked back at the imposing outline of the space station. Some clear signs of the attack by the Iron Hornets remained visible, including shrapnel holes and pockmarks across the outer shell. But the regolith radiation shielding had absorbed much of the onslaught.

Ben was silent for a bit as the drama of the panorama sank in.

"I want to get to that ridge over there," he said, pointing to a truncated hillock sticking up on the skyline. "The view will be fantastic, and it will show us how big the asteroid is."

"Yeah, I've never been that far," said Nevaeh, aware that her boss had told her to do the minimum to keep Ben happy and then send him on his way.

"Can we go any faster?" asked Ben, with a thrill in his voice as he took in the vastness of the scene.

"We're not allowed to stir up the dust. It gets inside the bots and makes them malfunction."

"You know, thousands of people on Earth invest in these asteroid mines and are making a fortune. But they've no idea what they look like."

"How many have you visited?" Nevaeh asked, curious.

"I don't get to ride across one that often," Ben said. "Most of my interviews and inspections are by video conference. Investors want to know what the returns are, the mineral composition, how much silicate rock, what type of precious metals. They don't treat it as a travel destination. But this time, I took a chance and here we are," he said with a grin. "Guess I got lucky!"

As they lurched along across loose slurry and stretches of sand and boulders, they came across two bots digging a trench.

"What are they doing?" asked Ben.

"Getting samples for the next dig," said Nevaeh.

"Got to take pictures. It's great against that amazing background."

"Halt, transporter," Nevaeh ordered, and the transporter lurched to a stop, somewhat awkwardly, on a slope. "Parking mode on."

Ben got out, made sure the ground was firm, and walked a little bit away. The bots were drilling a long hole.

"It's a Ditch Witch, they call it," shouted Nevaeh.

Ben crouched on the crusty regolith, his space suit scraping the surface next to an old lava channel. "Wow, it's fantastic! So stark," shouted Ben.

"Be careful, the ground can be very unstable. The bots can grip with their claws."

"Just a couple of minutes and I'll be done."

"I'll be here if you need me. Just shout! I'll be working on some files."

Ben took a couple of steps toward the retreating bots, noticing changes in the way he moved as he tried to get used to his weightless body.

"My legs don't seem very useful in space," he muttered as he lolloped along. "I'm not sure why I brought them with me. But a stabilizing tail might be helpful because three points of stability is better than two."

Suddenly, he felt his foot tread through nothing, like missing a step on a flight of stairs. He somersaulted over and landed on his head. Stunned, he scrabbled for a rock but couldn't find a hold. His body was being sucked down as if it was in quicksand on the edge of space. His heart began to race, beads of sweat collecting on his visor. He tried to signal Nevaeh, but she couldn't see him. He was slipping more and more quickly. Was there a cavern beneath him? His feet couldn't get a grip. His visor was fogging up, and he screamed into his mouthpiece.

"Ben, are you okay?" Nevaeh asked, looking around.

"Negative in the extreme. I'm in deep shit."

"I'll move the transporter over so that we can help," she replied calmly.

When she got closer, she could see him half submerged where the ground had given way.

"I can't get a grip," shouted Ben. "I'm getting sucked down. It's like it has its own force."

"I'll call Joe for help."

"We don't have time. I'm getting crushed."

"Okay, I have a metal bar we can lay across and you can haul yourself out."

She slid the bar out of the transporter and over the crumbled regolith toward what she could see of Ben. He attempted to pull his torso out of the hole. He inched upwards, straining, but couldn't sustain the lift.

I wish I'd done more weight training, he thought. *This is going to be my end. A moron lost on the edge of space after taking one small step.*

"Joe, come in, Joe," Nevaeh called on the radio communicator.

"What is it?"

"We're in trouble, Joe. Can you help? Ben is stuck in a cavity and getting sucked in."

"Wait. Don't move. Be very still," commanded Joe, suddenly sounding authoritative and taking control.

As they waited in the dark stillness, one of the two bots sidled over to them. It looked down at Ben, gave an apparent snort, and wrapped its proboscis around the bar.

"Tell Ben to hold on," said Joe.

It heaved backwards, stirring up pebbles and sand from the regolith that splattered Ben's visor like hail.

"You're going to hurt him," screamed Nevaeh. "Be careful!"

At first, it just seemed to stretch him like a medieval torture machine, but gradually Ben began to edge upward. The bot dragged him onto a more stable patch of ground, and he lay there panting, spread-eagled like a drying animal skin.

"He's free, Joe!" Nevaeh shouted, a little too loudly. "You've done it."

"Great! Now take care, y'all. It's wild out there."

Ben lay still on the fine powdered surface, shards of silica pointing up like acupuncture needles. Nevaeh examined Ben's space suit.

"It's punctured, and I can see some blood. Can you get up?"

Ben struggled to find his feet but gradually managed to stand erect.

"Careful where you tread," said Joe.

Nevaeh helped Ben back to the transporter, eased him into the seat, and helped him settle. They made the journey back to the station in silence. Ben had his eyes closed, so he didn't see what looked like something green and shimmery in the hole he had gotten stuck in.

Maybe just a trick of the light, thought Nevaeh.

After Ben went to a room to get cleaned up, Nevaeh contacted Joe.

"You again!" he shouted.

"Joe," responded Nevaeh softly. "You may want to check out the spot where Ben slipped in the regolith. I think something may be in there, perhaps buried. I'm pretty sure it's worth investigating."

Nevaeh's mind was in overdrive. What would cause that weird glow? It seemed like a portal to another world, a portal that was beckoning her.

103
The Chat

"JEEZ, THAT WAS A bit of a comeuppance," Ben said, trying to make light of the incident.

"A what?" Nevaeh asked, puzzled.

"A dumbass humiliation."

"Yeah, well, you survived. Maybe you're luckier than you know."

"I think I stepped into a black hole! Thanks for saving my life. I thought I would slip below the surface and be engulfed in an asteroid."

"That would have been a story for your readers!" Nevie grinned. "But the bot saved your life, not me. Maybe you should thank Joe."

"I did already. He told me to go screw myself!"

They managed a laugh.

"But I feel great, like I have some superpowers. Don't know what it is."

"Okay then, so why don't we change the subject? Why don't you use your powers to tell me about life on Earth?" enquired Nevaeh.

Forehead creasing in confusion, Ben said, "What do you mean, precisely?"

"What's it like there? What's your favorite thing to do?"

"Oh! So you've never been there. How weird!"

Nevaeh shook her head. She had often dreamed of visiting her "home." Everything she'd read about Earth was beautiful: The stories, the people, the cultures. Even the history and fairytales were enchanting. When she was growing up, she'd read about witches, sorcerers, and magic spells.

The animals that roamed there were fascinating to her too. She had particularly liked the *Babar the Elephant* series, although she could never understand why anyone wanted to shoot an elephant. Elephants were so noble, clever, and dignified. Some people even worshiped elephants, which she could understand.

She'd been told that on Earth people slept horizontally on big, comfortable mattresses (sometimes with a pea under them), instead of the cramped, almost vertical cubicle she was used to, and she wondered what that might be like. She had tried horizontal before, but it didn't feel right.

She often imagined strolling through the woods, hearing the birds chirping, feeling the rain on her face, and plucking fresh, succulent strawberries from a field. She hoped to one day swim in the sea, her body immersed in salt water and brushed by the foam of the waves. But that idea seemed less likely as time went on. She didn't know how to swim, and there was far too much work here for her to consider a visit to Earth.

Ben's voice brought her back from her musings. "I love everything. I love breathing in the morning air. The seasons, and the flowers. I love being on the water. Out here is awesome, with the light and the stars, but on Earth it's more tactile."

Through the exterior porthole, Nevaeh could see Joe and the bots excavating something from the regolith and boxing it up.

Ben paused as he watched her attention focus elsewhere, then continued, "The other thing I love is the smell of freshly cut grass when someone is mowing the lawn and the earthy scent you get when rain falls on dry soil."

She glanced back toward him. "Yes, I know what that is," Nevaeh said, finding a connection to her pent-up knowledge. "Petrichor. The smell is caused by an oil exuded by certain plants during dry periods when it's absorbed by clay-based soils and rocks. During rain, the oil is released into the air along with geosmin, a metabolic by-product of certain actinobacteria, which is emitted by wet soil, producing the distinctive scent."

"I didn't know that," said Ben. "You are a mine of information!" He grinned at her.

Captain Zephron passed by their table, carrying gear and equipment.

"Hi, Guy! I thought you left ages ago."

"Yes," replied Guy. "I'm not here. Or I'm outta here. Was just moving something with Joe for Commander Bancroft. Safely in the hatch now, or soon will be. I'm headed to Halona to see Howie. First time in LEO for ages!"

"Okay, good luck," said Nevaeh.

Guy waved.

"Now you tell me something about you," Ben said, picking up from before the interruption.

"Well, I was born in space, on Quivira. One of seven experimental babies. We were the 'Magnificent Seven.'"

Ben's eyes widened. "I heard one of the seven had an accident?"

"Well, he's here actually. Meet Ved." She waved at Ved, who was having a snack nearby. "He's a bit of a cyborg," she whispered. "Some even say he has alien blood." She paused. "I was brought up in the Quivira space colony, taught everything either remotely or by tutors. Have you been to Quivira?"

"Yes, of course. I've been to Quivira and most of the other space colonies. Isn't Quivira run by the famous doctor?"

"Dr. César?"

"Yep, he's the one."

"He was my doctor, who pulled me from the incubator."

"Actually, he was the one who put you in the incubator," said Ben. "Yours is a famous story. Everybody on Earth knows it. That's why you were called Nevaeh. You were the first heavenly child. You are literally world and universally famous."

Nevaeh looked down, her thin hands grasping the tabletop firmly until she could feel the cold edge cutting into her skin. "Well, everyone might know me, but I know little about myself. We're a little cut off here, and I don't get the time to do a lot of research. I don't even know who my mother was."

"You mean the woman who contributed the egg for the fertilization? That's what they call her."

"Yes, I mean that," said Nevaeh sharply.

"According to the accounts, she had just arrived on Quivira. I think her name was Taylor, or Tessa, or something similar. Some T word. She was selected because she was young and healthy and had good characteristics."

"Sounds rather clinical," said Nevaeh. "And where is she now? I'd like to know her."

"I've no idea."

Nevaeh turned wide eyes to him. "Maybe you can help me find out?"

"I know a pianist who might know," said Ben without further explanation.

A chime on Nevaeh's wrist communicator told her the commander was calling. She knew what it meant: A radiation leak exposed somewhere in the ship.

104

The Find

ElleWon, June 2101

"HELLO, COMMANDER," NEVAEH SPOKE into the comms without taking her eyes off the boots she was adjusting.

"I need you down here in five," the commander ordered immediately.

"The leaks again?" Nevaeh asked.

"Something different," Bancroft replied. "I'm pretty sure you'll want to see this."

"Okay, Ben. I must go. Ved will take care of you. You can ask our resident alien a few questions."

Nevie approached the port-side hold below decks, where Commander Bancroft was waiting. She was standing in front of a wooden crate, the contents of which gave off a greenish glow. Eyeing the box, Nevaeh walked forward slowly.

"I've never seen anything like it," Commander Bancroft murmured. "The density, and that incandescence; there's something metallic about it. It seems to be a rock, but also almost alive."

Nevaeh kept her gaze focused firmly on the spherical stone about the size of a soccer ball inside the box.

"Any ideas where it's from?

Nevaeh shook her head. "I'd need to run some tests to determine that."

"And what is this greenish glow?"

Nevaeh poked the rock, and it emitted a burst of light. The ship's generator groaned, and the power surged. There was a loud whine as the external radiation shield was automatically reinforced and covered all parts of the station.

"Intriguing," Nevaeh muttered. She pulled out an instrument and began to take some readings.

The surface looked like an old mineral deposit from an exploded star or maybe a protoplanet. She tapped a small hammer lightly on the stone. A bright light surged for a few seconds before fading. Shocked, Nevaeh jumped away from the stone, breathing heavily. If a single tap could make it surge that much, there was no telling what the actual power of this stone might be.

"So, is this what the bastard was after?"

"Maybe, but how did he know about it?" asked Bancroft. "Say nothing of this to anyone!" she snapped suddenly. "No one must know we have this here, not even the Space Consortium and Howie Rich."

Nevaeh nodded. "Are you sure they don't know about this already?"

"Nobody has reported back to the Consortium about the crate. Only about securing the asteroid. If my suspicions are right," whispered Bancroft, "this stone is a relic from the old worlds. This may be a lost treasure or some unidentified object from a distant solar system. Maybe it fell off a spacecraft like a bouncing bomb."

"We need to run more tests," Nevaeh continued. "We don't know what could happen once we access its full potential."

"Oh, I know what will happen," the commander protested. "People will be dropping by to collect it."

Nevaeh nodded thoughtfully, eyeing the green glow. "I think there might be some sort of radiation leaking from it," she told Bancroft. "It's best if we both go for decontamination."

Using her protective gear, Nevaeh put the stone back in its casing and stored it in a secure locker. She made sure all the lights were off before she left the storage room and headed to the gym for her routine exercises.

105

The Fix

Marius Hills, June 2101

T HE TRITANS WERE GETTING agitated. Their spirits had been buoyed by
news of a rescue mission, led by Captain Calytricx Draeven. The *Arc-
turus Pathfinder 4* was nearby. Arrival was imminent. Then sudden gloom. The
Pathfinder had hit an asteroid. Asimov had tried to make contact with them, but
it was proving difficult. Two ships down. Maybe it was a pattern. Maybe it was
sabotage.

Noel noticed how the Tritans' spirits rose and fell with each fresh piece of news.
He made repeated visits to the Tritans to continue his studies, taking absences from
his teaching work at the university. Meanwhile, Teagan fulfilled her duties as their
priestess, performing the traditional rituals prescribed by Asimov.

The longer they waited, the more attached the Tritans became to Teagan. On
Clara's urging, Teagan at one point asked when they would let her leave.

Asimov was silent for a long time. Then he spoke softly and slowly, but she could
not mistake the subtle tension in his voice.

"I am afraid we cannot let you leave. This is a great time of need, and there are
things that only you can accomplish. There will be a time when you are no longer
essential, but that time is not today. My people are far from home without much
hope. You give them that hope. Please do accept my apologies for the discomfort
that it has caused you, but when we are called in the path of the divine traveler, it is
not an easy one and there are bound to be obstacles."

Teagan stared at him, then turned and walked away. She did not want him to start
dissecting her thoughts.

Noel was torn between attempting to arrange as quick an exit as possible and
trying to find out and document as much as he could about the Tritans. As it became
increasingly clear that the Tritans were not going to compromise over Teagan, Noel
and Clara began to talk together about alternative ways to arrange her escape and
return to Earth.

"We can't ask the Chinese again," said Clara. "They think we still owe them for
the failure to produce sellable human organs."

"We can't just bust out. The Tritans will track us down. Teagan's like a goddess to them."

"What powers does she have? Maybe she can order them to let her go."

"I don't think that'll work," Noel said, shaking his head. "They won't let her go until they have a way home. They need repairs to their propulsion system. The anti-gravity mechanism is blocked. Stupidly, they don't seem to carry a spare. *Plus ça change*."

"I'm going to contact that woman who helped us get into César's lab. Zeitan. She's linked to the Iron Hornets. They'll do anything if we pay them enough."

"You want them to break us out of here? That's crazy."

"Maybe while you and I are away. All they have to do is grab Teagan and get her home."

"It's worth considering," said Noel. "But I doubt they'll do it. We have nothing to offer."

The Tritans did not know how long they'd now have to stay in the Marius Hills. Their rescue ship had been damaged in a violent solar radiation storm. It had hit an asteroid that was being towed across its path and lost the crystal stone that was an essential part of its navigation equipment. Someone had been towing the asteroid on an uncharted path. Without the powerful stone, the craft could not navigate effectively. The ship had, however, been able to land on the lunar surface, near them in the Marius Hills area. With the damaged ship hidden by a cloaking shield, the two crews were in contact.

"The good news is that we can use parts from one ship to repair the other," Asimov told Noel, showing him how the bright-cut crystal slotted into the top of the navigation system. When he turned it on, it gave off a striking, luminous glow. "That can help us chart the way home through the cosmos. But it needs a functioning guidance system."

Noel summed things up succinctly: "You have the guidance crystal, they have the needed operating parts."

The Tritans quickly got to work, hoping that they would be able to fix their ship by pillaging the other. They could no longer rely on a reliable rescue.

Unsure how long all this would take, Noel and Clara needed a backup plan. Clara contacted Hunter.

"Do you know how we can find Zeitan again? We badly need her help."

Hunter stared at his parents, not sure how to respond. They were desperate, and he didn't want to disappoint them.

"I'll see what I can do," he said. Hunter wanted to get in touch with her as well. "I'll try to find her, Mom. But no guarantees."

"I want my daughter back!" pleaded Clara. "It's like we're in a brainwashed cult."

106
The Power

ElleWon, June 2101

O N ELLEWON, LOUD VOICES erupted in the storage room where Nevaeh had left the stone stored in its crate. She heard the sound of shattered glass.

Stealthily walking down the darkened corridor, she heard a man and a woman shouting at each other. Someone had left the door to the storage room ajar. Feeling her way past boxes of supplies and equipment, she moved quietly forward, aware that whoever was in the room could have a weapon ready to fire. She strapped on a gas mask that was kept at the entrance to the room.

As Nevaeh edged in, she heard a large crash. One of the station's crew members, Tina, was standing before the case, her hand on the stone. The stone began to glow with a strange incandescent light as she held it tight.

"Tina!" Nevaeh called out loudly, forgetting her caution. "Don't touch it. You need gloves. It's radioactive."

Startled, Tina turned toward her, her mouth opening to speak. Instead, her head began to split open. A fissure snaked across her skull like a lava flow, and Nevaeh could see Tina's brains surging as if someone had deliberately set them on fire. Her hands glowed so brightly that Nevaeh had to cover her eyes. Tina let out a weird, prehistoric gurgle and collapsed.

"What the hell are you doing?" Nevaeh managed to ask the man next to her as he went to pick up the stone. "No one was to enter here."

He only managed one step forward with the stone before he also collapsed to the ground. His body melted right into the floor, leaving the stone in its stead. A pungent smell filled the room, and Nevaeh had to use the gas mask to breathe properly.

She used her protective gloves to pick up the stone and return it to its case. Then, she left the room, reported Tina as "missing," and called for clean-up. Commander Bancroft would have to sort it out.

Nobody can be trusted on this space facility, Nevaeh thought.

107

The Appointment

Tricala lunar base, June 2101

H UNTER HAD MANAGED TO set up a rendezvous with Kiana. His fingers
tingled with excitement as he typed out the coordinates for their meeting
spot: The remote Tricala base, nestled on the desolate far side of the Moon.

He couldn't believe Kiana had agreed to rendezvous with him there. It was a risky
move, but he was willing to take the chance. He wasn't sure what she'd look like or
whether she'd still feel the same way about him. Or had time changed everything?

Flying over the Rich Industries helium fields on the Moon, Hunter saw the
rampant pollution and discarded waste already building up on the lunar surface.
Despite regulations—mostly ignored because they were unenforced—the company was polluting the lunar surface with abandon. Ever since they had closed down
Jared Lansky's Space Disposal Inc., the pollution had gotten worse, and more
blatant.

Hunter had been attracted to the shapes on the Moon ever since his father had
taken him to the Mount Lemmon observatory. Hunter had always been passionate
about protecting its environment and despised those who took it all for granted.

This has to stop, Hunter thought. He ran through the other planets mankind had
visited—Earth, Mars, Venus—and how every one of them was already blighted by
humanity's pollution. *We're going to wreck every planet we visit if we don't change
our ways.*

The problem on the Moon was the extraction of helium-3. It was abundant,
but huge amounts of regolith had to be mined to get to it, leaving terrible scarring
on the surface. Huge buckets scooped regolith from the surface and deposited it
on giant conveyor belts for processing. The regolith was then heated to extract
the helium and cooled during the huge nighttime temperature swings, resulting
in preliminary isotopic separation, before being put through a cryogenerator to
achieve maximum helium-3 concentration.

It was just like the old days at Arizona's Harmony Mountain mine. Rich Industries only cared about making a quick buck and leaving, with little regard for
the ecological consequences. With fossil fuels running out on Earth—or politically

impossible to use—and the need for cheaper alternatives, demand for helium-3, used in nuclear fusion, was soaring, along with solar energy.

The Tricala base was a desolate and lonely place, with half-finished buildings and a dusty landscape stretching out as far as the eye could see. By the time Hunter got there for his meeting with Kiana, he was getting more and more worked up. The sound of his own breathing echoed in his helmet, a constant reminder of the vastness of space.

"We've got to do something about Rich Industries," Hunter said when they'd found each other. "They'll wreck everything."

"Calm down, boyo. It's not that bad."

Hunter snorted, almost forgetting his real purpose, but got back on track. "Look Kiana, my family needs your help again."

"We got your sister out, didn't we? That should be worth something to you."

"Yes, I'm really grateful," Hunter said.

He'd heard about what went down at the lab. "But I haven't seen her. And my parents say she is missing again."

"That seems careless."

"My parents are desperate."

"Where is she now?"

"We don't know."

"How will you pay me?" She winked at him playfully.

"What would you like?"

"A little payment in kind would be appreciated."

"How kind? he joked.

"A small kiss or two would be appropriate. It's lonely out here on Tricala."

"Understandable," he said. "It's the far side."

Their faces drew together like magnets, their lips just a mere inches apart. It had been a long time. His gaze locked onto hers, and Hunter's lips curved into a playful smirk. She caressed his shoulders. Without hesitation, he leaned down and pressed his mouth against hers, igniting a spark of electricity that traveled through Kiana's entire body, a sensuous kiss that was brief but lingered between them, inviting them both to do more.

"I've wanted to do that for a long time," Hunter whispered.

"Me too," Kiana replied, wrapping her arms around his neck and pulling him closer as they kissed again.

Kiana's soft hands gently caressed the back of Hunter's neck as his fingertips traced the curves of her face. His hand cupped her cheek, his thumb gently stroking her skin. Kiana's heart raced, feeling the intensity of their connection, the desire for more growing with each passing second.

Finally, they broke apart, both of them winded. "I'd no idea how much fun the dark side is," whispered Hunter.

Kiana looked up at him. "I love you," she whispered. "I have since you knocked all my stuff over in the corridor. You were so adorably clumsy and apologetic."

"I've loved you since I spotted you at the kennel on Epona. That ass is a work of art!"

She laughed. "You looked so confused then too!"

"Me and Chester!"

They burst out laughing.

108

The Crystal

Halona, July 2101

H OWIE RICH WAS EXHAUSTED; he'd had a hectic week. First, an asteroid cave-in had caused significant damage to some bots and broken the mining supervisor's femur. It had caused an unnecessary--and expensive--delay. On top of that was something personal: His Oudry painting had gone missing. He assumed someone had stolen it. Maybe it was a warning. The fact that someone could break into his suite without showing up on his security cameras or triggering his silent alarms was worrisome. Howie felt violated; the Oudry had a special significance for him.

And he still didn't have possession of the mysterious stone he'd heard about. News of the stone's power had reached Howie's ears on Halona, but nobody would give him a clear idea of where the stone was. Bancroft was holding out on him.

"I've heard this crystal is one of the most powerful elements in the universe," Howie told Ofentse. "Anyone who manages to harness its power can navigate the galaxies. We don't want that power falling into the wrong hands now, do we?"

Howie gave instructions to drill the lunar asteroid to its core, believing the stone was located there. But the drilling had not yielded any results yet. The thought that the stone might not be in the asteroid was deflating to Howie; he was thinking about involving General Lin Wenyi. To do that, however, he needed to narrow down the stone's possible locations. Howie was already working on that. He didn't care what it would cost him. He had to get that stone.

As for the missing Oudry, Howie had already upgraded his security, decommissioned his securitybots, and put the word out to all fences on Earth. If anyone came in with his Oudry, he would hear about it at once. When he caught the thief, Howie promised to give whoever it was the slowest possible death.

"Get me the latest report on the caved-in asteroid. I also want the manifests for all crafts and shuttles that arrived a day before my suite was broken into, the day it was broken into, and the day after," he said to Ofentse. "And ask people there if they saw anything strange."

Usually, Ofentse didn't question Howie's authority, but this time he had to ask.

"I've gone through all the manifests a week before and after the theft. I didn't find anything out of the ordinary, just a few bots going backwards and forwards, maybe cleaning; I also went through all footage of arriving and departing shuttles. Maybe the painting has been misplaced on Halona."

Howie stared at Ofentse. "Since when do you get to question my authority?"

"My apologies, Howie. I will do as you instructed."

"Great. And please get me General Lin. I think we also need to have a chat with that Russian scientist, Polyakov. Arrange a visit for her to Halona as soon as possible." As Ofentse started to leave, Howie called out to him, "Ofentse, I'm sure you know the value of discretion in this matter."

Ofentse nodded. Privately, he thought Howie was losing his mind. What a jerk, to talk to him like that in such a condescending manner. Ofentse resolved to do something about Howie when this was all over.

109

The Prize

B AOLIN'S DREAM WAS TO take over ElleWon, one of the richest mining operations around. It had become an all-consuming obsession.

He wanted to teach the Space Consortium a lesson. But his team needed more discipline and coordination. He had tried to attack an ore-rich asteroid on its way to ElleWon, but he and his Iron Hornets had been beaten back. There was too much firepower against him.

Taking over ElleWon would be a fitting tribute to his mentor, Han Bai. It would make all members of the Iron Hornets rich, and would turn him into a legend; his story would be told millennia after his demise. He only needed information about armaments and defenses.

He had tried to get information via Ming Fan, but her intel was dated.

What he needed was someone on the inside who understood all the workings of ElleWon. He thought for some time, then called his deputy, Wu Zeitan. General Lin said she had recruited Zeitan, named after a former Chinese empress, to bring some professionalism to the Hornets.

Zeitan was as fearless as he was, cunning and smart. She always liked to be prepared. Her planning was meticulous.

She looked at Baolin, her dark eyes wary as she watched her commander, who was in a pensive mood.

"I need someone," he said, "on the inside of ElleWon, someone we can bend to our will. I prefer someone who has a grudge, not just someone who wants money."

"I'll look into it," Zeitan replied.

"Use all resources at your disposal. I expect something concrete by the end of the week."

Zeitan nodded and turned to leave, but Baolin called her back. "And Ze?" She turned back to her commander as he played with the jade handle of a knife. "This stays between us. I need the utmost discretion on this. Don't involve anyone else."

Zeitan nodded again and saluted. "Yes, Commander. I will not fail you."

Baolin stared into space after she left. He knew she would come up with something. With that settled, he cast his mind to other things. He knew of a possible treasure transporter that was lightly defended and ripe for the taking.

But this time, the security teams were waiting for him. It was as if they had someone on the inside who knew their operations. Both the Space Consortium and national governments started to reinforce patrols that would ensure freedom of skies and sweep away the raiders.

After a second failed hijacking attempt, Baolin's anger boiled over. He screamed as he dropped his laser gun on the table with a bang. The others moved as far away from him as possible, watching warily as he collapsed in a chair.

Baolin wasn't angry that the ship had escaped. He was furious about how it had happened. One of his own men had fired a canon that ripped the spaceship apart with Baolin and the rest in it. Baolin had managed to get out of the burning carcass because his carbon mask also came with a respirator. The others had been less fortunate.

He asked one of his bots to bring him something to drink. "Five years of drills and training, and it's all the same!" he shouted.

The bot shuffled forward gingerly with the drink. Baolin saw the bot's hesitation and became even more irritated. He grabbed the machine roughly by the shoulder and drew it closer.

"Why the hell are you so slow?!" he yelled, bringing his laser up and disintegrating the bot in front of everyone. It lay in a crumpled heap, particles and wires spinning sharply across the floor. The beam had also penetrated a human just behind the bot, felling him in an instant. Baolin's voice echoed in the silence that engulfed them. He breathed heavily as his crew cowered behind each other.

"Now, which one of you was foolish enough to fire that canon when I specifically ORDERED YOU NOT TO?" Baolin thundered.

His face mask glinted, giving him extra menace. "You are the Iron Hornets, the most ruthless and dangerous pirates that have plagued this galaxy. How did a tiny number of men manage to escape your grip? How?!"

As his anger began to subside, he asked, "Where is Ryder?"

The others pointed to the lifeless human on the floor directly ahead of him, and Baolin sighed theatrically. He returned to the chair and sat down again.

The mission had been a failure, and he'd lost the quite large percentage he would have made. But capturing ElleWon would make up for it tenfold.

110

The Solution

Hornets' pilot ship, August 2101

Almost a month later, Zeitan approached Baolin with some trepidation.

"Commander, I am sorry for the delay; it proved more difficult than anticipated. However, I think I've found a solution."

Baolin's face was expressionless. "I hope for your sake it is not a waste of my time."

Even though she had been his deputy for almost three years, Zeitan still found looking at a maskless Baolin an unnerving experience. "I'm sure you know about the seven children born on Quivira?"

Baolin made an impatient gesture. "What is this, a pop quiz? You know my history. I don't have time for stupidity, Zeitan. Do you have someone of interest or not?"

"Those children are now adults, just like you. The musician Ming Fan informed me that one of the children has been seeking information about her possible egg donor, Teagan Ward."

Baolin looked at Zeitan, suddenly interested. "Go on," he commanded.

"Apparently, the mother's being held on the Moon. She was originally in the lunar prison, serving time for trying to kidnap one of the babies. Now, Ming Fan tells me Nevaeh wants to meet her mother. I was thinking that if we offered to find and locate her mother and get her out, in return she might give us a way into ElleWon."

Zeitan wished she could read Baolin's mind as he gazed into space.

"Who is holding the mother now?"

"I think the Chinese have her. They freed her from the detention center in the Marius Hills, but continued to hold her because they felt she or her parents had reneged on a deal. I don't know the details."

"Well, that's out then. I don't think we can take on the Chinese government. Most importantly, how do we know this girl will betray her people for a woman she's never met? She's been on ElleWon for some time?"

Zeitan nodded; she'd considered these possibilities. "Ming Fan's source claimed she was desperate to meet Teagan Ward, and referred to her several times as her mother. I believe she'll play ball."

Baolin stared at her again. "Are you a mind reader, Ze? How can you assume what she will or won't do? You're trusting the word of Ming Fan, who hasn't even talked to her. Zeitan, I need a concrete plan, not hopes and conjectures."

Stung by the rebuke, Zeitan said, "Begging your pardon, Commander, but I believe with planning, and a little luck, we can do this."

"Maybe, but we've failed before."

"Commander, you gave me this responsibility; trust that I will never fail you."

Baolin brought out his knife with the jade handle. Fearing the worst, Zeitan moved back. He looked directly at her. As so often when she saw him directly, she was both repelled and drawn to the contrasting features of Baolin's face.

With his voice low and dangerous, Baolin told Zeitan, "Very well, you have my blessing. Keep me updated on the details. I need a concrete plan in a month."

When Zeitan left, Baolin went over her plan again in his mind. There were a lot of ifs and buts, but it might be workable.

He walked over to a bank of computers and said, "Computer, run a simulation of these factors and give me a percentage of success." He put in the variables and waited a few seconds while the AI ran the numbers.

The first results gave him hope. He rearranged the parameters and told the computer to run another simulation. The numbers were better. He smiled; Ze might just be onto something. He instructed the computer to send the scenario, probability, and parameters to Zeitan.

When Nevaeh and the other six were born, there had been a buzz all over the world. The heavenly babies, they were called. Baolin knew he was originally one of them. But privately, he thought they were freaks of science, little better than Dolly, the original cloned sheep. He was glad that the Hornets had rescued him.

But one of those sheep might just provide a way for Baolin to write his name in history.

***

Nevaeh herself couldn't understand her obsession. She thought about her mother every day as she went about her daily routines. She had been doing fine without Teagan Ward, so why did she want to alter her life so drastically for someone she didn't know? Someone who might not care for her or have any interest in meeting her.

She wished she could confide in any of the others, but she didn't know how they felt about finding their mother; or, as they might put it, their egg donor. They treated each other like siblings, but who knew if there was just one donor or many. Were they all related at all? Ved particularly––although they were good friends and would do anything for each other––was different and didn't seem to be part of her.

None of her research had turned up anything useful. She had even asked the AI to run searches in restricted files through back doors she had created and commanded it to keep on a background search undetected while it carried out other operations.

What she had found was that Clara Ward worked at the Malapert base, and Nevaeh was certain Clara was Teagan's mother. Maybe Clara had access to the Chinese base. But, just as Benjamin Taylor had told her, she couldn't get a pass to visit the Shackleton base, where Teagan Ward was probably being held, without arousing suspicions. Even if Nevaeh claimed she was on a research project, there was still no way she could get approval to visit her.

The weight of uncertainty pressed on her. She found herself caught in a web of questions without answers and a viable plan.

Even Bancroft had noticed something was wrong. She asked her in the galley one morning, "What's crawled up your backside recently? You've been acting like you're suffering from radiation poisoning."

Nevaeh murmured something about considering a professional matter and beat a hasty retreat. Later, as she stared at the report in front of her, Commander Bancroft appeared in her office.

"Just the person I was looking for. Get dressed. You and I are going to Halona for training and, as a bonus, a Ming Fan concert."

Nevaeh looked at the commander in confusion. "I didn't volunteer for a training trip to Halona or a Ming Fan concert."

"Well, I was invited—more like ordered—by Howie Rich to come discuss some things and attend the concert. Since you're a huge Ming Fan enthusiast, I thought you could tag along and have yourself a great time. Heavens know you need it. Plus, there's some training for radiation officers that you might need. Good networking."

Nevaeh didn't know what to say. She wasn't in the mood to go to Halona or attend any concert, even if the artist was the super-talented Ming Fan.

Bancroft seemed to read her mind. "If I can't tell my boss 'No' then you sure as hell can't either. I will see you at the bridge in an hour."

111

The Approach

Halona, September 2101

T HE CONCERT WAS GREAT fun, particularly the laser harp. Nevaeh enjoyed
herself more than she had expected.

It was an intimate group of about a dozen people. Ming Fan's incredible playing thrilled everyone, including the grumpy Bancroft. After the concert, everyone
gathered for a fabulous dinner by the famous chefbot, Yum Yum.

To Nevaeh's surprise, everyone treated her like a minor celebrity. They all wanted
to know about her work and how it felt to be a heavenly baby. Much of the adulation
was encouraged by Benjamin Taylor, who was there for a visit.

She had stayed in touch with him since their encounter on Valdenia 53. At first,
she'd just wanted to make sure he was okay, but their communication soon evolved
into a friendship. She still wasn't sure she trusted him—he was too enigmatic to be
trusted, too much a journalist. Maybe he was just after another story. But she liked
being around him.

By the end of the evening, Nevaeh had to admit that she had enjoyed herself. She
liked seeing Benjamin again, and he'd introduced her to Ming.

Just before they were about to board the elevator to head back to ElleWon, Ming
Fan approached her. "Ms. Nevaeh, I've been looking for an opportunity to talk to
you privately. Would you mind if we step into the bathroom?"

Nevaeh frowned, confused, but followed the woman. When they got there, Ming
Fan locked the door and produced a very thin foldable tablet and what looked like
earmuffs.

Smiling at Nevaeh's curious look, Ming said, "I'm sorry for all this cloak and
dagger stuff, but there's someone I'd like you to speak to." Handing Nevaeh the
muffs, she tapped on some buttons and the image of a slim woman with cold, dark
eyes appeared on the screen.

"Hello, Nevie. May I call you Nevie?"

Nevaeh nodded, noting that there was a slight delay between when the woman
spoke and when she heard her voice. She inferred that the earmuffs were translators
or scramblers.

"I'm sorry for the inconvenience. I've heard that you want to meet your mother," the woman said bluntly. "I can help you with that."

Nevaeh felt a cold thrill of excitement run down her spine. "How can you help me?"

The woman held up a finger and said, "Before we talk about that, there is something I need from you."

"What would that be?"

The woman gave her a smile that didn't quite reach her eyes. "I need an unrestricted tour of the facility in ElleWon, including high-security areas."

Nevaeh had started shaking her head before she'd finished the sentence. "I don't have the clearance to do that. The only people that can authorize that are—"

The woman cut in. "Your mother was imprisoned because she craved contact with you and Liam. Imprisoned because she broke into the nursery and tried to carry you in her arms. All she wanted was to hold her baby; to hold *you*."

"How do you know all this? Who are you?"

The lady gave a fake smile; all teeth, no mirth. "All these questions are unimportant, Nevie. The important question is: What sacrifice are you willing to make for your mother? She was imprisoned for you. Will you do the same for her? I must go now. Think about it. Our mutual friend will be in touch."

Just like that, the woman was gone. Nevaeh removed the muffs and handed them and the tablet to Ming Fan, who smiled at her and said, "I will be in touch." She left the bathroom, leaving Nevaeh with more questions than answers.

While Commander Bancroft slept all the way back to ElleWon, Nevaeh ruminated. Was it true her mother was in a lunar prison because she had tried to see them? What kind of heartless bastards would deny a woman the chance to see her offspring? Nevie knew the woman she'd spoken to must operate on some level with the Chinese government. That was the only plausible reason why Ming Fan would be a go-between. She also knew that, despite their denials, the Chinese government supported those ragtag armies of bandits that attacked moon stations and the lunar industries.

Entering into a deal with this mysterious lady with cold, dark eyes was like allying with the enemy. She had heard what those bandits did to their captives. She had even seen one of them in the hospital on Quivira. Nevaeh didn't think seeing her mom was worth all the lives on ElleWon unless she could make them promise not to harm her colleagues when they took over the facility.

Nevaeh couldn't believe she was considering handing over an important asset to the enemy, putting the lives of others at risk, fraternizing with the enemy. Maybe she deserved to be in lunar prison with her mother.

112

The Next Move

ElleWon, September 2101

N EVAEH TOOK THREE AGONIZING weeks to decide what to do.

Finding out about the mysterious woman was easy enough; Nevaeh had used her considerable hacking skills to gain access to a secure facial recognition database. Inputting the woman's description, Nevaeh was surprised to find her so easily. Her name was Wu Zeitan, deputy commander to Baolin, her very own brother and now the dreaded leader of the Iron Hornets.

The Iron Hornets weren't trustworthy. No way they would promise not to hurt anyone and keep their promise.

Despite her lack of connection to her mother, Nevaeh longed to discover her story, who she truly was. Even though she hardly knew her, there was something inside Nevaeh urging her to find out more about where she came from, a profound longing simmering inside her for a connection to her roots.

Nevaeh analyzed a proposal, attacked it relentlessly and, when she saw a chink in the armor, she tore at it until it came apart. Then she thought of another plan and repeated the process. When the final idea for her plan eventually came, she was doing her round of radiation checks.

It was so simple, it seemed it couldn't work. But she thought it through, and it stood firm. She attacked it more relentlessly; still it stood firm. She went through it a third time, her computer-like mind imagining scenarios, and it still seemed viable. Satisfied that she had a workable plan, Nevaeh went about putting it into action. The first thing she did was organize a video conference with Wu Zeitan.

If she was surprised by the call, Zeitan didn't show it.

"Nevaeh, to what do I owe the pleasure?"

Before she could say anything, Zeitan made a gesture for her not to speak. Then she ended the call. A few seconds later, Nevaeh received a notification for another video call. When she selected it, it was Zeitan again.

"Hello Nevie, this line is free from prying ears."

"I want you and the other Hornets at ElleWon in three days. I will have deactivated the security system and disarmed the bots. All I need is your word that you won't harm anyone here and that you will hand my mother over to me in person."

Zeitan gave Nevaeh that enigmatic smile again. "Nevie, I don't know what you've heard or read about us, but we're not heartless. Once your people understand who's in charge, then you'll have nothing to fear. I'll be in touch. You've made the right decision."

That was all.

Nevaeh felt relieved. The plan was in motion.

***

"Commander, I talked to Nevaeh. She'll be ready for us in three days."

Baolin stared intently at the screen in front of him. He looked limp and dejected.

"What's wrong?" Zeitan asked.

"I just heard from my friend, Alimjan. His mother is dead. She wasted away. Such a proud woman. She gave me so much when I was young. She died of addiction after they released her from detention. That terrible cordyceps combo they're pushing."

"Combo?"

"It's an addictive drug they're pushing to make populations compliant, complacent, and unchallenging. They're using it against the Uyghurs and other minorities."

Baolin sat silently. Zeitan had never seen him so down.

"I loved her like a mother," he whispered. His scarred face looked raw and inflamed.

Zeitan waited for him to compose himself, then said, "We must make them pay."

Anger darkened his face. "They will definitely pay. I will eliminate this drug factory, wherever it is. So, you have news?" he asked finally.

"We heard back from Nevaeh. She expects us at ElleWon in three days, with her mother."

He nodded and said, "Good. How are we sure it's not a trap?"

Zeitan already had an answer. "I'll be leading the pilot ship, with your permission, Commander. If it's a trap, I'll make sure I take down as many as I can along with me. If it isn't, then I'll inform you."

Baolin shook his head. "That is reckless in the extreme. I will not let you risk your life. We put her mother on an unmanned flight. If it's attacked, we know it's a trap;

if it isn't, then we know we can take her at her word. When are we securing her release?"

Zeitan nodded, pleased by the emotion in her Commander's voice. "I'm leading a team to Huashan tomorrow. We should be able to smuggle her out undetected. We can hide on the dark side of the Moon until everything blows over."

Baolin smiled. Zeitan had never seen him do that.

"Good job, Zeitan. You've impressed me with your dedication and resourcefulness. I will see you in three days." Then, to the crew he said, "Gather yourselves, pussies. We're going hunting."

113
The Trail

Tricala, September 2101

ONCE SHE LEFT BAOLIN, Kiana came up against an immediate problem. Contrary to what the Hornets thought, she found out that the Chinese were not holding Teagan at the Huashan base. In fact, nobody had seen her for a long time, maybe since her rescue.

Kiana put out feelers to her sources. What had happened to Teagan after she was released from the lab? How had she just disappeared? She herself had seen Teagan in Noel's arms when they raided the lab. What had happened to her after that?

She tried to contact Polyakov, thinking the professor might know, but couldn't get hold of her. Through his old boss, General Lin Wenyi, she was able to contact the scientist's assistant, Li Jie.

"Li, have you any information about where Teagan Ward is?"

"I've no clue. She's probably dead."

"We need to find her."

"Last I saw her was in the Marius Hills. Why not start there?"

***

Kiana, supported by a couple of securitybots armed with lasers, decided to reconnoiter the Marius Hills complex for signs of Teagan, trying to recreate what had happened to her after the escape.

Kiana drove close to the entrance of Dr. César's lab, then headed south. She realized that the trail was probably dead and that Teagan was elsewhere, maybe even in a different habitat by now, but she had to start somewhere. She had heard tales from miners of an abandoned alien spacecraft nearby. Perhaps she could spot that.

Sitting in her vehicle, she launched a surveillance drone high into the sky, hunting for signs of where the aliens may have hidden their spacecraft. Using the ion-powered device, she flew backwards and forwards over the vast sea of ancient lava, scrutinizing deceptively attractive depressions and the long shadows cast by the descending sun.

Spotting something, she instructed the navbot to go lower. It hovered over a large pit, but Kiana didn't recognize any signs on the ground of aircraft landing or being maneuvered. No tracks, no scorching. She pulled the drone up and flew further along a gulley.

Then she noticed something else. It glinted in the disappearing light.

She came in lower and could see the dome of a craft, slightly exposed, protruding from a small outcrop. Dipping the drone lower, it stuttered in the Moon's ultra-thin atmosphere, the ion engines trying to gain traction.

Then: Plop! The drone crashed to the ground, and the visual transmission abruptly halted. She tried adjusting the frequency, hitting the "On" switch, boosting the power.

Nothing worked. She had lost contact. Was it a malfunction, or had some force jammed the snooping aerial surveillance drone?

Kiana drove into the tunnel system, navigating toward the coordinates where the drone had gone down.

114
The Exchange

Marius Hills, October 2101

As Teagan became more familiar with her responsibilities as a priestess, she began to feel conflicted. On the one hand, she was experiencing a powerful spiritual awakening, feeling connected to something greater than herself through her mantras and meditations. But, on the other, she feared becoming too attached to the Tritans, who looked up to her for guidance. She struggled to achieve a balance between being their leader and not wanting them to begrudge her for withholding her advice, although she wasn't always sure what guidance they wanted.

She therefore tiptoed the line between connecting with the Tritans and keeping a necessary distance, finding pointers from an inner radiance that helped her judge the boundaries. She was a bridge between worlds, able to guide the Tritans through isolation; a salve, a balm that comforted the lost. The Tritans relied on her for counsel and solace during their long periods of sequestration underground.

Teagan led the group in a series of meditations, guiding them into a deep state of trance. Together, they tapped into an inner light that connected them to the unseen realm. Her hands trembled with energy as she led the ceremonies, her fingers gliding over the rough surface of the cave, connecting with the patterns in the ancient lava.

But for Teagan, these rituals were physically and emotionally draining. She poured all her energy into helping the Tritans find peace and balance, as Asimov wanted, often leaving herself exhausted and depleted. As she walked the bridge between the seen and unseen worlds, Teagan was torn between her own needs and the needs of those she had committed to serve.

Afterwards, the Tritans would graze on the minerals from the lava walls, using their long index fingers to extract small filings and feed each other.

Sometimes, as she meandered across a span in the lava tunnel, Teagan would feel something stirring inside her. The octopus spirit was speaking to her. She sensed a new beginning, and she knew that it would soon be time for the Tritans to leave.

One afternoon, she sat inside a chamber that the Tritans let her use at the rear of their craft. She was lethargic, dreaming about her babies from long ago. Beautiful

Nevaeh, golden Liam, and Ved, her wonderful Ved; they were all smiling at her. She was so out of it that she didn't hear the rising murmur nearby.

Something was approaching through the labyrinth of tunnels, not in a vehicle, but on foot. The Tritans could hear footsteps getting stronger, the person not even trying to disguise their presence. They came forward, their steps crunching like a discordant drumbeat on the lava floor.

Out of the darkness, a woman emerged, alone and unguarded. They could finally see her clearly—she was tall and strong, with an air of authority. She approached slowly but surely until she was standing in front of them. The Tritans watched her as she moved toward Asimov, unprotected and carrying nothing.

Noel and Clara had gone on trips for research and provisions, so Teagan was on her own--though DiaLog was still around, so that he could translate if needed.

The woman held up a hand in greeting. Asimov raised his hand in return.

"I am here on a peaceful mission. I have come here alone in search of something very precious," she said without breaking eye contact. "And if you can help me find it, I promise that no harm will come to you."

"We will listen."

They all stood motionless.

"I have a proposition," the woman said. "I know that you are far from home and need help. We have something that may be useful to you, but seek something in return."

"We are still listening."

"One of your transports misplaced the powerful crystal that I assume you use to guide the ship. We can locate it and return it to you. In return, we would like you to hand over Teagan Ward to us, so that she can be with her daughter and other offspring."

Teagan, some distance away, started when she caught her name and the mention of her children.

"She has a daughter?" Asimov asked.

"Yes, she works aboard the ElleWon space station at L1."

"They have the stone?"

"They can locate it," the woman stated cautiously, not wanting to open up the possibility of a retrieval mission by the Tritans to procure the crystal. Asimov had been in contact with the damaged rescue ship and knew the navigation crystal was missing after the *Pathfinder* had scraped over an asteroid.

A wave of energy surged through the Tritans. Asimov appeared to consult with some of the group. There was unanimity that the crystal must not be allowed to fall into enemy hands. It could be used to track and pursue the Tritans. Somebody mentioned their enemies, the crested Draxid.

"We are interested. We cannot allow an enemy to have the guidance crystal. How do we arrange the swap?"

"I will be your intermediary. I guarantee that you can trust me. If you allow it, I will take Teagan with me, and return to you with the stone."

Asimov stepped forward, his antennae twitching in concern. "Why can't we do a simultaneous exchange? We don't even know you."

"They want to see her alive first before giving up the crystal. It's reasonable. She should be checked."

"We all love Teagan. Why should we let her go?"

"It may be your only chance to take the crystal with you. If not," she mentioned, "we will auction it to the highest bidder on the international market."

Again, a surge of energy went through the Tritans. They were trapped in a barren hole. They wanted to head home. They were willing to take the risk.

"I give you two days," said Asimov. "After that, we will track you down. If you double-cross us, we will be swift. Remember, I have access to Teagan's consciousness. And I will destroy her if you double-cross us. I do not say that lightly."

Teagan guessed it was an empty threat, but didn't say anything.

"I assure you, you can trust me."

"I do not, but fear may keep you honest."

Asimov stood aside to let Teagan step forward.

"We shall see you again," he told her. "I will send for you."

Teagan bowed to him.

The woman faked a greeting for Teagan. "Ms. Ward, how lovely to see you again. You seem to have made yourself at home here."

Teagan looked puzzled, not recalling who this person was or the role she had played in her liberation from detention. She looked across at Asimov for guidance.

"We need to be on our way. We have a bit of a journey. Soon you will see Nevaeh, your daughter."

The woman thanked Asimov again and asked DiaLog to convey greetings to all the Tritans. Then she walked up to Teagan, deftly injected her in her neck with a nerve-paralyzing agent in case she changed her mind, and placed a supportive arm around her to march her out to the vehicle parked out of sight down a short tunnel. Teagan did not look back.

"We'll put you on the SkyLift and you'll be on ElleWon pretty shortly," the woman told a comatose Teagan.

***

Nevaeh was walking around the now-deserted ElleWon when she received a request for a video conference from Zeitan. She hastily answered, but it wasn't Zeitan on the screen. Instead, it was an underweight woman with a lined face. She looked nothing like the pictures of the youthful Teagan Ward from the files. Nevaeh looked at her intently, trying to ascertain if she was the right one, not a trick by the Iron Hornets.

Zeitan's face showed on the screen. "We have kept our end of the bargain. How far have you got with yours?"

Nevaeh felt a pang in her heart: Teagan had gone through so much. Willing the tears not to fall, she said in a husky voice, "ElleWon will be ready for you when you get here. But I would like to request a slight change of plan."

Zeitan looked up, her brow furrowing.

"I need you to deliver my mother to Quivira, to the custody of her father, Professor Noel Ward. No deal without that. I can't keep her on ElleWon. The Consortium will close everything down after your visit."

Zeitan nodded.

"I need confirmation from her when you deliver her to Quivira and she's safely with Professor Ward. He's expecting her."

Noel had been unsure about the consequences of freeing his daughter and exposing the Tritans, but he also knew that Clara would be mad at him if they refused to seize the opportunity. He had, however, insisted on one condition.

"My grandfather insists that you say nothing about the alien craft until they are able to leave."

Zeitan nodded again and said curtly, "Of course. See you soon."

115
The Deal

Epona, October 2101

K IANA ABRUPTLY APPEARED ON Hunter's screen, her grubby clothing and the dark circles under her eyes making him frown in worry.

"We've found her," she stated baldly. Her voice sounded hoarse.

A knot formed in his stomach. Teagan could be heading home. "Where is she?"

"I can't give you any details. Just that she's been located. We'll have to extract her," Kiana said, not wanting to mention that had already been done.

"Will it be risky?"

"I'm not sure. It's unpredictable."

Hunter didn't like the sound of that. "Don't put her in any more danger."

"We'll be careful. Plus, there's a quid pro quo."

"A what?"

"We need you to do something in return."

"Kiana, you know I will if I can."

"We'll have an important package for you to deliver," Kiana said, her voice low. "Just a heads up. Be ready."

"Is it a body?"

Kiana chuckled. "No, it's a package in a crate. It needs to be delivered directly to Howie Rich on Halona."

"I'll ensure it's delivered directly to the bastard."

Hunter knew how important this package must be if Kiana was asking him personally to deliver it. With any luck, it would win Teagan's freedom.

116

The Emergency

ElleWon, October 2101

"COMMANDER BANCROFT, THIS IS an emergency. I need to see you at the reactor now."

"What is it, Nevie? I have a real emergency here; the powers that be are bitching over the pace of the metals extraction operation."

"Lynn, there won't be much metal to extract if you don't get down here now. Radiation levels have been rising for the past two hours."

Now she had Bancroft's attention. "What do you mean, radiation levels are rising? It's your job to keep radiation levels acceptable and safe. Do your blasted job."

She heard Nevaeh sigh. "You have to begin evacuation procedures. That is standard operating procedure."

"Don't tell me about SOP, Nevie. I've been in charge of this ship since before you were pulled out of the incubator. I'm not evacuating this ship just because you say so."

Nevaeh exhaled audibly. "I'm coming up." The voice in Bancroft's ear went dead. She muttered a string of curses and waited for Nevaeh to arrive. When she did, Bancroft rounded on her. "Nevaeh, you might be the best at what you do, but I will not have you give me orders."

Instead of replying, Nevaeh dropped an instrument on her desk. "That's a Geiger counter. I calibrated it myself. The best of its kind; it's never given me an incorrect reading."

Commander Bancroft cut in, "Will you get to the point today?"

Instead of answering, Nevaeh brought out another Geiger instrument and said, "Normal readings should be around thirty-two counts per minute." She pointed to the second counter, which showed that readings were climbing. "This is what the radiation levels are at the moment, 460 counts per minute and rising. Two more hours of this, and the results might be catastrophic. I need run of the place to fix leakages this huge. If you evacuate immediately, I can fix this in a few days."

Next was the hard part.

She looked at Bancroft directly and said in a brisk tone, "It's your call, Commander. What's it going to be?"

Commander Bancroft stared as if she was trying to read her, then said, "You have three days. I'll leave three bots with you. Get to work."

As Nevaeh was leaving, she heard Bancroft's voice on the speakers. "All units begin evacuation protocols. This is not a drill. I repeat, this is not a drill."

Nevaeh smiled to herself. Her plan was moving along beautifully. In three days, she would be long gone.

Then Bancroft called her back. "To be safe, I think Kim and I should stay aboard to help out."

The climb in the SkyLink elevator for Teagan was long. She was bundled into the passenger car. The carriers, for both cargo and humans, were rocket-assisted on the way up, guided by a tether made of high-tensile single-crystal graphene. The elevator included a sleeping car and a restaurant section.

By the second day, the drugs Teagan had been injected with had worn off, and the woman named Zeitan told her what was happening.

"We're getting an immediate connection to Quivira," explained Zeitan. "Then you can meet up with your family. I'm sure you're very excited."

"I've seen them," she said simply.

When they reached the top, the SkyLink docked with the ElleWon station. Buffers ensured a safe connection, and three layers of doors opened in sequence: First the car's inner door, then its outer covering, and then the connecting door to the station.

Teagan stepped out onto the sky bridge, ready for the onward connection. She was already apprehensive about renewing human contact.

117

The Welcome

Quivira, October 2101

A JOYFUL NOEL WAS there to greet her when Teagan docked at Quivira. The Hornets had kept their side of the bargain.

"Long time, no see." He smiled and hugged her tightly. "I'm sorry, but you'll find no disciples here!"

Noel noticed she was a little groggy. Probably the effects of space travel, he thought. He then called Nevaeh to confirm.

"The Eagle has landed."

Motoko hugged Teagan. "Nice to see you after so long! You're looking good. Please follow me," she said. "We have a bit of paperwork to complete. I know it's very boring, and I'm sure you must be tired, but we need to get the red tape out of the way."

Teagan frowned. "Not again! I don't want to sign my life away a second time."

"Don't worry, Teagan. Just follow me." Motoko led the way down a long corridor. It was dark and quiet. They skirted past some pallets of dried plants until they reached an unlit room. Motoko ushered Teagan inside. She could feel a big space with the air conditioning humming in the background. It was pitch black and nothing moved. "This is mysterious," Teagan said uneasily.

Suddenly, all the lights went on and everyone shouted, "Surprise!"

Teagan's mouth fell open, and she grabbed a desk to support herself.

A huge crowd of Quivira residents was assembled. In the front was a group she recognized: Liam, Tara, Gabby, and Ved. They were all applauding her. To the side were Noel and Clara together, beaming with laughter. And just behind them, Benjamin Taylor, the journalist who had stayed in touch with Nevaeh. "I invited as many of the babies as I could find," Motoko said.

Teagan burst out into a huge smile as tears rolled down her cheeks. "I can't begin to say how wonderful this is. I've dreamed of this for so many years, to meet you all together."

"Arturo is with Howie on Halona, Nevie on ElleWon. I'm not sure where the infamous Baolin is. Here, you may have heard of Shiko." Shiko smiled and waved.

"I have no words to express how happy and proud I am. I am so proud to be your mother."

Clara smiled at her. "So proud of you," she signed.

Teagan looked around and asked with trepidation, "Where's Dr. César?"

"He has many projects," said Motoko. "He's only here sporadically."

"So here's to the absent magician, with us in spirit. May he be absent long." They cheered. "And also to Maureen, who kept us all on track," said Noel. Maureen waved, so happy to see everyone. From the back of the crowd she moved forward, pushing a wheelchair. Seated comfortably was Julian, one leg bandaged. When she saw him, Teagan screamed. "Oh my God, what did they do to you?"

She rushed forward and hugged him. Everyone clapped and whistled. "How I've missed you," Julian said, his arms going around her.

MB-13 pushed him to the center and Maureen clasped MB-13's hand. Julian kissed Teagan amid shouts of "Get a room!"

"What happened?" asked Teagan. "I'll tell you all about it some other time."

"I'm so happy. I can't tell you. Thank you all." Teagan beamed, tears of happiness streaming down her face. "Just a couple of days ago I was with a bunch of aliens," Teagan said, before catching herself. "Ha, ha, just kidding," she said, glancing nervously at her father. "I mean, the Chinese base."

"Yes, we've all felt like aliens recently," interjected Noel, saving her from her mishap. Clara hugged Teagan and kissed her on the forehead. "Let's eat and celebrate," she said, and they all tucked in to some of Yum Yum's specialties. MB-13 sidled up to Julian to ask how he was doing.

"Much better," said Julian.

"By the way," said MB-13, "that picture you mentioned you wanted, we now have it."

"Fantastic!"

"Courtesy of the old bots network!" Julian nodded. "I appreciate it, old bot!"

That night, it was difficult for Teagan to sleep soundly, despite her exhaustion. She kept on thinking of the Tritans and her time as their priestess. She found herself questioning everything––her purpose, her beliefs, and her place among the Tritans. Why had she been selected? It was a restless and uneasy slumber, plagued by doubts and uncertainties.

As much as she tried to push them away, they continued to nag her, like a persistent tide that refused to be ignored or recede. She was sure they'd meet again.

118

The Takeover

ElleWon, October 2101

NEVAEH HAD BEEN PACING the bridge for the past two hours. Zeitan and the rest of her crew were supposed to be here by now. She fidgeted with a food sachet but was not hungry.

She was just about to check the radar again when she heard, "This is White Tiger for the Iron Hornets, requesting permission to dock," over the channel she had blocked off for Zeitan.

Eagerly, she responded, "Permission granted."

She guided the lead ship through docking protocols and ran to it as it coupled to the dock. When the hatch opened, she expected to meet Zeitan or Baolin. Instead, a mild-mannered bot walked out.

"I'm Sparkus. I hear you have a radiation leak that needs fixing?"

Nevaeh started laughing. "Very funny!"

Meanwhile, on the lead ship of the Iron Hornets, Baolin and Zeitan observed as the pilot ship docked successfully and there was no violent reaction. A combined force of bots and Hornets secured the station.

"Looks like everything is okay," Baolin said excitedly. "It worked, Zeitan! ElleWon is ours for the taking." He immediately ordered a search of the station. "We need that stone intact!"

Zeitan began combing through the lower reaches in search of the crystal but encountered a locked door. "We need a code."

Flanked by a couple of armed bots, Baolin walked into the control center and came across Kim and Bancroft.

"Commander Bancroft, I presume," Baolin said. "Very nice to meet you. Impressive operation you have here. Now, first I'm going to ask politely. Where is the stone?"

"There is no stone. The asteroid is outside."

"Being smart! Maybe you'd like it rough?"

Baolin instructed the two bots to "ask" Commander Bancroft.

"You can't do this!" Commander Bancroft screamed as the first bot threw her hard against the wall. Just as she managed to get on her feet, the other one landed a heavy blow on her face. A smudge of blood splattered against the wall.

"So they really do bleed red." the first one remarked to his partner.

Bancroft wiped her lip. Before she could react, the two bots picked her up and dragged her toward the security door. One of them held her head toward the security scanner to pick up her retina. If anyone knew where the stone was, it was Bancroft.

As this was happening, it occurred to the commander that this must be an inside job. How else would these people know about the stone, or gain access to their station so quickly? Who had ratted?

"I'm going to ask you again, where's the stone?"

"There's no stone. I don't know what you want."

Baolin's eyes fell on Kim in the corner, and he grabbed her by the neck. "If you don't talk, I'm going to sever this woman's neck in front of you."

Bancroft's gaze went to Kim's, and then back to Baolin's. She tried to stall, hoping Nevaeh had found a good place to hide the stone.

"You're quite a woman, I must confess," Baolin said to Bancroft. "The mighty Commander Bancroft, willing to throw her colleague's life away because of something that never concerned her to begin with."

"I've told you already," Bancroft answered weakly. "I don't know where the stone is. We don't know about any stone. Please don't harm Kim."

"But you know who has it," Zeitan countered, joining Baolin in the control center. "You know who that person is and you're trying to protect them with your own life?"

"The station has been evacuated. We had a radiation scare."

"Just tell me who has the stone, and you can go back to the life you had before," Baolin stated. "Otherwise, Miss Kim here will pay for your lack of cooperation."

"Sir," a commando called out as a message popped up on his screen. "The sweepers have found some matching DNA in the aft section of the space station."

Baolin handed Kim to Zeitan and grabbed the tablet from the soldier. There was no evidence to suggest the man had been alive recently, but there were small traces of his DNA scattered all over a chamber in the station.

"What happened to him?" he asked the sweeper on the other end.

"Appears to have been some sort of chemical obliteration," the woman answered. "He's totally gone, but his DNA still exists. The chemical compound is relatively unknown, but there are traces of it all over this space station."

"Any leads?"

She rummaged through a carefully folded pile of clothes. "See this?" she asked, holding up a work overall. "The DNA on this cloth doesn't match that of our dead guy. My guess is that there was a second person on the scene."

"Run that through all the software you can get your hands on," Baolin commanded. "Whoever was on the station probably tried to destroy the material either to hide evidence of their wrongdoing or something else."

He ended the connection and handed the tablet to Zeitan. Then, he moved closer to Bancroft and spoke softly to her.

"You see? If you don't start talking, I'm going to make sure you disappear completely without a trace."

Zeitan ordered the bots to increase the level of pain.

Despite her commanding air, Bancroft did not have a high pain threshold. She began to wail, a deep and agonizing sound that caught Baolin off guard.

Unable to take it, he walked out of earshot. When she wouldn't stop wailing, the guard struck her from behind, and she passed out. Baolin sighed loudly and asked the bots to find a location where she could be held securely.

Bancroft's entire body ached from being thrown against the wall, taped, beaten, and choked. But she wasn't ready to give up on life yet. She still had one trick up her sleeve. All she wanted was a way to ensure she could survive another ordeal and gather her wits. She wanted so badly to give these assholes everything they had given her. But she still needed to keep her strength, at least until the right moment.

Bancroft hung there, inert, blood trickling from her lip and her left shoulder. Her hair was matted and covered in grime. As the bots took her away, she looked like a boxer about to pass out.

Zeitan turned to Kim. "Why don't you save your boss, little girl?" She took out a knife and put the tip close to Kim's eyeball, by the tear duct. "Otherwise, your eyeballs will be on the floor, and I'll have the pleasure of squashing them."

"We can use them as pucks for ice hockey!" one commando said.

Zeitan applied pressure, nicking the skin ever so slightly. Enough that blood streamed down Kim's face.

Kim was ashen, as though she was about to faint. Beads of sweat rolled down her back. In a rasping voice, she said, "The back locker."

"Hang on, she's saying something. This better not be a hoax."

A commando went to search through the lockers, throwing the contents on the floors. After some time, one called out, "There's a wooden box hidden behind some joggers."

Out in the corridor, the guard holding Bancroft looked down at his screen, and Bancroft saw her chance. She moaned weakly and turned on her heel, pushing a tiny button at the edge of her last toe. The tiny, embedded syringe she kept there for emergencies shot straight through, injecting her feet with a super serum. Immediately energized, she shot up and grabbed the guard who'd kicked her earlier, hitting his head against the wall, then the floor.

The other guard quickly produced a taser from her pocket and aimed it at Bancroft.

"Let him go, now!" she ordered.

With the serum fully kicking in, Bancroft snapped the guard's neck and dropped him like an empty sack. "Like that?"

The other guard made the mistake of firing the taser. Bancroft swerved to avoid the electric charge and punched her in the chest. Wheezing loudly, the guard crashed to the ground. She tried to get up, but Bancroft held her down and clamped one hand over her mouth while squeezing her throat tightly.

The guard went limp, and Bancroft stripped her naked and dressed herself in the guard's uniform. She marched outside.

"Where do you think you're going?" another guard barked as she made her way through the doors.

"There's a prisoner on the loose!" Bancroft fired back. "We need more hands!"

Too confused to stop her, the other guard ran in the direction she had been coming from and found the naked body on the floor. Bancroft, meanwhile, evaded a couple of guards and made it to a space cruiser parked alongside ElleWon. She fired up the engine and was about to close the hatches when Zeitan appeared, jumping on a wing and thrusting a weapon through the closing hatch, jamming it.

"Not so fast, my dear!"

Bancroft looked up but, before she could move, Zeitan raised her weapon and shot her straight through the skull. Blood splattered the back of the contoured chair.

"Don't worry," Zeitan said to the dead woman. "We found it. You can go now."

Bancroft's body slumped forward at the controls, lights flashing garishly against her frozen, lifeless face.

119

The Asteroid Strike

ElleWon, October 2101

"Y OU WASTED HER? THAT'S insane. She might have been useful. We could have traded her."

Baolin slammed the metal butt of the laser against the wall and smashed an attached screen. Parts of the folding stock clattered to the floor.

Zeitan stood in front of him defiantly. "It was necessary. She was trying to escape."

"She could have been a good bargaining chip, you moron. Why is everyone so inept around here?"

Letting his anger get the best of him, Baolin broke a nearby bot's fingers straight off; they dangled helplessly from their interior wires. He slumped into the chair in Bancroft's command center, checked the radar for any incoming craft, and looked across at the large expanse of the Valdenia asteroid, where the mining bots were still working as usual, vacuuming up the metal-laden ore. Baolin adjusted his face mask, scratching underneath.

Looking more closely at the radar monitor, he spotted an incoming craft about eight minutes away. It looked like reinforcements coming to the defense of ElleWon.

"My God! Can't we do anything right today? Jesus! We can't even take over a space station that was handed to us without a fight, and now it looks like we'll have to defend ourselves."

He watched the incoming craft on the sensor. It didn't take any evasive action.

"Must be a trap. They're as brazen as hell."

Zeitan sounded the alarm.

Guy Zephron, returning from Halona on a scheduled trip, headed toward Elle-Won, oblivious. He hadn't heard the series of alerts about the radiation risk on ElleWon. Even if he had, he may not have complied.

Guy was looking forward to an early meal and a rest. He pulled into the docking bay and got off the craft.

"Looks like a bit of malarkey is going on," he muttered to the navbot.

He was surprised to be challenged as soon as he docked.

"Hands up and don't move."

Guy put his hands in the air. His padded spacesuit glistened in the light. "What's going on? I come here every three months."

"Let him go," instructed Zeitan. "He's just a lone pilot. No threat on his own."

Back in the command center, Baolin couldn't contain himself. "How can we let someone just sneak up on us like that? We need a bit more discipline here. I can't stand being surrounded by idiots. But worse, I can't stand unjustness. I'm going to kill them. I'm going to annihilate them."

He flicked his jade-handled dagger across the room and sliced off a bot's antenna.

"I am going to wipe them off the face of the universe." Baolin picked up the chair and slammed it against the wall. "Nobody does that to my friends."

Zeitan returned and calmly watched him, standing off to the side. "Baolin, you sound like you're losing it," she said bluntly. "Who has done what to your friends?"

"They killed Alimjan's mother." Tears ran down Baolin's face. "They heartlessly fed her addictive drugs and she died."

Baolin had been ruminating about this ever since he heard about her terrible death. Now his grief came out in a torrent.

"This lab is a cancer. It is destroying people's lives, turning them into mindless slaves and killing them. I swear on the lives of Alimjan and his family, I will not let this rest. It must not happen anymore. It's a plague. This terrible lab and its evil doctor must be wiped out, eradicated from the face of this earth. I want it done immediately." He slammed his jade-handled dagger into a sideboard, which splintered into pieces.

"Yes, boss, but how do we do that? We don't have a missile big enough to do the job."

"Look outside. What do you see?"

They looked, but nothing struck them.

"We control the Valdenia asteroid, don't we? Yes. Is it worth anything to us? No. They've exploited most of its potential. It's been sucked dry. So, let's use that as our weapon. Asteroids hit the Moon all the time. This time, it'll come from a different direction and obliterate the lab. We will wipe them out. I'll lead the attack," volunteered Baolin.

Zeitan shook her head. "You can't do that. It's certain death."

Everyone looked toward Zeitan to suggest a solution, but she did not volunteer herself. Instead, she said, "I'm sure we can automate an attack. Just put the tug on autopilot."

"Yes," interjected Guy as he stepped forward into the room. "But someone needs to know when to release the tug so that it slingshots the asteroid into the lab at the right angle. Just hitting directly from the heavens won't do the trick."

"Let's just strap Bancroft into the pilot seat and say she went berserk," Zeitan suggested.

"But Mr. Zephron's saying that a direct hit will just damage the lab, not obliterate it. We need to come in from the side, where the walls are weaker," said Baolin.

"Yes, correct," said Guy, who had finished cleaning himself up and was reporting back to the control. "It requires pinpoint accuracy."

"So who can do it? Maybe one of the bots?"

"I think it's better if I do it."

"You?" Baolin looked at Guy quizzically.

"I have more experience with guiding asteroids. I'll ensure a clean and accurate hit. And I know the right trajectory to be able to maneuver out of there once the asteroid is successfully released. Plus, it's time I took care of my conscience--all those drowned babies. Maybe saving a few now will balance out the ledger."

Neither Zeitan nor Baolin knew what he was talking about. They didn't know what had happened in the Great Cyber War. But they didn't enquire about Guy's motives.

"I'll help you," Nevaeh offered, coming into the control center after attending to some damage on the exterior skin. "I hope that guy César fries. It's because of him my mother was imprisoned."

"No, this is something I need to do myself. After what I've done in my life, saving people from whatever this lab is doing is the right thing to do."

Baolin knew Guy was the right man and they agreed he would take command.

"The Valdenia is all yours, Guy," Zeitan said once Guy's tug was firmly in control of the asteroid. "Good travels and come back safely. Just deliver that motherfucker!"

Guy ordered the AI to chart a course for the Marius Hills.

"That's a collision course," the AI warned. "I cannot chart that. We will be obliterated."

"Don't worry, navbot. We'll adjust before hitting the ground."

Guy entered a manual target code. Fifty-nine thousand kilometers to travel before impact. He would decouple within good time to avoid any blast.

As he slowly unleashed the throttle, the wires tightened around the asteroid and Guy's tug began hauling the Valdenia on its final journey. The jagged silhouette of the rock pulled away from the familiar outline of ElleWon, leaving an empty void that seemed strange to the crew who had grown accustomed to the giant's presence adjoining the space station.

As the Valdenia drifted away from the L1 point, Guy took a sip of the lemon-flavored water he kept velcroed to his discolored control station.

Soon the Moon's gravity took over and the Valdenia picked up speed heading for the basalt cupolas of the Marius Hills. The instruments showed they were traveling at more than 2,400 meters per second. Guy turned on the music.

"Decouple. Decouple," the AI warned. "Collision course. Collision course. Manual override needed, urgently." The AI sounded panicky.

Satisfied the asteroid was on target and had enough momentum for successful impact, Guy told the AI, "Release lines and head back for ElleWon. We've done our job."

There was a pause as the asteroid gathered pace.

The AI initiated the automatic release, but nothing happened. It tried again. Still, the lines remained stubbornly attached.

"The lines seem stuck. We cannot decouple," the AI said blandly.

Guy frowned. The Marius Hills were quickly approaching. "Try some more. Get those lines off or we'll get incinerated!"

"Something is wrapped around a protrusion on the Valdenia. It will not release."

Cursing, Guy went back to the aft cabin to try to sever the lines. Built for tensile strength, the lines were almost impossible to cut. He tried a laser, but it would take hours––time they did not have––so he resorted to an old-fashioned axe. The blade just bounced off the taut line.

He looked out the side windows. The Moon's contours rushed toward them.

"Just loosen the line as much as possible," he said, going back to the controls. "That might help."

But the bot's attempted maneuver was too late. Nothing could free the line.

Clearing his throat, Guy stayed resolutely guiding the asteroid in as they hurtled closer and closer to the surface of the Moon. He stretched out his hand to hold the navbot.

"I'm sorry, old mate."

"I understand."

***

Down below, in their subterranean lair, Dr. César was working in his lab, programming the bots to fulfill a new order after an acrimonious discussion with General Lin, who was visiting to firm up production rates and deliveries.

"You are too slow," Lin had shouted. "We need faster production."

"This is a small lab. We are doing our best." Li had smiled at her.

"At least get me a tea. I need my Longjing."

Li had instructed a bot to bring her some tea to her liking.

Apart from the robots working as usual in their regular rows, interrupted by nothing, the lab seemed empty. They were all oblivious to the imminent attack.

Dr. César, trying to calm down a little before going back to see General Lin, who was talking to some ants that were trying to edge through a crack in their container.

"Now, don't go there. You can have a bit of sugar water."

Then he headed for a corner corridor to stretch his legs. He noticed the lab rats getting agitated. They sensed from the vibrations that something was imminent. Maybe another moonquake. César knew where to hide. He scuttled along to his emergency escape pod and opened its reinforced side door. At least he could get a break from General Lin's piercing voice.

Inside the lab, the monitors issued a frantic warning. Emergency lights began flashing, and the shaking had become so violent that Lin could no longer stand. Then, the huge bulk of the asteroid struck the labs directly, like an avalanche with the force of a nuclear thunderbolt.

Something in the lab ignited, and a fireball ripped through the tunnels of the Marius Hills, incinerating everything in its path. Rows of bots melted at their workstations, their metal frames dripping onto the floor in twisted heaps. Emergency lights flickered on, casting an eerie red glow over the scene. Smoke billowed from the wreckage, and the acrid smell of burning wires filled the air.

General Lin screamed and tried to run, but the kinetic energy of the asteroid obliterated everything in an instant. The vortex threw her petite body across the room, and she slammed into a wall, crippling pain shooting through her back. Searing heat peeled the skin off her face and hands, curling up like crispy bacon, and her eyeballs melted in their sockets as she was vaporized along with the rest of the station.

Nothing was left but charred debris and a cloud of dust. The Controller's abandoned station crumbled. Large slabs of regolith crashed onto the unmanned desks as everything turned to dust.

As the inferno cascaded down the tunnels, César pressed the eject button to hurl his escape pod into space. Below, the lab disintegrated like a crumpled box, returning the land to how it was before the brief time that humankind had intervened. Beyond the lab, the ball of flame tore through the narrow tunnels and lava crevices. To any observer, it appeared like just any other asteroid strike—one of the thousands over the Moon's multi-billion-year history.

120
The Handover

ElleWon, October 2101

B AOLIN AND ZEITAN WATCHED from the ElleWon control center as the intense ball of flame tarnished the Moon's surface and incinerated César's lab.

"Ha, ha! That's what victory looks like!" Baolin punched the air. "That is Alimjan's revenge."

He hugged Zeitan, who looked over his shoulder coldly at one of the bots, as she replied, "Mission accomplished, boss!"

Leaving him there, Zeitan retrieved the crate from the storage locker. She opened it, and a dazzling bright light blinded her before she quickly shut the lid and carried it back to the control center.

"This is for Howie Rich," she told Baolin. "Hope he likes it."

Baolin looked triumphant. "A mission accomplished," he mused. "Just imagine what more we can do together."

Zeitan looked at Baolin sadly. She really liked him, but orders were orders, and hers were clear. She moved behind him. Before he could blink, she swung a graphite cord around his neck and tightened sharply.

His hands shot up to his neck, trying to remove the cord as she throttled him. His mask dropped down, and his reddened jaw exposed his titanium teeth. Despite the strength in his arms, Zeitan had better leverage, and he couldn't escape the chair, which had become his death chamber.

Zeitan saw the shock in his eyes. "I'm sorry, Commander, but we have new orders. The Iron Hornets have a new Commander now. They think you're too unstable. We need someone steady in charge, not a sentimental, unreliable maniac."

He tried to grab for the jade-handled knife, but it was just out of reach.

As the cord tightened, his hand fell. She felt him grow limp. Zeitan laid his head on the armrest of the chair and said to White Tiger, "Order the pilot ship here. We're going home."

White Tiger simply answered, "Yes, Commander."

121

Howie Wins

Halona, October 2101

WHEN HE GOT TO Halona, Hunter didn't waste any time. He'd been asked by the Hornets to deliver the box directly to Howie in his high-security quarters. Hunter's eyes had locked on Kiana's as she handed over the stone, unaware of her earlier commitment to the Tritans to give them the stone in return for Teagan's release.

Boris showed Hunter to the space station's inner sanctum and gestured for him to take a seat. "Howie will be with you shortly," said Boris.

"Ah, so here's the delivery boy," Howie said when he finally entered the space. "Why don't we go into my quarters? Please follow me."

Hunter followed Howie into a large suite. As they sat, Hunter glanced at the impressive art collection on the walls.

"You have something for me?"

Hunter placed the crate with the crystal inside carefully on the table. "This is from General Lin and the Hornets."

Howie's eyes filled with excitement. "I've been waiting for this." He opened the box, and the room was filled with a green glow. "Extraordinary."

Hunter watched as greed and desire battled each other in Howie's eyes. Since the days of the cowardly attack on Misericordia Farm, Hunter had despised Howie Rich and knew him to be a man who lacked morals and empathy. But now, seeing him gloat over the acquisition of this rock, Hunter's anger welled inside him.

Howie leaned a little closer. "The rumor is that this stone is one of the most powerful elements in the universe. I've heard that anyone who manages to harness its power can destroy civilizations in the blink of an eye, conquer galaxies, and become one of the most powerful beings anyone has seen."

"General Lin sent a message," said Boris. "She said, 'Our deal is satisfied. I think we are even'."

Howie could barely contain his excitement. With this crystal, he was jubilant and confident of his future. Confident he would continue to outwit the greedy Jack Rushes of this world. Confident that he would continue to control the Space

Consortium. Confident he would always win. "Congratulations, sir," Ofentse said from where he stood in the corner. Howie grinned at Ofentse and said, "Get us a drink; we're celebrating."

Hunter sat silently, his eyes on the kris daggers Howie collected—weapons known for their sharpness and precision.

"Long may we cooperate for our mutual benefit," said Howie.

Hunter had always considered himself patient. He was the kind of person who could wait for days, even weeks, before taking action. But now his anger began to boil to the surface. "Mutual benefit!?" he shouted. "Can you hear yourself? Do you know how much calamity you've inflicted, the damage, the hurt, the wounds?"

Howie and Ofentse were shocked by the seemingly unprovoked outburst. Hunter hadn't meant to say anything, just be a good messenger, but seeing the man celebrating was too much for him.

"You are a selfish monster, willing to trample over anything just to get your way. Do you know any of your victims? You have wrecked my sister's life. You definitely know her! Have you met a small baby called Katrina? And do you remember Misericordia farm? Dozens of people were killed. Her mother was shot to death by your murderers."

Hunter looked at Howie, who was unmoved.

"Not just killed. No. On your orders, they strung a woman up on a cactus bush, half-naked, and then used her for target practice, shooting off one toe at a time. Can you imagine how agonizing that was? No, of course not. You have never suffered. You have never been poor. You have never known what it's like to go without food, without love, without anything.

"But that mother knew love. She had taken care of her baby. Katrina. She had left her in a latrine for protection. The dirt was her savior. She was the only survivor on Misericordia farm. You ordered everyone to be wasted for a minor transgression. You didn't care. It was part of business. Part of your way forward toward dominating the universe. Part of the march toward some stone in a box with strange powers that even you don't understand."

Howie realized that he wouldn't stand a chance in a fair fight. He considered his escape routes or calling the guards, but there was something in Hunter's eyes that made him hesitate. It was almost as if Hunter wanted him to dash, to give him an excuse to chase after him and hurt him.

So, instead, Howie stood his ground and waited for Hunter to make the first move. The seconds stretched out, the tension palpable in both of their faces.

Finally, Hunter clenched both hands into fists. "You're going to regret ever crossing me and my family," he growled. With one kick, Hunter swept the box containing the crystal off the table and sent it crashing to the floor.

Howie sat impassively, but Ofentse dashed across the room to retrieve the box and set it upright.

"You're a coward, Howie," Hunter spat, advancing on the other man. "You only pick on the defenseless."

"What would you know about courage?" Howie sneered. "You're nothing but a garbage collector."

"You are a slimeball. A monster. And one way or another, you're going to pay, I guarantee it. I hope you burn in Hell."

He picked up a kris dagger and threw it across the room. But they weren't designed as throwing knives, and the kris bounced harmlessly off a chair, hilt first.

"Call the securitybots," Ofentse, circling around to protect his boss, said to Boris.

Realizing he was cornered, Hunter made a dash for the door. "See you in Hell, dickhead," Howie shouted after him.

Boris began cleaning up after him, leaving the room in silence. The diaphragm doors hissed shut behind Hunter.

"Increase security to Threat Level Eight," Howie instructed Boris impassively. "Arrange some sort of an accident for that guy after he's left the vicinity. Then you can close down for the night." He stared across at Ofentse. "Well, that was a bit of a show. "

"Glad he got that off his chest. Why was he talking about this farm? And who was Katrina?"

"No idea."

122
The Celebration

Halona, October 2101

H OWIE BEGAN DRINKING, ENCOURAGING Ofentse to join him. Howie liked the amber-colored small batch E. H. Taylor Kentucky Bourbon whiskey, which, despite weight restrictions, he'd had shipped out to him personally. "Here's to the Colonel," he'd say.

Ofentse was not a whiskey drinker, and if anything preferred Scottish whisky, but he took a shot. It tasted good. A bit of caramel corn sweetness, mingled with butterscotch and licorice. "Not bad!" said Ofentse.

"Let's have another," said Howie as he poured. They clinked glasses.

Howie noticed that Ofentse's biceps gave a pleasing contour to his upper body. He had been working out.

Ofentse took another sip but didn't want to match Howie, so he put his glass down. "Such a wimp!" Howie said, riled up and wanting to get back at someone. "Can't even push the boat out when we need to celebrate."

Ofentse said he'd prefer some water and keep hydrated.

"Now you're embarrassing me. Not much of a man, are you?"

Ofentse walked away, edging toward Howie's collection of ceremonial daggers, ostensibly to tidy the mess.

"How's that girlfriend of yours?" Howie asked. "Toni, I think?" Ofentse didn't look up from what he was doing. "She's well, thanks."

"You know, I fucked her for you one time when you seemed to be neglecting her. She didn't seem too happy and needed some attention; a bit of a tune up!"

Howie was clearly trying to stir up some trouble. Winning the precious crystal had made him feel invincible.

Ofentse tried to imagine what an all-powerful Howie would look like. Even worse. Ofentse was now as tense as a wound-up spring. His anger boiled inside him, and he tried to suppress it, gripping the cabinet, but failed.

"Howie, you are such a bastard. I have worked for you loyally. I have supported you and helped you. I've helped you trample your way to everything like a rogue elephant. You have no right. YOU HAVE NO RIGHT! You need to be put down."

Howie continued to needle him. "She liked it when I went down on her. Her pussy was delicious."

Ofentse swung round, his eyes blazing. He was about to strike him when an apparition interrupted them—Clara Ward, fresh off the flight from Quivira, walked in, clearly unaware of the earlier visit of her son. She was wearing a light jumpsuit and carrying a coffee she'd just picked up on the way.

Howie paused.

"Knock, knock. Hope I'm not interrupting anything important."

The securitybots blocked her entry.

"Mrs. Ward," Howie said. "To what do we owe this unexpected pleasure? I was just describing to my good deputy here the art of pussy licking."

Clara raised an eyebrow. "Can't be civil even for a second, can you?"

Unused to being rebuked in front of others, Howie's face turned white.

Clara put her coffee on the table and walked forward. She was clearly on a mission.

"You are a vile piece of shit," she said. "You don't deserve to be alive or walk in this universe."

"What have I done to you?"

"You've only wrecked my daughter's life, you asshole." She glanced across at Ofentse. "You had her almost raped, lured her to Quivira under false pretenses, had her exiled to a lunar prison when she became inconvenient, and then your lackey, Dr. César, conducted various sick experiments on her while keeping her in solitary. You run a sick organization. We are going to sue your ass off. You won't be able to do business in this world or the next."

"You are misinformed, Mrs. Ward. I've only tried to help you and your family. Your daughter was sent to jail because she murdered someone—one of my employees. In fact, she should be in jail now, if you hadn't paid for Zhang to spring her."

"You are a corrupt and despicable killer." Her nostrils flared, and her eyes flashed with defiance. "You trample over people to grab whatever you want and only think of yourself. I will see to it that your empire comes down in tatters."

"Ofentse, I think we get the drift. What is this, Ward Family Complaint Day? Please throw this lady out."

Ofentse, who had kept as still as a pillar of salt during Clara's sermon, moved toward him. "You know, Howie, she's right. It has to end somehow."

Howie glanced in his direction, sensing fresh trouble.

Without warning, Ofentse picked up the jewel-handled kris that Hunter had thrown and ran at Howie. With full force, he plunged the dagger into his body, right up to the hilt.

Howie looked at him in shock. "Motherfucker," he muttered.

He tried to get up but had difficulty raising his large body off the couch. He ripped out the kris, and blood spurted across the room.

"You're going to die," Howie shouted at Ofentse. He grabbed Ofentse by the neck and tried to throttle him.

Ofentse swung at Howie, but the other man was ready for him. They fought fiercely. Ofentse wasn't sure how it happened, but suddenly he was on the ground, with Howie looming over him, beating him viciously.

"Get up," Howie taunted him, punching him in the face. "Show me how brave you are, you little turd."

Ofentse's face began to swell up as Howie beat him, and his vision began to blur. He knew he was going to lose consciousness if he didn't do something quickly. Elbowing Howie in the stomach, he managed to break free and scramble across the floor as Clara hid behind a desk. He didn't dare look back at Howie. His heart was pounding as he tried to find something to retaliate with.

His hand reached out and his fingers clasped the small meteorite studded with green crystals that Howie kept on the counter. He gripped the brownish-grey rock in his fist and smashed it down onto Howie's bulging neck.

Something snapped, and Howie's body crumpled to the floor, his gaping wound still spouting blood. His vision went hazy, as in an underwater dream. Ofentse's piercing voice echoed incomprehensibly and faded. Howie's legs would not support him. His arm clawed ineffectively at the chair.

Ofentse watched him like a man who had just harpooned a whale. Howie briefly twitched and a trickle of blood oozed from his mouth. Then he became still. Ofentse was unsure if he was breathing. He didn't want to bend down close enough to check, in case Howie was feigning.

Panicking, Clara said, "We've got to get out of here. Boris will alert everyone if he finds us."

Ofentse rearranged the room to cover his tracks, put the meteorite sample back in its place, and removed the second whiskey glass, wiping away any prints. Together, Ofentse and Clara pulled the body over to the door to Howie's living room. Ofentse opened the diaphragm shutter, then switched it to close. The thin blades snapped shut over Howie's limp body, cutting through the space suit and into the flesh, as though Howie had been trapped while stepping out of his quarters. Not very believable, but it would have to do.

Then they left the suite and locked it. They probably had a few hours before the body was discovered.

123

The Reaction

Quivira, October 2101

N EWS OF THE ASTEROID strike struck Noel like a sledgehammer, knocking the breath out of him. His legs turned to rubber. For some time, he didn't know what to do. He felt weak, as if his heart had been pierced by a bullet. A bitter, metallic taste filled Noel's mouth mixed with the salty tang of blood and tears. It was the taste of despair and hopelessness. Years of research down the drain. No one would believe him.

He had no way of knowing if the Tritans had escaped in time. After studying them and talking with them for so long, he had grown to love and admire them, even if he still didn't fully understand them.

But now, he couldn't shake the fear that they may not have escaped in time. Those beings that he had spent so much time studying and conversing with had become like family to him, making this devastating news all the more unbearable, the thought of having lost them sending shivers down his spine.

"Did anyone check? How are the Tritans? Were they there?" he asked.

His life's work had gone up in smoke, and no one had checked because no one knew about their existence.

"We did record an asteroid strike. Not a very big one," Alain Gagnon confirmed. "Not far from the Marius Hills."

"He keeps talking about the Tritans," said Motoko, mystified. "I think he's going crazy."

Noel, still working from Quivira, sent a search team of bots to the Marius Hills, but they reported finding no sign of the strange beings. Video footage showed a barren landscape. The lava tubes were empty.

"Maybe it's all in your imagination," said Motoko.

"I met them. I didn't imagine it. I have my research. I'll publish that. Then you'll see." He began to panic as waves of doubt flowed through him. "DiaLog must have records."

Maureen swept in. "Where was César? Did he survive?" she asked.

"His body hasn't been found. Everything was burnt to a crisp. We must assume the worst."

"A Chinese team has combed through the site as well," Clara said on a video connection from Malapert, where she was acting as if it was business as usual. "Nothing. Nada. Zilch. It's like it never existed. I'm so relieved you weren't there when it hit," Clara told Noel. "You know you're everything to me."

"Love you!" said Noel.

"See you again soon."

He blew her kisses.

"I'm going to see off Nevie now," Clara said. Her granddaughter had reached out to her not long ago and, after meeting her, Clara had changed her stance on the babies. "She's visiting Earth for the first time. She's so excited."

"Don't tell her about this. I'm sure Teagan would be devastated."

"I won't tell her until we know what happened. They might have escaped before it hit. They had a ship."

Noel could only hope that was true.

124
The NDE

Halona, October 2101

ARTURO SMELLED IT FIRST, a mix of blood and puke. The bots couldn't discern the acrid aroma, but Arturo started to retch as soon as he entered Howie's quarters. Howie's blood trickled into the corridor and pooled on the floor. One arm stuck out incongruously from the shuttered door like a Halloween dummy. Arturo couldn't see Howie's face but knew immediately that this was a scene of death and foreboding.

He tried to force open the titanium door, but it wouldn't budge. He called a securitybot for help, and it forced open the door with one arm, tearing back the diaphragm shutter.

Arturo, who was visiting Halona on an art scholarship arranged by Howie, broke down in shock at the sight of Howie's body, penetrated by the shutter door. He'd always treated Howie like an uncle—a rich one. He had never imagined a scene of such carnage. The blades of the door had closed over him, slicing into part of his body.

Arturo ran screaming from the room into the corridor. "Help, help! Howie needs help."

A cleaningbot moved quickly, stuffing a cloth into the wounds, maintaining pressure to stop the blood.

It called the medibots, who rushed to the scene in a couple of minutes. Somehow Howie wasn't dead, and they swiftly escorted his limp, corpulent body to the medical ward, where they put him on life support.

"We must give him all medical support available. Maybe we should fly him back to Earth?" Arturo asked.

But a medibot declared him in too much danger to risk moving. "He can't handle the pressure. We can treat him here, although it would be better on Quivira. Maybe we can get him there. He wouldn't handle the reentry to Earth."

Medical ward personnel managed to stop any further damage from occurring with their timely arrival. First, he was gasping; they helped him breathe better with an endotracheal tube and got him on a ventilator. Then they managed to stabilize him by using balanced IV solutions and blood transfusions, followed by an IV maintenance drip, with dextrose to support the brain function and reduce secondary neuronal injury.

When Howie emerged from his coma, his head pounded, and his mouth was like cotton wool. The haze of pain blurred his vision, and he could barely make out the figure in front of him. It took him a moment to realize that the figure seemed to be holding a knife. He began to thrash, scared he would be stabbed again. But the medibots held him down. "You're okay now," they told him.

Word of what happened quickly spread among the top executives of the Consortium.

Carl Howard, head of the moon mining operation, was desperate to prevent Ofentse from taking over. They had never got on well, and Carl knew he would be sent back to an Earth job.

"I'll send Professor Polyakov. Maybe she can do something."

"Just keep him alive," counseled Chris Stackpole, the Canadian responsible for running the three biggest mines on the Moon. "Get Polyakov now."

Polyakov was able to provide video instructions to the medibots to buy Howie time.

"Because of Howie's obesity, this will not be easy, but you must continue adequate oxygenation and circulation. If needed, place him on extracorporeal membrane oxygenation or ECMO. Then, you must expediently assess for and stop any major vascular bleeding and reduce the fractures—so I would do a full body scan, cut off clothing, and cauterize or clamp any major arterial bleeding, internally and peripherally. Next, align the fractures as much as possible."

"Understood," said one of the medibots.

"After that, I would use nanobots via the IV to "mend" or stabilize the microneural and vascular connections, and institute robotic surgical assistance to monitor and adjust extracorporeal membrane oxygenation, as well as provide any further cardiovascular interventions that might be necessary. Finally, use the nanobots to help establish the initial connections with AI."

Once Howie was stabilized and on life-support, Polyakov coordinated with Maureen Grau to arrange for his transportation to Quivira, where Dr. César's facilities were the best available anywhere.

Maureen flew urgently to Halona. After discussing with Professor Polyakov, she agreed this was to be kept top secret. Polyakov arrived shortly after Maureen, and got Howie ready for the flight.

When things were calmer, Maureen went back to Howie's quarters to inspect the scene. Everything in Howie's chambers had been scrubbed clean. But she found a wooden box on the sideboard, next to the kris collection. She put the box in a strong duffel bag with some papers on top, also removing the map from the wall and rolling it up, before rejoining Polyakov.

"Ready to depart, Professor?"

Howie was strapped on a gurney, attentive medibots by his side. As they boarded the shuttle, Maureen knew she had missed MB-13.

125

The Comeback

Quivira, October 2101

A FTER BEING FLOWN TO Quivira, Howie was hooked up to a battery of monitors and devices to keep his respiratory, cardiovascular, renal, and gastrointestinal systems functioning while Polyakov assessed the damage.

At first, Polyakov thought Howie might survive. He would have to undergo extensive surgery, but he might have a chance. But soon it became clear that efforts to control his internal injuries were failing and his clotting system was becoming overwhelmed—his organs were shutting down and he was bleeding out, despite the ECMO.

An alarm alerted the crew that the vital signs were bad. "We're losing him. I don't think we can save him. He has too much microcirculatory damage, and the bots cannot get the bleeding under control," said Polyakov.

"He's not dead yet. I'm sure you can save his brain at least," intervened Stackpole.

"I can try."

"Then he could still run the Consortium. Nobody would know he doesn't have a body. We could fake it," Stackpole mused. "All his meetings are by video."

"If that's what you want. But it would be an extremely limited and limiting existence."

"For him, yes. But it will avoid a trillion-dollar civil war, and maybe the collapse of the Consortium. It will buy us time."

Polyakov, supported by the medibots, operated on Howie for six hours. They inserted a cannula into Howie's nose, feeding cooling nitrogen gas directly to the base of the brain. "If you get cold fast enough before the heart stops, the vital organs, particularly the brain, can tolerate cold without blood flow for a time," she explained to the bots assisting her.

To support Howie's mind, she attached a bypass machine to his carotid and vertebral arteries, and prepared a solution of oxygenated artificial cerebrospinal fluid for cushion and nutrition for the cryo-preservation, all while she worked on the best way to connect the brain to a computer. Once the body was bypassed and the brain isolated, his limbs and trunk were cut away. Maureen arranged for the body to be cremated.

"We want the strictest secrecy. It's your head if word gets out," Carl warned.

Preserving the brain was the complex part. It took Polyakov and her expert team some time to get Howie stabilized and connected, and work out the kinks by providing the necessary inputs and sensory stimulation. But, after intricate surgery and preparation, Polyakov thought she had done it.

"Let him stabilize and monitor the connections for a bit." She was exhausted, and became aware that she might need a change of clothes. "Let's take a break," she said.

After a brief walk to her assigned room, Polyakov collapsed on a bunk and slept for fourteen hours.

She was envious of bots; they did not have accumulated pent-up feelings and anxiety. She had never done anything like this before.

She wasn't even sure if it was sensible, saving a monster. But he had saved her career, and she had taken an oath.

Polyakov ate a hearty breakfast before she went back to the operating theater where Howie remained hooked up to the equipment. It was time to see if what she had done would be successful, or if the Consortium literally needed a new head.

Tentatively, Polyakov typed into the computer, *Hello, Howie. This is Olga.*

The monitor was blank for an agonizing few moments.

Then, *Hello, Olga, it is good to be alive,* appeared on the screen.

Olga smiled, and Carl appeared relieved. Even the bots cheered.

"A miracle! We live to fight another day," Stackpole said. "How does it work?"

"Tiny sensors implanted inside his brain translate his brain activity into messages that can be read on a computer screen. The computer can send back messages, creating a conversation."

"So we could make it look like he's still running a meeting, maybe by synthesizing his voice?"

"We can do that, but it will only be audio."

"That's enough for now. Maybe we can create a Howie avatar later. I truly appreciate it. You've saved us. Neat job, Polyakov."

The computer screen, now hooked up to a rotating camera, burst into action again.

It seemed just like the old days, but different!

126

The Double

Epona, October 2101

WINGTIP LOOKED UP AT Hunter after reading his report on the Hornets' operation.

"So, do you have anything to add?"

"Sir, I can officially confirm that Mr. Rich is a monster and Ms. Madison is not to be trusted," Hunter answered, still officially out of the loop.

"Yes, Kiana has done a good job, hasn't she?" Wingtip responded, pulling at a long eyebrow hair.

At a loss for words, Hunter could only shake his head.

"Seems like she's dismantled the Hornets and taken out their leader."

Hunter frowned. "She was working for us?"

"Yes. You were right about the double agent. She's been working for us all along."

"My God!" Hunter said, his whole body relaxing with relief. "That's amazing."

"Yes, she is. In fact, you can tell her so yourself."

"She's here?"

Kiana stepped into the room, smiling at Hunter.

"This calls for a celebration," said Wingtip. "Three mizuna juices, please."

Hunter smiled at Kiana, relieved that they were on the same side after all.

"To the demise of the Hornets," said Wingtip.

"I'll drink to that."

"And the excellent work of Zeitan, or whatever her name is."

Kiana erupted into laughter. Hunter loved that huge smile.

"Thank you," Hunter said simply, not knowing what else to say.

After some pleasantries by Wingtip about the protracted operation, Kiana whispered to Hunter, "Let's get out of here."

"If you will excuse us?" Hunter said to Wingtip.

"Be my guest." He smiled at both of them like a bemused bishop.

Once out of sight of Wingtip, Hunter looked over his shoulder to make sure they weren't being watched before he pulled Kiana closer. He wanted nothing more than to press his lips against hers, and yet something held him back. He nervously rubbed noses with her, then smiled before giving her a hesitant but passion-filled kiss.

"I owe you so much. I owe you my sister's life."

Kiana smiled back at him. "Yes, you do, Buster. So, pay up."

"It may take some time."

Hunter hugged her tightly, feeling relief and happiness submerge him. They had finally made it through everything, and they were together.

Then Hunter took a pace back. "I do have one person to thank who played a bigger role."

He took her through a familiar labyrinth of corridors back to the kennels, where Chester greeted him as though he hadn't been away even a day.

"Hello, Chester. Remember me?" asked Kiana. Chester didn't care and licked her anyway. "I really miss Xeno. But Chester is almost as good."

Hunter gave her a smile. "No way," he said. "Chester rules!"

127
The Key

M AUREEN'S FINGERS BRUSHED AGAINST MB-13's smooth, metal arm
as they sat together in her office. Her mind was filled with conflicting
thoughts. She was torn--part of her wanted to stay with MB-13, while another
part wanted to start a new life on Earth. And then there was the question of
what others would think of her retiring with a robot as her companion.

Yet, despite all these doubts, Maureen couldn't deny the strong bond between her and MB-13. Maybe it didn't matter what others thought.

After more than thirty years running Quivira, she had finally made up her
mind.

Maureen and MB-13 had formed an unlikely bond, finding solace and companionship in each other's company amid the trauma of tending for Julian.
They had become more than just human and machine--they were friends.
They even loved each other, although Maureen realized that might mean different things to the two of them.

"You know, MB-13, I've been thinking. I think it's time to retire on Earth.
Teagan's joyous homecoming had been a sort of climax. And you have already
made such a significant difference in my life. I am sure you will do the same for
others on Earth. Let's embark on this new journey together."

"I think we care for each other. I want you to be with me," said Maureen.
MB-13 agreed.

Maureen paused for a moment before adding, "To mark this, I want to give
you a name. From now on, you shall be known as Harlee."

MB-13's face lit up at the new name. "Harlee? I quite like that name. Thank
you, Maureen. It feels more personal than just a machine designation. Maureen
& Harlee."

Their decision to share their lives on Earth was a significant one, but it didn't
quite fit the traditional concept of marriage as it applied to humans. MB-13,
after all, was not a human, but a highly advanced artificial intelligence with a
unique consciousness.

They decided to consult with legal experts to formalize their partnership through a Companionship Agreement, a pact that was growing in popularity. This agreement allowed individuals, whether human or artificial intelligence, to formally commit to living together, sharing their lives, and taking care of each other's well-being. It offered the legal protections and rights typically associated with marriage, such as inheritance, medical decisions, and property sharing, without the traditional romantic and familial connotations.

She leaned across and gave Harlee a kiss. Harlee's face beamed with delight.

But before formalizing her union, Maureen had one other thing to do.

She tracked Ved down in the cafeteria, where he was drinking mizuna juice.

Ved smiled at her. "I thought you were leaving?"

"Yes, it's time I retire. But I have one last thing to do." She paused and he looked at her. "Ved, you know I've always loved you, all this time."

He nodded.

"I have lost several people I've loved in my life, but I have always looked out for you. Dr. César also loved all of you, in his way. But after your accident, Ved, he may have gone too far."

Ved wasn't sure where this was leading, so he said nothing.

"I know that he gave you this exoskeleton suit to make up for your accident. But there was something else."

Ved frowned, and she could tell that she was starting to worry him when he asked, "What?"

"He tried to give you superhuman powers by injecting you with alien DNA. If you feel different, it's not just the suit. Ved, you are different."

The color in his face drained. "I knew there was something about me."

"As you know, Dr. César is now presumed dead, so we can't know for sure. But there is something I want you to have that may help you track down your people."

She presented him with the crystal in the wooden case from Howie's office. "This stone has created lots of trouble. But it's also the key for you to return home. I believe they'll welcome you. Keep it safe, and use it when the time comes. It will unlock your future."

Ved looked at the box encased in the duffel bag, shaking his head. "How will I know where to go?"

"Teagan will know. Get in touch with her."

Maureen kissed him gently on his forehead and left without looking back.

128

The List

California, November 2102

HUNTER INSISTED ON ESCORTING Nevaeh for her visit to Earth. "I'm your uncle. I'd love to show you around."

Ben also joined them––he expected to make a bit of money from the pictures of her swimming in the ocean for the first time.

Her dream of going to Earth was finally becoming a reality, but Nevaeh was still nervous. She had frequently dreamed of returning "home". But she had never been to Earth. It was just a dream, a strange attraction, like the seas had for the Moon. She was glad for Hunter's help—she needed a guide to this strange place of blue oceans, white icecaps, dark mountains, rambling prairies, lush green jungles, and brownish-yellow deserts.

After securing the release of her mother, Nevaeh was determined for a real-life meeting. But all travel had been restricted by the Space Consortium for several months after the attempt to kill Howie. So, the return had had to wait.

Ben had been partly instrumental in helping Nevaeh secure her mother's release, so she thought it sufficient compensation for him to accompany her for their reunion. Besides, they got on quite well.

"You know I'll do anything for you after you saved me from my comeuppance," he told Nevaeh with a chuckle. Ben was, however, amazed by how little she wanted to take with her. "You know that Earth doesn't have a controlled climate. Temperatures can vary," he explained.

She watched as Hunter programmed their destination into the spaceship before he took his seat. They fastened their seatbelts and allowed the machines to take over. The spaceship took off from Quivira, the familiar silhouette fading into the distance, and headed for Earth.

The spaceship was faster and more advanced than she was used to. It was not a long journey.

"Brace yourself," Hunter suggested as they neared the reentry point. Protected by the rocket's heat shield, they entered the Earth's atmosphere at around 17,500 miles per hour and immediately began plunging toward the Earth. Hunter initiated a retrograde engine burn to aid deceleration. Nevaeh gripped the armrest and closed her eyes. It wasn't the smooth journey she was used to. The spaceship jerked and shuddered as it passed through the clouds. Nevaeh used every bit of control in her to keep herself from screaming.

The spaceship kept plunging until it adjusted onto its new flight path and broke into direct sunlight.

"Everything's fine now," Hunter said, and Nevaeh slowly opened her eyes. She watched in awe as she saw the brightness all around. The spaceship hadn't landed but was now moving horizontally.

"Wow," Nevaeh said as she stared through the glass panel. "It's even more beautiful than I imagined. Where are we?" she asked Ben.

"Over the United States. We're headed for Arizona, to meet Ming Fan," he said.

Nevaeh could see the rugged landscape below, ranging from desert land and scrub to majestic mountains, punctuated by striking geological formations and vibrant colors. The interplay of natural beauty and geological diversity was mesmerizing. "I think you will be able to spot the Grand Canyon on the left," said Ben.

From above, Nevaeh observed the winding river snaking through the canyon's depths and the intricate patterns of erosion that had shaped its walls.

Too quickly for Nevaeh, the spaceship sped to its destination, and they got to Arizona's main spaceport.

"Wow," Nevaeh said again as the spaceship got lower and she saw the impressive buildings of the spaceport's main terminal. She had never seen structures so tall.

"You should see New York and Shanghai," Hunter said, landing the spacecraft softly. "We're here," he announced before the seatbelts unclasped from around them.

Nevaeh grabbed her bag, and Ben did the same. Hunter pressed a few codes before the door opened, and they stepped out. Robots were waiting for them at the doorstep of the spaceship to check them in.

Nevaeh walked toward the open doorway and gasped as a ray of sunlight hit her face. Fresh air hit her nostrils. It was like nothing she had experienced before. She felt light, and took a moment to close her eyes. Ben suggested that the bots get a wheelchair for her until she got used to the gravity.

"My feet feel so heavy."

"Yes. Your heart will take time to adjust. It takes more effort to pump the blood, and it begins to pool in your feet. So you need to take it very easy, particularly for the first few days," explained Hunter.

"You'll have to get used to it and adapt. You might feel some back pain. Your bones are probably weaker than those of humans on Earth. You'll have to exercise and build muscle."

Hunter allowed her to adjust to the new environment for the first few moments before he called her name. Nevaeh's eyes snapped open, and she properly took in her surroundings.

"Don't want to disillusion you, but it will probably take months of rehabilitation, if not years. Want to go back to ElleWon yet?"

"No, this is amazing!" She tentatively took her first step, expecting to float as in space. To her surprise, her leg touched the next step, and she smiled. Even though she had read about this, it was surreal.

"Nevaeh," Ben called out.

She realized the bots were waiting to scan her. She took slow steps until her feet became accustomed to the surface.

"Place your palm there," Ben said as he pointed at the palm of the security-bot.

Nevaeh did as instructed; it was all it took for the bot to scan Nevaeh's identity. The bot did her health check as well, and it was confirmed that she was free of any disease.

"Identity and health check confirmed," the machine said before Nevaeh retreated her palm. "Identity number is 161803398."

Hunter signaled for them to head for the checkpoint. They met another set of robots that scanned their luggage. It took a few minutes to pass through the various checkpoints before they got out of the port.

"That was a bit hectic," Nevaeh said.

"Trust me, this isn't half as hectic as what we go through when we want to go into space," Hunter said as he got into the next available vehicle. "Come on." He signaled for Nevaeh to get in.

"Welcome on board. Your destination, please," the cyborg driving the vehicle asked.

Hunter input his address on the screen beside him. The seatbelts automatically clasped around their waists before the vehicle started moving.

Nevaeh stared in amazement as she saw people walking past shops and cafés while robots moved along as well. There were robot cops, just like in space. Nevaeh's eyes widened when she saw a dog. Of course, she had come across bot dogs, but had never seen a real dog going for a walk.

The vehicle arrived at their destination and they got out. Nevaeh stared at the large gate before them.

"It's beautiful here," Nevaeh whispered as she kept glancing around. People kept glancing in their direction because Nevaeh was tiny, and her skin was paler than everyone else's.

"Yes, it is. Let's go in before it gets dark," Ben said.

"Is this her residence?" Nevaeh asked.

"No, we'll be lodging here. Ming Fan chose to see us here," Ben said.

***

"Welcome to the *Hill Springs Hotel*," the robot at the receptionist's desk said as they entered.

"Thank you. We'd like to have two rooms," Hunter said.

After the robot passed them two transparent key cards, Hunter led Nevaeh to the rooms where they would meet Ming Fan.

Opening the door to her room, Nevaeh took in her surroundings. She had never seen such a big bed.

She touched the bedspread and withdrew her hand almost immediately as she felt the softness.

She gingerly took a seat, and her eyes widened in delight when the bedspread felt cool against her palm. She recalled dreaming about how it would be to sleep horizontally. Slowly, she leaned on her back, and soon, she was lying on the bed. It felt strange and weirdly wonderful. She snapped her eyes back open and sat up. It didn't feel right. She had previously always slept vertically.

Hunter and Ben both grinned at her. "Ming Fan is on her way," Hunter said, and not two seconds later, there was a knock on the door.

"Please come in," Nevaeh said as she stepped aside to let her in.

Ming Fan and Ben took their seats on the chairs, while Nevaeh sat on the bed. Hunter went out for a walk. The three silently stared at each other for a while before Ming Fan said, "Are we going to sit here staring at each other all day?"

"Of course not. Nevaeh will ask you her questions now," Ben replied as he pointedly stared at Nevaeh to prompt her.

"I was wondering what you know about the woman who gave her eggs for my birth," Nevaeh said.

"You mean your mother?" Ming Fan asked.

"Yes," Nevaeh whispered as she tilted her head to the side.

"I know a lot," Ming Fan said with a distant look. "I shouldn't be telling you this, but I have nothing to lose. Besides I stopped being a spy the moment I left space."

"A spy?" Ben asked, confused.

"Yes, a spy. I was a Chinese spy," Ming Fan said, and Nevaeh gasped. "I was asked to infiltrate the Consortium. They knew about Howie's fetish for great talents. They knew he would come for me, so they asked me to give information about the Consortium's plans," Ming Fan said with a shrug.

Ben and Nevaeh glanced at each other.

"I did it for a while, but it got boring. However, during that time, I had a glimpse of who Dr. César was, and I knew he was up to no good while pretending to solve the world's medical problems. Being one of the mothers too, I was able to get more information about him than I could otherwise."

Nevaeh and Ben were stunned.

"Teagan said she was our mother."

"Yes, she was your mother," Ming Fan told Nevaeh. "But she was not mother to all seven. Dr. César liked to hedge his bets. And he wanted different ethnicities. His aim was to populate space."

"What do you mean?" Nevaeh asked.

"I'm Baolin's mother. That's why General Lin intervened when he got into trouble and secured his future. But I think he went insane with power."

"And who was the father?" asked Ben.

"Howie admired Guy Zephron, so he encouraged César to use Guy as a sperm donor. That's why the children are so good-looking."

"Guy was my father?" asked Nevaeh. Ming Fan nodded. "Yes, you can be proud of him. He was an honest, decent man.

"I wrote out a list after Howie told me once when he was drunk." She showed them a handwritten page.

Nevaeh—Teagan, Guy

Liam—Teagan, Guy

Arturo—Teagan, Howie

Baolin—Ming, Guy

Ved—Maureen, César

Tara—Toni, Guy

Gabriella—Toni, Guy

Shiko—Motoko, César

"Ved's mother was Maureen? No wonder she was devasted by his accident."

"This is incredible," said Ben. "Nobody will believe all this."

"And Art is Howie's son? Does he know?"

"Of course. That's why he is so protective."

They studied the list in silence. Things were starting to click now that Nevaeh could see the connections. Why Maureen loved Ved, why Howie was enthralled by Art.

"This makes a lot of sense now," said Nevaeh. "How about Hunter?"

"He may have heard some things, but does not know everything." Ming Fan paused. "Anyway, I have to be on my way now. Give my love to Teagan when you see her in Bolinas."

"Thank you," Nevaeh said, her mind whirling with all the new information it had gotten.

After Ming Fan left, Nevaeh was practically bouncing with energy. She wanted to go and find her mother immediately, but Ben convinced her to be patient.

"You just got here, Nevie; your body isn't strong enough for more travel. You should get yourself in better shape before the next stage."

Nevaeh looked at Ben in exasperation. "Ben, I'm grateful for all you've done for me. However, I don't think I have the patience to wait. I need to see my mother."

Ben smiled and held her hand. "Nevie, I know how you feel. But I know the physical exertions gravity does to someone like you who isn't used to it. Check with Hunter. Your face is recognizable. We can't be seen moving around. We need a plan. Howie's tentacles still spread far, and this is his home turf."

"It seems that he has many 'home turfs.'"

Nevaeh had always prided herself on being reasonable; even in the heat of everything that had happened on ElleWon, she had led with her keen mind rather than her emotions. She let out a sigh; Ben was right. She also realized she needed him to move around. She didn't know Earth very well. It was best not to irk him.

"Alright, Ben, you win. Do you have a treadmill?"

Ben, obviously relieved he didn't have to butt heads with Nevaeh over the matter, smiled.

"I can do better than a treadmill. In the basement, there's a gym with a virtual assistant that will help you with various routines to achieve your exercise goals. I'll show you to the gym when you're ready."

129

The Ocean

California, December 2102

The journey to Bolinas was a discovery for Nevaeh. She had watched and read so many things about Earth. Seeing it for herself firsthand was another experience entirely.

"If Earth is this beautiful now, how was it before the Great Unraveling?" Nevaeh asked.

"It was beautiful; Earth is still beautiful. The greatest problem for planet Earth is the fact that we humans live on it," said Ben. "We have scoured, pillaged, and raped the Earth. Even now, with resources scarce and the weather becoming an enemy, we still harm her."

They drove past fields of ripening strawberries, being picked by machines running on wheels along the rows. They stopped at a roadside stall selling roasted almonds and walnuts, and picked up some delicious oranges.

Based on the information Hunter had gotten from Desiree, they tracked Teagan down to a little yellow shack close to the beach. The shack required some repair and looked as though a good wind might blow it away. But, apparently, it had been there many years.

The white sands of Bolinas Beach were at the mouth of Bolinas Lagoon, in a spot where waves wrapped around the point and rolled in softly. It was known as a great surfing beach, especially for beginners, and was also popular with dog owners since pets could roam off-leash.

It was the first time Nevaeh had seen the ocean, the endless white sand, and its gentle waves lapping on the shore. To Nevaeh, it was heaven.

Behind the shack was a little inlet. The air smelled of seaweed, the breeze stroked her face, and Nevaeh felt she could live forever.

She had found home.

Nevaeh stood in front of the shack, unsure how to approach.

"I don't even really know what she looks like now," she told Ben.

"Maybe she'll think I'm just a stalker, or worse, someone sent by Howie to harm her."

Hunter suggested they take a stroll before going to see Teagan.

They walked around Bolinas, taking in the sights. The town had only one restaurant, a bar, and a couple of cafés. While they were drinking, the café proprietor told Nevaeh that most inhabitants were either writers, artists, or environmentalists.

Ben and Nevaeh wandered around town and found little shops that sold crafts and artisanal goods on the only commercial street in Bolinas.

In one of the shops, Ben bought Nevaeh a beaded blue and green necklace. In another, they found a beautiful old wooden cage hanging from a brass hook.

"What's that?" asked Nevaeh.

"It's a cage that Chinese people keep singing crickets in as pets. They're meant to bring good luck."

"Let's get that for my mother. She can hang it in her home. Look at the beautiful carving."

Ben paid for the present, and the saleswoman put it in a bag.

"Do you think that's what we are? Just crickets kept in a cage for someone's amusement?"

"The secret is to escape without getting stamped on!"

With her courage built up, Nevaeh decided it was time.

They marched toward the house. Hunter knocked on the door but then stepped back so that Nevaeh was the first person Teagan would see. The door opened slightly and timid eyes peered through, but nothing was said.

Nevaeh was unsure, but then she blurted out defiantly, "Hello, Mother."

The door opened a bit more to show Teagan, looking surprised and unsure what to say. At the party on Quivira, she had longed to see Nevaeh. Now, she was desperately tired and full of doubt.

"Nevie?" she asked.

Nevaeh glanced toward her, pleading through her eyes.

The floodgates began to collapse open. "I only wanted to hold you, and they wouldn't let me," Teagan said finally, as memories cascaded through her mind in waves.

Nevaeh rushed forward and bent down to hug her. "I know, Momma. I know."

"They kept me away from you. I only wanted to see you."

Teagan looked at her. "My, how beautiful you are. My daughter. So beautiful and alive, right here in California."

"Yes, Momma, I'm here with you now."

Tears fell down their faces and mingled as they hugged.

Hunter looked on as Ben stood by awkwardly.

"Hi," Ben said to Teagan's companion, who had stepped up next to her. "I'm Ben."

"Julian."

Hunter grinned and hugged Julian, who had been equipped with a prosthetic leg.

They all stood outside uncomfortably. A couple of pintails flew overhead.

"We bought this for you," said Ben, handing over the wooden cage. "It's for your new home. It's meant to bring good luck."

Julian admired the work.

"Hunt, you're here. Why didn't you say?" asked Teagan when she spotted her brother. She hugged him and almost refused to let him go. "I haven't seen you for ages."

At Teagan's urging, Hunter, Nevaeh, and Ben entered the house and stood inside. Julian made some space for them to sit.

"We have so much to discuss," Teagan said softly. "I'm not sure I have the energy."

"We'll take it slowly," said Nevaeh.

They sat down and began talking about how Teagan had got to Quivira, their memories of Maureen Grau and Dr. César, where Noel and Clara were now, how all the other children were, and so many other things. So many details. So much catching up.

"Where's Maureen now?"

"I hear she lives in the mountains," said Teagan. "They used to call her the witch!"

"Yeah, she bought a small spread and struck it rich," interjected Ben.

"They say she found some Spanish loot in the bottom of a lake on the property she bought. The lake had dried up because of climate change. In the silted-up bottom, they found a rotting oak cask filled with old coins. Or at least that's the story. She lives with a bot called Harlee."

"I liked Harlee," injected Julian.

"Where's the place?" asked Teagan.

"*Ojo del lago*," said Ben. "It was a crater formed ages ago by a small asteroid."

"What's that mean?"

"*Ojo* is 'eye' in Spanish, so it's Lake Eye or Eye of the Lake."

So, is that what the old man was talking about? The treasure you seek lies beyond the eye, Teagan wondered to herself.

They talked well through the night. The men slunk off to their beds, but Teagan and Nevaeh stayed up late.

In the morning, Nevaeh found herself asleep on the couch.

"I love it here," she said as she glanced up. "All life is here."

Nevaeh stretched and yawned. What a beautiful morning. She walked over to the verandah, sniffed the air, then breathed in deeply. She descended the wooden steps and then started running across the sand like a wild horse.

Ben walked to the porch and watched Nevaeh, clad in just her underwear, yelling in happiness as she jumped into the shallow water of the beach. Happy with how everything turned out, Ben said to himself, "Welcome home, Nevie."

A little later, sunning on the verandah, Ben asked Julian, "How did you two meet?"

"Halona," said Hunter with a grin. Julian sighed, telling Ben the whole story.

The five of them talked through the morning, until Nevaeh heard something that made her pause. It started as little drops, but soon it was a downpour.

She turned to Hunter with wide eyes. "Is that rain?"

He nodded. Nevaeh stood and walked toward the door. Fascinated, she watched the fat drops fall to the ground and into the ocean. Small pools filled up near the door. In amazement, she started to take her outer clothes off once again. She turned to her mother and smiled.

"I'm going to take a dip in the ocean. I always wanted to dance in the rain and bathe in the ocean. Now I can be an earthling and do both."

She pranced like a child down the sand and into the water, enacting years of childhood dreams in a few seconds. Excitedly, she splashed in the sea as though she was five, with Ben gleefully watching from the water's edge and sharing her excitement.

"Come in, scaredy cat," Nevaeh said, waving to Ben.

"Let's swim too," Teagan said to Julian and Hunter.

"I'm sorry. I have to go," said Hunter. "I'm meeting Kiana."

He hugged Teagan again. "Don't be a stranger." He kissed her on the cheek. "Next time I'll bring Chester."

"You better!"

Ben also took his leave. "I'll be back," he said with a grin.

"Take your time," responded Julian, barely audibly.

A couple of minutes later, Teagan was out, dressed in a bright yellow flowery swimsuit, Julian in shabby pants. Julian led Teagan to the back of the house where the inlet was.

Together with Teagan, he showed Nevaeh how to swim. He gently lifted her in his arms and held her at waist level, showing her how to kick her legs and use her arms.

Then, he carefully picked up Teagan and lowered her into the water, as though he was anointing his priestess. After a few seconds, she broke the spell and splashed over to Nevaeh. The three of them spent the next quarter of an hour enjoying the togetherness, the waves lapping gently against Teagan's head and Nevaeh splashing around. Then, Teagan stood up, put her hands around Julian's waist, and kissed him gently.

"You are my love. You know that, don't you?"

Back in the house, after a beautiful dinner of freshly caught tuna, they decided to have an early night. Nevaeh took the couch.

In the bedroom, Julian yanked off his prosthetic leg, adjusted a sock over the stump, pulled back the bed covers and got in beside Teagan. He snuggled up to her, switched out the lights, held her in his arms, and breathed in her scent as they both looked up at the strange painting on the wall of a swan that was retrieved from Howie's quarters by an agent of MB-13. The painting seemed to connect them all.

She mumbled to herself: "Behold the bird that cannot fly; the treasure you seek lies beyond the eye."

I have found my treasure here, she thought to herself.

Along the beach, children in wetsuits surfed a gentle wave and a dog played in the sand. It looked a lot like Chester. A grizzled man in a flat cap sat on a rock eating a sandwich, while the fin of a great white cruised ominously offshore.

Amid the golden sky of the setting sun, a saucer-shaped object dipped behind a cloud.

A lanky, long-necked white egret waded through the shallow waters of the lagoon and, overhead, a brown pelican started his dive, scooping up fish into his large pouch as the crescent moon shone on the horizon. To the left, maybe that was a white octopus in the darkened pool.

A perfect end to the day on an imperfect planet.

"The Sun, with all those planets revolving around it and dependent upon it, can still ripen a bunch of grapes as if it had nothing else in the Universe to do."

Galileo Galilei, Astronomer, 1564–1642

Epilogue

California, March 2103

Three months later, Teagan sat on the verandah, cradling her early morning tea. She breathed in deeply. The air was fresh.

An ant was struggling up one of the white posts.

"Hi, Felix!" she shouted. "You made it here."

She smiled to herself as she watched the determined ant continue its ascent.

Teagan took another deep breath, her hand gently resting on her abdomen, where a new life was growing. She was pregnant, and in this peaceful moment on the verandah, she felt an overwhelming sense of gratitude and anticipation for the journey ahead.

As usual, she checked her morning messages and the news on her screen. She took a quick sip of the hot liquid.

More news about the Space Consortium's exploration of Mars, a war between two African nations, revelations about a songwriter's affair with a well-known politician, and updates on the revival of the gold market.

The screen abruptly went blank.

She hit the escape key and cursed. Nothing was working. She turned the screen over. Nothing, except a message reading,

"ERROR. NO SIGNAL."

Then, as if on an old-fashioned manual typewriter, letters began appearing on the screen one by one.

I KNOW WHERE YOU ARE. YOU HAVE SOMETHING OF MINE, AND I NEED IT BACK.

Who is this? Is this a joke? she typed, trying to stay calm.

Nothing happened. She could hear the waves gently lapping the beach.

Then it burst back into life:

THIS IS HOWIE RICH. RETURN TO ME WHAT YOU'VE TAKEN. I WILL TRACK YOU DOWN. MARK MY WORDS. NOWHERE IS SAFE.

Teagan looked frantic, and a sickness welled in her stomach. She began to shake, and her eyes rolled into her head. The teacup slipped from her hand and shattered on the floor, its hot liquid scalding her thigh.

Julian rushed out. Teagan silently pointed, tears running down her face. Julian and Teagan looked at the computer screen as it went blank again.

Teagan clutched Julian's arm. "He's coming for us," she said. "I know it. Can't he ever leave us alone?"

"How did that prick find us here? Wasn't he killed?"

"He can't track us down here, can he?" Teagan implored.

"Someone's just messing with us. Let's go inside and rest."

Julian looked around, half expecting Howie or one of his proxies to appear from the bushes or from behind a rock on the beach. Then he noticed Teagan was still trembling all over.

Willing himself to calm down, he hugged Teagan, kissed her hair, then her lips, then her earlobes.

"Nothing is going to happen to you," he whispered.

"Howie is far away, and that's if he's alive in the first place. I'm going to keep you safe. I promise. We don't need to fear an avatar."

When Teagan was calmer, Julian led her to the bedroom, hugged her, gave her a deep kiss, and made sure she slept.

Then he called Hunter.

"Do you think there's a risk Howie is still alive? I thought he was dead."

Hunter's response was instant. "I was told he was killed in an accident. It's possible that it was a crank call. Maybe it's that deputy, Ofentse. I'll look into it and get back to you. Relax, Julian; I'll make sure you guys are safe."

Lying in bed, watching the ceiling fan go around, Teagan asked Julian, "What do you think he wants?"

"The Oudry painting, probably."

"Why does he want that old thing?"

"Because it's not a dead swan. It's the key to a map of the Orion constellation, buried in a painting.

The real treasure is not what Maureen found at *Ojo del lago*. It's beyond the eye in Cygnus. That's where we discover the treasure."

Behold the bird that cannot fly; the treasure you seek lies beyond the eye.

"Well, I'm a little busy today," yawned Teagan, now more relaxed. "The treasure will have to wait."

"Or maybe we already have it here," she added, patting her small developing stomach bulge, and smiling.

"What I crave right now is a large plate of Claw's delicious spaghetti."

###

Acknowledgements

Thanks go to my father, who stimulated our imaginations as children by telling us engrossing stories to entertain us on long car journeys, and to my son-in-law, Jason, who got me interested in writing science fiction. I'm also grateful to Craig Martelle for the inspiring 20Books conventions in Las Vegas, which made me realize the scale and possibilities of the indie and self-publishing industries.

I'd like to thank several people in the space industry and related academic fields for helping with background and ideas for the book, including: Angel Abbud-Madrid, President of the Space Resources Roundtable at the Colorado School of Mines; Al Globus of the San Jose State University, for his work on space settlements; and Nitin Arora of Georgia Tech. Several people were involved in guidance on technical details in the manuscript, including Martin Meinshausen, who assisted with many mining and lunar questions, and Kathleen Ranney, who helped with medical possibilities and specifics. My apologies if I have overly conflated particular issues.

I'm indebted to a number of people for editorial help: especially Parisa Zolfaghari, who knocked the overly long manuscript into shape by eliminating unnecessary chapters and providing greater focus; to Kerry Cullen, who provided excellent character analysis; and to Laura Soppelsa, who delivered a thorough copy edit and additional suggestions.

For the early stages of the manuscript, I would like to thank Stella Wilkinson, who helped shape the character arcs; Garry Buden, who saw the possibilities of Teagan as an alien priestess; and Matt Patterson-Muir, who gave helpful feedback on an initial draft, as well as several friends who provided comments. Thanks also go to cover designer Liam Relph, who provided stimulating suggestions and analysis about covers and current approaches in the genre.

I am also part of several social media groups for writers that keep members up-to-date on trends and new approaches. Many thanks to all the members for the entertaining and stimulating feedback.

About the author

Jeremy Clift is a science fiction author and former journalist. A fan of Adrian Tchaikovsky, Mary Robinette Kowal, Cixin Liu, and Andy Weir, he is keenly interested in how space exploration will change humanity over the next 200 years. His first work of fiction, *Born in Space*, is part of his Sci-Fi Galaxy series of novels, built around the growth of orbiting space habitats and the exploitation of asteroids.

A former non-fiction publisher at an international organization, he is a communications consultant and writing coach who has also worked in magazines and as an international news correspondent for Reuters. A graduate of both the London School of Economics and George Washington University, he has lived in a variety of capitals and cities around the world. He now resides in Virginia.

Leave a Review

Reviews help writers

If you enjoyed *Born in Space*, please help others to appreciate it too:

Recommend it. Help others find this book by recommending it to friends, readers' groups, and discussion boards.

Review it. Take a few moments to write a review, telling others why you liked this book.

Contact. You can find me at jeremycliftbooks.com

Also see my Amazon author's page.

or Goodreads

Free downloads

Check for free downloads of related content.

Get a free intersecting side story with **"Born in Space"**
or an unpublished chapter
Log in to jeremycliftbooks.com to sign up for

"Collision in Space: The Tritan Scoutship Chronicles"

Printed in the USA
CPSIA information can be obtained
at www.ICGtesting.com
LVHW031754250524
781139LV00006B/215

9 798990 010734